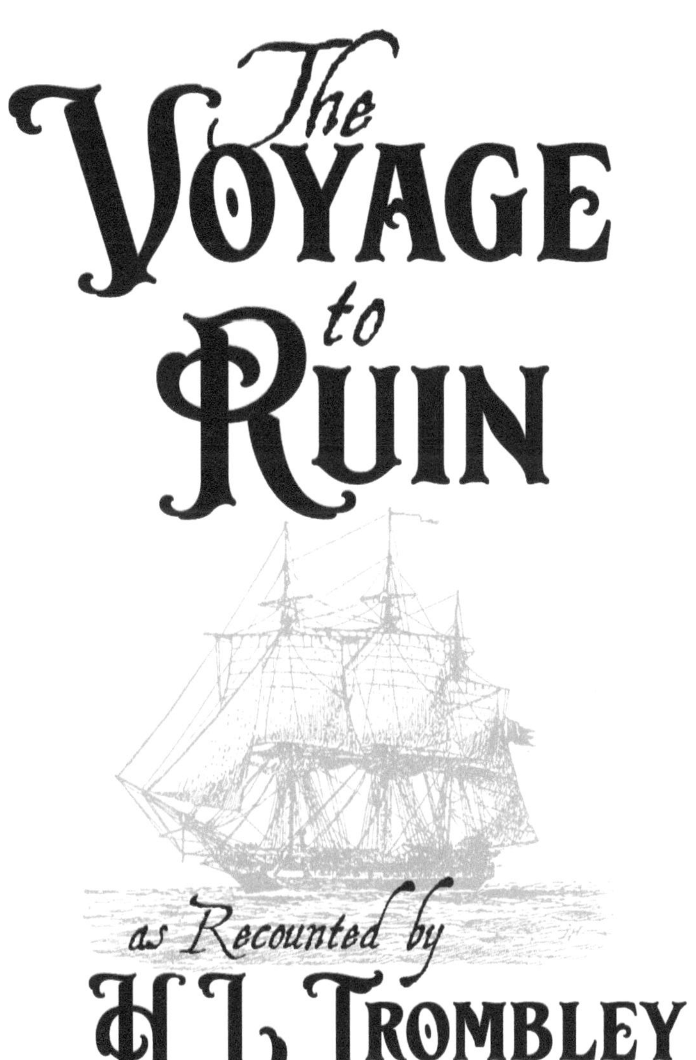

The Voyage to Ruin

as Recounted by

H. L. Trombley

The Pirates of the Eschaton
Book One

Decorative ship elements are the font *Ships N Boats* by Manfred Klein

Ultimate Revised Edition 2025
ISBN: 978-0-615-14612-6

Wicked Windlass Press
Irving, Tx USA

For my family—

And most especially

For the memory of my grandfathers:

May angels lead you into Paradise.

Oh, let me midlife mourn by the shrined
And druid herons' vows
The voyage to ruin I must run,
Dawn ships clouted aground...

- Dylan Thomas, "Poem on his Birthday"

Eschaton
The
VOYAGE
to
RUIN
being a True, Compleat and Accurate
Account of the scelerous Knaves of the
Pyrate Ship Eschaton
Recounted by H.L.
TROMBLEY
HMS Circe

Rjomaskyr
Mordghre
Riesling Sea
Bordeaux Sea
Chamomile
Umeboshi
Port Cullis
Charolais
Elhard
Pistou
Eclaire
Chai
Pekoe
Urd
Furikake
Erris
Camembert
Port Manteau
Melysion
Erdbeere
Shiarau
Shiraz Sea
Selsig
Schlagsahne
Tawney Port
Edamame
Garam Masala
Comino
Chianti Sea
Cilantro
Korma
Parmigiana
Parmigiana
Porta Bella
Zabaglione
Gouda
Feta

The Quadra Terrarum

Supported at its corners by the four pillars of the elements, the Quadra Terrarum itself supports numerous and diverse forms of life, from the dragonfolk of Stratocumulopolis to the deep-sea dwellers off the Fetan Coast, and of course human beings in all their multitudes, with their short and busy lives. The dome of the sky covers the mountains and seas of mortal lands, while the fixed stars hang above in their harmonious spheres. Under the hills lie the perilous countries of Faeriekind. And deep, deep below all, so legend holds (for no mortal being has ventured thence, or thence returned), the fiery pit of Tartarus itself.

[...]

In the year 426 (by the Camembertian calendar) the sea captain Nicolas Osbert, in the ship *Copernicus*, confirmed once and for all that the world is, in fact, flat, thus silencing a long scholarly debate on the topic. Round worlds have been postulated, but no evidence of their existence has ever been found.

- From *A New Cosmology of the Quadra Terrarum*,
by Keo Arnwulf, Scholar of Elhard

TABLE OF CONTENTS

Lost at Sea

Captain Flynn Freeborn sat with his feet on his sea chest and his boots on the deck, trimming his toenails with a boarding axe. He hummed in a cheerful baritone as he worked, and the occasional lyrical phrase slipping free revealed that he sang one of those sea shanties of which sailors are so fond—yet not just one sea shanty, but a thematic fusion of all the sea shanties in Captain Flynn's considerable repertoire, the very apotheosis of all sea shanties:

"Hmm-hmmm drunken sailor … rant and roar hmm-hmmm … drink up, me hearties, yo ho!"

He reflected as the nail parings fell down to the deck on the keen, almost unparalleled pleasure, so often unappreciated, of neat, trim toenails—a pleasure, alas, that many of his men did not share with their captain. Why, there was many a salt on the *Peregrine* (an otherwise taut ship—or as taut as one of its kind, with such a captain, could be) with horny old growths covering his toes, yellowing carapaces as tough as rhinoceros hide and as long as the tusks of an oliphant. Yet they skittered up and down the masts never batting an eye—or breaking a toe—and padded about the deck barefoot, unabashed by their lack of pedicurial hygiene. It was not a thing he could easily understand.

The boarding axe, honed to a razor's sharpness, shaved off the last crescent of nail. Captain Flynn, well satisfied, leaped to his feet, thrust the weapon through his belt, and bellowed out in a voice that would have put the mightiest lungs on the stages of Parmigiana to shame, "O where are me boots, me noggin, noggin boots?" The answer, of course, was "on the deck, right where you left them," but Flynn preferred the less accurate but lyrically more appropriate, "All gone for beer and tobacco!"

He continued to sing in a roar that could have been heard at the foretop in a howling hurricane as he pulled on the aforementioned footgear, and would have gone on to wonder about not only his boots but his shirt and his bed had not an even louder shout, hoarse and irritable, overridden him. Extracted from the sailors' cant and obscenity, the gist of the message was this:

"The First Mate's compliments, sir, and would you kindly belay that atonal howling and come up on deck?"

Flynn emerged from his cabin, inhaling of the clean, salt air and smiling. This was the pinnacle of life, it was—sailing large on a bright morning, brisk air quivering with the promise of a glorious day. The men working the ship were singing of women and grog, the quartering breeze hummed through the rigging, the pellucid waters rushed and gurgled along the *Peregrine*'s side. A glorious day!

"Well, Jem," he said, ascending to the quarterdeck, "what's afoot, then?" The word afoot particularly delighted him, and he repeated it with a chuckle to himself, knocking his freshly trimmed and shod toes against the plank beneath him.

"Sir," said the First Mate, making an abortive gesture towards a non-existent cap. "Sail to leeward, sir."

"Now, Jem Starboard," said Captain Flynn, distracted for a moment from the interesting question of a strange sail in their cruising ground. "There's no call for such formality, so there ain't. You're a free man now, you are, a gentleman of fortune, not one of the Admiralty's sad slaves!" He clapped the younger man's shoulder. "So belay that sirring and saluting and carrying on, and speak to me in plain language."

"Aye, sir," said Jem Starboard. Flynn cast him a wry look, and his face (usually rather pasty, with freckles) turned bright red. "Uh, I mean—er, Captain. Mad Dog sighted a sail just off the larboard beam, sir—uh—Captain. Sir."

"Ah!" Flynn's eyes lit. "A chase? A fat, foolish merchant wallowing in our waters, loaded with silk from Chai or gold from the Queen's own coffers?" The light dimmed. "Or a warship to harry us away from our rightful cruising ground, the braggartly buggers?"

"Perhaps you ought to have a look, sir," suggested Jem Starboard, for a moment forgetting himself. Well, old habits, as they say, die hard, and before he became Jem Starboard, First Mate of the *Peregrine*, he had been Jeremiah Starkey, a Lieutenant in the Royal Navy of Camembert, and he would no more have gone without saluting than he would have gone without pants.

Flynn forbore to comment. Flynn's attention was, in fact, wholly taken up with the prospect of a prize. "Aye!" he said, "a prime idea!" And at once scurried up to the maintop, his spyglass in his teeth.

The distant ship leapt into focus, hull-down on the horizon. From the trim of her rig, no merchant at all, but a ship of Her Majesty's Navy. He frowned, sweeping the blurred indigo line of sea and sky with the glass, and when an accompanying squadron did not appear, a moral dilemma did. Even a lone Navy vessel could give his sweet-sailing *Peregrine* a tense moment or two, with no pecuniary benefit to himself or his men. And yet—his ship had the weather gage of her, with the breeze right where she liked it, and it would be easy enough to rake her with a broadside or two, board her in his own smoke, and take her while those Navy dogs still had their hands in their pockets. "Aye, there's glory for you," he said to himself, stroking his chin while he considered. Then a thought occurred to him, and he leant down and shouted towards the deck, "Jem Starboard!"

"Aye, sir?" The mate's head appeared almost at once at the edge of the swaying platform.

"Tell me, Jem," said Flynn, passing the spyglass, "what does your keen and professional eye make of yonder bark?"

"Sir," said Jem, having looked, "that is Her Majesty's Ship the *Pegasus*, a frigate of thirty-six guns. I'd stake my—" he almost said "I'd stake my career on it," but since his career was long since dust and ashes, he swallowed the words and finished, "my ears on it, sir."

"That's a considerable wager, Jem, as you've got the biggest jug-handles I've ever seen in all my days," said Captain Flynn. "But you've confirmed my own suspicions, that you have. And who captains H.M.S. *Pegasus* these days, if you can recall?"

It was well known on the *Peregrine* that Jem Starboard still knew the Navy List by heart.

"Captain Bayard Rangle, sir," said Jem at once. He sounded a little wistful. Perhaps he missed those regimented days of eight-bell watches, hardtack and salt horse, stiff collars and silly hats. Perhaps he was thinking of the Admiral's broad pennant he'd never hoist, the well-bred young lady he'd never marry, all because he'd sent a ship to starboard when he should have said port, running her aground, dismasting her, sinking her, the culmination of a series of disasters that drove him to resign his commission and seek alternate employment before he could be hanged, decommissioned, flogged round the fleet, or simply tossed over the side by his own men, a sacrifice to propitiate the heathenish gods of the sea.

Flynn nodded to himself. "Cousin Bayard," he said. "Always exact to the moment." His face split in a huge, white moon of a grin; hurling himself down towards the deck he cried, "Listen up, then, mates! That's Cousin Bayard on yonder ship, so it is, and I don't doubt we'll be seeing a bit of action before the day is out, and then perhaps the good captain will be joining us for our evening victuals. So let's give those Navy dogs a good show, eh?"

The *Peregrine*s roared their approbation, and all through the long, golden afternoon they packed on as much sail as their ship could bear, the whole shooting match, t'gallants'ls, royals, skysails and all, a gleaming, towering pyramid of canvas. Oh, the glorious living speed, the white foam rushing along the *Peregrine*'s side!

"If she don't decline to fight," said Jem Starboard, "we'll be up on her by sunset, sir."

"She won't, not she," said Captain Flynn, squinting up into the maze of rigging and white, white sails. Was that great mass of canvas pressing her down a trifle at the head? He thought it might be. He shouted an order, and the grinning men obeyed (they knew their captain's motions, they)—and yes, now her motion was easier, freer. Now she more than sailed—she flew. "Not with Bayard Rangle in command. A more bellicose, warlike, battle-hungry, pugilistical bastard you'll never meet, nay, not if you lived a thousand years." But he was smiling as he said it. After all, had not Cousin Bayard's love of a dust-up been what reunited them in the first place?

The Navy ship had certainly sighted them by now; she was beating toward them, tack upon tack, not merely accepting battle but welcoming it, hurrying it on. What a lovely vessel she was, a trim little frigate, and how well handled! She and the *Peregrine* were much of a size, but what a difference high discipline and fast gunnery made! She'd be a tough nut to crack—if Captain Flynn really intended to crack her, that was.

"Let's show her our true colors, shall we, Jem?" said Flynn, grinning at the mate.

"Aye, sir," said Jem, touching his forehead—but he was smiling too. Striding forward, "Hoist the colors!" he bellowed. The ball of black ascended to the mizzen-peak, then snapped out, flapping and streaming in the joyous wind, the jolliest Roger you ever saw: a grinning, winking, pig-tailed, earringed skull that bore a remarkable likeness to Captain Flynn himself—or Captain Flynn as he would look in a century or so, his bones nibbled clean by the fishes—and wearing a shabby tricorne hat.

"Ahhh!" cried Flynn, watching the flag and laughing out loud. "What a fine thing it is, what a fine thing indeed!" How many fat merchants had wept at the very sight of those colors? How many tried to flee, all too late? 'Twas a fine thing, a fine thing indeed, to sail under such colors!

The *Pegasus* closer now, as white daylight deepened to gold, every line and spar of her visible in almost painful detail, her open gun ports glaring. Flynn watched as she went about, staying in her own length, as graceful and lively as a cutter, shouldering the turquoise-and-amber seas aside as though she would reach her foe by sheer willpower alone. Twice more, he reckoned, she'd need to tack, and then he'd be upon her.

"Not long now, Jem Starboard," he said, rubbing his hands in his eagerness.

"Aye, sir," the First Mate replied, watching the approaching ship with wide and wishful eyes.

In later years, when the name of Flynn Freeborn had passed into history, and from history into legend, when Captain Bayard Rangle was an old, old man, an Admiral whose grand-children were captaining ships of their own, the battle they fought that day would be remembered as the battle, the decisive battle, the final battle of the Royal Navy's war on piracy. Oh, you could say with perfect accuracy that Vandemar Broadside continued his rampages for years afterwards, but, for all his infamous violence, he was merely raging against the dying of the light (as it were). With Lucenza di Ladro dead and Cornelius Cid given official pardon by the Crown of Eclaire, Flynn Freeborn was the last of the great pirates—and with his passing, so passed an age.

Scholars, historians and enthusiasts in later years pored over the battle's least details, as though knowing where the *Pegasus*'s yeoman of the sheets was standing, or the type of coffee Captain Bayard had drunk that morning, would increase their understanding one iota. Papers were written on the topic—monographs—whole dissertations. Leon Ampersand, the scholar of Elhard whose name you may have heard in connection with other matters entirely (for it was his knowledge of both mechanics and magic that helped make Cornelius Cid's first airship sky-ready), wrote the notable work, An Humble Proposal Regarding the Mysterious Disappearance of the Famed Pirate Captain Flynn Freeborn (available, no doubt, at your local bookseller).

These things being the case, there is little need to go into great detail here. The details have been enumerated elsewhere, and they are not, no not by a chalk as long as your arm, the point of our excursus. The battle is not the point. While other authors may attempt to impress their readers by flashing out a host of technical terms, swamping them with jargon that mystifies rather than clarifies, laying them quite by the lee, such is not our intent. We will be clear, concise, brief, succinct.

To lay the scene:

The *Peregrine* had the weather gage, and was going large with the wind on her larboard quarter, throwing up a fine, white wave that smothered her bows in foam. Her guns, twelve to a side, were run out, each attended by a grinning crew of hardened, desperate, perilous scoundrels, scallywags and poltroons. Captain Flynn himself stood on the quarterdeck, a song bubbling in his heart if not quite to his lips, his hands clasped behind him, an antic light in his eye. Now and then he laughed out loud, for no reason anyone else could see.

The *Pegasus*, meanwhile, beat up toward her foe with all the spirit that was in her. She was a stiff, modern frigate, very fast, very weatherly, and she was as close-hauled as ever she could be. The captain had beat to quarters long since; there were sharp-shooters in the tops, slow-match smoldering in tubs on deck, filling the air with its heart-quickening reek, and (just as on the pirate ship) the gun crews waiting, waiting, a-waiting the order to fire.

In that golden hour, with the sun gliding down towards the horizon, turning the sky to amber and the sea to bronze, the two ships converged in almost perfect silence. They might have been the only things moving in an otherwise motionless world; the sky was empty of birds, and even the sea might have been merely a picture of water. But the two ships raced toward each other with swift grace and deadly intent, white-winged, glorious, and it was a matter of moments until battle was joined.

The *Pegasus* went about, showing the *Peregrine* her starboard broadside. The gap between the two ships was narrowing. Neither had yet fired.

"Flynn Freeborn!"

The dark-haired captain of the *Pegasus* had a carrying voice, and his speaking trumpet carried it farther still. "Surrender now," he bellowed, "and I guarantee your death will be quick and merciful!"

"Surrender ain't a word in Cap'n Flynn's prodigious vocabulary!" Flynn returned, his own voice crossing the gap between ships without the aid of a megaphone. "So you can just be takin your surrender and—" But there is no need to repeat exactly what he said, which was not the sort of thing one would say with ladies present. The pirates let out a bellowing jeer, and the sailors roared their disapprobation.

"And I'll remind you," Captain Flynn continued, "that God reserves the lowest, deepest, blackest, foulest pit of hell for traitors and kinslayers, so if you'd not see your immortal soul damned for all eternity, you'll let us by in peace!"

"The hell I will!" cried Captain Bayard in a fine froth of indignation. "You're a pirate, Flynn, a disgrace to our family honor, and your poor mother would thank me for bringing you to justice!"

"Let's give her a shot, now," Flynn murmured to his gunner, a wild-eyed, bearded fellow named Hieronymous London. "Can you be pitching it right over the quarterdeck, between the Captain and yon redcoat? Give him a scare, like."

Hieronymous grinned, revealing a black, mostly toothless gap in his wiry grey beard. "Can I?" said he, chuckling. "Just you watch, mate." He set his piece with particular care, squinting down the sight while his crew poured in the powder and rammed in the shot, Flynn looking on with the pleased anticipation of a boy about to get a particularly fine birthday present. The gunner stepped aside and jerked on the lanyard. The gun went off with a bang, kicking back with the force of the powder's explosion, and hurled the ball in a fine, sweet arc straight toward Bayard Rangle, passing so close by him it knocked the hat from his head.

"A fine shot, indeed!" Flynn cried, laughing, as Bayard (his scowl visible even from this distance) bent to retrieve his now-mangled hat. "Never have I seen a finer!"

"O' course," said Hieronymous London, modestly.

Leaning forward, Flynn shouted, "That for speaking in such a blaggardly fashion about my sainted mother! Stand and fight, you cowardly dog, and we'll show you what your honor's worth!"

"I'll see you hang, Flynn Freeborn!" Bayard cried, voice cracking with rage. "Fire!"

The *Pegasus*'s broadside disappeared in the smoke of the simultaneous crash of guns. Roundshot whizzed through the rigging and thudded into the *Peregrine*'s hull. Men shouted, ropes parted, and dismounted blocks came tumbling down. One landed at Flynn's feet. He picked it up and regarded it, like Hamlet contemplating the skull of poor Yorick.

"You know what to do, Jem Starboard?" he said, tossing the block to his mate.

"Aye, sir!" Wielding the block like the orbis mundi (or, more properly, the cubus mundi, I suppose), the First Mate of the *Peregrine* strode along the deck, shouting above the din of the battle begun: cheering men, the crack-crack-crack of musket-fire, and once every two minutes (damned quick gunnery) the enormous, shattering crash! of the *Pegasus*'s broadside, intercut with the *Peregrine*'s more ragged, irregular replies.

"Prepare to go about!" Jem Starboard cried, and at once the rigging darkened with men hurrying aloft. "Lay aloft, lay aloft, you slubberdegullions!" he roared, with the furious passion of first naval officers throughout history. But when everyone was in position (and it took less than a minute, even with the firing of the guns, the hurrying and scurrying of the powder-monkeys, and the general hullabaloo), the *Peregrine* began her turn. First her head came up into the wind, the hands at the braces cheering and yo-heave-ho-ing for all they were worth, her leeway drifting her nearer to her foe—and then, when all the way was almost off her, and her sails were shivering, Flynn Freeborn winked at Jem Starboard, who gave a quiet order.

The *Pegasus* let fly another broadside.

The *Peregrine* shuddered, hesitating between the old tack and the new, and then slowly began to creep back into the old. The *Pegasus*, not slow to take advantage of the opportunity, kept up a hot fire, pummelling the defenseless pirate. Several spars, shot away by the latest volley, crashed down toward the deck. Men lay here and there in heaps, groaning, while others ran this way and that, waving their hands in the air and hooting in their panic, slipping in the blood that soaked the deck.

Flynn Freeborn was clutching his belly, laughing so hard he could barely stand, while the tears rolled down his cheeks.

"Sir?" It was Jem Starboard, whose blood-daubed cheeks gave him the aspect of some fierce barbarian chieftain from ancient times. “Should we strike the colors?”

“Eh?” And when Jem had repeated his question, Flynn wiped his eyes and said, “Oh, aye, to be sure, to be sure. No sense in postponing the inevitable, so there ain't.”

For such a short battle, the carnage on the pirate ship was shocking. Captain Rangle, who had seen many a hot action in his day (several of them against this selfsame buccaneer), was hard-pressed to contain both his face and the contents of his stomach as he stepped across to take possession, accompanied by his bosun, his third lieutenant, and a file of marines. The deck was awash in blood, blood oozing down the masts, blood dripping from the rigging, blood jetting from the scuppers into the sea. Dead men lay in heaps, and the wounded too, and they filled the air with their cries, for there was no one alive to help them.

Captain Flynn stepped up to greet the conquering heroes, a sad figure just as battered as his ship. One of his coat sleeves hung empty, and there was a bloody bandage wound round his head. His face was greyish-white, the stubble showing black by contrast. An attentive observer, however, might have noticed the wry sparkle, ill-concealed, in his eyes.

“So, Flynn Freeborn,” said Bayard Rangle, “you see what your arrogance has brought you.” Captain Rangle, of Her Majesty's Royal Navy, was a tall, dark-haired, well-made man, only a few years older than Flynn himself. He came off very well by contrast, however, as he was relatively clean, his curly hair neat, his uniform impeccable. The file of marines didn't hurt, either.

“Aye,” said Flynn, hanging his bloody head. “'Tis a new word I've learnt today, so it is. I'll not soon forget the lesson you've taught me.”

Nearby, one of the wounded pirates let out a loud and piteous groan.

“Hush up!” hissed the corpse next to him.

“Which I'm just trying to add a note of verisimilitilitude,” the other casualty retorted, hurt.

“Bugger your very-sery-melly-tude,” said the corpse, whose front was all one stiffening mess of red. “We're just set dressing, we are.”

"Bugger your own self," said the first pirate, but his heart wasn't really in it.

"You'll wear a hempen necktie, Flynn," said Bayard, in strong, comminatory tones.

"Aye, no doubt," Flynn replied, his hand straying to the necklace of braided beads and hemp he wore, as so many pirates did, to remind him of the fate that awaited him if he were caught. His fingers brushed the ornament, and he swayed on his feet, his face turning the color of whey. With a muffled groan, his eyes rolling back in his head, he keeled over, landing with a thump on the deck.

"Damn!" said Bayard. "Pass the word for the ship's wizard. Hurry!"

"But, sir," said the third lieutenant. "If we're just going to hang him anyway—"

"His fate is for the courts to decide, Mr Chay," said Bayard piously. "Would you like to deprive Her Majesty of the pleasure of condemning the most infamous rogue this age?"

Queen Leonara's temper, and her hatred of pirates (this pirate in particular), was legendary. Mr Chay, only recently passed for lieutenant, had not the least desire to do any such thing, and he ran at once to fetch the *Pegasus*'s wizard, who clucked and tutted over the comatose captain, then appointed several of the beefier marines to carry him down to his cabin.

Bayard accompanied the party, abjuring the men who remained above to "make sure these rogues don't try anything." Since the rogues seemed disinclined to try anything but lie on deck and expire, the marines were not displeased with their lot.

Not, that is, until the dead pirates suddenly rose up, overwhelmed them, wrested their weapons from them, and threw them overboard.

"Cousin Bayard!" cried Flynn when they were alone in the cabin, wrestling his arm out of his coat, where he had put it for very-silly-milly-tude.

"Cousin Flynn!" cried Bayard, and the two men threw their arms around each other, embracing and pounding each other's shoulders and grinning like fools.

"Ah, that was grand!" said Flynn, laughing. "That was the best one yet!" He went to the sideboard and poured two glasses of wine, offering one to his cousin.

“Wasn't it?” said Bayard, looking pleased. “I particularly liked the bit about the hempen necktie.”

They toasted the success of the ruse and drank off their glasses, and Bayard said, “I was impressed, cous, by how quickly your men got those spars down, and how natural it looked—almost as though they really had been shot away. You've been practicing, haven't you?”

“Oh, aye,” said Flynn, refilling his cousin's glass. “The lads, they enjoy a bit of drama, they do. Did you notice the blood on the deck, at all?”

“I could hardly have avoided it, could I? Pigs' blood, I suppose?”

They toasted the success of the ruse, drinking to each other's health three times three, laughing and reminiscing about past encounters.

“Ah, cous,” said Flynn, chuckling and wiping his eyes. “What larks, eh? What grand larks indeed! More wine?” He offered the bottle, which Bayard took. But instead of pouring himself another glass, he frowned, his lips pursed and a little line between his eyebrows.

“Er...” said Flynn, looking at the motionless wine bottle.

“You almost took my head off with that ball, you know,” Bayard said, rousing himself from his brown study.

Flynn laughed. “Ha ha! Aye, indeed! What fun, eh, cous? Eh?” Bayard, however, did not join in the merriment; Flynn, at last catching on to his cousin's mood, leaned forward and said, “Cous, what fashes thee? Art sick? Art vexed? 'Twas only a joke, so it was!”

With a sigh, Bayard put down both the empty wine glass and the far-from-empty wine bottle. “I can't do this any more,” he said.

Flynn blinked.

“I—I can't!” said Bayard. “The—the lying, the deception, the—” He was on his feet, pacing, waving his hands. “Do you know,” he said, turning towards Flynn, “I have falsified my own log books. I have lied in my reports to the Admiralty about you. That alone would be enough to have me court-martialled, stripped of my rank, probably shot if not flogged round the fleet and then hung! I take my life into my hands every time I set foot on this ship, cous.”

"I've risked me own life for you many and many-a time," Flynn remarked, mildly enough, helping himself to more wine. His eyes narrowed with a pleasant recollection, and he chuckled. "D'ya remember that time, off the coast of Erris—"

"Aye, but, Lysander—" Bayard began, then checked himself. Flynn had frozen, the wine still pouring from the mouth of the bottle and into the glass—over the rim of the glass—onto the spotless deck. Bayard sighed. "Flynn, I mean. Cousin. I can't be thinking only of myself. I have a family, responsibilities. What will happen to them if I'm caught?"

Flynn did not respond. His face was dark. The wine was a red waterfall over the edge of the glass.

"Your mother sends her regards," Bayard said.

At that, Flynn was out of his seat like a shot, knocking bottle and glass alike to the deck, a fine spray of broken glass. "So it's this again, is it?" he cried. "This same tired old worn-out theme? I gave you me answer on that long ago, cous, long ago, and I've not changed me mind—nay, nor ever will!"

It was an ancient argument between them. Long ago Bayard had ceased to press the issue, valuing his cousin's good will too much to risk alienating him in such a high-handed fashion—but this time he was determined, his mind was made up, and a stubborn hope flared in his breast.

"Will you not?" he said now. "If not for your own sake, then for the sake of those you've left behind?"

Flynn stuck out his jaw—a sure sign he was feeling mulish, obstinate, intractable and contumacious. "And who would you be referrin to, then?" he asked.

"Oh, for God's sake!" Bayard burst out, throwing his hands in the air. "Your mother? Evie?"

"Ah," said Flynn, and if the name moved him he gave no sign. Meeting his cousin's eyes he said deliberately, knowing it would wound, "Is she still alive, then?"

"How dare you!" Bayard hissed, stopping his fist mere moments before its impact with his cousin's face.

"I'll tell you how," said Flynn, putting his face right next to Bayard's. "Because I am a pirate, cous, a lawless rogue, and I answer to no man but myself. This may not be the life I would have chosen for myself, but it's mine now, so it is! And I don't require your help, your assistance, or your damned interference!"

"If that is the case," said Captain Rangle, drawing himself erect, strong chin jutting in a way that increased the resemblance between them, although they were not in fact related by blood, "I'll waste no more of your valuable time, Captain." And he turned to go.

"Wait, now, cous," said Flynn, and although he did not follow Bayard, or offer to touch him in any way, he did hold out his hand, and on his face was regret. "Let's not be parting in anger, not after all we've been through. Are we not cousins, and closer than brothers? Look." He turned his hand palm-out, showing the round, white scar there.

"You must think me a sentimental fool," Bayard said, but he halted, turned, looked. His lips tightened. There was a similar scar on his own palm, got when he and Flynn were children, playing a foolish children's game.

"Never in life!" cried Flynn. "Never in life, cous!"

"So you'll do it? You'll give up your life of crime, recant, go home? She has been waiting a long time." He did not say the name a second time.

"Fifteen years," Flynn said softly, looking down at the mark on his hand. "A long time, in very deed." He glanced up. "And what has one such as I to offer her? I, near thirty years old, an unrepentant sinner. Nay, cous, nay. I'll not go to her."

She's no younger, Bayard thought but did not say, and she has been waiting all this time. Unhappy but by no means surprised, he said, "Farewell, then, cous. The next time we meet, if ever we do, it won't be a mock battle. I have my duty."

"Aye." The two men shook hands, and Flynn mustered a smile. "And how shall I be ridding myself of your intolerable presence this time?" he asked. "Will you walk the plank? Or would you like to be shot from a cannon again?"

"No." Bayard shook his head. "It took months for my ribs to heal the last time. Perhaps you should just heave me overboard?"

"Well, it's not as entertaining for the lads, so it isn't, but if it's your preference—"

"It is."

"Then I suppose it's into the drink with you, cous. You're not wearing your best coat this time, are you?"

"No. I've learnt my lesson."

"Well. Good-bye, then, cous."

"Good-bye."

The crew of the *Pegasus* watched in horror as their captain went sailing over the *Peregrine*'s rail, arms and legs flailing, tossed with many an imprecation by a band of grinning importunate cutthroats, and landing with a glorious splash in the water below. And with many a bark of piratical laughter ("yar-har-har!") the *Peregrine* slid out from under the *Pegasus*'s lee, her spars miraculously healed, and swept out into the open ocean. The *Pegasus*, busy hauling Captain Rangle (who could not swim) out of the drink, did not give chase.

Having ascertained that Bayard was in no danger of drowning, Flynn clapped his spyglass to and turned from the rail, deep in thought. Many of the things Bayard had said, he had said before—and many of Flynn's replies had been his traditional responses as well. Like two musicians improvising together, they played endless variations on the same theme, handing the argument back and forth, one to the other, but never altering its essence.

The men were already at work cleaning up the mess of the battle. Sailors, like cats, are fastidious creatures; unlike cats, they can tolerate a fair degree of squalor (and pirates rather more than ordinary sailors), but the blood in the standing rigging was, they felt, coming it a bit high. And with Jem Starboard (once an active, zealous lieutenant in Her Majesty's service, with all that implies) in charge, the work moved along at a brisk pace. By morning there would be no sign that a battle, even a mock battle, had ever taken place.

Sighing, walking heavily, Flynn stepped up and took the helm from the sailor stationed there. Balm for the soul, it was, to feel the spokes of a living ship's wheel beneath his hands, but at first, his soul was not balmed. Bayard's words stuck like a fishhook in his mind, niggling away at him. He was not a man much given to introspection, and the unaccustomed work brought him lower and lower, until his heart might have been dragging along the bottom of the sea.

Gradually, however, the ship's lively motion, the purple breeze of evening, the singing of the crew as they worked and the wind in the rigging, the dazzling emergence of a thousand stars, worked upon him, and his native optimism reasserted itself.

"And after all," he said to himself, "everything that starts must have its end, and nothing's eternal in this valley of shadows and tears."

Another man might not have found this thought comforting, but to a creature like Flynn, who lived almost exclusively in the present moment, it was exactly the sort of reflection he needed to break free of his blue mood entirely (like a tired swimmer who requires a friendly hand to heave him above the water's sparkling surface), and once he had thought it, he smiled to himself. What a lovely evening it was, to be sure! How gentle the breeze, like a mother's kiss on his cheek! How immeasurably precious the world, how clear and distinct and as it were real everything appeared, how three-dimensional, how perfect. Every spar, every shroud, every backstay, was diamond-edged, standing painfully distinct from a sky that was no mere background, but real and thriving and present, close enough (he would have said) to touch. A soaring happiness filled his soul, and if you had asked him then, he would have told you how he wished life could go on like this for ever.

I must pause here and confess, dear readers, that I am puzzled as to how I should continue. In fact, a part of me wishes I did not have to continue at all. I would much prefer to leave you here, with the charming image of Captain Flynn at the helm of his beloved ship: a man in the prime of his life, rather good-looking, made handsomer still by his evident happiness—a man, it must be admitted, of no particular virtue, but in whom a certain dash and ebullience of spirit might almost have obviated the need for virtue. I would like that of all things, because the events to come are unpleasant in the extreme, and will no doubt be as disagreeable for you to read as they are for me to relate. However, to leave you with the impression that Captain Flynn's story ends here would be iniquitous, vile, false. We must remember that the service of truth sometimes requires the endurance of suffering, and if things become too frightening, we will hold each other's hands for comfort, like children lost in a dark wood.

It was past midnight when Flynn sought out his bed at last, weary but filled with a sort of subdued joy that hummed in his soul like a melody played on the violoncello. He swung up into his cot, and no sooner had his head touched the pillow than he was asleep.

He woke with a start sometime later. It was still dark, and the *Peregrine*'s easy motion had not changed, but something was out of joint. He had been dreaming, he thought, but of what he could not have told you; the 'cello's voice had been tuned down half a step, and no longer spoke of present joy, but of grief to come. There was a strange smell in the air, a damp, marshy, greyish-brownish odor, like a graveyard in a swamp. And had he heard a noise—a thick, muddy, sloppy, slurpy sound, like a swamp monster dragging its oozing pseudopods across the deck?

Heart a-thrill with superstitious fear, he fumbled for a candle-end and a lucifer—found them both—popped the match alight with his thumbnail. In the sudden blaze of gold he saw—

"Oh, God!" The words were wrung from him unwilling, but he could not unsay them now. The thing—there was a thing in the cabin, what in God's name was it?—hunched and awful, dragging with it tendrils of seaweed and the muck of the ocean floor, turned to look at him—

With a sputter the match went out, burning his fingers. He dropped it with a cry and quickly reached for another.

This time he thought to light the candle, and as it spread its infinitely welcome, sane by all that's holy, warm golden gleam through the cabin, he laughed out loud with relief. There was nothing there!

Nothing there? Why, of course there was not! What could have been there? How would it have got there?

Someone pounded on the door, and Jem Starboard's voice carried through the thick wood: "Captain? Is everything all right?"

"Aye, all's well..." he began to say, but the words died on his lips. There on the deck—the clean deck when he went to bed—was a wide, glistening, greyish puddle. There was grit and sand in it, and a long purple rope of seaweed.

"Captain?" Jem's voice held a note of panic now.

Shaking off his paralysis, eyes still fixed on the telltale pool, "Aye, Jem," Flynn called. "'Twas only a bad dream, so it was. Don't fash yourself."

"Aye-aye, Captain!" Jem's relief was palpable. "Well—sleep well, sir."

"Aye," said Flynn, mostly to himself. "Aye, no doubt."

Nothing more transpired that night, Flynn's rest was deep and dreamless, and in the morning he was inclined to view the whole thing as the product of an overactive imagination and unacknowledged guilt.

Or he was, until the glassy puddle of seawater on the deck, even more inexplicable in day's clear light, confronted him. And then, in the great cabin, he found one of the stern windows open, letting in the fresh morning breeze. Letting in now. What else had it let in, in the deepest watches of the night? He shuddered to think of it.

"No, sir," said Jem Starboard, when asked. "I didn't hear a thing. Nothing," he might have added, "except you yelling and carrying on."

Flynn grunted. "When we sight the tip of Garam Masala," he said, "if this wind holds, let's take a north'ard turn. Who knows but that we might meet a fat merchant, loaded down with pearls and ambergris, bound for Chai? And then," he added, mostly to himself, "there's always Eclaire. They do a brisk trade themselves, this time of year."

"Aye, sir," said Jem, regarding his captain with a little frown between his eyebrows. He did not point out that Eclaire's principal export was wool, and that the trouble of disposing of a cargo of sheepskins would far outweigh the trouble of taking it in the first place. He confined himself instead to saying, in a casual tone, "Eclaire's far out of our usual cruising grounds, sir."

"Aye, well," said Flynn, taking off his hat and running a hand through his long, long hair, "I've a longing for a change of scene, so I do."

"Aye, sir," said Jem Starboard. What else could he say?

That night again, Flynn's rest was broken by fell dreams—closer now they were, hull up on the horizon of his soul. Again he woke with a startled curse on his lips, again he felt with horrible certainty that he was not alone in the cabin. And this time he heard, accompanying those glutinous footsteps, a harsh, raspy, thick and awful sound, like a drowned corpse trying to breathe. It was very near at hand—it was almost in his ear.

He sat up with a shriek, lighting a candle with a speed born of fear, certain he would see some Horrible Thing looming over his cot, grinning at him with barnacled teeth.

But there was nothing there.

Nothing but a spreading puddle on the deck, in which a small sea animal flopped and wriggled, drowning in the cabin's air.

"Oh, by all that's holy," breathed Flynn, clutching the candle-end with one hand, pressing the other to his pounding heart, "what is it that's haunting me?"

The question before him was threefold: 1.) What was it? 2.) Why him? and 3.) How could he be rid of it? He scrounged about in the cabin until he found a pen, an inkwell and a sheet of paper, and wrote the three questions large at the top. Then he set about trying to think up the answers. He screwed up his face with the effort, but after a long time and a great deal of determined thinking, he had made no progress whatever, and given himself a throbbing headache in the process, all that unaccustomed effort having strained his brain muscles, one supposes.

"Nay," said he, crumpling the paper (a handbill offering substantial rewards for his own capture) and tossing it into a corner. "Nay, that's not the way to be going about it, so it isn't. Thinking never was your for-tay, Flynn Freeborn." So he took himself out of the cabin and climbed up the shrouds, up to the maintop and then, without a pause, higher still to the topgallant masthead, a hundred feet up and more, swaying with the roll of the ship, commanding a magnificent circle of empty sea (not a sail, not a sail for miles) and empty twilit sky. He hooked an arm around the mast and settled himself as comfortably as he could, drawing his pipe out of his coat pocket.

Brief gold flared in the gathering gloom as he lit it, and burning tobacco glowed red as he inhaled a deep draught of fragrant smoke, closing his eyes with pleasure. He blew it out in a white ring, smiling as it dissipated against the darkening sky. The first stars were emerging—there, orange against the indigo, was the Fishhook, which the ancient Fisherman used to catch the souls of those who died at sea.

"By Heaven," breathed Flynn Freeborn, taking the pipe from his mouth. "Lucenza!"

There are few today who have not heard of Lucenza di Ladro, the self-proclaimed Queen of Pirates, whose beauty was matched only by her ferocity in battle. She was not one to offer clemency to those she captured, not she; the flag that flew at the main of her ship, the *Stella Maris*, bore no device at all: it was black, plain unornamented black, and its meaning was simply: Death.

Or it had been. For now Lucenza di Ladro herself was dead.

"But surely..." said Flynn, shaking his head. "Surely ... surely she wouldn't blame me for it, and me as innocent as a newborn lamb?"

For almost a year they had sailed together, the *Peregrine* and the *Stella Maris*, for if one pirate ship could wreak havoc on trade, then what could two in company do? And then, there were other benefits to such an arrangement (Flynn, remembering said benefits, grinned to himself). What times they'd had! But a squadron of five ships of the Royal Navy had been sent to put a stop to the pirates' capers, and although Flynn and the *Peregrine* had escaped to fight another day, a spark in the *Stella Maris*'s powder magazine blew Lucenza, and her crew, and the ship that had pursued her, as high as Heaven (although Heaven was far from her final destination).

Flynn had turned to look back, had seen the pillar of smoke like a huge black thumbprint spoiling the sky's flawless blue; bowing his head and removing his hat, "Sorry, lass," he said. "No hard feelings, I hope."

Hard feelings, however, there were in plenty. What Flynn did not know, because he wasn't there, and had no convenient narrators to tell him, was that, in the moments before the *Stella Maris* exploded, Lucenza had turned to stare with narrowed eyes at the fleeing *Peregrine* (hotly pursued by two ships of the squadron). "I hope they kill you, Flynn Freeborn," she said, "and if they do, I'll see you in Hell tonight. And if they don't—I swear I'll haunt you to the end of your days, and see you down to Hell myself!"

The moon hove up over the horizon, swollen, misshapen and gibbous, looking for all the world like an enormous rotting orange. Flynn, lost in recollection, scarcely noticed. He sucked on his pipe, found it dead and cold, and chomped on the stem instead. Aye, it was just like Lucenza, that proud hasty impetuous ill-tempered miss, to blame a man when he was blameless. And stubborn! Stubborn mulish obstinate and obstreperous to boot! It was just like her to come back from the dead and be tormenting a man, when he had much more important things to be attending to!

"Well," said he, grasping a backstay and sliding down to the deck, "if she comes back tonight I'll be ready for her, so I will!"

If he had seen the orange moon's gleeful goblin grin, a clear omen of disaster if ever there was one, he might have been much less sanguine about his chances.

Before retiring to his cabin, Flynn went below to where the foremast hands made berth (pirates are less strict about such things than the Royal Navy, which seems to delight in making up rules and regulations, and many of the men slept up on deck when the weather was fine, but many more were deserters or mutineers or former Navy seamen fallen on hard times, and they liked the comforting familiarity of slinging a hammock in the traditional fourteen inches). He crept through the rows of swinging hammocks, like the cocoons of some enormous insect, until he found the man he wanted. "Pope!" he hissed. "Oy, Pope!"

The sailor known as Pope snored on. The exhalations of his breath were like the fumes of a distillery, eye-wateringly strong. Wrinkling his nose, Flynn leaned closer, grasping the fellow by his shoulders and giving him a good shake.

"Pope!" he roared in a whisper (a neat trick, if you can do it). "Pope, wake up!"

But there's no sleep so strong as the sleep of the grape, and Pope did not so much as flicker an eyelash.

"Well," said Flynn to himself, "there's no help for it, so there ain't. 'Tis my immortal soul that's imperilled, after all."

He gave a mighty heave, dumping Pope out of his hammock and sending him sprawling on the deck. Even this extremity was not enough to rouse the fellow, who at once squirmed into a more comfortable position, sawing logs the while.

"Lumbermills ain't in it," said Flynn, regarding the sailor with some vexation. He scratched his head beneath his hat, sighed, cleared his throat, raised his left eyebrow, and at last squatted down, putting his mouth right next to Pope's rather crusty ear.

"Pope," he said. "Pope, listen! The magistrate's a-coming, so he is, Pope! He knows what you've done, and this time you'll hang for sure!"

With a terrible shriek, still half-dozing, Pope leapt to his feet—knocking his head on the low beams above hard enough that Flynn saw stars and cuckoo clocks and little tweeting birds. Wavering on his feet, rubbing the sore spot, Pope squinted at Flynn through the gloom.

"What the hell did you do that for, Cap'n?" he demanded. "I was sleeping!"

"Aye," said Flynn, "and if you slept much deeper, we'd be sewing you into your hammock and heaving you into the yawning black abyss, so we would. Come along now, Pope, and bring your little book. I've a task for you, I have."

Pope shot his captain a narrow-eyed glare. The existence of Pope's little book was of course common knowledge on the (men cannot live for months and months in such close proximity without learning all of each other's most intimate secrets, as if by osmosis), but it was considered bad form to mention it. Flynn, however, had not become captain of his own pirate ship to be cowed by the ineffectual glowers of half-mad one-foot-in-the-grave sheep-stealing so-called hedge wizards, and raising one eyebrow he said mildly, "Show a leg, now, Pope; 'tis a matter of some urgency, so it is."

Grumbling, Pope dug around in his effects, coming up with a slim book with a battered leather cover, adorned (though you couldn't see it in the murk tweendecks) with cabalistical symbols. Slinging a satchel over his shoulder, he indicated with a grunt that the captain should lead, and he would follow.

"Listen now, Ezekiah Pope," said Captain Flynn, when the cabin door had closed behind them. "I'm being a-haunted, so I am, and I do fear me that tonight the malevolent spirit will be a-coming for me soul. So if you'd just be obliging me with some spells of protection..." He flapped his hands in a spell-cast-y sort of way.

Pope was a frowsty bugger, with a long white curly beard, a cast in one eye and a paucity of teeth. He squinched shut his eyes as he worked through Flynn's words—but when he had ferreted out their meaning, his ugly face broke into a smile that was almost beatific. "Aye, Captain!" he said. "Aye! Much obliged!" He began to turn the pages of his little book, lips moving, until he came upon the page he wanted. Slinging his satchel round to his front, he began to rummage through it, pausing only to look up at his captain and say, "Stand in the center of the room, there, Captain, if you please," in a brisk and business-like tone.

"Aye," said Flynn, rubbing his hands. Here was something! Here was taking action! Aye, and he'd see some magic in the bargain!

If Flynn had paused to reflect, it might have occurred to him that the charge for which Ezekiah Pope had nearly been hanged was not sheep-stealing (although of that he certainly was guilty) but fraud (and, it was rumored, some other crimes far less mentionable): to wit, wandering the countryside posing as a magician, offering curses, hexes, protective spells, charms, potions, philtres and so on, all of which proved (once Pope had wandered to the next town) to be so much snake oil and deceit. But the question of whether or not the charms of a charlatan would be equal to the wrath of a dead woman scorned never entered Flynn's mind. He stood in the center of the room with perfect confidence and good cheer, and watched as Pope went through his manoeuvres.

First he took a piece of pink chalk from his satchel and commenced to drawing around Flynn an intricate symbol: a circle filled with so many whorls and lines and curlicues it looked more Art Deco than Abracadabra. That being done, he chalked some very magical-looking runes and figures around the edges, then stepped back to admire the effect.

"You understand, Captain," he said, "this is a little off-the-cuff, most of my really powerful reagents having been taken from me when I was unjustly condemned."

"Oh, aye, to be sure," Flynn murmured, as Pope took a grey-green frond from his satchel, lit it at the cabin's lantern, and wafted the smoke through the air. "Emonsday!" he declared in a loud voice, reading (one must assume) from his book. "Egonebay! Eavelay isthay oorpay anmay in pacem!"

He continued on in the same vein, now capering about the cabin and gesticulating, spreading the dense, spicy smoke everywhere he went. Very impressive it was, with Pope's loud hoarse voice chanting the words of the spell, Pope's long white beard a-wagging, Pope's knobby old arms a-waving this way and that.

"Aye, aye, no doubt," said Flynn, when Pope had come to a halt, spine bowed, limbs all ahoo, panting for breath. "Most impressive, most magical indeed, to be sure! I feel a thousand times safer than I did before!"

So saying, he seized Pope's hand and gave it an enthusiastic wringing. "Thank'ee, Pope!" he said. "A thousand times thank'ee!"

"Oh, Captain," said Pope, hanging his head and blushing like a maid. "'Twas the least I could do." But before he would consent to leave the cabin, he insisted on pressing into Flynn's hand a number of items: a holy book, a flask of water blessed by the Pontiff in Comino, a little green sachet that smelt strongly of limes and lavender, hung on a leather thong, and a blue glass eye such as jewellers in Feta give away free with a purchase of their wares. "Be safe, Captain!" he kept exclaiming. "Be safe!"

"Aye," said Flynn, somewhat taken aback by the man's effusion. "Aye, thank'ee, Pope, I shall."

Quite overcome, Pope daubed at his eyes, snuffling, and backed out of the captain's cabin.

Flynn looked down at the rummage sale in his hands. His eyebrows knit, and began to drift slowly up towards his hairline. And then at last he laughed out loud, dancing an impromptu hornpipe in his delight.

"Ah-ha-ha-ha!" he cried. "Protection by the bale! She'll not take my soul this night, that she won't!"

He went to sleep that night with the green sachet under his pillow, the glass eye in his left pocket, the book in his right, and the little flask of holy water clutched in his hands much as a toddler might clutch a well-loved teddy bear. He fell asleep at once, smiling with such sweetness and innocence you would not have believed, to see him, that this man had committed enough crimes to keep a whole benchful of judges employed until the final trumpet's blast. Whether the effects of Pope's charms were actual or merely psychosomatic, he slept soundly and dreamed fair, a sweet melody like the lullabies his mother had sung to him (long long ago, in another life it seemed) running like a bright ribbon through his head.

No dark dreams intruded on his rest that night, no strange noises jolted him from slumber. Above, on deck, the watches changed, the helmsman sang to himself a song they sang in the home he had left long ago, to which he could never return. The moon rode high across the black velvet sky, shrinking from a vast, engorged yellow orb to its more orthodox silver coin. The wind backed a point, the watching men altered sail accordingly, and Flynn's sleeping mind noted the change in the sound of the *Peregrine*'s rigging, the gurgling song of the water rushing along the ship's side.

So relaxed was he, dipped in sleep's warm and blissful balm, that the sound of someone entering his cabin did not awaken him. Even when that someone climbed into his hammock and settled beside him, he barely opened his eyes.

"Why, there you are, lass," he murmured, gathering her up in his arms. "How long it's been since I have seen thee!"

She smelled good, dusky and sweet, her rich black hair like silk against his face, tickling his nose. Her long, smooth limbs were bare. She leaned over him to whisper in his ear, "Have you missed me?"

"You know I have." He smiled sleepily at her.

"Good." Her answering smile was a fierce white flash in the dim room. "That's very good indeed."

In his previous life, Jem Starboard had been a cheerful, good-natured, sanguine youth, full of hopes and plans and dreams of future glory. Leaving the Navy had been like cutting open his chest and pulling out his still-beating heart—but it was easier than staying, with the men calling him Jonah to his face and his superiors eyeing him as you might a sack of burning dung some mischief-maker has left on your front doorstep. Resigning his commission had been a blow that even time and the resilience of youth could not quite heal, and his old friends in the service would not have recognized Jeremiah Starkey in the lean, hard-faced, slouch-shouldered pirate who walked the deck of the *Peregrine*. Sometimes, indeed, he hardly recognized himself.

"All's well," came the cry from aloft, echoed from lookout to lookout. All's well, all's well ... but Jem, hunching his shoulders inside his peacoat, felt a shudder of dread. Something had driven him up on deck in the middle of the night (in the old days, he had never suffered from insomnia), a sense of something amiss, or about to be.

"Clear night," remarked the man at the helm.

"Aye," said Jem, squinting up at the sky. The stars blazed unwinking, each as clear and as cold as ice.

"Heard we'll be sailing north soon."

"That's up to the Captain," Jem said.

"Lads don't fancy chasing after boatloads of sheep," the helmsman commented, mildly enough.

"The Captain will make it worth our while," Jem replied. The Captain could turn lead into gold, if it so suited him, Jem sometimes thought.

The helmsman grunted, turned his head, and spat. (Jem's inner First Lieutenant cringed.) Wiping his mouth with the back of his hand, he said, "The lads think—"

The world froze. For a long moment, stretching onward into infinity, Jem thought he had died, or gone mad, his mind splintering to fragments under a terrible pressure. It was only when it stopped, and time resumed its usual forward march, that he realized the cataclysm had been a sound, and the sound had been a scream. The silence that followed was shrill and tinted red.

"What the devil was that?" said the helmsman, picking himself up off the deck. Across the ship, similar questions were voiced, rather too loudly, by the other deafened men.

"It came from the Captain's cabin!" shouted Jem.

"Eh?" said the helmsman.

But Jem was already sprinting that way, as fast as his gangly legs would take him, bursting through the cabin doors at the head of a stream of bewildered, consternated pirates.

"Captain!" he cried. "Captain!"

The cabin was empty. One of the stern windows flapped open, and a gritty pool of water glistened on the floor, but Captain Flynn was gone. It was as though he had never been there at all.

Jem put the *Peregrine* about, searching the waters they had already sailed. On such a quiet night, someone would have heard if the Captain had fallen overboard, but Jem did not let the still, small voice of logic impede him. He scoured the waters of the Chianti Sea until his eyes bled, but not a trace of Flynn Freeborn did he find, not a strand of his hair or a scrap of his clothes, nor a bleached-white skeleton washed up on some distant shore. In his twilight years he became famous for waylaying hapless travellers and demanding of them, "Have ye seen Captain Flynn?"

He ended his days in a ramshackle bar in Porta Bella, dead for thirteen hours before a barmaid noticed he was gone, but of Flynn Freeborn himself, he never saw another trace.

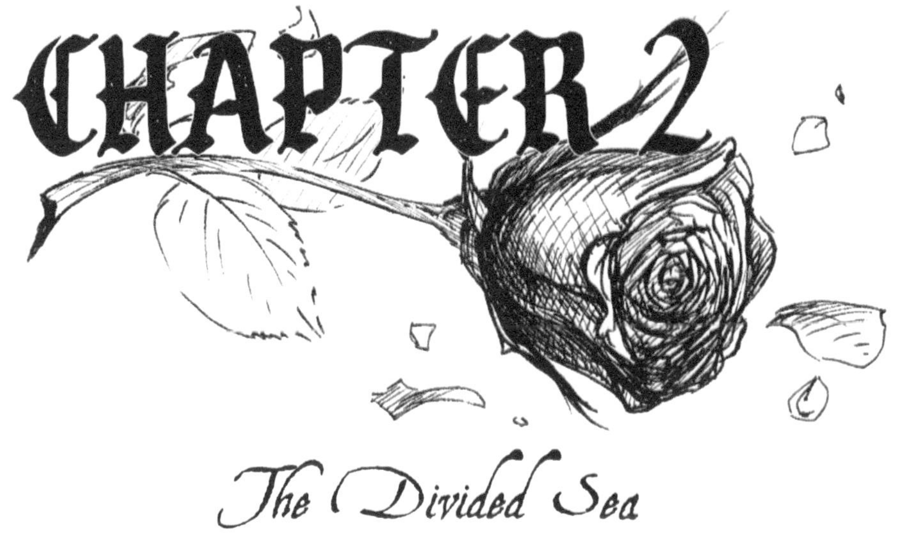

I. Ruses De Guerre

There is something terrifying about a court-martial. The phrase conjures up images of stern-faced old men in uniform, glowering from an august, awful height onto some unfortunate creature, judging him with inimical eyes. The very sound indeed smacks of the Inquisition. And yet, when one breaks the phrase into its component words and contemplates their meanings, it is nothing but a military tribunal, a gathering of officers convened to investigate some aspect of the service or another. There is nothing in the phrase (two innocent words, three syllables) to suggest doom or death.

But perhaps it is that first word, "court," with its implication of judgment. Even a civilian court is a frightening prospect, for no one is so innocent in his soul that he does not fear judgment. Indeed, we avoid judgment whenever we can, preferring to sail through our lives without contemplating our actions any more than we can get away with, and our spirits quail to think that, someday, we will stand before that Eternal Judge and, perhaps, be found wanting.

From the expression on Captain Acheron Zeal's young, open face, he might already have been condemned to the depths of Tartarus, although the court-martial did not convene for another turn of the glass. He sat on a hard wooden bench, dressed in his best uniform, his gold-braided hat a twisted ruin in his hands. That his judges, senior captains all, would find him at fault he had no doubt; his only comfort was that officers were rarely executed by hanging.

In an agony of anticipation, he imagined the Admiral leaning across the table and growling (Captain Zeal's sentence already written behind his glaring eyes), "Tell us about your encounter with the *Eschaton*."

It was the fairest of all fair mornings, the sort of dizzyingly clear day that becomes more and more common as one sails east, nearing the Pole of Water, when the vaulting sky above is so high and blue, and the sea around you so vast, that you feel you might spread your arms and drift up and up, unhindered by gravity, wafted by the freshening morning breeze, up among the clouds themselves, and see that, truly, the universe has no end.

Captain Zeal paced the quarterdeck of the *Kraken*, a cup of coffee in his hand. They had entered the cruising ground of the *Eschaton* sometime in the watches of the night, and he had been on deck since then, although he had his sharpest lookouts above, ready to sing out at the first sight of a sail. He could have slept, knowing that he would be awakened when the time came—but anticipation quickened his pulse and his thoughts, and he was no more capable of sleep than he was of growing an extra arm.

"Good morning, Captain Zeal," greeted the first lieutenant, one Thomas Morrow by name, as Captain Zeal ceased his pacing and came to stand at the rail beside him. The lieutenant was a long, lean, gloomy man, and the bright day only made him seem gloomier by contrast. The anticipation of an engagement with the enemy did not suit him, nor did the sleepless night.

"Good morning, Mr Morrow," Captain Zeal returned. "We should catch our first glimpse of him soon, I believe."

"Indeed so, sir." As Mr Morrow mouthed the words, his long face lengthened still more, giving him the look of an old, grey, dejected hound. Captain Zeal was young and eager for action (and in a world that was more or less at peace, action was hard to come by), and he was not very good at being comforting (especially to a man old enough to be, if not his father, then at least his uncle), but he said,

"Don't worry, Mr Morrow. The plan is a good one. God willing, we'll be sailing home with a fine prize under our belts."

Morrow swallowed hard, surreptitiously reaching out and touching the nearest piece of wood (easy enough, when sailing in a wooden ship), to belay any ill fortune that might follow his captain's words. He was spared any further attempts at encouragement by a shout from the top.

"On deck there! Ahoy, the deck!"

Captain Zeal's head came up, like a hound catching scent of the fox. "What is it, Mr Childe?"

"A sail, Captain!" The young lookout's voice was shrill with excitement. "Just on the horizon, two points abaft the beam!"

"It's him!" Captain Zeal breathed, and before Mr Morrow could voice a protest, he found himself holding the captain's coffee—the captain being in the process of climbing up to the top to see for himself.

"Lend me your glass there, Mr Childe," said the captain, appearing so suddenly that Mr Childe squeaked with surprise before recovering enough to stammer out something that might have been "Yes, sir" and passing the glass to his superior officer.

Not so very long ago, Captain Acheron Zeal had been a midshipman just like this lad, and it seemed he'd spent half his life in the foretop. He was untroubled by the pitch and roll of the ship, peering through the glass, and … there, just there! A sail indeed, barely visible on the pale horizon.

"Good eyes, lad," Zeal said, and Mr Childe flushed with delight.

A sail on that horizon, with trade as depleted as it was these days, and with the rest of the fleet patrolling to the east, could mean only one thing. It was the *Eschaton*.

Captain Zeal hurtled himself back towards the deck, hands and feet scarcely touching the ratlines or the shrouds, and the moment his boot touched wood, he was snapping orders in his best captain's voice, swelling with excitement and authority, sending the hands running this way and that in perfectly orchestrated chaos.

The *Kraken* was a tight ship, an orderly ship, a tidy and disciplined ship—but within a short interval it was transformed. Gone was the precise, military neatness, gone the strict discipline. The neatly hung sails were slopping off the masts as though set by drunken squirrels, and laundry flapped off every spare inch of rigging. Haphazard heaps of canvas and slapdash coils of rope hid the guns—but the camouflage could be removed and the guns brought to bear at a moment's notice. The hands, as well, abandoned their habitual restraint (a restraint inspired, no doubt, by the knotted ends of the bosun's rope), and lounged about the deck, smoking thin cigars and shouting to each other in loud, indolent voices. The Royal Navy's *Kraken* no longer, she had undergone a marvelous sea change and was now a mere *Calamari*. Captain Zeal viewed the metamorphosis with satisfaction. Mr Morrow looked as though he might cry.

"Excellent," said Captain Zeal, rocking back and forth on his heels in his excitement. "Perfect, in fact." He clapped Lieutenant Morrow on the shoulder (something that Lieutenant Morrow despised with a hatred so pure, it was almost holy) and said, "Now when our friend sights us, we shall appear a ripe prize, easily plucked." He grinned, seemed on the verge of whistling (Mr Morrow winced at the very thought—all they would need was a priest, a corpse and a woman on board to maximize their ill luck), but checked himself before he had blown the first note and said, "Now I shall go below to shift my jacket. Carry on, Mr Morrow."

Captain Zeal was a young captain, an enthusiastic captain—a zealous captain, even, one might say—but in many ways he was not a satisfactory captain. He was entirely too voluble for Lieutenant Morrow's taste, showing an inclination to chat not at all in keeping with a sea captain's traditional dignity. And the way he squirreled about in the rigging, as though he were a mere lad! Perhaps age and the service would settle him, but Lieutenant Morrow did not hold out much hope for it. The captain longed for distinction and glory, in this age when all wars had already been fought, when all pirates had been exterminated, and all the world was at peace. His (doomed to be, Mr Morrow feared, unrequited) love of military prestige made him even unsteadier than he might otherwise have been. Mr Morrow frowned, sighed, and stared into the white froth of the ship's wake.

By the time the unsteady and ambitious captain returned to the deck, having exchanged his blue captain's uniform for a taupe-colored jacket, the distant sail was visible not only from the masthead, but from the deck—near enough to confirm that she was, in fact, the *Eschaton*. She was a slender sloop, with the strongly raked masts and narrow beam of a privateer, trim, manoueverable, built to take maximum advantage of even the slightest puff of breeze, and flying the distinctive black flag, the rose and skull that was her captain's emblem. Captain Zeal admired her out loud, and Mr Morrow raised his eyebrow (he had but one, a furry bar across his forehead) and said, "But—with all due respect, sir—she's a pirate!"

"But a damn fine sailor, all the same, Mr Morrow. Look there, she's spotted us at last—see the way she tacks!" He lowered his glass, smiling like a boy who's got exactly what he wanted for Christmas. "Time to run away," he said.

The *Eschaton*, cruising between the rich harbors of the Chai Republic and a small, out-of-the-way island in the middle of the Shiraz Sea, spied the unwary merchant ship and tacked to intercept it. The merchant—keeping infamously poor lookout—all but squawked in surprise when the pirate was at last spotted, and at once set every sail she could hang on a spar or a mast. It was hopeless, of course; no fat merchant could hope to outrun the predatory *Eschaton*, even with a fresh breeze, a following sea, and a thousand sea-miles between them.

"And yet," said the captain of the *Eschaton*, in a rich, amused sort of voice, "she might as well fly a huge banner with 'Bait' written on it in big, black letters."

"Bait?" echoed the first mate.

"Oh, aye." The captain appeared unconcerned. "There's a ship of the line lurking somewhere up ahead, I've no doubt, ready to batter us to splinters. Keep your eyes open, Chance."

"Aye, Cap'n."

Ah, the marvelous chase, both ships flying over the glinting sea under such a fine, white, beautiful press of canvas! The hands on the *Kraken* waited at their stations, ready at a moment's notice to tear off the camouflage and run out the guns—and, as the *Eschaton*'s captain had said, pound the pirate into driftwood. On the deck was an air of tense expectation; Captain Zeal had, once again, to master the urge to whistle.

The gap between the two ships grew narrower, the captain (who was not as young as Lieutenant Morrow despaired, having made post four years ago and being fully entitled to the two gold epaulettes on the shoulders of his uniform jacket, and having besides been at sea since he was nine) employing every trick he knew to make it seem as though the *Kraken* were making all speed, when in fact she was ambling along as casually as a courtier on holiday, her hands in her pockets, whistling a jaunty tune (figuratively speaking). The crew were having a grand time, running back and forth, waving their arms and hooting at each other—putting on a marvelous show of confusion for the pursuing pirate.

A puff of white, the thunderous report of a gun, and a jet of water just off the starboard beam—the *Eschaton* was firing her first ranging shots. If Lieutenant Thomas Morrow had been a praying man, he would have fallen to his knees, and if he were a nail-biting man, his fingers would have been raw to the quick, but he was neither of these, and simply clenched his jaw until it ached while his captain capered about like a schoolboy.

"Remember your orders, men!" he shouted, still tapping his feet to a tune only he could hear. "Let her come in a bit closer … now, Mr Morrow!"

"All hands!" bawled the first lieutenant, and gave the order to tack, sending the men scurrying, some aloft, some alow, a perfect cacophony of motion, completely confusing to an untrained eye.

From the *Eschaton*, the pirates watched as the merchant ship, the innocent *Calamari*, attempted to tack—that is, to change course by turning her head into the wind, a much swifter manoeuvre than wearing (turning the ship downwind), but less certain, and in this instance completely inexplicable.

"God's blood," swore the first mate, "what in hell is she doing?"

"Missing stays, I believe," said the captain.

Indeed she was. Her bow turned directly into the wind, the *Calamari* floundered for a moment, suspended between the old tack and the new, before flopping back into her previous course, her starboard gun-ports glaring blackly at the approaching *Eschaton*.

The pirate captain swore, and the first mate turned to raise one thick, black eyebrow.

Whatever the captain might have said, however, was lost in the first thundering crash of the *Kraken*'s broadside as her guns were brought to bear.

"Hoist colors, Mr Tallis!" Captain Zeal roared; "Aye-aye, sir!" the signal midshipman replied. As the golden eagle of Camembert ascended the flagstaff, Zeal cried: "Fire as she bears! Handsomely, handsomely—wait for the roll—FIRE!"

The shattering boom of the broadside—the most magnificent sound in the world! He could listen to it over and over, especially when accompanied by the music of shrieking foes and splintering wood, and the solemn creak of the enemy's mast falling, falling, landing on deck with a terrible, beautiful, tortured crash.

"The dog!" swore the *Eschaton*'s captain in a rich voice that was no longer amused. "He was the man-of-war, and I never once suspected!" The crew were busy with their axes, clearing away the wreckage of the mast before it could cripple the ship. The *Kraken* let loose another broadside, and as cannon balls whistled overhead and splinters flew (some of them as long and as deadly as arrows), the captain shouted, "Lay her alongside, Chance! We'll have to board her!"

"Aye, aye, Cap'n!"

It was a bold manoeuvre, and perhaps a mad one, but the *Eschaton* was known for such daring moves; even outgunned, she had never yet lost a single-ship action. If she could only survive the pounding she was receiving from the *Kraken*'s guns (and what a pounding it was! Captain Zeal was passionate about gunnery, and had drilled his gun crews day and night to achieve a level of speed and accuracy so brilliant, it was one step shy of perfection—it would have been perfection, if it had been humanity's lot to achieve it), she could board and slaughter her foes without mercy. From a ship that flew the black flag, no quarter could possibly be given.

"Prepare to repel boarders!" shouted Captain Zeal as the two ships' courses converged. The *Eschaton* was still firing, and a cannon shot whizzed over his head, parting lines and plowing holes in sails. His face was black with soot, and there was a bleeding slice across his forehead, but his teeth shone white in a manic grin as he called out, "Cheerly, my lads, cheerly! We'll show these brigands how we do it in the Navy!" He brandished his sword, and the sailors all cheered.

The two ships came together not with a gentle kiss, but with a horrible rending crunch, and the pirates came swarming aboard. But the *Kraken*s were waiting for them, and on the deck there was smoke and blood and confusion as the battle raged, and the *Kraken* and *Eschaton* each tried to batter the other into submission.

"Capture the leaders if you can!" Zeal hollered over the din, ducking the saber-swipe of an ear-ringed rogue and stabbing him through the middle. All around him was the smoke and chaos of battle, and the deck was awash with blood. His men were fighting and dying on all sides of him—and his boys, too. He saw Mr Childe fall, savaged by a pirate's boarding pike, but he had no time to react, lest his own life be lost.

But somehow, amidst the thunder of cannon and the crack of sharpshooters in the tops, the clangor of steel on steel and the shrieking of the wounded, amidst the arid scent of gunpowder and the tangy reek of blood, amidst the infernal raging anarchy, the battle was thinning. Most of the barbarous figures on board the *Kraken* were no longer moving, and on the mizzenmast of the *Eschaton*, the black flag twitched and began to descend.

"She's striking her colors, sir!" exclaimed Mr. Morrow, who came lurching up out of the smoke, a bloody saber in his hand. His coat was slashed, soot-stained and bloody, but there was a light in his dingy eyes that Zeal had never before seen.

"So she is," the captain agreed, biting his lip and frowning. It was unlike a pirate to surrender, especially unlike everything he'd heard about the *Eschaton*. They would fight until every last one of them was dead, rather than face the (highly theoretical) mercy of Her Majesty's courts. Better to die in battle than to hang, after all.

Zeal narrowed his eyes, watching the sea, the ship … awfully quiet on board the *Eschaton*, there...

"Your glass, Mr Morrow!" he said.

As soon as it was clapped into his hand, he was scowling into it, scanning the sea to leeward... "There you are!" he hissed. The black speck leapt into focus—a boat with a handful of people aboard, one of them in a magnificent red coat.

He glanced up at the *Eschaton*. Completely unmanned…

Or was it?

The spyglass slammed into Mr Morrow's arms, nearly breaking his ribs, as Captain Zeal shouted, "All hands! Wear away, wear away as fast as ever you can!"

As the weary men struggled to follow the order, and the Master at the wheel started to turn—

The *Eschaton* exploded.

"There she goes, Cap'n," said one of the pirates, a massive, scarred woman with a peg leg, an eye patch, and a determinedly square chin.

"Aye?" said the captain without interest, hunched inside the magnificent red coat. Hunks of burning debris caromed past the boat and landed hissing in the ocean; from behind them, clearly audible, came the crackling roar of a burning ship, and the screams of terrified sailors.

"She was a sweet old barky to be sure, Cap'n," said another pirate, a slim young dark-skinned woman with tattoos covering her arms from wrist to shoulder, "but don't you worry, we'll find another soon enough."

"Aye, I suppose."

A third survivor, a skinny lad with an enormous head and an improbable haystack of bright orange hair, did not speak, but made comforting noises in the captain's direction.

The boat pulled for the nearest port, confident that it would not be pursued. The handful of pirates who survived gradually began to talk and laugh with each other, grateful for their lives—but the captain sat, sunk in brooding silence at the bow, and said not a word.

A handful of days later, the *Kraken* put into Umeboshi Bay. She was a pathetic limping shadow of her formerly grand self, scorched half to death, jury-rigged fore and aft with a temporary mast and sails made from stitched-together shirts and trousers, pumps clanging night and day to keep the poor wreck from foundering. They had been blessed with fair breezes, an easy sea and few casualties, or they'd not have made it into the bay. As it was, the sad hulk of a ship staggered within hailing distance of the port and promptly sank.

"...And it was thanks to the quick thinking of the people of Umeboshi, my lords, that any of us are survived to tell you what happened," said Captain Acheron Zeal, lately of Her Majesty's Ship the *Kraken*. "All manner of fishing boats and other such vessels put out from shore and rescued my men. Captain Fletcher was so good as to pick up my first lieutenant and me in his own boat." He bowed to the captain in question, who gave a jerk of his head.

Captain Zeal fell silent, acutely aware of the closeness of the air in Admiral Tannin's after-chamber, aware as well of the stern, immobile expressions on the faces of the captains behind the bench. The silence in the room went on and on, the scratching of the secretary's pen as he took down Zeal's words only emphasizing the dreamlike stillness. One of the captains stifled a cough; another toyed with the edge of a paper. A model of the Quadra Terrarum (a very handsome one of its kind: the cube of the world suspended in an elongated sphere of glass, supported by a carved column of colored crystal at each corner, representing the four elemental poles) sat near the corner of the long table, where one of the junior captains pinged his fingernails against its brass base. At last the secretary's scratchings ceased; the Admiral looked a question to him, and he nodded.

"Very well," said the Admiral. "Have you anything to add, Mr Zeal?"

Zeal's voice stuck in his throat. He tried to clear it surreptitiously, certain the noise was as loud as an oliphant thundering across the deck. "No, sir." His stomach was clenched with dread—Mister Zeal, not Captain!

"Very good. You will wait outside whilst we deliberate."

"Aye, sir. Thank you, sir."

Wringing his hat, Zeal took himself outside to wait.

II. Sorrow and Rue

The evening bells were ringing out over Umeboshi, and they might have been ringing for him, so light and carefree did he feel. Reflections of the city lights rippled in the bay, stirring his soul with a poetic impulse hitherto unknown and unexplored. Cheerful voices and golden blazes of light spilled from the windows and open doors of the inns, taverns and pubs that lined the streets that led to sea. Some of the voices hailed him, calling him by name, but he simply waved and continued on his way.

Acquitted, by God! He breathed in the word with the bracing air. Exonerated! Cleared of all charges! It was like, very like—he groped for the poetic phrase—like being reborn, all the grit and dirt and worry and care of the previous life washed away by the pure waters of a second chance!

He grinned at his own cleverness, called out in response to an invitation from a nearby inn, "Give you joy, Mr Chandarlis, but I'm overdue for an engagement as it is!" and ambled along the quay, whistling jauntily (and off-key-ly, for Acheron Zeal was never one who could carry a tune), his heart filled to bursting, to be alive in a world that had such joy in it!

The surge of wild joy had mostly subsided, but a sweet hum of contentment remained, by the time he sat down to dinner at the home of Lord and Lady

Wainscott. Famous entertainers, the Camembertian ambassador to Chai and his wife had collected everyone who was anyone in the entire Umeboshi region, politicians, merchants, assorted naval officers, knights and soldiers, even a celebrated actress of the local theatre, for a celebration of Queen Miranda Regina Allegra Felicity Cardamom's fifty-second birthday. A sea captain fresh from a stunning victory against nefarious pirates (especially a young, handsome, personable sea captain) was a gem in the diadem of celebrity, a prize to be proudly displayed at the Wainscotts' dazzling board.

His private source of happiness sustained him through the discourse of his companion on the right, a dewlapped banker with a passion for the stock exchange, even enabling him to nod and smile and interject appropriate comments with all appearance of complacency. "Mark my words," the banker rumbled, helping himself to his fourth glass of wine, "if this unrest in the Diet continues, we'll have a new regime in Chai by Michaelmass, and then you'll see the prices plummet!"

"The ... Diet?" said Zeal, who had not been attending.

"Aye, the Diet! The Chai parliament, or whatever strange democratical organization they have running their country." The banker snorted into the rim of his crystal wineglass. "Give me a decent autocracy any day of the week, eh? As a ship's captain, I'm sure you agree, eh?"

"Er," said Zeal. As a true son of Camembert, he of course loved his Queen and country, but he couldn't honestly say he'd ever given the more abstruse questions of government any thought at all.

"But," said a rich voice from his other side, "would the Chai people accept an autocracy?"

Zeal and his neighbor both turned to the left and attended to the new speaker. This would have been worth doing in any case, as she was a lady of remarkable beauty: tall, poised, with the most perfect alabaster skin you could imagine, and a joyous profusion of sunset-colored curls pinned on top of her head in the Chai fashion, held in place by delicate stillettoes. She smiled apologetically. "I do beg your pardon for cutting in on your conversation, Captain, but the question of the government of Chai is of particular interest to me."

The banker harrumphed and quit the field, turning to address the fellow on his right.

Zeal, not sorry to leave the 'change behind, said, "I believe I must beg your pardon in turn, ma'am. I don't believe we've been introduced."

"A matter of a moment to rectify." She held out one slim, gloved hand. "Espera Amica, of House Phinoparos. I am the envoy to the Chai Republic from Stratocumulopolis."

"A dragon?" Zeal cried, pressing her hand and, in his astonishment, forgetting to release it. "But—this is remarkable! I am very pleased to make your acquaintance indeed!"

She laughed, a lovely ringing. Blushing, Zeal released her hand—almost dropped it—and attempted to recover. "Er, that is—"

"Please, Captain," she said, "don't be embarrassed. I'm sure you have a great deal of natural curiosity about us and our city."

"It's true I've never been privileged to visit there," Zeal said. "Please, is it true—is the city truly built of cloud? How is it kept aloft? Are the streets solid—could a human walk on them?" His questions crowded forward, jamming the entrance of his mouth like an inconsiderate crowd of shoppers on the day after Thanksgiving.

"Enough!" cried Lady Amica, laughing, holding up her hand. "At least, Captain, allow me to catch my breath!"

"I beg your pardon, my lady," he replied, his blush returning and bringing several of its friends, and bowed. "I don't mean to weary you with questions. Indeed, interrogation is a poor form of conversation."

"Indeed?" But she was smiling. "To be honest, the ways of humans are as foreign to us as ours seem to you; if I am allowed to respond question-for-question, I shall be perfectly content."

"An equitable arrangement."

By this time, the dinner-party had devolved into small knots of conversation, as the guests waited for the next phase of the evening's entertainment. Servants passed around sweet coffee, port, bubbling wine or brandy; Captain Zeal absent-mindedly drained his glass of port, listening to Lady Amica describe the white pillars, the gleaming colonnades, the sunlit plazas and shining temples of the dragon city.

"But tell me," he said, "and I beg your pardon if my question is impertinent—er … dragons, you know … that is, I'd always thought…."

She laughed and held up her hand. "You want to know why I'm not sixty feet long and covered in scales." Quite red, he nodded. "It's no mystery," she said. "The ability was given us to assume human form at need. In my true shape, you know, I could not sit at this table, or drink this excellent wine." Which, smiling, she sipped.

"Given?" said Zeal. "By whom?"

But before she could answer, their host rose from his seat at the head of the table and clapped his hands.

"My lords and ladies, assembled guests," he called, "the ballroom is prepared. Would you not care to dance?"

A general murmur of assent, a disorderly procession to the ballroom. Zeal rose and offered the lady his arm. "Shall we?" he asked.

She smiled. "Gladly."

They had the first dance together, a brisk minuet that had the more portly guests flushed and panting, and then Lady Amica excused herself to speak to a couple of locals—the mayor of Umeboshi, dignified with his black coat and long moustache, and his wife. Zeal took himself over to the table where drinks were being served, helping himself to a glass of the sweet wine, distilled from plums, native to the area. Thus provided, he sipped from his glass and watched the crowd.

There were few people he knew here—Admiral Tannin was in attendance, and a handful of captains senior to him on the list, with their wives. There was the usual complement of young maidens, some comely, some rather less so, and young gentlemen vying for their attentions. A man by the window wore the red cross of the Knights of St George on his breast; noticing Captain Zeal's attention, he raised his glass in an ironic toast. Zeal inclined his head.

The rest of the crowd was an even mix of colonists from Camembert, comfortably fat from rich living, and local dignitaries, functionaries, breviaries and so on, all of them somber black blots against the foreigners' bright-colored finery.

"There you are, Ash!" cried a voice from behind him.

"Kermit!" Zeal turned, grasping his friend's wrist. "I had no idea you were here. What brings you to this side of the world?"

Captain Kermit Feldspar, a friend of Zeal's since their boyhood days (they had both served as midshipmen in the old *Arquebus* frigate) shrugged his round shoulders. "Convoy duty, I'm afraid. My poor old *Prometheus* has sailed from pole to pole more times than I can count, herding merchants. But perhaps," he grinned, clapping Zeal's shoulder, "now you've won your famous victory, they might grow a bit less timorous."

Zeal chuckled. "Merchants will never grow less timorous, not until the last pirate is swept from the seas."

"So long as it means continued employment, I suppose I shouldn't complain." Captain Feldspar sighed. "I long for a good war, don't you?"

"Oh, yes," Zeal said fervently. Exterminating pirates was all very well, but nothing to engaging her Majesty's foes in right honorable and glorious combat.

"But tell me all about your mighty battle! The only people I've spoken to couldn't tell a frigate from un fromage, you know."

"Well," Zeal said, and began the tale. By the time he'd half finished, he'd collected a little avid crowd, other Navy men, and a flock of young ladies who had gathered to see what all the excitement was about.

"So you are the captain who sank the *Eschaton*?" asked a black-haired young beauty whom Zeal had not previously noticed.

Having once noticed her, he couldn't see how he might have overlooked her in the first place. She had a fine, proud look in her green eyes, a wry smile on her perfect pink lips. Her easy posture and her lithe figure bespoke a natural, unconscious grace, and he had a sudden, acute longing to see her dance.

"I am, Miss...?"

"Drake," she said, lowering her eyelashes with maidenly modesty, and holding out one slender hand. "Franceline Drake."

"A pleasure," said Zeal, bowing over her hand, just brushing her knuckles with his lips. He raised his eyes to look into her face—and saw, with a pleasurable jolt, that she was looking back at him. He felt his face grow warm; the other young ladies surrounding them murmured with disappointment and began to disperse. He straightened, only reluctantly releasing her hand.

"An heroic feat," she said, and he was struck by her voice—rich yet sweet, it pulsed in his blood more strongly than the wine he had drunk. "And yet—your own ship was badly damaged, was it not?"

"She sank as soon as we entered the bay," he said, and was rewarded with a concerned little gasp, a charming moue on the young beauty's lips. Warming to the story and the attention (and, to tell the truth, he was already quite a bit warm from the alcohol), he raised his hands to demonstrate just how the poor, battered wreck had limped into Umeboshi Bay, pumps clanging away, the carpenter reporting three, four, five feet of water in the hold. He caught and held the black-haired beauty's eyes, was on the verge of asking her to stand up with him for the next dance, when one of the other captains cried, "Three cheers for Zeal and the *Kraken*!"

Amid the enthusiastic response, the young beauty escaped, and when the furor of congratulation had died down, he could not find her again.

The young beauty had escaped to Lord Wainscott's well-kept garden, where she paced among the lemon trees and the chrysanthemums, worrying her white lace gloves off one finger at a time, then replacing them, muttering to herself the while, "Hell and death! Now what shall I do?"

In such a state of nervous excitement, it's really no wonder that she was unaware of the presence of another in the garden until a loud, deliberate step on a twig called her attention to it. She whirled about with a gasp, only relaxing when the other had stepped into the light of a nearby paper lantern.

"Oh, Mother," she said. "Don't do that!"

Lady Espera Amica smiled, taking her arm and guiding her toward a marble bench situated in a clump of ornamental shrubs. "I'd wondered how long it would take you to notice me," she said. "You are distraught, my dear."

"Shouldn't I be?" Miss Drake returned, sitting down with ill grace. She waved one hand toward the house's lighted windows, where the laughter and gaiety of the party inside could clearly be seen. Her gesture was aimed in particular towards a certain arrogant, blond-haired captain, although she couldn't see him. "I've just met the most horrible, the vilest, the wretchedest scoundrel who ever crawled across the face of the Quadra Terrarum!"

"Captain Zeal seems a pleasant fellow," murmured the envoy with a faint smile.

"Mother!" Anguish, swift and acute, shone on Miss Drake's face. "You know what he did!"

"Hmm…" Lady Amica tapped her lips with her fan. "He dances very well," she said. "And he is a pleasant, if vigorous, dinner companion. Perhaps you refer to the way he wears his hair, which is not up to the current mode? Or, no … I seem to recall something about a certain pirate ship…"

Rage flashed in her daughter's eyes. "How dare you talk about it like that?" she demanded, springing to her feet in her agitation. "As though it were an amusing joke! He killed Random, Mother!"

"Random?" Lady Amica blinked.

"Random! Random Chance, first mate of the *Eschaton*, whom you met!" The girl clenched her fists and looked down at the marble bench, her jaw tensed, her beautiful lips trembling.

Unspoken between them, though not uncontemplated, was the thought that Lady Espera Amica of House Phinoparos was unlikely to recall one scruffy, shabby pirate above the crowd of men who had passed through the doors of the envoy's mansion. Franceline looked down at her hands, scowling.

"Don't frown so, darling. You'll wrinkle your brow."

The rebellious scowl deepened.

"My dear." Rising, Lady Amica put her arm around her daughter's shoulders. "Have you slept at all since it happened?"

"What?" A sniffle. A handkerchief produced to stem the incipient tide. "No.

Couldn't."

"Then here is what I suggest." She waited to make sure she had her daughter's attention. When Franceline had looked up, she continued, "Go to your father. Ask you him what you should do. He'll have good advice for you, I'm certain."

"Go to Dad?" The young lady swallowed a hiccup. "How? I don't have a ship."

Amica thought about it. "There will be a ship carrying despatches back to Camembert regarding the state of affairs here in Chai, and of course the sinking of the *Eschaton*." The young lady winced at the casual mention of that unhappy event. "I will impress upon the admiral that it is vital you should be returned to Camembert as quickly as possible. He will be eager to cooperate, I'm certain." She smiled, pleased with her plan.

Not so her daughter. "Mother!" she cried. "You want me to take passage on a royal ship? Me? A passenger of the Royal Navy?" As though there were nothing more ludicrous in the entire world.

"Unless you'd rather swim, my darling. Or fly."

A sulky look. "You know I can't."

"Then it's settled. I'll speak to the admiral at once." She rose with the perfect, unconscious grace of her people, leaving her daughter alone in the garden with her thoughts and her memories of the dead.

Three-quarters of the *Eschaton*'s crew lost: shot by royal marksmen, slashed by royal sabers, dismembered by royal cannon, drowned. One boatload escaped before she exploded, a spark in her powder magazine blowing her high as Stratocumulopolis before the   had the chance to pursue the fugitives.

Random Chance, the first mate, cut in half by a cannon ball before his captain's disbelieving eyes.

"Listen up, mates," said the captain, resplendent in plumed hat and fine red coat, "we're down, but we're not defeated. I've a plan to get us a new ship."

The survivors of the *Eschaton* gathered in a dirty dockside tavern in Umeboshi, glasses of harsh liquor leaving sticky rings on the already-filthy table between them. There was anger in their eyes, anger and hatred of the Navy dogs who had dared to harm their beloved barky. Any plan their captain had, they'd listen.

"It'll take cunning and cleverness on your parts," the skipper continued, "but you're my crew, so it goes without saying you're twice as clever and three times as cunning as any Navy dog." Shouts of approbation, glasses lifted, fiery beverages quaffed. The captain grinned, and when their glasses had been renewed, leaned forward and explained the daring plan.

"I cannot begin to thank you enough, Captain," said Lady Amica, her magnificent hair a russet aura around her fine head.

Captain Zeal bowed. "It's a pleasure to be of assistance, my lady, truly," he said.

Both of them looked at the envoy's black-haired daughter, the very same beauty who had so intrigued the young captain at the Wainscotts' dinner party. Miss Drake smiled wanly. She was just as beautiful as he'd thought the night before, but in the clear light of morning she was revealed to have a thin, pale look about her, and purple umbrae shadowed her eyes.

"It is, of course, essential that she be returned home as quickly as possible," said Lady Amica. "You understand."

The captain bowed once more. "Of course."

In truth, it had been something of a surprise that the Admiral had first honored him with the duty of carrying despatches home in the sleek, swift-sailing Scylla, and then further entrusted him with the safety of the envoy's own daughter. Captain Zeal was nothing if not adaptable, however, and sailing to Camembert in such a fine craft as the Scylla was infinitely preferable to being stuck on land for any length of time; he was only amazed at his own good fortune.

To Miss Drake he said, "I'll see your dunnage brought aboard, Miss, and my steward will show you where you and your maid will berth. That's nautical speech," he added, "for where you'll sleep, of course."

"Of course." A thin smile. A sailor heaved her trunk up onto his shoulder, and the steward, a lean, rawboned fellow named Duffy, gestured to her. "This way, Miss."

She followed Duffy up the gangplank, disappearing from view, and Captain Zeal turned to the envoy. "It was your influence that got me this opportunity, I realize," he said. "I'm more grateful than I can say."

She smiled. "You are doing me a favor as well, Captain," she said. "Any debt between us is cleared."

Up on deck, Mr Morrow was yowling sourly at the hands. Zeal smiled to himself. To her, he said, "I'd best get aboard, my lady. We sail with the tide."

A smile, a bow, a kiss on the hand, and all the proper formalities had been observed. Captain Zeal propelled himself aboard with enthusiasm and, well, zeal, lungs drawing in the sweet, clean air of the sea, feet revelling in the feel of the living deck beneath him. How good it was to be going to sea!

Franceline Drake woke in the middle watches of the night with a gasp and a start, clutching her blanket to her breast. Subsiding back into her bed in the captain's cabin (the captain having taken the first lieutenant's cabin, the first lieutenant then taking the second lieutenant's and so on down the chain of command, until some poor junior officer had to sling his hammock in a fourteen-inch cubby), she stared open-eyed at the deck overhead, seeing not smooth planks washed blue by darkness, but the smoky deck of the *Eschaton*, red with blood. And Random, tall and dark-haired and handsome and bold, waving his sabre and shouting, "We'll show 'em for sure, Cap'n, just you watch—" and no more than that, because then the cannon ball came hurtling through the smoke and confusion and severed his top half from his bottom, and a look of pained consternation came over his tanned, handsome face, and then he died, and his blood stained the deck along with all the rest.

She found to her supreme dismay that she was sobbing, tears sliding through the fingers that covered her face as though to block out the terrible vision.

"This will never do," she said to herself, and sat up, dabbing her eyes on the sheets.

It was cruel of her mother to send her to sea with the man who'd sunk the *Eschaton*. No doubt she thought it amusing to do so, a bit of elliptical draconic humor. To someone who had not lived for nine hundred years, however, it was not amusing in the least.

Franceline climbed out of bed and wrapped a dressing gown around herself. She would go up on deck and take the air. It would clear her head, enable her to sleep.

Unless, of course, Captain Acheron Zeal happened to be there as well, his hands folded behind his back, pacing back and forth along the windward side of the quarterdeck, the captain's canonical place. Seeing him, she almost turned and went right back down to her cabin—but before she could escape he had seen her, and he approached with a concerned smile.

"Miss Drake," he said. "Are you all right? Is there anything I can do?"

"I—" she said, caught off-guard by his kindness. "No. That is—it was … it was stuffy in my cabin. I thought perhaps some air…"

"Of course." Another smile, this one full of understanding and perhaps (it was difficult to tell in the chancy moonlight) a hint of condescension. Any liking she might have had for him dissipated at once. "It is rather close in there, especially if you're not used to it."

Several things occurred to her at once, then. The first was that Captain Acheron Zeal's solicitousness was not condescension at all, but polite concern. The second was that it was not merely polite concern. The third was that Captain Zeal was not an unattractive man.

Lastly, the thought struck her that perhaps her mother had done her a favor after all.

"Miss Drake?"

She turned her face up towards his, smiling to herself. "I'm sure you're very busy, Captain," she said, "but it would be … comforting if I could stay here for a little while. Do you suppose that would be all right?"

"Of course!" he hastened to say. Nothing he should like better, always at the lady's service...

"I don't want to inconvenience you..."

No inconvenience, none at all! Sailing the Sea of Bordeaux was the easiest thing in the world—a child could do it. Would Miss Drake like a proper tour of the ship? He could point out certain improvements made to the masts and the rigging that she might not find too awfully dull.

She smiled and took his arm. "I would like that of all things," she said.

Golden evening in Tawney Port, Scylla lying at anchor on a gently heaving sea. Beyond the smooth, gold-tinged curve of the sails and the stretch of wine-colored water, the white bulk of the Sea Wall loomed against the purpling sky. Between ship and shore the captain's barge plied its way, the captain himself in the bow, resplendent in his best dress uniform. His lady passenger, too, was aboard, looking as sweet as springtime in a white lawn dress and matching gloves. The playful breeze kept snatching at her hat, and she, laughing, kept snatching it back.

Adorable creature, thought Captain Zeal, casting her an affectionate glance. At dinner in his cabin last night, he had dared to take her small hand and press it with his own. Perhaps, he had said, after his mission was completed, he might be allowed to call on Miss Drake? It would be an honor, he assured her. Miss Drake had laughed, and curtained her vibrant green eyes with her long, dark lashes, and said that the good captain might indeed.

"I shall, of course, escort you to your lodgings, Miss Drake," said the good captain, giving her a hand up onto the dock. Her tiny protest, her "Oh, that won't be necessary," had not begun to be uttered before Zeal called out, "Duffy, look sharp, there, and bring along the lady's things."

Together they proceeded to Miss Drake's lodging-house, the Unspotted Lily, a respectable place on a respectable street, where Captain Zeal bowed, kissed her hand and wondered if he might have the pleasure of dining with her, since she embarked for Stratocumulopolis early the next morning.

"I know a place not far from here: the Three Sisters. Perhaps you've heard of it? A perfectly unexceptionable place for a young lady such as yourself to visit. Since my business with the Admiral is already concluded, I am a free man until he decides what next to do with me."

He little realized it, but the Admiral had already decided what to do with

Captain Acheron Zeal. Though the unfortunate *Kraken* had been sunk, her captain had shown remarkable clearness of head in the heat of battle, and a keen grasp of the somewhat unorthodox strategies necessary for fighting pirates. Further, his report indicated that the *Eschaton*'s captain had survived, and such a heartless arrogant rash impetuous buccaneer would certainly not take the loss of his ship with a bow and a smile. No doubt he was already planning his revenge. It was the Admiral's thought that Captain Zeal was just the man to track down the corsair and neutralize him before such revenge could be effected.

The young captain, however, knew none of this. He only knew, as evening sank down into star-strewn night, that he was in the company of a young, beautiful, charming, vivacious, captivating young woman, and he meant to enjoy every minute of it before they had to part.

"A toast," he said, filling first her glass and then his own with the Three Sisters' wonderfully sweet, light wine. Raising his glass, he met her eyes boldly and said, "To beauty, that it may ever inspire men to strive for glory in great deeds."

Flushing, she looked to the side and said, "Pray, Captain, do not say such things. It … it is not proper."

Stunned, and suddenly almost as embarrassed as she was, Captain Zeal cried, "Oh, Miss Drake, I meant no importunity. Forgive me—let us drink to something else." Racking his brains, he stuttered the first words that tripped forward, the traditional Navy toast: "To the Queen, and confusion to her enemies."

The flush changed to a swift pallor, and a strange dark unreadable look, but Miss Drake took up her glass and said, "The Queen," in a perfectly normal voice, taking a sip of wine, and Zeal reasoned that he must have imagined it, after all.

Yet the memory of that look of rage (for rage it had been, murderous but tightly controlled) remained with him, though not for some while would he understand its source.

III. The Rose and the Skull

That same night, much later, a slim figure in a magnificent red coat walked through the doors of the old shabby-elegant public house known as the Baron. It was not in what one would call the nice part of town, being situated down near the wharves, where rats both bi- and quadrupedal scurried through the filthy streets. The Baron itself was down one of the narrower and darker of these, and its exterior was nothing to look at, but inside all was genteel quiet: the gleam of lamplight on old wood, the scent of pipe tobacco and mellow brandy, the clicking of two old sailors playing draughts at a table near the door.

The figure in the red coat approached the bar, where a man who must have been ancient when the first animals thrust their heads up out of the sea attended to the polishing of glasses. "Aye?" he said, not looking up at the stranger's approach.

"Captain Cid. Is he here?"

The bartender pointed, and Red Coat nodded a thanks and turned and walked that way, stopping at a table in the back where sat a lone old man with an amazing salt-and-pepper beard and curious eye-pieces that gave him the aspect of a startled mallard, nursing a drink.

The captain of the *Eschaton* (for so it was) slid, uninvited, into the seat across from him.

Cornelius Cid II, former privateer for the king and queen of Eclaire, famous adventurer and inventor of the world's first flying ship, the *Miracle*, glanced up. His be-goggled eyes went wide, and shoving his eyepieces up onto his forehead and starting out of his chair he cried, "Why, it's never my dear Francie! Bless my soul, sweetheart, is it really you?"

"Hi, Dad," said Franceline Drake. "I need a ship."

Acheron Zeal was not a poetic man—his vessel was his verse, the sea his stanza, the deck his dactyllic hexameter—nor one given to hopeless maundering after women (and that his cause with the draconic envoy's daughter was hopeless he had no doubt), but all the same, after his morning pot of coffee (drunk while the sun was a mere hazy streak on the eastern horizon) his feet informed him that they would like to take a walk about town, and his heart (that most contumacious of man's organs) supplied the direction. His brain, however, was a little bit startled when he found himself looking up at the sky-docks on the northern edge of town, where the noble flying ships at their moorings bobbed on the morning airs.

A few words about flying ships, or sky-sailers as they are sometimes called. They were conceived in a fit of madness (or genius if you prefer; indeed, there is very little difference) a mere quarter-century earlier, when the infamous warlock Baron Felix von Death stood poised to overrun Camembert with his armies of doom—and indeed, the first flying ship, the previously mentioned *Miracle*, was instrumental in bringing about his defeat. It was not an easy task to get the *Miracle* off the ground; back in those days, magic of any kind, but white magic especially, was rare (owing to Baron von Death's systematic destruction of the world's wizarding schools), and of course nothing but magic could induce a three-masted sailing vessel to quit its aqueous home and take to the skies. Captain Cornelius Cid was nothing if not determined, however, and following the amazing success of the *Miracle*, airship technology quite took off … so to speak.

Now winged ships sailed between every nation of the world, their white sails gleaming in the sunlit lands above the clouds. Piracy became obsolete; not only was it difficult for pirates to persuade white wizards to ship with them and help them fly, but those pirates who still plied the waves found themselves at a distinct disadvantage against the airborne ships of the Royal Navy. O happy world, united in harmony by ships borne on wings of air! And woe betide he who should attempt to disrupt that joy!

Captain Zeal (who knew how airships worked, though he was such a junior captain, with so little influence, that he had small hope of obtaining such a prime command, even after sinking the *Eschaton*) shaded his eyes against the rising sun, looking up at the row of sky-sailers where they floated at anchor some several hundred feet overhead. Which one was her ship, he wondered? Would the slender Cirrus return her to Stratocumulopolis, or was it the bluff and broad-beamed Phaeton that would bear her to the city in the clouds?

As long as it's not the Icarus, he thought with a shudder. Someone should have thought twice about giving a ship that ill-fated name.

Just then a blow from behind sent him sprawling; springing to his feet, he cried, "I beg your pardon!" and turned to see who had assaulted him.

"I beg yours," replied the grinning young woman before him, whose bare arms were tattooed to the shoulder. "Didn't see you standing there." She grabbed him by the shoulders and began vigorously brushing the dirt off of him, busy dark hands flicking over his fine blue jacket. "Shipping out today, are you?"

"Not I," said Zeal, narrowing his eyes and wrenching himself from her grasp. He straightened his coat and by his scowl attempted to drive her away—but she took no notice.

"That's a right shame, it is, Cap'n. I wouldn't mind sailing with the likes of you. Eh, Lilly? Ain't he a fine-looking cove?" She laughed and jabbed her elbow into the side of her companion, a woman at least seven feet tall and proportionally broad, as covered in scars as the smaller woman was in tattoos. No doubt she had seen some terrible battles, for she also wore a patch over her larboard eye, and instead of a leg on that same side she had a carved ivory peg. Like her companion, she was dressed in sailors' clothes: duck trousers, blouse and tarpaulin jacket, little black slippers for shoes.

This giantess, this Lilly, gave no reply, merely a grunt, the expression on her square face never changing.

"Well," said the smaller woman, never losing her sharp grin, "never mind it. Lilly don't speak much, though when she does it's best to attend to it." She paused and said, "Say, now, before we take our leave of you—you wouldn't be Cap'n Acheron Zeal, would you?"

"And if I were?" said Captain Acheron Zeal.

"And if you were," said the young woman, taking a saucy, hip-twitching step closer to him, "I'd congratulate you on the finest piece of sailing this age." She took another step. Captain Zeal took a deep breath and stood his ground. "We never thought no one would ever do for the ol' *Eschaton* like that, did we, Lilly?"

She was quite close enough by now for Zeal to see every tooth in that broad white grin of hers, even the one each side that was capped with gold—and before he could react, she had grabbed the back of his head and planted a wet kiss on his mouth, then spun away, laughing, dangling his gold chronometer in her hand.

"Here, now, you—!" he cried, wiping his mouth with the back of his hand.

She danced just out of his reach, swinging the timepiece by its chain. "Seems to me, Cap'n, you'd best watch yourself. Wouldn't want anything bad to happen to you, now would we?" And she whirled the chronometer around by its chain, letting it slide through her fingers and sending it hurtling back towards him.

He caught it and started after them, but of course by then they were far away, lost in the gathering crowd. His face was the ugly red of shame. He clutched the gold watch until its edges bit into his palm. "Damned pirates!" he swore. And then raising his voice, "Tell your captain," he shouted after them, "I'll see every last one of you hang!"

The only reply was the faint sound of mocking laughter—and that might have been his imagination.

"That was stupid," observed Lilly Bones, who ran with remarkable agility and speed for a one-legged woman.

"Stupid?" Luna Shee laughed, skipping and dancing down the street now that all chance of pursuit was gone. "Didja see his face? I'd do it again, if I had the chance."

"I'd want to kill you, if I were him," Lilly Bones observed.

"'Course!" Luna grinned, narrowing her strange pale eyes. "That's the idea! He's angry, and angry people do stupid things—right?"

"Do they?" said Lilly Bones. "I wouldn't know."

"My lord!" cried Acheron Zeal, banging into the offices of the Admiral of the Fleet, a harried functionary clinging to his coattails, "I beg you will give me a ship!"

"Zeal." Admiral Edwin Crandall, a sad-faced fellow with the pendulous jowls of an aged hound, raised one eyebrow at the importunate young captain. "Good day to you."

"Oh!" said Zeal, whipping off his hat and bowing. "I beg your pardon, my lord, but—" advancing, hat in hands, "—it is imperative that I have a ship. Please, my lord! Those—those contumelious pirates—they must be brought to justice, my lord!"

"I tried to stop him, milord," said the cringing functionary, "but he came bellowing through here like an 'urricane, roaring and squalling like a most tempestuous blow, an I'd sooner try to rope the Funnel than to stop him, milord, all carrying on about pirates..."

"This is highly irregular, Zeal," said the Admiral. "One does not simply burst in on one's superior officer and demand a ship—it is not proper, it is not decorous, and it is not done. Do you understand?"

Zeal stammered something that might have been acquiescence, wringing his hat.

"The Admiralty..." continued Admiral Crandall in his rough, jowly voice, "the Admiralty, I say, does not hand out commands to any young post captain who happens to request it—can you imagine, Zeal, the state of the service if we did? Chaos, disorder and confusion! We might as well be a democracy, if that were the case! No, no, no, Captain Zeal," he said, his voice falling with Zeal's hopes and his heart, "it cannot be done."

Unnoticed by the desolate Zeal, the Admiral here exchanged a sort of sly grin with his secretary who, undismissed by his lordship, had neglected to take himself from the room. But Zeal was too busy wrestling with a great welter of emotions roiling in his breast, a tumult of thoughts thundering through his brain. Miss Drake—the wreckage of the *Eschaton*—the poor *Kraken* sinking forever and aye—the pirate wench who mocked him. After considerable struggle, but before the Admiral could speak, this nascent storm burst forth, and:

"Oh, sir!" cried Zeal, throwing himself to his knees before the startled Admiral's desk (that is, the desk of the startled Admiral, not the Admiral's startled desk) and holding out his hands (one still full of hat) in supplication. "Please, I beg you, give me a ship to hunt these lawless rogues, and I shall see them brought to the Queen's justice, sir, I swear it!"

"Hang 'em yourself, would you, Zeal?" said Crandall, having regained some measure of composure. He had seen post captains weep like little girls, or turn stark white with dread, or stutter as though stultified with terror, but never in life had he been so passionately accosted as today.

"If … such is the will of the Admiralty, of course," Zeal replied, getting back to his feet with a wince (he had hit the deck rather hard). His earlier exuberance and (shall we say it?) zeal were gone, and he blushed like a maiden at the way he had addressed his commander. He'd be court-martialed, hanged, flogged round the fleet...

"You know, Zeal," said the Admiral, levering his burly, jowly, ponderous mass into a standing position, tucking his arms behind his back and pacing in the manner of admirals throughout the ages (even Odysseus must have done so, when addressing his men), "there are many captains above you on the list."

Zeal swallowed. "Yes, my lord. I do realize."

"The capture of this anachronistic buccaneer and his crew could make a man's career, were it done in a sufficiently glorious and … hrm … spectacular fashion."

Another swallow. Poor Zeal's collar seemed to have shrunk since the start of the interview, and his neck cloth was far too tight. But one did not loosen one's neck cloth in the august presence of the Admiral of the Fleet.

"I understand, my lord," he said. "Such a mission must go to..." He paused, swallowing once more to dampen the desert of his throat, "Someone..."

"Someone with wit," the Admiral broke in. "Someone clever and cagey and quick-thinking. Someone, also, enthusiastic and … may I say? … zealous."

Hope's first rays broke over the horizon of his soul. "My lord…" began Captain Zeal.

The Admiral raised his hand. "I will be frank with you, Zeal," he said. "You are all those things I named. But you are also rash, impetuous, hasty, arrogant, insubordinate, impulsive … and young." Clearing his throat, he continued, "You have very little influence with the Board—you come from a family of no particular note—the fourth son, I believe?" Zeal nodded. "Where was I?" muttered the Admiral, ticking off points on his fingers. "Young … impetuous … no influence … ah, yes. You are also, Zeal, a glory-hound, and that is a dangerous thing to be these days. There is no glory to be had. The war ended before you were born. Piracy became a thing of the past while you were still a squeaker in short-pants." He spread his hands. "All the world is at peace.

"Furthermore, as you know, sailing ships are becoming obsolete; the last one built in Navy dockyards was the *Circe*, two years ago. It's airships these days, Zeal—airships for diplomatic missions, airships for merchant convoys, airships for exploration—and unless something goes horrifically awry, that's the way it will continue. That is not to say that the oceanic fleet will disappear, by no means—but we must look to the skies!

"And, as you know, Zeal," he finished kindly, "airship commanders are men of high rank—not junior post captains."

"Sir—my lord—" said Zeal, whose mouth had gone dry after such a lecture, "I realize all of that, of course. But—"

"Hasty, I called you, and I stand by it," said the Admiral, though over the course of his speech he had diminished, become less an awesome, terrifying creature and more of a humorous, paternal human being. "But you have great potential, lad, and though I can't give you an airship—" he reached behind him and took a folded paper from his desk "—I do have orders here that you are to take the *Circe*, fit her out, and take her to hunt down those pirates you missed the first time." Here he handed Zeal the parchment sealed with good wax and the official stamp of the Admiralty.

Zeal took it in trembling hands, and any artist could have used his face as a study for the full range of human emotion—or at least the positive ones: like the rainbow following the tempest's blast, hope and joy and eagerness and relief all beamed across his radiant face. He could not speak, beyond wringing the startled Admiral's hand (that is, the hand of the startled Admiral, not … well, actually, the hand might have been startled as well, given the happy ferocity with which Zeal wrenched it) and saying, "Thank you, sir, thank you!" But at last he recovered his dignity and said, "I shall not disappoint you, my lord."

"No, Zeal," said the Admiral, massaging his hand, "I imagine you won't."

The *Circe.* Thirty-two guns. Two hundred crew (she was slightly under-manned). Seven-hundred and twenty tons of timber, sailcloth and cordage, a towering, swift-sailing, fighting machine.

Much as a new mother cannot help but caress her newborn infant, so was Zeal, on his inspection of the ship, unable to keep his hands off her. Every backstay, every belaying pin was an object of perfect beauty, and even the reek of the orlop deck (where the surgeon, a small, white-faced creature in a dark coat, gave a bow that was proper, but clearly impatient for the captain to quit his, the surgeon's, rightful territory) was like roses to him.

"Excellent, Tom!" he kept exclaiming. "Really, really excellent! Perfect, in fact! We'll wrangle those rogues this time, just see if we don't."

The long-suffering First Lieutenant Thomas Morrow, who despised familiarity in a captain, bit back a sigh. "Aye, sir."

Back on the quarterdeck, where the fresh breeze was as a gift from Heaven, and the cloud-streaked sky was the faultless blue of the raiment of angels, Zeal drew in a deep breath and exhaled it with a happy grin. Here, here was the apex of existence: here on the deck of a fast-sailing ship with the living motion of the sea beneath his feet (how the landbound could bear to walk about on that hard, dead, inert stuff was beyond his ability to fathom), the white blooms of the sails above him, and the sun beaming down like a blessing over all. Ah, the thrumming of the wind in the rigging, the thump and bustle of men going about their duties, the crash and splash of the waves…!

Ah, the rhythm of life at sea, the ringing of the ship's bell and the changing of the watch, the singing of the men before the mast when the day's work was done. The succession of dinners—alone in the great cabin, or aft looking out the stern windows, or in the gunroom where the officers messed. The evening gunnery practice, *Circe*'s cannon throwing twelve-pound shot, roaring and banging away like the drums of some giant's army, while the gun crews sweated and cheered. The sweet, easy, rhythmic passage of days and weeks, almost unnoticed but for the laconic entries in the ship's log: Weather fair. Bearing ESE, 7 knots.

Until one morning, almost two months later, the captain stood on the quarterdeck, morning cup of coffee in his hand, watching the sky overhead flush to blue with the rising of the sun. The last stars faded from view, the sun shrank from a giant orange ball to its accustomed small yellowness, and Zeal sipped his coffee, thinking he might like to take a swim.

"Sail ho!" cried the lookout.

"Where away?" returned Captain Zeal.

"Eh—" The mid in the foretop hesitated.

"Quickly, now, lad!" cried Captain Zeal.

But by then the great, dark shape overhead had blotted out the sun—a brief eclipse, for the airship crossed the sky on swift wings of sailcloth and magic, and every man who could spare a moment paused to watch her pass.

Zeal had his glass out and pressed to his eye, trained on the fast-moving sky-sailer. When she had dwindled to a black speck on the horizon, he lowered it, and the men (most of whom had sailed with the captain before) could feel the wave of tension that emanated from his tall, blue-jacketed form.

"Did any of you lads," he said in a voice that carried to the top of the tallest mast, "happen to catch a glimpse of the colors that ship was flying?"

Grumbles, hesitation. And then a hairy old salt piped up, "Aye, Cap'n. She flew the Jolly Roger, she did. The rose and skull."

"The rose and skull," Zeal repeated, his voice rising. "The rose and skull! And what ship, gentlemen, flies the rose and skull?"

No one ventured to guess. "No takers?" cried Zeal, pacing in his agitation. "Well, I shall tell you what ship. The *Eschaton*! The *Eschaton* which we sank but weeks ago!"

Stunned silence on deck. Zeal stomped a few paces more, then stopped, his back to his crew. His shoulders were shaking.

"Captain?" ventured Lieutenant Morrow, reaching out a hand.

Captain Zeal turned, and Morrow quailed at the look in his eyes. "Sir?" he said.

Then Captain Acheron Zeal laughed out loud, raising his hands to the sky. "It's perfect!" he cried. "Can you imagine anything more glorious, man, than a sailing vessel capturing a sky-sailer? Thank God this chance has come to me! Thank God!" he repeated. "Now, men! Follow that airship!"

Resisting the urge to shake his head, or burst into tears, or both, Mr Morrow made the only response he could. "Aye-aye, sir," he said.

CHAPTER 3

Three Sea Songs

One. Warlike Seamen

Stavros Parhelion had once been a good man, a righteous man, a man with a home, a family, a few modest ambitions, and one fervent hope. When he went to church (and he went often), he clasped his hands before him, knelt down before the altar, and prayed before God, "O Lord, deliver your people!" For Stavros Parhelion was a native of Feta, and Feta, a tiny island in the southernmost waters of the Chianti Sea, whose principle resources were olives and goats, was a possession of Parmigiana.

Not that Parmigiana had much use for Feta. Parmigiana, that wealthy nation-state, had plenty of olives of her own, and very little need of goats. But she also had a greedy, tight-fisted, avaricious, grasping, rapacious, covetous Prince, the Doge, Lorenzo di Capellini, and it was whispered in Feta (whispered in very low tones indeed, lest the Doge's secret police, the Carbonara, hear) that Lorenzo di Capellini would never rest easy until not just the Formaggio Peninsula, but the whole world, lay in his iron grasp.

Thus did Stavros pray that his beloved homeland, with her rocky hills and her gleaming shores, her blue waters, her ancient temples (remnants of an unknown race), might be delivered from the tyrant. But the years went by, and God seemed disinclined to do anything about the tyrant at all, and Stavros Parhelion lost hope.

And then one day, the day his life ended, he decided he'd had enough.

He was making his way down to the shore, to the place where his little boat was moored (like most Fetans, he was a fisherman), when a black-clad Carbonara stepped into his path. On what pretext, he could never afterwards recall, but it was in the time when even the least murmur against the Doge was sedition punishable by death.

In that moment, he decided he would no longer cringe and scrape before the Doge's dogs. No more would he grimace and grovel and groan—he was done with it. And so he said, distinctly, to the (not-so) secret policeman, "Piss off."

"What did you say?" growled the policeman, his color coming high.

"Perhaps you mistook my meaning, you great hulking meathead," said Stavros Parhelion. "I said 'Piss off.' In other words, begone with you, you odious pile of excrement. Go to hell, you heap of dung. May your entrails rupture, you muck, you filth, you iniquity! And the same to your master, that despotic fiend!" And Stavros took his tackle box (a big, heavy thing, made of metal), and swung it at the Carbonara's head.

The Carbonara's eyes rolled back to the whites, and he toppled like a very large, very stupid-looking tree.

Stavros took one look at what he'd done—

And ran.

Happily, his boat was near; he splashed out into the surf and shoved off, pulling like mad for an inlet he knew, a secret cove where he could hide, all the while hearing shouts and the sound of pursuit behind him.

His first fear was not for himself, but for his family: his foolish outburst, however satisfying it might have been, had rendered not only his own life, but the lives of his wife and his little daughter worthless, should the Doge's men find them. He cursed himself for a narcissistic nitwit. And when he reached his hidden cove, he dragged the boat onto the shore and hid it among some rocks, then crawled into the little cave (smugglers had used it, long ago), lay down on the sandy floor, and wept.

"Stavros! Hey, Stavros!"

"Gyaaaaah!" shrieked Stavros, sitting bolt upright and nearly braining himself on the low cave ceiling. "Who's there?"

Night had fallen, and the figure in the cave mouth was dark black, except for a faint halo of starlight. "It's me, Demetrius!"

"Demetrius?" For a moment, Stavros felt a warm glow of hope. Then he flopped back on the sand and groaned, "Demetrius, why will you associate with a dead man? Go away!"

"I came because I want to join you."

"Join me?" said Stavros. "Join me where? Here in this miserable cave? On the gallows, the gibbet, the block?" Never had any man been as miserable as poor Stavros Parhelion.

"No, you dummy! In your fight against the tyrannical oppressor!"

This was news to Stavros. Last he had checked, he was on the lam, not leading a crusade. "Fight?" he cried. "What fight? There is no fight! We try to fight, we get embarrassingly squished, and our families with us." He sniffled. Poor Phaedra. Poor little fuzzy-headed Carina....

"Your family's fine!" Demetrius hissed. "Nikkos smuggled them out of town as soon as he heard what happened."

"Praise be to God!" cried Stavros.

"Praise be," Demetrius responded. "Now listen, Stavros. This is our chance to bring down the evil overlord for good and all! There are others who want to join, too! We'll get a ship—we can hide in all these little secret coves and inlets around here...." Demetrius babbled on.

"Demetrius," said Stavros Parhelion. "What in the sixteen holy names of God are you talking about?"

"I'm talking," said Demetrius, "about becoming pirates!"

Yes, Stavros Parhelion had once been a good man, a law-abiding citizen. But Stavros Parhelion was no more. In his place: Sundog, the most terrible pirate of the southern seas!

"That's the third one this week," said Phaedra, peering through her spyglass. Phaedra's position aboard the *Leukothea* was unclear. She was Cap'n Sundog's wife, of course, and could run the rigging as nimbly as any man aboard, but she had no official status. Some of the men whispered that she was a sorceress, possessed of mighty powers of dubious origin, but if she could indeed command the elements, she kept that knowledge to herself. Mostly, she served as lookout, advisor, quartermaster, anything that was needed. Currently she stood at the *Leukothea*'s rail, watching the burning wreckage glide astern.

"Any survivors?" asked Stavros—that is, the fearsome pirate Sundog—hopefully.

Phaedra scanned the wreckage, giving Stavros' heart time to lift ... and then shook her head. "No. Anyone who might have survived has either drowned or burned to death or been eaten by sharks by now."

Stavros drooped.

And then, just when it looked like Phaedra was going to have to put down her spyglass and comfort him (her usual method was to pat him on the shoulder and say "There, there." She was not much for either giving or receiving comfort), he clenched his fists, raised them to the heavens, and cried, "Who is this fiend in our cruising-ground, who slaughters our rightful prey? Who dares poach on the territory of the fearsome Sundog? Who? Who-oooo-oooooo?!?" Hooting like a demented owl, he turned to his wife. "We will hunt this marauder down and make him pay!" he said, waving his fists.

"We will?" said Phaedra, blinking in surprise. And then she grinned. "Oh, yes," she said. "We will!"

You must understand, gentle readers, that the only ones who thought the fearsome pirate Sundog was particularly fearsome were Parmigianese merchants, and the Doge—and the Doge didn't so much think "fearsome" as "annoying." Sundog and his crew had effectively embargoed trade with Parmigiana, capturing any merchant vessel that dared to enter Fetan waters—but he was the gentlest pirate you ever saw, cowing the unfortunate merchants with the singularly gruesome and bloody Jolly Roger that flew at the main, taking their ships without ever a shot being fired, and then setting them all afloat in their ship's boats while he and his crew took the booty. Which booty, it must be added, he and his men then distributed among the native Fetans for whom it was destined anyway, but without the egregious tariffs and fees imposed by the Doge.

It was a good system, and it had worked pretty well for the last year and more, but now some other pirate (a real pirate, the crew of the *Leukothea*—and her captain as well, it must be admitted—were thinking) was poaching on their territory, killing and burning, leaving shattered wreckage and drowned, bloated bodies as the only evidence of his passage. Such impertinence must be dealt with.

But how to find him? And how to deal with him, once found?

Stavros put his head in his hands. "I'm not suited for this kind of thing," he said.

"Oh, my dear," said Phaedra, and stopped, and smiled. Her look was kind. "No," she said, "you're really not."

Look ahead, look astern, look a-weather and a-lee, goes the old sailing song. Ahead was the *Circe*'s bow-wave, foaming high and white against the sparkling, milk-warm waters of the Chianti Sea, aft the *Circe*'s wake, miles long and as straight as a ruled line across the sea. To windward, a sad wreck, smoldering only a little now, as wretched a sight as a bird with a broken wing, flapping and flailing on the ground, wounded member held out straight as it tries its best to fly. No sign of any survivors. And to leeward a sail, a sail (nay, a whole ship!), white against the faultless blue sky, a chase on which Her Majesty's frigate the *Circe* was bearing down with swift grace and deadly intent.

"A pirate for certain, sir, unless I mistake," said First Lieutenant Thomas Morrow. "Not our pirate, though," he could not forbear to add, in a gloomy undertone.

He needn't have bothered. "No, indeed," said his captain, the keen-eared

Acheron Zeal, clapping his spyglass to and turning to look at his premier. "And not the one who did all that damage, not with those popguns." (They were both thinking of the *Eschaton*, whose handiwork they had seen often enough to recognize by now.) "But we'll take her just the same, Mr Morrow. Thou shalt not suffer a pirate to live, you know."

"Aye, sir." Mr Morrow did stifle a weary sigh, but only just. He also refrained from correcting his captain on the exact wording of the proverb, as officers who made a habit of correcting their superiors tended to have short careers, and if Mr Morrow did not die an Admiral, he'd rather just die now and get the sorry business over with.

Besides, all of Captain Zeal's attention was focused on the chase. A polacca, by her rig, with that antic lateen sail on the foremast. She had obviously sighted the man-of-war, and was making all speed to escape—and escape she would, for although *Circe* had the weather gage of her, there was the dreadful loom of land to lee ("th' impervious horrors of a leeward shore," as the poet once said), and the polacca, with her shallower draught, could slip among the shoals and reefs and be safe where the larger ship would run aground.

Ah, but if he could engage her ... ah, then the battle was all but won! (He reached out to touch wood, automatically, without noticing what he did.) In manpower they were almost equal, polaccas requiring a larger crew, but in broadside weight of metal this puny pirate could not touch the *Circe*. Therefore Zeal urged his dear ship on, his attention wholly taken up by her every motion. The pull of the sails, the tautness of the backstays, the hum and surge of the waves along her sides—nothing escaped him. He was, in a way, one with her—could feel the tension in her rigging as though it was his own—and when he gave a quiet order, his men, perhaps sensing this mystical union, leapt to obey.

"Come on, girl," he whispered to the *Circe*, clenching his stomach muscles to make her go faster (it might not have really worked, but on the other hand, it might. At any rate, it was almost purely instinctive, just as you cheer your loudest for your favorite sports team when you watch them on television, even though you know they can't possibly hear you). And whether it was the tightening of his abdomen or his hawk-like attention to the tiniest details of her rig, the *Circe* was, hand over fist, overhauling the smaller vessel.

The *Leukothea*, for her part (for of course it was she), had not seen the Camembertian frigate coming until it was almost too late. At first she thought to try to fool her foe by throwing up all sorts of false signals, claiming to be an Eclairesian merchant struck with the plague (among other things), but the man-of-war was far too canny for that sort of skullduggery, and bore down with the implacability of Divine Judgment. The pirates started their water, they threw their cannons overboard, they jettisoned their shot and their stores, but to no avail. The *Circe* had the weather gage, and with a deft manouevre she cut the *Leukothea* off from land and escape, and let loose a devastating broadside across the pirate's bows.

Sundog fell to his knees on the deck and began to pray, raising his clenched hands to heaven and sobbing.

"Get up, you coward!" Phaedra snapped, grabbing him by the scruff of the neck and yanking him to his feet. "Will you not stand and fight?"

"With what?" cried Sundog. "We have no weapons—we threw them overboard. And they would slaughter us if we tried."

"Slaughter be damned—" began Phaedra, but the other pirates were of the same opinion as their captain. They raised their hands in the air, shouting surrender, and someone was hauling down the fearsome Jolly Roger.

"We will be hanged," Phaedra snarled at her husband, as the *Circe*'s officers and men came across and took the defeated pirates in hand, "and Feta will never be free."

Sundog just hung his head and looked miserable.

It was, all in all, a disappointing battle. The only shots fired was the *Circe*'s first broadside; the very threat of being peppered with roundshot, dismasted, sunk, had been enough to inspire the pirates to capitulation. The only one who had shown any spirit at all was the lone woman aboard, who had wrenched free of her captors and leapt on Captain Zeal who, she rightly supposed, was the author of her present misfortune. Shrieking curses, none of them intelligible, she attacked with the fury of a wounded wildcat, going straight for his eyes with crooked claws—but Captain Zeal was lean and wiry and the veteran of many a scrap, and soon had her by the wrists, keeping her well away from his sensitive organs of sight, while she still struggled and hissed and spat.

"Little hellcat, isn't she?" said he, in tones of mild disbelief and disapprobation. "Perhaps the surgeon can give her something to calm her down."

"You know these wild southern women, sir," said Lieutenant Morrow—who immediately wished he hadn't.

"Hmm," said Captain Zeal, while his captive continued to wrench against his grip. "Mr Torrin!"

"Aye, sir?" said the marine officer.

"Take our guest here and see that she's made comfortable. And when you have done so, go to Dr Foxglove, with my compliments, and see if he doesn't have something that might calm her nerves."

"Aye, sir." And to the woman, "Come along then, ma'am, we're not going to hurt you."

But the moment that Zeal relinquished his hold on her wrists, she spun away, slapped him across the face, whirled, kneed the unfortunate marine in the groin, and dashed to the *Circe*'s rail, all before any of the men around her could do more than emit shocked and startled (and in poor Torrin's case, pained) cries.

Leaping up onto the rail (the *Circe*s gasping in amazement and awe), she whisked around to face her erstwhile captors. "Feta will be free!" she cried, in accented but perfectly understandable Camembertian. "The tyrant will fall! A curse on any who stand in the way of freedom!"

And then, while the men aboard were still trying to digest her words, she spun about and dived off the rail, into the turquoise sea.

One of the prisoners, a small man whose dark hair stood in wild tufts around his head, sank to his knees on the deck, groaning aloud, raising his bound hands to Heaven. The *Circe*s, who had never seen such a drama, were whispering amongst themselves in low, shocked voices. The marines were gaping like carp.

Captain Zeal was the first to recover. "Right!" he roared. "Back to work, you lot! Marines, get those prisoners below! (Mr Torrin, are you quite all right?) Mr Blake," to the second lieutenant, "if you please, take a party across to the prize and make her ready to depart. Mr Lucas," that was the bosun, "if any man is caught lolly-gagging about, I'll see he gets two dozen at the grating. All you men—you know your duties, I suggest you return to them."

There was a great rush and stamping of feet as the men hurried to obey. Captain Zeal, nursing his cheek (the woman had cut it with her nails when she slapped him), turned to his accustomed stretch of the quarterdeck—and scowled when he saw that Lieutenant Morrow had followed him.

"Yes, what is it, Mr Morrow?"

"Captain...." Morrow hesitated, then said in a rush, "Am I not to take the prize in, sir?"

Captain Zeal's temper, already suffering from the disappointment of the non-battle, had not been improved by the pirate woman's display, and so he can perhaps be forgiven for the brusqueness of his response.

"Are you questioning my orders, sir?" he said, his face dark. And then, at the appalled look on Morrow's face, "Look here, Tom. It's no snub against you. I need you here—every captain has to have a reliable second-in-command. Don't look so crushed. Think: it mayn't be too long before you're bringing in the *Eschaton* herself." He thumped Morrow companionably on the arm (at which the poor lieutenant was hard-pressed to hide the look of pure loathing that crossed his features). "Now, this is of course the last time we'll discuss it. Prepare a course for Porta Bella. We'll intercept the squadron there and give the Admiral our prisoners."

"Porta Bella, sir?" said Morrow, a very picture of morosity and resentment. "Aye, sir. Very good, sir." He turned and shuffled away, and in a few moments his voice, as grey and gloomy as the man himself, could be heard barking the orders that would take the *Circe* home.

Two. The Hanged Man's Hornpipe

Captain Acheron Zeal was, if only he knew it, a maiden's dream.

Standing at the wheel of the *Circe*, his strong hands gripping the spokes, he looked off into the distance, his eyes fixed on something only he could see. The breeze that belled out the *Circe*'s white sails stirred his long, golden hair and toyed with the hem of his blue uniform coat. But even an ugly man can have long, golden hair and a well-tailored (if slightly shabby) coat; he can even have piercing eyes that gaze poetically into the distance, and strong, lean, sun-browned hands that lie gracefully on the polished wood of the ship's wheel: such things are accessories, mere constituent parts, and do little to describe the beauty of the whole. Captain Zeal was, however, far from ugly, although he didn't know it and wouldn't have cared if he did, his thoughts being far from his own physical beauty.

In fact, at the moment there was little on Captain Zeal's mind at all. The *Circe* was running free before a frolicsome southern breeze. After the tedious business of beating south, tack upon tack, day after day, lying as close to the wind as ever they could, they had rounded the point of the Formaggio Peninsula at last and made their northward turn. The anticipated trouble with the Fetan pirates had never come, not even when Feta itself was a low, purple hump to larboard, and now it never would; Zeal had deposited his prisoners with the Admiral of the Parmigianese fleet—liberated from one more nuisance.

"Well, Zeal," the Admiral had said, "I could wish for you to stay for their trial, but your report will stand you in good stead—and you have other rogues to collect, unless I mistake."

"Aye, sir," said Zeal, hat in hand. "Thank you, sir."

And now—and now—homeward bound! Not for long, of course, for after a refit in Tawney Port there were pirates to catch and glory to win, but those considerations were still well in the future. Now there was only the perfect breeze, the spirited motion of the *Circe* as she shouldered gaily through the waves, the clear sky overhead, so blue, so unimaginably vast, the white clouds that speckled it only emphasizing its hugeness. Oh, the perfect euphony of such a day, when the living motion of the sea seems the apotheosis of happiness, when the joyous lift and surge of the ship is nothing to the lift and surge of your heart, when even the bosun's hoarse caws are like a song! On such a day, what can you do but close your eyes and drink in the beauty of it, like tangible light?

Yes, Captain Zeal was a handsome man, a very Adonis, and the sight of him now, with his young, open face beaming out happiness, would have sent many a maiden's heart a-fluttering, her blood pulsing faster through her veins.

Indeed, there was at least one young woman in the Quadra Terrarum (though, alas, dear readers, it has been many a year since we could in honesty name her "maiden") whose heart raced at the thought of Acheron Zeal, whose stomach fluttered, whose hands shook—but, despite her recent masquerading and his fond hopes, these were not the physical manifestations of love. Even as *Circe* raced northward across the Shiraz Sea, her captain at her helm, her wake a white furrow in the living waters, a red-hulled sky-sailer flew down the Parmigiana coast like a sea-hawk seeking her rightful prey. There Captain Franceline Drake paced the boards of her own quarterdeck, nursing her hatred of Zeal like some foul and twisted changeling at her breast, and from her mouth poured words that had no business in any well-bred damsel's vocabulary. So ferocious were her curses, the hardened pirate at the wheel actually hung his head and blushed.

"Cap'n." A brown, tattooed arm slid through hers, and Luna Shee matched her steps to Drake's. "You're upsetting the crew, you are."

A thin smiled twitched the corner of Captain Drake's mouth. "Am I, Luna?" she said. "Perhaps I should exchange them for less timorous souls, the next time we make port."

They walked in silence for a few steps. Drake's boots thudded against the white planks, but Luna's bare feet made no sound. "You know, Cap'n," she said presently, "revenge is a fine and pleasant pastime, but it don't put coins in a person's pocket."

Drake snorted. "As if I cared for that."

Luna snorted in return. "You'll care for it quick enough, when you have no crew to fly this fancy boat," she said, and poked Drake's arm with her forefinger. "You need a better plan, Cap'n, than 'run at 'im and kill 'im'."

"I suppose Lilly put you up to this?"

"Oh, no, Cap'n!" said Luna, her eyes earnestly wide. "Lilly's all for the 'run at 'im and kill 'im' plan. It's Moonhart and yer dad who're urging you to subtlety—and you know your dad, he'd rather you didn't kill 'im at all," Luna added.

"Subtlety," Drake said, as though the word had a rotten taste. "It's a good thing I like you, Luna, or I'd heave you over the rail for this."

Luna's teeth flashed, pointed and very white, in her dark face. "Aye, I know it, Cap'n. It's why I made bold to approach you."

From for'ard came a shrill cheeping, gibbering sound; the young lookout was jumping up and down in the bows. Before Drake had time even to furrow her brow, someone shouted from above: "Cap'n! Toggle's sighted someone down on that rock below—should we take a look?"

She glanced over at Luna, who widened her eyes and shrugged. "Oh," she said, "why not? Take her down."

"Aye-aye, Cap'n!"

The refugee proved, when the *Eschaton* had descended from the sky, to be a woman. A wet, angry, wretched, bedraggled woman, who greeted her rescue with the sort of cold courtesy one might expect from a monarch, one who is not particularly impressed by the subjects she is faced with. She was taller than Captain Drake, with the sort of womanly figure that certain prose stylists call "ripe," olive skin, and a mass of wet, black curls. Her Camembertian was tinged with the accent of Feta.

"Thank you for the rescue," she said. "Now you must take me to Porta Bella!"

"Ma'am," said Drake, "we mustn't do anything. You may not be aware of what sort of ship you're on, but we do what we damn well please, and we don't take orders from waterlogged castaways. We've rescued you out of the kindness of our hearts, and you'd do well to show proper humility and gratitude."

Murmurs of agreement from the crew. Aboard the *Eschaton*, Captain Drake was as good as a Queen—better, you might say, for the *Eschaton*s had no use for Queens, or anybody else who tried to tell them what to do—and you just didn't talk to her like that. Not if you wanted to live to see your grandchildren.

"Forgive me," said the woman, though her tone was hardly what you'd call contrite, let alone humble or grateful. Urgent. Frantic. Imperious. But not humble. "But they have taken him—to Porta Bella, I'm certain. It may be too late! He may already be hanged!"

"He?" said Drake, quirking her eyebrow. "Hanged? I'd hear this tale. Why don't you come down to my cabin and tell me about it. I'll get you some food, wine, fresh clothes. How does that sound?"

Putting her arm through the other woman's, she nodded to two of her crew. One would bring clean clothes the right size for the castaway, the other, victuals for the hungry woman.

Down in the captain's cabin, dry and fed, the woman introduced herself as Phaedra Parhelion, and told the story you already know, gentle readers, how her husband's ship, *Leukothea*, was captured by a ship of the Camembertian Royal Navy—and, being pirates, he and all his crew were sure to be hung.

"Hmm," said Drake, lighting up her pipe. As clouds of fragrant blue smoke surrounded them, she said, "Can you describe this ship?"

Phaedra considered. "A frigate. The ... the *Circe*, I believe." Drake shrugged. "Her captain was an arrogant young man. Yellow-haired. Wore a little goatee." She drew her finger and thumb down her chin, indicating the shape of the captain's beard. And then she smiled with bleak satisfaction. "I struck him," she said.

Drake felt herself go still—much as you may have seen a cat do, when it senses prey is near. "This captain," she said, casually, "did you happen to catch his name?"

"I did," said Phaedra. "It was Zeal."

After that, there was no question about helping her. Even now, if she closed her eyes, she could see it in her mind: the bright day, its beauty a mockery of the slaughter on the *Eschaton*'s decks, the sprays of blood obscenely red—and still the *Kraken* kept up its relentless fire, thump-thump-thump-thump-thump of broadside after broadside, the *Eschaton* shuddering as blow after blow struck her hull.

It was Random who saw how the battle would end, Random Chance, her first mate, who suggested blowing their own powder magazine rather than surrender to the Royal Navy. "After all," he said, "the least we can do is take 'em down to hell with us, eh, my lass?" She had been caught by the breath-taking insanity of it, had given the orders that would make it so. As the *Eschaton* altered course to close with the man-of-war, she had seen the cannon ball that killed him come hurtling out of the smoke, cutting him in two just as he gave the order to board.

After that, what did anything matter? It would have been better, she sometimes thought, to have died in the battle rather than live on without him—but her crew, damn them all, would have none of it.

"Can't have your revenge, can you, if you get killed now?" said Luna Shee.

"Revenge," agreed Lilly Bones, her sister in spirit.

They spirited her away in one of the ship's boats, while most of the crew stayed behind to keep the navy dogs occupied (a sacrifice they made willingly, the mad zealots) and blow the dear old *Eschaton* to the sky. And the *Kraken* with it, they had hoped.

Except the *Kraken* had not sunk, and her captain, damn and blast him, had survived. If it was her last act upon the earth, she would see him pay for what he had done to her.

So there was really no question but that they would help Phaedra. After all, they had the same goals.

There was just one little problem. If Captain Zeal had had enough time to deposit the pirates with the nearest Naval authority, they were most likely already dead and adorning a gibbet somewhere, a grim example to others who would thwart Her Majesty's laws.

"No!" said Phaedra. "He is alive! He must be!" But she had no reason why this must be so, and when pressed, would only say, "I would know it if he were dead."

"Well, then," said Captain Drake, tapping the ashes of her pipe out the stern window, "our first task must be to find out where he would have taken his prisoners, and what would have happened to them after that."

They were almost too late, as it turned out. Even during the so-called "Golden Age" of piracy, when Flynn Freeborn of the *Peregrine*, Lucenza di Ladro of the *Stella Maris*, Cornelius Cid of the *Winged Hope* and, most recently, Vandemar Broadside of the *Obliterator*, performed the dastardly deeds that made their names resonate through the ages, civil authorities had been quick to denounce their depredations, and naval authorities even quicker to neutralize their menace. And now, in these latter days of peace, though piracy was by no means unheard-of, it was all the more condemned as a violation of the natural order, and those guilty of such crimes were swiftly punished.

Thus Stavros Parhelion, otherwise known as the fearsome pirate Sundog, scourge of the Shiraz Sea, handed over to the Admiral of the fleet stationed near Porta Bella (Camembert and Parmigiana being, at that time, allied states), was handed by that worthy in turn to representatives of the Doge. The Doge, who hadn't gotten to be the Prince of a small but influential nation-state by being a dummy, knew a political opportunity when he saw one, and threw the captured pirates a huge, lavish and very public trial (some people throw parties—he threw trials) in which their many crimes against the state were enumerated in detail. And if a lot of details that never happened got added by witnesses who were never present, well, that was justice in Parmigiana. The public particularly liked the testimony given by a young "merchant seaman" whose ship had been "captured by those barbarous pirates," who said his captain and shipmates had been "most cruelly ill-used" at Sundog's hands, and who had only escaped by head-butting his captors and diving overboard.

Only two days later, Stavros Parhelion stood on a gibbet at the water's edge, his hands bound before him, listening as the charges were read: Burning, Sinking and Destroying those Innocent Merchant Vessels Such as Happened in his Way, Piracy, Theft, Murder, Treason Against their Most Just and Lawful Ruler, the Doge, and Enmity To All Humankind, for which, he was Sentenced to Die. His comrades, Nikkos and Demetrius and all the rest, were equally sentenced, but the death of the pirate Sundog was the spectacle for the day, the reason for the crowds that stood on the shore, the wharves, on boats just out to sea. A weathered figure in preacher's garb (who looked, despite the broad-brimmed preacher's hat, less like a priest than an opera critic) stood in one of the boats, haranguing them to repent of their heinous sins.

Stavros was only grateful that Phaedra had escaped. He hoped, if she were still alive, that she never found out what had befallen him.

The moment came. The charges were read. Stavros stepped forward, clearing his throat. Some memorable last words were expected of him.

"Today the Doge destroys me," he said, raising his voice to be heard to the farthest edges of the crowd, "but he cannot destroy the longing for freedom that beats in the breast of everyone who calls Feta home! His tyranny will fail! We will be free! FREEDOM!" he shouted, raising his bound fists to the sky.

Just then, it began to rain fire.

"Keep her steady!" Drake shouted. To her gunners: "Aim for those buildings, to larboard!" And to her wizard: "You're not any good to me if you keep fainting, man! Stand up straight!"—grabbing him by the hood of his robe and hauling him to his feet.

"F-forgive me, Captain," said the wizard, Elian Scuttlebutt by name, a plump little man with a bald head and a shiny face. "My! This is hard work, isn't it?"

"You'll find it even harder with my dagger in your throat," said Drake. "Can you make lightning strike that group of men beside the gallows?"

"And keep the ship in the air?" said Scuttlebutt. And then, at the snickt of a knife being drawn, "Y-y-yes, of course, Captain."

"Good." Drake turned to Phaedra Parhelion, who was waiting nearby, her black eyes calm, her face perfectly composed. "It's your turn," she said.

Phaedra nodded.

"Once you've got him, you're on your own," Drake said. "I can't be hanging around waiting for you. I've concerns of my own." The Camembertian fleet, far below and astern of the *Eschaton*, was performing the manoeuvres that would bring it in close; one lucky shot was all they needed to bring the pirates plunging from the sky. The tiny black dot against the clouds to larboard was no doubt an airship of the Royal Navy whose wizard had somehow sensed the ruckus, and was coming up fast to investigate. "But," Drake added with a small, wicked smile, "I can promise you that everyone will be much too busy to worry about you."

Phaedra nodded again. "I understand. Thank you."

Drake's own nod was more of a jerk of her chin. "Indeed." Phaedra stepped up onto the rail, balanced on that slender piece of wood for a moment, hundreds of feet up in the air. She could see the chaos below her, crowds of little ant-like people milling about in confusion as the *Eschaton* continued to spurt fire from her lower guns—and there, on the gallows at the low tide mark, as clearly as though he stood close enough to touch, Stavros, looking up at her.

"I'm coming, my love," she said.

She jumped.

"My!" exclaimed Elian Scuttlebutt. "What a remarkable woman!" He mopped at his forehead with the sleeve of his billowing robe. "How—" He stopped, shaking his head. "I could never—"

Drake strode forward and seized him by the throat. She was a small person, and slim, but he was smaller, and his feet came up off the deck, to flop and dangle in the air.

"Where the devil," said she, "is my lightning?"

He choked and sputtered, his face turning a remarkable rainbow of colors.

With a curse, she set him back down. "Lightning!" she snapped. "Now!"

"Y-y-yes, ma'am," he said, though it came out as more of a wan cough.

"Uh, Cap'n?"

Drake rounded on the new interruption, eyes blazing, and the unfortunate speaker retreated a step. "What?" she snarled.

"It's just ... we've got company, Cap'n."

Indeed they had. The squadron had got into position, and, with its guns trained as high as they would bear, was opening fire. Dense white clouds spurted from the cannons' mouths, at this distance looking like tiny puffs of cotton—and with each cloud, a lance of flame, and the deep, sky-shattering boom of the gun's report.

"They'll not hit us at this angle," said Drake, and indeed, the shot arced through the air well below the *Eschaton*'s hull. But to her own gun-crews she shouted, "'Vast firing!" To her first mate she said, "It looks as though we're no longer welcome here, eh, Moonhart? Let's away to more congenial skies."

"Aye-aye!" Albius Moonhart, a long, lean, sallow fellow inherited from her father, clicked his heels and did not—quite—salute. He strode along the deck, shouting the commands to luff up and bear away, leaving the Royal Navy and their impotent gunnery far behind.

Captain Drake had, however, forgotten the imminent presence of the Naval sky-sailer, and when the first shots twanged through the rigging, she shouted, "Hell and death! Return fire! Luna, port your helm! Moonhart, get us the devil out of here!" The pirates scurried to obey, and the *Eschaton* began to sheer away, declining combat with the heavier ship, gathering speed as she angled out to sea. Drake, once more grabbing poor Scuttlebutt by the throat, pointing with her free hand at the fast-approaching Navy vessel, "And give me my god-damned lightning, or by all that's holy I will kill you with my own two hands!"

"Y-yes, Captain!" gasped he, sliding towards the deck.

Captain Drake cannot entirely be blamed for what happened next, although her famous and conspicuous red coat was partly at fault. However, if the Navy sharpshooter had aimed a little more to the right, much that transpired later would have been averted—although we would have had much less of a story to tell. He was in the fighting top of the approaching ship, rifle in hand, and he was aiming for the *Eschaton*'s captain. Perhaps it was a trick of the wind, or the unpredictable motion of the pirate ship. Perhaps it was fate. He breathed a prayer and squeezed the trigger. The gun went off with a clear, bright crack!

The red-coated captain remained standing. But the other pirate, who stood not a foot away, fell.

"Hell!" cried Drake, as Scuttlebutt's head dissolved in a red spray. She dropped the corpse and shook the blood off her hands—and felt the deck beneath her feet begin to slant—almost imperceptibly at first, then faster and faster and more and more as the magic that maintained the ship's altitude dissolved at the wizard's death. "Hell and death!" Drake cried, and began to spit the orders that would keep them all from dying when the ship hit the ocean, fathoms below.

"Somebody get Cid up here! Moonhart, see that the wings are fully extended! Set every stitch of canvas we have! Jettison everything we don't need—every ringbolt, every ha'penny nail, every chest, every gun! Dead-Eye!"

A seedy fellow with a scraggly beard and one blind eye stepped forward. "Aye, Cap'n?"

"To the top with you! See if you can't return the favor."

Dead-Eye grinned. "Aye, Cap'n!" Taking his trusty gun, a rifle whose bore was grooved to throw the bullet farther and with much more accuracy than a smoothbore weapon, he hurried away.

"Captain." That was Moonhart, standing at her right shoulder, urgent. "If we abandoned ship now, some of us might survive."

"He's right, lass." Stumping along the deck—which now was slanting like a cathedral roof—was a squat, square, bearded man in aviator's leather cap and grease-stained coveralls. "We've got no choice."

The look Drake shot him was compounded of affection and irritation. "Dad," she said, in decided tones.

"Your mother'd have the hide off me if I let you get killed, my Francie," Cid told her.

"Pfft," Drake said. "She'll hide us both if I crash this shiny new ship you gave me, and you know it." The *Eschaton*'s downward dive was growing steeper by the second, her masts and rigging taking on an ominous note as the wind wrung them out of true.

"Take the gliders, lass," Cid urged. "I've built five. If you hurry you'll still be safe."

The gliders were Cid's latest invention, light wooden frames with canvas wings that would waft a rider along with currents in the air. As good as a parachute, you might have said, except no one had quite thought up parachutes yet.

Captain Drake's face was scarlet as her coat. "No!" she cried. "Damn and blast you both! I will not abandon my ship! I will not let them win again!" She gesticulated toward the Navy sky-sailer, now right aft.

"Why, bless me, lass—" Cid began.

"Get into the control room," said Drake, her voice like a hawser stretched to breaking. "Do what you can to slow us down. Moonhart, I believe I gave you your orders."

The older men nodded, and turned to obey.

The *Eschaton* fell from the sky like a slow-arcing comet, and hit the Shiraz Sea with a splintering crash. Her mainmast snapped like a toothpick, and her bowsprit shattered, and water came gushing through the terrible wounds in her hull.

"That's torn it," said Captain Heywood, of H.M. airship *Helios*, in tones of deep satisfaction. "We'll see no more of that parcel of rogues. Let's go home, Jim."

"Aye, sir," said his first lieutenant, and gave the orders. Soon *Helios* had worn, leaving only the Shiraz's shining waters behind.

"Why, bless me, lass!" cried Cornelius Cid, eyes round with awe, "I didn't know you could do that!"

"Nor I," said Moonhart.

"Nor I," Drake agreed, her face white with strain. The *Eschaton* was hovering less than a man's height above the water; she began to drift downwards, and landed as gently as a leaf on a still pond.

"Where's he goin?" asked Luna Shee, pointing up at the swiftly-departing sky-sailer.

"He thinks we crashed and sank," said Drake, whose voice was growing fainter with every word she spoke.

"Did you do that, too?" asked Luna, amazed. But Drake's eyes had rolled back into her head, and with a quiet sigh, she collapsed.

Three. Heart of Oak

The pirates clustered around the cabin door. Was the captain all right? Would she recover? Would she die? The *Eschaton* had no physician, not even a surgeon or a horse-leech (the wizard would have served the purpose, but he was no longer fit for duty), so when Cid emerged from the cabin, his face (what could be seen of it through the enormous beard) grey with worry, the gathered pirates assaulted him with questions.

"Peace, now, mates," said Cid, raising his hands. "She's sleeping, but it's peace she's needing if she's to recover. Back to your duties, now."

"What I want to know is, what happened back there," someone said.

"Aye, that's what we want to know," others agreed.

Cid and Moonhart had already consulted on the point, and now Cid said, "Why, bless me, lads, if I know! But it could be that there was just enough magic left in the ship to keep us from crashing. It could be (and I'm merely theorizing, I am, so don't hold these words against me if I'm wrong, bless me!) that the ship herself saved us from crashing, once the wizard was dead."

The explanation, spurious though it might have been, satisfied the pirates, and they said, "But what do we do now?"

Moonhart and Cid, and Luna Shee and Lilly Bones, had consulted on that point as well. Now Cid puffed out his chest and said, "This here vessel's as taut as any could wish. We'll sail her home, aye, and find ourselves a new wizard, and before you know it, we'll be soaring high and free once more. Now get to work, you lot! Let the Cap'n sleep!"

"My lord, my lady," said Captain Acheron Zeal, bowing, "I am honored."

"It is we who are honored, Captain Zeal." The woman had been a beauty once—was a beauty still, in fact, though no longer young. Her hair, they said, had been as red as flame, but now it was silky and white, like spun ice, worn coiled in an elaborate braid on the top of her head. Her husband, something of a poet (but, he always said with a self-deprecating grin, "a very little something") had written poems about the change, autumn giving way to winter; indeed, a volume of his verse had been published only a few months before, to ecstatic reviews. If there were a more famous couple in the entire realm, it could only be the Queen and her Prince-Consort themselves.

Lady Althea Goodheart-Smythe, now the Queen's Champion, and her husband Sir Gregarius Ignatius Smythe, head of the Knights of St George, had played key roles in the defeat of the warlock Baron von Death twenty-five years before. The stories said that Sir Gregory had duelled the dark wizard Falco Malvens to a standstill, bearing the holy blade of his ancestor, St George himself. Captain Zeal looked around the room, hoping for a glimpse of the legendary sword, but there was no sign of any magical artifacts at all in the Smythes' neat, rather spartan parlor.

"You have a reputation for courage, dash and bravery—" Althea continued.

"And zeal," put in her husband with a small grin.

Lady Althea smiled and touched his shoulder, then turned back to Zeal (who had, of course, never heard that one before). "We're only happy we weren't too late," she said.

"My lady." Zeal paused, cleared his throat, wondered about the best way to phrase his next words. "My lady," he tried again, "my lord, there are other ships, other captains. When I received your letter, I was of course pleased and grateful, but—"

"But why you?" said Sir Gregory. He was not wearing the full ceremonial armor of the Knights of St George, but a soft white surcoat with the symbol of his order embroidered on the breast. Zeal nodded. The knight considered, folding his hands behind his back, then said, "When you were a child learning to read, were you given the classics of literature right away, or were you first taught the alphabet?"

"The alphabet, of course, my lord," said Zeal, baffled.

Sir Gregory nodded. "And isn't it true," he said, "that the principles of flying an airship, a sky-sailer, are based on, derived from, the principles of sailing ships?"

"Ah," said Zeal, understanding dawning at last. "Yes, it is true."

"Then," said Sir Gregory, "isn't it best for one to learn the most basic principles first, before being thrown into more complex operations?"

Zeal bowed.

"Not to mention," said Sir Gregory, with a sly grin, "you do have a reputation for adventure, Captain. That was, ah ... a prerequisite."

Meanwhile, the object and the purpose of all this discussion stood a little to one side, small hands folded before him: a boy, perhaps ten years old, with wide blue eyes and fine blond hair, dressed in the uniform of a midshipman. The formality of blue broadcloth jacket and white breeches made him appear absurdly young, and far too beautiful for a human child.

"You will take good care of him, of course?" said Althea, a mother's anxiety entering her demeanor for the first time, as she gestured the lad forward. "I realize that many things are beyond your control...."

"Now, love, don't fret," said Sir Gregory, turning to her and taking her hand. She raised her eyes to his, and was caught there. They might have been the only ones in the room, so intense and private was that shared gaze. Zeal averted his eyes.

He found, to his surprise, that the child was looking at him. He quirked his eyebrows towards his parents, as though to say, "They do that all the time," and shook his head. Zeal suppressed a grin.

"Of course," said Lady Althea, smiling, in response to the words her husband had not needed to speak. And to her son, "Peter, say hello to Captain Zeal."

"Hullo, Captain Zeal," said the boy, with a neat little bow. "I'm very pleased to meet you."

"The same," Zeal replied. "Come now, let's get your dunnage and be off." To the parents (and there was a hint of anxiety in Sir Gregory's face as well, now) he said, "Forgive me for hurrying him away, but time and tide wait for no man, and I have received some intelligence about the *Eschaton*'s latest position."

"Of course," said Sir Gregory. "Pity those other pirates escaped."

"Indeed." Suppressing a grimace, Zeal turned to the *Circe*'s youngest young gentleman. "Come along, then, lad," he said, "and I'll show you your new home."

It was unusual for the parents of a new midshipman to meet with his captain in person, but Sir Gregory and Lady Althea were an unusual pair. It was a lucky stroke, Zeal reflected, to have their patronage, especially after that damned unfortunate business with the Fetan pirates escaping from the very gallows. And who had engineered their escape, who had made it possible? The *Eschaton*, of course. The *Eschaton*. The thrice-damned, blasted, accursed *Eschaton*. He was beginning to hate the very sound of it.

Captain Heywood, of the *Helios*, claimed he had shot the *Eschaton* out of the sky—but not two weeks later, fishermen in southern Camembert had seen a sloop with a red-painted hull, matching the *Eschaton*'s description exactly, sailing north toward Unicorn Bay.

"If only I knew where she made berth!" said Zeal.

"I beg your pardon, sir?" said Mr Midshipman Peter Goodheart-Smythe.

"Nothing, lad. Just thinking out loud."

Of course, being much too young, Mr Midshipman Peter Goodheart-Smythe was a midshipman at all, but a first-class volunteer, and so he was rated on the ship's books. But given a couple of years, he would be a midshipman in thought, word and deed, and given four more after that, he could go before the Navy Board and be examined for Lieutenant. With such parents as those, it would be a wonder if he weren't commanding a sky-sailer by the time he was twenty, if he didn't prove an utter booby.

He didn't appear to be a booby, though a little delicate. Well, time at sea would change that, especially under the tyranny of Wakeman and Vaughn, the eldest of the *Circe*'s mids. Zeal showed the boy the midshipmen's berth himself, noting how his eyes grew wide (amazement, or dismay?) at that dank hole, abjured him to make friends with his shipmates, and excused himself. He had duties, urgent duties, to which he must attend.

The notice hung between an advertisement for Gruver & Fritch, Ltd., Shipwrights, and a poster announcing available berths aboard H.M.S. *Prometheus*, bound for adventure in the far north, inquire with Captain Feldspar. There was also a broadsheet requesting anyone with information regarding the whereabouts of the pirate ship *Eschaton* to come forward. But the notice with which we are concerned is the one in the middle:

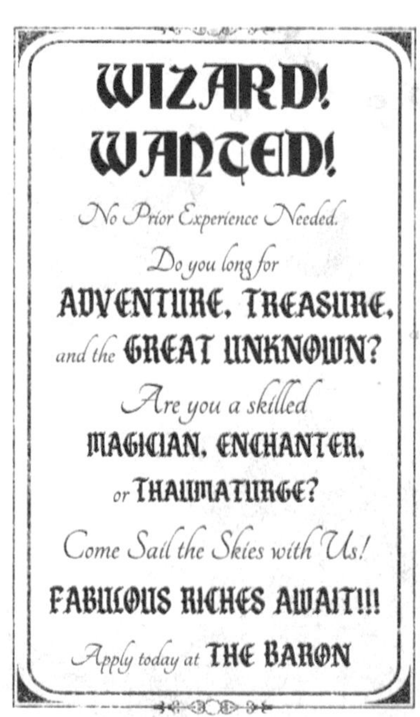

The man reading the sign was tall and thin, with hair the color of straw. By his dress, especially the absurd buckled hat he wore, tall and wide-brimmed, and the mud still on his enormous boots, he was recently arrived from far inland, Camembert's agricultural heart. He tugged at his right pigtail, scratched his chin, rubbed his head beneath the ridiculous hat, and removed the notice from the wall. Rolling it up and putting it in his pocket, he set out in search of the Baron.

"Yes, thank you," said Captain Drake, exchanging a weary glance with her father. "We'll be in touch."

The person before them, shrouded in innumerable filmy veils of various colors, bobbed a half-bow, half-curtsey, and departed.

"Next, please," Drake called.

They were in the back room of the Baron, a ramshackle waterfront public house, and they were auditioning wizards. It was, however, not going at all well.

The next candidate strode forward. He was a tall man with an enormous mop of wild black hair and a hawk-like nose, dressed in flowing robes of black velvet. Raising his arms, he proclaimed in a deep and mighty voice, "I am the great dark wizard Falco Malvens! No wizard has ever surpassed my powers!"

"I thought Falco Malvens was dead," Drake whispered to her father.

Cid's eyes were sad. "Aye, lass, that he is. This many and many-a year."

"For many years," 'Falco Malvens' continued, striding about the little room and gesticulating, "I have held myself apart from humanity! But now—I shall deign to accept the work you offer me! I—oops!" The toe of his shoe had caught on a loose board, and he tripped spectacularly. The black wig came tumbling off his head, the false nose popped off, and he went sprawling at Drake and Cid's feet, looking for all the world like a spider someone had squashed.

"Er..." he said, in a much different voice. "That is...."

"Thank you, Lord Falco," said Drake. "We'll be in touch."

"Well," she said, when she and Cid were alone, "that was a bloody waste. Aren't there any competent wizards in the world?"

"Patience, Francie," her father said, patting her shoulder. "We'll find someone yet. Or he'll find us. It hasn't been so very long that wizards could walk freely in the world again, you know."

"I know." She sighed. "It's just—"

"Hello?" called a new voice, and a face peered around the doorjamb. "Beg pardon. Is anyone here?"

Drake's heart, which had fluttered to life again, now died within her. "If you're looking for the kitchen," she said, "it's—"

"Ain't lookin for the kitchen," said the newcomer, coming round the door and into full view. "Heard someone round hereabouts was lookin for a wizard."

He was, of course, the fellow previously described: tall, skinny, bony, ugly, with a prominent nose (a real one this time) and an asymmetrical face. His hands were in his pockets. All that was required to complete the image was a pitchfork, or a piece of straw dangling from his lip.

"Oh?" said Drake, with forced politeness. "And perhaps you know where we could find one?"

"Am one," said the hayseed. "I'm applyin for the job."

Franceline Drake was much too well-bred to laugh in his face ... but she laughed in his face. "You?" she gasped. "Oh, heavens! That's—" But whatever it was, was lost in another gale of laughter.

Until now, he had remained in the doorway, but now he stepped into the room and closed the door behind him, striding forward (a smooth and purposeful walk for such an ungainly fellow) and looking her right in the face. Her laughter stilled. "I think—" he began, and then stopped. His eyes were perfectly colorless—not grey or white, for grey and white are both colors, but clear as water or quartz. "You don't need me," he said at last.

"Certainly not!" said Drake, shaken by the intensity of his gaze.

"No." He shook his head. "Don't need me—don't need a wizard 't all. Unless a ship's cap'n cain't be ship's wizard, too." His eyes never left her face.

"How..." she said. "How did you know that? It wasn't on the notice."

He shrugged, and began to turn away. "Not magic, if that's what you're thinkin," he said, starting for the door. "Logic. But I won't waste your time,

Cap'n." He waved. He was almost gone.

"Wait!" Drake cried.

He paused.

"What makes you think I don't need a wizard?"

He turned. "Got your own magic. Stiff with it. Coming outa your ears. What d'ya need me for?" Tipping his hat, he said, "Good day t' ya."

His hand was almost on the door handle when Drake said, "But I don't. I haven't got any magic. And even if I did, I wouldn't know how to use it."

That gave him pause. "You don't say," he said.

She lifted her chin. "I believe I just did."

"Well." He paused to consider, then strode back to her, stretching out his hand. "In that case," he said, "I believe I will take the job." He shook her hand. "Dallon Moral," he said.

"Franceline Drake," she replied.

It wasn't until much later that she realized she'd never actually offered it to him.

Captain Zeal had not thought about Miss Franceline Drake for many weeks—or, if he had, it was with a sort of dim regret. She had sailed to Stratocumulopolis to live in her mother's house there, and she was as lost to him as if she'd flown to the moon, and his hope of her had been a faint one to begin with.

Imagine his surprise, therefore, when he saw her walking down the lane in Tawney Port, even more beautiful than he remembered. She saw him, too, and her eyes grew wide—and then she inclined her head, inviting him to approach and speak to her.

"Good day, Miss Drake," he said, removing his hat.

"Good day, Captain Zeal," she replied. "I am surprised to see you here. I thought you were off hunting pirates."

"Indeed," said he, falling into step beside her, "this is a brief but necessary stop. We put out to sea tomorrow."

"Ah," said she.

How lovely she was! He had quite forgotten the delicacy of her features, the rich blackness of her hair—blacker than anything, made blacker still by contrast to her fair, fair skin. And the grace of her slender figure, her tiny gloved hands as they held her parasol, the little feet just peeping beneath the hem of her gown.

"I suppose," said Zeal, after an awkward pause, "it would be terribly impertinent to invite you to dine with me?"

Her eyes flicked sideways, regarding him from beneath her thick lashes. "Terribly impertinent, Captain Zeal," she said. "Most improper."

"Ah," he said, deflated. "I thought it would be."

"But," she said, with a rosy smile, "I would be happy to accept."

Joy—pleasure—rapture! Would seven o'clock be acceptable? It would. Would Miss Drake be averse to dining on board the *Circe*? It was a marvelous ship, a magnificent vessel; Miss Drake would be fascinated, he was sure, to see some of the improvements he'd made. Miss Drake said she would be honored. She would be aboard the *Circe* at seven o'clock.

"I know how punctual you Navy men are," she said, lightly touching his arm. "I'll be certain not to be late."

It was, of course, unthinkable that a young woman of Miss Drake's breeding and station should go unaccompanied to dine with a young man, and so Captain Zeal was by no means surprised to see another woman, this one a square-jawed, stern-faced matron, being helped up the *Circe*'s side, with many an exhortation to "mind the roll, now, ma'am, just wait for the opportune moment." Miss Drake, however, leapt over like a born sailor, you might have said, and Zeal thought, with her pink cheeks and her laughing eyes and the sparkle of spray in her hair, she had never looked so fine.

She continued to look fine throughout the meal, which they took in his dining cabin under the watchful eye of the bulldog-like matron. She took no part in the conversation (she was, in fact, mute, but Zeal had no way of knowing this. Lilly Bones had offered to come instead, as being the most imposing member of Drake's crew, but since Lilly and Zeal had met before, it was deemed unwise)—

but conversation was not why she was there. Her purpose, sole and entire, was to ensure that the young man didn't try any "funny business" with the lady.

Of course Zeal would never have offered Miss Drake the least importunity, whether they'd been alone or surrounded by an army of chaperones, but the rules of propriety had to be observed, down to the last punctilio.

Indeed, at first Drake found his relentless courtesy wearying; she had always believed that politeness in men was a sign of weakness, or a lack of interest in her. But as dinner continued it became clear that he was not uninterested, nor even disinterested. The way his eyes lingered on her face—never long enough to be construed as staring, but with unmistakable avidity—the way he spoke her name, even the way he poured the wine: all these shone as clear as stars in the night sky as proofs of his growing and ardent affection for her.

She was charmed by his politeness. No man had ever before treated her with such amiable civility, such kindness and solicitude. Certainly Random had never addressed her as Captain Zeal did, as though—as though—as though she were a lady!

Damn him, thought Franceline, I'm supposed to be charming him, not the other way round!

But when he raised his eyes to meet hers, she had to look away, and felt an unwonted blush rise to her cheeks.

"Miss Drake?" said Captain Zeal, and she realized he had asked her a question.

"Oh," she said, "I'm sorry. I ... was thinking."

She saw by his downcast look that he was charmed, that he was, if she wanted him, completely and entirely hers. "I merely wondered if you might like to be shown round the ship," he said.

It was not the first time she had been made to realize her power, but it was still a heady draught, more dizzying than wine. If she smiled at him—like so—and gazed up at him through her eyelashes, as though shy—this she did—his flagging spirits would falter, his hope renew. And if she said in her sweetest tones, "Why, Captain Zeal, I would like that of all things," then the trap was closed. He was hers. He stood and offered her his arm. She took it and rose.

"This way, then," he said, in the voice of a man in a dream.

He showed her the *Circe* from stem to stern, pointing out certain improvements he had made in the rigging (she noted them, as they appeared very useful innovations), explaining the uses of various ropes and blocks and things, and he would no doubt have shown her down to the very hold, to demonstrate how proper stowing of cargo could improve the ship's trim and enable her to lie as much as half a point closer to the wind, if Drake had not pled the lateness of the hour, saying that she must return to her lodgings before much more time had passed.

"Oh!" cried Captain Zeal, blushing. "Forgive me, Miss Drake. I've been babbling on about things that can't possibly interest you."

"Oh, no, Captain," said Miss Drake prettily. "I am interested, if only for your sake."

This produced a deeper blush. And then she saw him take a slow breath, stepping closer to her, daring the displeasure of the ever-watchful chaperone. "Miss Drake," he said, the flush quite vanished, "you know I must proceed to sea tomorrow. But I would be honored, truly honored, if you would allow me to write to you."

There was a queer pressure in her chest, and she was having difficulty keeping her own breathing steady. What was this—this rank betrayal on the part of her emotions? It was not to be borne!

"I think, Captain Zeal," she said, looking down, "that I might."

She did not offer him her hand, and he did not offer to take it. He did not touch her at all, except to help her into the boat that would row her back to shore, but his face was radiant with happiness. He bowed to her, and then the boat was disappearing into the darkness, and she waved and waved and waved until she could see him no more.

The wizard Dallon Moral hummed to himself as he tinkered about in the *Eschaton*'s engine room. It was not an engine room as my readers today might understand it. It was not, for example, filled with steel mechanisms that dripped various liquids, or furnaces of glowing coals, or drums of oil, or boilers that oozed steam. There was an array of odd gadgets and gizmos, gears and cogs, tubes and wires and other such things, but this was the marriage of magic and science, and, as such, was strangely beautiful.

He was working by candlelight, as the sun had long since gone down, and he was oblivious to the fact that anyone might be watching him. "The problem," he said to himself, as he contemplated the huge crystal, surrounded by a web of wires, that served to harness a magician's energies and allow the ship to fly, "is clearly one of power storage. Stop feeding it with magic, and boom, that's it, no more power, goodbye clear skies, hello painful death."

"Aye," said a voice behind him, "bless me, 'tis ever been the difficulty! But 'tis baffled I am to discover a solution—bein no sort of magician meself."

Moral whipped around. In the doorway stood Cornelius Cid, who, besides being the father of Captain Drake, was the father of the modern airship. Others had dreamt it, but he had realized it.

"Well," said Moral, "seems to me ... mind if I borrow this?" There was a wrench sticking out of the front pocket of Cid's coveralls. The lanky wizard snatched it and turned to the crystal and its web. "Seems to me," he said, swiftly dismantling the apparatus, to Cid's unspeakable horror, "that oyou're onto something here, but the application's not—quite—right!" He grunted with effort, and the crystal came free. "Hold this, please." He dropped it into Cid's hands. "Look. Hook these together like this," he did so, "reach that tube across here, give it a coupla twists, and then—" he took the crystal out of Cid's hands and slid it into the altered device, "just a coupla words...." He spoke, then, in a language that Cid had never heard (it was Latin, in point of fact, a favorite language of magic-users. Others can of course be used, and spells spoken in plain Camembertian are no less effective, but the Latin just sounds better), holding his hands above the crystal. Flaming gold letters appeared on its surface, blazing for a moment brilliant white, then growing cool and dim. By the time the wizard stopped speaking, they had disappeared entirely, and you could not have said, to look at it, that they'd ever been there.

Cid opened and closed his mouth several times.

"There," said Moral, putting his hands on his hips. "That oughta do it. It won't be perfect, I'm afraid, but it should be enough to keep this boat in the air for a little while, even if something happened to me."

"How long?" Cid asked.

The wizard shrugged. "Couple days? A week at best, I reckon. I'll do some research. There's gotta be a way to make it permanent."

"Amazing!" Cid breathed, reaching a hand towards the crystal but not—quite—daring to touch it. "You're a real wizard, so you are, bless me! Only one other wizard I've met could do a thing like that! A dark wizard, he was, and his brother a paladin. But a good man, despite his malevolent ways, God bless him."

A queer expression passed over the wizard's face. "I heard," he said. "You sailed with Falco Malvens, didn't you? During the war."

"Aye," said Cornelius Cid. "Into the teeth of the Funnel itself. Bless me! What an adventure that was!"

"And—" said Moral. And you fought against him at the end, he had been about to say, but he never got the chance. There was a knock at the door, and Luna Shee poked her curly dark head round the corner.

"Wizard here?" she said. "Aye, I see he is. Cap'n wants you. Her cabin."

"The Captain?" said Moral, in some surprise. "Why?"

Luna shrugged. "Didn't say. Are you coming or not?"

"Of course." He took his jacket from the hook where he'd hung it, tugged it on, and followed.

The captain's cabin, when he had knocked and gained entry, was dark, the only light faint starlight coming through the stern windows. Dallon eased himself inside and shut the door behind him. "Captain?" he said, waiting for his eyes to adjust.

"Here," said her voice.

There was a dim shape seated at the table. It might have been hers.

"Why're you sittin here in the dark, Cap'n?" he asked.

"I'm trying to light this candle with my brain."

She hunched forward in her chair, her elbows on the table before her, her chin resting on her arms. There was a candle in front of her. She was glaring at it hard enough to make her eyes cross.

"Here," said Moral, coming to stand beside her. "That's no good. You'll just give yourself a headache. Like this." He concentrated briefly, and the wick burst into golden flame. "Do you see?"

"No," she said. "You've blinded me."

"That's not what I meant. Do you have another candle?"

"Over there." She gestured. He went to fetch one, and held it out before her. "Do you understand what to do?"

"I ... I think so."

"Give it a try."

So she did. She concentrated until she was half-blind with headache, but the wick would not light. Tears burned in her eyes.

"It's no good," she said, her voice low and wretched. "No good at all. It's true. I really am worthless."

He stared, uncertain how they'd gotten from lighting candles to worthlessness. And then he saw the first tear slide down her cheek, and the next, and the next, until the dam broke, and she lay down her head and sobbed, weeping as though her heart would break.

"Cap'n..." he said, kneeling beside her, using the soothing voice that had worked so well on the horses back home. "There, there. Why don't you tell me what this is really about, hmm?"

In a choked voice, she did. Not all of it made sense to him, but he understood enough for one thing to be clear. The real problem, as was often the case, was love.

"I'll kill him," she wept. "I really will. I'll kill him!"

Women, in Captain Zeal's experience, were not creatures to be understood. Certainly he had never understood his mother, who was apt to fly into hysterics at the least provocation (he had once dropped his best gold-laced uniform hat in her presence; the resulting fit had lasted almost a week), and the last time he'd seen his sister, she had been a mere slip of a thing, far too young to have anything like a personality. Indeed, was it even possible for a woman to have a personality? He'd never been sure.

But Miss Drake. Oh, Miss Drake! Miss Franceline Drake! He wanted to think logically about her, but he always got stuck just saying her name, over and over. It was like music, like fine wine, like sailing so fast over a running sea that it felt like flying. Miss Drake!

"Mr Morrow?"

"Aye, sir."

"Have we completed our stores?"

"Aye, sir. All but a ton or so of water, sir."

"We can easily complete our water later on," said Zeal. "We must make haste! The *Eschaton* will be heading north, and we must catch her. There's not a moment to lose!"

Privately, Morrow agreed, but you'd never hear him say such a thing out loud. "What about the men still ashore, sir?" he asked.

Zeal considered. "Send Blake and a file of marines after them. They should be easy enough to find. There can't be more than half a dozen of them, at any rate."

"No, sir."

"Well, Mr Morrow," said Zeal, slapping his shoulder (Morrow averted his face and bared his teeth), "make it so. And let's to sea!"

To sea! Where the *Eschaton* was waiting. And when he'd caught her, why, perhaps promotion! A penniless sea-captain couldn't hope to marry a lady like Miss Drake, but the captain of a sky-sailer ... especially one with great deeds to his name...!

"But first," said Captain Zeal, "the *Eschaton*!"

"Well," said Stavros Parhelion, to the raggle-taggle band that surrounded him. "Now what?"

Phaedra's astonishing dive from the sky-pirate's lofty deck (no chance of her hiding her abilities now, not when an ordinary woman would have been so much flotsam after such a stunt) had saved them all, and several harrowing weeks' travel had brought them here, to a cramped room in a tiny inn on the Cilantro side of the Prosciutto Mountains. Little Carina slept in Phaedra's arms, rescued from the relatives with whom they'd left her.

"Now what?" said Demetrius, in a low voice that was no less fierce for its lack of volume. "How can you say that, Stavros? The Doge still rules. The people of Feta are still enslaved. What do you mean, 'now what'?"

"I just..." said Stavros, looking to the side. "I don't think I make a very good pirate."

A tiny fire burned in the grate, its glow painting the dark faces around him amber and bronze, the dancing flames reflecting in each pair of disappointed eyes.

"I am not a leader," he continued, looking away from those reproachful gazes. "I am a simple fisherman, who loves his homeland very much. But one man like me cannot topple a tyrant. I am not ... I cannot...." He paused, took a deep breath. "I just want to go home," he said.

It was Phaedra who reached out and touched his shoulder, Phaedra, who was not much for giving or receiving comfort. "And you will," she said. "We all will. There are just a few little things we have to attend to first."

Stavros (or should we say, the fearsome pirate Sundog?) looked round at the circle of faces: smiling, eager, unafraid. Slowly, he too began to smile. "All right," he said. "When do we sail?"

They were massive, craggy, ragged things...

Chapter 4

The Fisher of Souls

"You know," said Random Chance, first mate of the *Eschaton*, "you can make grog out of anything, you try hard enough."

"Anything, eh?" said his captain, leaning against the taffrail and watching the ship's wake slide by.

"And why not?" Random was a big, broad-shouldered man with thick, dark hair and a ready grin. It showed white against the gathering dark of twilight. "Had a mate one time on the Cyrinx; we put him ashore on an island in the middle of the Shiraz Sea with a pistol and a single shot—you know, traditional-like." The captain nodded. "Come back a year later, and hadn't he just set up a bloody distillery, turning all the coconuts and wild yams and whatnot into liquor? So we figured we could use a man of his whadyacallit—his ingenuity on our ship and took him back on board. Cried for days, he did, and wouldn't touch a drop of rum. Said it didn't compare to his coconut grog."

"Hmm," said the captain. "Are you sure you're not making this up, Random?"

"And would I do a thing like that?" He moved closer, standing beside the slim, red-jacketed figure of the captain, and smiled. "Would I tell stories to my fine, bright lass?"

"You might," said Captain Franceline Drake, looking away. "You're a terrible liar, Random Chance."

"Not to my Francie, I'm not," he said, touching her cheek and smiling.

"That's Drake to you, sailor," she replied, but she did not move away, and she was smiling too. "What brought up this talk of grog?"

"It was on my mind, is all. A Random thought, you might say."

Drake giggled, then laughed out loud, and after a moment Chance joined her. When the merriment died down, she regarded him, her hard green eyes softening, and said, "How lovely it is to be here with you. Somehow … somehow, it feels as though it's been a long time."

"And so it has." Random's tanned, bearded face grew solemn and sad. "You're dreaming, love, and I'm dead. And in a moment you'll have a gruesome and disturbing visual to remind you."

"What?" She reached for him, but he was backing away. "Random—"

His face worked with pain, and he gasped out, "Francie—help me—"

And then his top half went sliding away from his bottom, and his face turned a ghastly shade as his torso landed with a splatter on the deck. His legs remained standing for a moment or two before they, too, toppled over, spraying her with blood as they fell. She pressed her hands to her face and closed her mouth tight, unsure if she opened it whether she would scream or be sick or both.

He looked at her, his face a hideous mass of corrupted flesh, nibbled on by fishes and other things that live in the deep. "Francie..." he said, his voice burbling up somehow from that ruined chest, "help me..."

Drake screamed—

And awoke with a gasp—alone, in her empty bed, in her dark cabin. For a moment she stared around her, confused, clutching the sheet to her breast, still seeing the shape of the old *Eschaton*'s cabin laid over the new. She blinked (a cold tear streaking down her cheek) and the illusion vanished, leaving only the present reality. The old *Eschaton* was gone, shattered and sunk to the bottom of the sea, and Random Chance with her.

"Damn you for that, Acheron Zeal," she muttered, her stomach clenching with hate.

Rising from her bed, she wrapped a robe around herself and went up on deck, where the stars were very bright and almost close enough to touch, and the sleeping world skimmed past miles below. Still new, thinking of ship's altitude instead of ocean's depth, but not unpleasant.

Those members of her crew who were awake and running the ship acknowledged their captain's existence, but did not approach, and she was left alone on her sacred stretch of the quarterdeck.

"Do you remember," she said softly, leaning her elbows on the taffrail and looking out across the dark stretch of earth below, "you always said it would end in tragedy for us. A pirate's life is a short and unhappy one, you said. And how could it be otherwise? We take what we want from life, and isn't that fine, and isn't it grand, but we pay for our sins in the end."

She fell silent. Below the whirring ship there might have been mountains or plains or ocean or nothing at all—it was far too dark to see.

"Cap'n?"

She had heard no sound behind her, no footfall, which meant—

"Oh," said Drake. "It's you."

She turned as she spoke, and Dallon Moral gave her a sheepish grin, taking off his ridiculous hat.

"It's me," he agreed. He tugged at his corn-yellow forelock as he neared.

"Traditionally," said Captain Drake, "crew members are not to approach the captain on her quarterdeck unless invited."

"A wizard," returned Dallon Moral, "goes not where he is wanted, but where he is needed."

He tried to sound lofty, but he only managed to sound like he was quoting something, and the hayseed accent didn't help. Drake suppressed a smirk.

"Wrong on both counts, then, wizard," she said. "I don't need anything from you at present."

Uninvited, he leaned his elbows next to his captain's, but instead of looking down at the shadowed landscape, he gazed up to where the fixed stars gleamed, each holding the post it had occupied since the beginning of time. Raising his hand, he pointed.

"You see that star yonder, Cap'n? The big, bright red one?"

She looked where he indicated. "Aye?"

"That there's Hamus, the Fishhook. The brightest star in the constellation called the Fisherman. You know the story of the Fisherman, Cap'n?"

"This had better have a point, Moral, or I'll pitch you overboard with my own two hands."

He grinned at her, unperturbed by the threat. The crew of the *Eschaton* had grown inured (though they'd never admit it) to their Captain's fulminations. "They say the Fisherman was a demi-god in days of old, back when demi-gods and dragons and whatnot wandered the earth and freely entered into commerce with us mortals. Well, this ol' Fisherman, he weren't too popular with the other demi-gods (nor with us mortals, neither), on account of his fondness for taking the souls of the sea-dead and distilling 'em into his favorite likker. So Leviathan, King of the Deep (of whom I'm sure you've heard, Cap'n), corralled this Fisherman and stuck him in a cave somewhere, and told him he could only drink those misfortunate souls what happened to get caught in the cages he set at the bottom of the sea. And there he sits to this day—and they say he's got a powerful thirst on him by this time, having been stuck in a cave for untold ages of man. And that's the story of the Fisherman, Cap'n, with all due respect." He tugged again at his hair.

The words sea-dead and liquor had stuck in her breast like arrows. She stared first at the Fisherman in the sky, the red star gleaming like a bloodstained fishhook, and then she turned her gaze on Dallon Moral and said with lips gone dry, "And why have you told me this story?"

He shrugged. "Came across it while I was studying. Felt it might be relevant."

"To what, exactly?" It was a struggle to keep her voice level.

He gave her a keen look—a wizard's knowing gaze, not the guileless stare of a hapless hayseed—and said, "Sometimes dreams are just dreams, Cap'n. Other times, they're messages. G'night."

He turned and walked away, his step so light it made no sound. Drake gritted her teeth against a sudden wave of tears. Her hands closed on the rail as though to let go were to fall into eternal damnation, and she slid slowly to her knees.

At the helm, Luna Shee glanced back at the quiet hiss and thump. "Cap'n's having another bad night," she remarked.

Beside her, Lilly Bones shrugged her huge shoulders. "Killing Acheron Zeal'd make her feel better," she said.

Miles away, pacing the quarterdeck of Her Majesty's Ship the *Circe*, Captain Acheron Zeal sneezed.

"God bless you, sir," piped the officer of the watch, Mr Midshipman Peter Goodheart-Smythe.

"Thank you, Mr Smythe," said Zeal, blowing his nose and stowing the handkerchief in the pocket of his woolen coat. "Bracing night, isn't it?"

The *Circe* was cruising the waters of the chill Riesling Sea off the coast of Erris. Recent reports put the *Eschaton* in the area, bearing towards the cursed Island of Mordghre and perhaps beyond to Rjomaskyr—God alone knew to what purpose. But where the *Eschaton* went, there the *Circe* would follow until the pirates were captured and given hempen neckties courtesy of her Majesty, Queen Miranda, or the naval ship was growing barnacles at the bottom of the ocean.

"Aye-aye, sir," said Midshipman Goodheart-Smythe, who had been shivering inside his own thick coat and knit scarf and fuzzy mittens (gifts from his mother before he put out to sea from Tawney Port).

"You were raised at Cardamom Castle, were you not, Mr Smythe?" said Captain Zeal. "I assure you, if you remain in the service long enough, you'll grow accustomed to all weathers."

"Aye-aye, sir," Peter agreed (it being long-standing naval tradition that one never disagreed with the captain, no matter how inane his conversation).

"I'm curious," said the Captain. "Your parents are both Knights of St George, correct?"

"Aye, sir." The ten-year-old's pride prompted him to add, "And my oldest brother was just knighted last year. Sir."

"Did you not wish to be a knight yourself?"

"Oh, no, sir," said Peter Goodheart-Smythe, his blue eyes wide and earnest. "I wanted to sail the seas and have adventures, like King Remington did."

At this Captain Zeal laughed out loud, his breath leaving great puffs of white in the air, and clapping the boy on the shoulder he said, "Well, perhaps you will, lad. Stay in the service, and you'll see all manner of strange and curious sights no lubber can lay claim to."

"Aye-aye, sir!" said Peter Goodheart-Smythe.

"Sir—you may want to have a look at this!"

Acheron Zeal not being one of your laissez-faire sorts of captains, he did indeed want to have a look at that, and up in the foretop, he trained his glass where the lookout pointed.

It was a clear night, and the stars were fully bright enough to illumine the two stone pillars jutting up from the sea before them.

"What in God's name…?" breathed Captain Zeal. "Those aren't on any of our charts!"

"No, sir." The lookout seemed pleased with himself. "Knew you'd want to see 'em for yourself, sir."

"Indeed..." Zeal looked through the glass a second time. He fiddled with the knobs on his telescope, and first one pillar, then the other, leapt into sharp focus.

They were massive, craggy, ragged things, as rough as though they had just been ripped from the earth's bosom. Starlight ran in silver rivulets down their myriad cracks and snags and bumps and jags—the hand of man, Zeal was certain, had never touched them.

A quick calculation confirmed that, on her current course, the *Circe* would sail right past, never closer than a biscuit-toss. Zeal frowned. The flame of curiosity that burned always in his soul, once banked, now flared into a bonfire. Besides, as a captain in Her Majesty's Royal Navy, was it not his duty to explore any strange and perilous object he encountered in Her Majesty's seas?

"Well done, Mr Barrow," he said, and slid back down a backstay to the deck.

Then striding aft, he cried, "Set a course for yonder stones. Two points north-northeast."

"Two points north-northeast," said the helmsman. "Aye-aye, sir!"

The *Circe* glided on through the night. When the sky began to grey with the approach of dawn, the two stones were still no nearer.

"Fifteen chests of gold doubloons," cried Luna Shee, raising her arms high. "Seven bolts of fine silk from Chai, twelve pounds of coffee beans, three bags of gold dust, assorted gems, knives, forks, watches, an antique flintlock, and a stuffed fox with glass eyes."

The crew of the *Eschaton* cheered. Behind and below them, a sinking, shattered, smoking wreck, a merchant ship foundered in the waters of the Chianti Sea, flying frantic distress signals for a rescuer who would never come.

"A fine haul, eh, Cap'n?" said Luna, bounding up to where Drake stood, arms folded across her chest, watching her crew's eyes turn to dollar signs at the sight of all the loot.

"Aye, I suppose," said Drake, turning away. "See that every man gets an equal share. We'll put in at a likely port and they can blow it all on rum and poxied whores."

"Cap'n!"

But Drake was already striding away, disappearing into her cabin and slamming the door behind her. On deck, Luna Shee shook her head. "Cap's depressed," she said.

"Killing Acheron Zeal'll make it all better," Lilly Bones said again.

Dallon Moral frowned. Kneeling beside the heaped-up booty, he plunged his hand into a chest full of gold coins.

"Oy!" cried Luna. "What're you at, mate?"

The wizard looked up at her. The coins in the chest went chink-chink as he rooted through them. There was a strange light in his colorless eyes.

And then he winced and bit back a gasp and yanked his hand out of the chest.

The gathered onlookers could see a bright bead of blood on his palm.

"What in the blazes…?" said Luna Shee.

"It would appear," said Dallon Moral, pulling something small and shiny out of his hand, "that you missed something in your inventory." He got to his feet and showed her.

"Well—" said Luna Shee, "what the hell does that mean?"

He shook his head. "Not sure. Gonna go show the Captain."

In his hand lay a barbed, gleaming fishhook with a drop of red at its tip.

"I think I'll retire," said Random Chance—or a memory of him, leaning against the bulkhead and watching the clouds flick past the aft portholes.

"Oh, aye?" said Drake, from her place on the bed. "And where will you go? A place where they won't execute you, I hope—I'd be awfully sorry to see you hang."

Random ignored the irony in her voice (though one large hand reached up to finger the braided hemp necklace he wore—a reminder of the likely end that awaited a buccaneer). "I think," he said, "I'll retire in Porta Bella. They still welcome a gentleman of fortune, I hear, and the Queen's arm ain't so long it'll reach down to Parmigiana. I'll dress in a different suit every day of the week, and I'll go see the opera, I will, with a fine lady on my arm."

Drake sniffed. "I'd like to see that! And where is the likes of you going to find a fine lady, I wonder?"

He turned and smiled at her, and her insides turned to water. "Already have," he said.

Drake rolled onto her stomach and buried her face in her pillows. "I wish you had retired," she told his ghost. "I wish you'd left me rather than died that way. I'd rather you were on the other side of the world than dead and gone forever!"

A knock sounded against her door.

Drake squeezed her eyes shut and willed all unwelcome visitors to leave her be.

The knock repeated, this time accompanied by a voice. "Captain!"

That damned meddling wizard! Drake lifted her head out of the pillow.

"Go away!"

"I ain't leaving 'til I've talked to you!"

"Then stay there until you rot, and be damned to your soul!" she cried, and this time she covered her head with the pillow to block out the noise. At least she'd locked the door; he wouldn't be able to get inside and bother her—

"I want you to look at this," said a voice at her elbow.

Drake shrieked and leapt out of the bed. There was a loud, ringing crackkkk! as her hand connected with his face, knocking his head back and sending his ridiculous hat flying to the floor.

"Get out!" she shouted. "Get out, get out, get out! How dare you come in here without my permission?"

"Captain," Dallon Moral said, facing her with a wicked red handprint splayed across his cheek, "I will not move from this spot until you listen to what I have to say."

She latched onto his narrow shoulders as though to give him a vicious shaking, but the strength ran out of her all at once, and she hung her head and leaned against him. One of his hands came up and patted her awkwardly on the back. She shuddered.

"Say it, then. Whatever you have to say, say it. And then get out."

"Look at me."

Her head remained stubbornly bowed, her rich black hair covering her face. Gritting his teeth and rolling his eyes, Dallon Moral reached down, grasped her chin, and brought it up to face him.

Her green eyes flicked to the side.

"You're behaving like a child," he said, and if she had been a little less distraught she would have noticed how the backwoods accent dropped away. "I don't care how young or old you are, or who your parents are, or where you come from, or whether you're the captain of a flying ship or a toy boat—you will listen to me now!"

She looked at him. Her lower lip trembled. "I'm listening," she said.

"Random Chance is dead."

Her eyes widened as though he'd slapped her. "I know that," she said.

"Perhaps you do," he said, "but you'd best accept it and soon, or your crew will elect a new captain and leave you to rot on some deserted island with only a sea turtle and an aged marmoset for company. Stop behaving like a spoiled child and get on with your life! People die all the time—deal with it!"

Her eyes were bright with pain and unshed tears, but her voice was soft as she said, "No—you don't understand..."

He sighed. Her hands still rested on his shoulders. His hand still curled around her chin. His other hand, without bothering to consult his brain, reached up to stroke her thick, black hair. She closed her eyes, and a tear spilled down her cheek.

"I miss him," she said.

"It gets better," he said. "Eventually."

She sagged against his chest and wept, and he closed his eyes as he held her. She did not cry for very long, and when she had finished, she took the handkerchief he offered, wiped her eyes and her nose, and said, "What should I do?"

"Be strong," he suggested. "I think he might need your help."

Her eyes grew wide, and one black eyebrow quirked a question.

He showed her the fishhook.

"Perhaps they're just very large," suggested First Lieutenant Thomas Morrow, "and very far away."

"Hmmm," said Captain Zeal, his glass trained on the two distant spires. "We would have sailed into the edge of the world by now, if they were that far away."

"Aye, sir," said Morrow.

All that long day the *Circe* had made for those two inexplicable stones, making a respectable six knots in an easy sea. They should have reached the pillars by now!

"Unless," said Zeal to himself, "they're an illusion, or we're not really moving at all. Well, let the men have their dinners—we'll not reach them tonight."

As Zeal was eating his own solitary meal, darkness fell with amazing suddenness, as though the world were a serving platter and some vast waiter's hand had slammed the lid over it (Duffy, his steward, had just taken away the remains of the meal). Napkin in hand, Zeal ran up on deck and saw the stars come blazing up out of the blackness—and then the round face of the moon bobbed up as though yanked by a string.

"Mr Morrow," he said to his lieutenant, choosing his words with care, "am I incorrect in thinking that yesterday was the new moon?"

"No, sir," said Morrow, his voice more subdued than usual.

"I thought not," said Zeal.

And then all lights—incongruous full moon, stars, ship's lanterns—went out. Some of the men shouted in alarm. Boiling up out of the sea came a vast, black wall of cloud, veined with sharp, purple bursts of lightning. Before Zeal could open his mouth to say "Reduce sail!" (or even "Re—!") the howling wind slammed into the *Circe*, batting her across the glassy sea and right between those two elusive pillars of stone.

The wind cut off with a last angry howl, but the lights did not return. Looming above them, they could see the ancient shapes of the stones, and behind them the seething purple cloud, but beyond them was neither sea, nor sky, nor howling void, nor anything at all.

"What in God's name is it, sir?" said Mr Morrow.

Zeal shook his head. "I don't know," he said in a creditable imitation of his usual voice, "but I think that we might reduce sail now, Mr Morrow."

"Aye-aye, sir," said Morrow, and gave the order.

The *Eschaton* set a course north for the Library of Elhard, where a scholar of Moral's acquaintance might be able to give them direction. Moral himself retreated to his cabin and his books and tried not to think about the singular softness of his captain's hair, or the smoothness of her skin, or the pink roundness of her lips, or anything else remotely connected to Captain Drake. He set himself to studying fifth declension nouns instead—his Latin had gotten rusty since he graduated from the Schlagsahne University of Magickal Arts. "Dies," he murmured to himself, "diei, diei, diem, die..." And then he fell asleep.

Captain Drake sat in her cabin alone, staring out the stern windows without really seeing the magnificent cloudscapes below. She lit her pipe and smoked it absently, filling the cabin with clouds bluer and more fragrant than the ones outside.

"I don't believe in ghosts," she said. "Or demons, or cursed demi-gods, or any of that."

"Oh, aye?" said a voice behind her. His voice. Her spine stiffened. "And didn't we always know we'd burn for the things we'd done?"

"You're dead," she told him, not turning to look. God alone knew what she'd see, if she dared to turn. Maybe nothing at all. "Go away."

"My body may be feeding the fishes at the bottom of the Shiraz, but what about my immortal soul, as the churchmen say? Where do you think that went, after all the men I've killed?"

"There's no such thing. Leave me alone." Her hand tightened around the stem of her pipe, the slender wood bending in her grip.

"And aren't you a silly miss?" he said, and now she could hear his slow footsteps shuffling across the deck, and she could smell a damp, muggy, graveyard odor creeping nearer. And what was that—that wet, slurping sound—as though a waterlogged torso were dragging itself across the planks?

She squeezed her eyes shut. "Go away."

"Closing your eyes don't turn out the lights, as me blessed mother used to say."

A chill breath on her cheek. The pipe stem snapped in her hand.

"Francie, help me. You're the only one who can."

"Leave me be!" she screamed, and in return a voice, a warm and living voice, muffled by the wood of the door, said,

"What, and is your own father no longer welcome here? Bless me!"

Drake's eyes flew open; she turned, and saw (of course) nothing but the empty cabin. Tossing the broken pipe aside, she ran to the door and opened it.

In the doorway stood no phantasm, only the homely familiar form of Cornelius Cid, goggles shoved up on his balding head, meerschaum pipe in between his teeth.

"Dad," said Drake, and fell into his arms.

"There, there," he said, patting her shoulder with his enormous hand. "It'll be all right, Francie, that it will. I promise."

"But are there ghosts?" Drake asked much later, drawing on her second-best pipe. "And the walking sea dead, and spirits that live in the deep, and all of that?"

"Well, as to that, my Francie," said her father, "I'm but an 'umble sailor, that I am, and though I've seen some sights in my day, sights to turn your black hair white, who am I to say 'Aye, there's these,' or 'Nay, there's none of those'? But that wizard of yours, he thinks something's afoot, he does, and that boy's got a head on his shoulders. Minds me of another wizard of my acquaintance, long before you was born—a dark wizard, he was, but the brother of a paladin. Bless me! I remember like it was yesterday. Have I told you about him?"

"Only about a million times." She regarded him with affection. "What do you think I should do, then?"

"Why, bless me, lass, if I know!" But he gave her a keen glance, his salt-and-pepper beard bristling with import, and gesticulated with his pipe. "But if there are ghosts to be laid to rest, then perhaps you ought to be doing so."

A few miles south of Elhard, when the crew of the *Eschaton* could see the crystal waters of Ceylon Lake shining like a mirror in the soft, green lands, the sky-sailer suddenly decided she no longer wished to go north. Like a contumacious filly not yet resigned to bridle and bit, she turned her head away from her rider's chosen course and broke away to the northwest, and nothing captain or crew could do would restrain her.

"What in the blazes are you doing?" shouted Captain Drake—yes, at her ship, as though hollering was helpful.

"Wheel's not responding, Cap'n," said the sailor at the helm, giving it a futile spin to illustrate the point.

"Dad," said Drake, and Cid gave a short nod, taking himself off to the engine room as fast as his short legs would take him. "You go with him too, wizard," she said, and whatever Dallon Moral might have been thinking, he restricted himself to a short, "Aye, Cap'n" before following the engineer. Drake did not pause to watch him go, but continued snapping orders to her crew. "Reef tops'ls!" she called. "Reduce speed!" The peaks of the Ironback Mountains were zooming below them at a hideous rate. "Draw in the larboard wing—we'll put her about manually if we must!"

Though the *Eschaton*'s crew ran about in a fine flurry of activity, however, their efforts were in vain. Whatever invisible hand had them in its grip, it would not be shaken off by such mortal striving as theirs, and all of Captain Drake's eloquent blasphemy could not turn the ship around.

"Captain, look!"

The sky had turned all manner of colors that the late afternoon sky should not—bruise-purple and sickly green and swollen black—and through the seething cloud, the red, engorged idiot-face of the full moon could be seen.

"Saints preserve us," she heard someone say.

"Fetch the wizard!" she shouted. "Get him up here—quickly!" And when Dallon Moral came panting up on deck, she rounded on him and demanded, "Explain this to me!"

He shook his head. "Cap'n," he said, "I ain't never seen nothing like it."

Faster and faster flew the *Eschaton*, hooked by cloud and reeled in by the wind, and the ground, and then the sea, blurred by below, and out of the froth of the ocean rose two great stone pillars, like the lintels of some giant's doorway. The *Eschaton* hurtled for the gap between them.

"Prepare to lower anchor!" cried Captain Drake.

"Captain, what—" said Dallon Moral.

She turned to him. "Whatever's through there," she said, "I'll see it in my own time, and not before."

Thunder roared; the tumid clouds were shot through with spears of lightning—purple, green and blue. There was a horrible crack, and a tearing noise like an arm being ripped from its socket, and then the wind gave a mighty shriek and the clouds opened up with rain. Not just rain—a curtain—a wall of water that turned the world black, that soaked clothing through within seconds, (Dallon's hat wilted on his head and commenced to dripping in his eyes), that stung against the skin as though made of stone.

The pillars rushed nearer. Moral squinted against the rain.

"Drop anchor!" Drake shouted above the screaming wind, the roaring thunder, the pelting rain.

Nothing happened.

"I don't think they heard you—" Moral was about to say, but then they both saw a flash of something through the rain—the anchor, arcing through the waterlogged air, clashing against the leeward stone, and bouncing away.

"Blast you, no!" shrieked Captain Drake.

He touched her arm, then stepped up to the rail. The anchor flapped uselessly at the end of its rope—the *Eschaton* would not heed it, and they would be sucked between those ominous stones.

"No, we won't," said Dallon to himself, setting his jaw. With a tiny inward prayer he gathered the magic to him; it came, filling the hollow places inside him, waiting for what he would do. He imagined what he wanted: the great anchor wrapped safe around the stone, the *Eschaton* secure and as steady as a ship at moorings in a calm harbor. There, he told it, pointing towards where the anchor flailed in the gale like the clapper of an enormous windchime. A twist of the wind could send it smashing through the *Eschaton*'s hull.

He felt his magic dash against the storm's rage like a breaking wave against a stone wall, and the wall held. Forked lightning split the sky, and he fell to his knees, gripping the railing so hard it drove splinters through his gloves and into his palms (though he would not notice them until much later). He shouted above the tempest's furious blast, a shrieking skirl of wind tearing the words away. It was like trying to drill a hole in adamant with nothing but a rotten carrot; it was like trying to lift a single hair from under the foot of a giant.

"Please," he begged, closing his eyes. His face was wet with rain.

The magic ran out of him all at once, with a color like silver and a sound like sweet voices singing hymns and a scent like incense and roses (though it was none of these, not a color or a sound or a smell, but a sensation in his mind that was like them). The *Eschaton* gave a horrid jerk, and for a moment he thought he'd failed in spite of his success, but rope and ship and anchor all held, and the *Eschaton* hung suspended in the darkness between the two giant stones.

The storm ceased at once, as though knowing it had been beaten.

Dallon drew a shivering breath, and then another. A hand appeared in his vision's periphery.

He turned and looked, and let Captain Drake help him to his feet.

"Good job, wizard," she said.

F

"Captain?" said a voice in the darkness.

"I'm here, Peter," said Zeal.

"What's going to happen to us?"

The words, "We'll all die, I expect," rose to his lips, and with an effort he swallowed them back down. But didn't the lad deserve better than a comforting lie? And yet … Zeal felt a mad grin stretching his face. "We're the Royal Navy, lad," he said. "We'll find a way."

"Lower a boat," said Drake—and even soaking wet, with her black hair a damp helmet plastered to her head, she managed to look fine and proud and beautiful. Her crew, all of them assembled on the deck, regarded her with awe and affection—this was the Captain! "We're going in." The *Eschaton*s cheered, and she raised her hand. "Not all of us. Some of us must stay with the ship, in case the others don't return." She pointed, indicating her chosen crew. "Lilly, you're with me."

The giantess inclined her massive head. "Aye, Cap'n."

"Luna, too."

The small, tattooed woman grinned and clicked her heels. "Aye-aye!"

Three others she named: the inarticulate Toggle, Dead-Eye Duvay with his rifle, and Rangle the admiral's grandson. Then she paused and considered the little band assembled before her, and added (almost as an afterthought), "Moral, you'd better come too. Who knows? A wizard might come in useful."

"You flatter me, Captain," the wizard drawled.

When it became clear that no more would be called upon to accompany the captain, the rest of the crew put up a piteous protest:

"Only six, Cap'n? Surely you'll need more than that! Take us, too, Cap'n! Take us with you!"

But Drake would hear none of it, and turned toward the boat.

"Captain." This was Albius Moonhart, the first mate—more like an uncle than a subordinate. He'd bounced her on his knee, and taught her sailor's knots when she was just a girl on her father's ship, the *Miracle*. Probably, Drake thought with a wry inward smile, the only one of her crew who could argue with her without getting shot for his pains.

"No more protests," she said, pitching her voice loudly enough that the entire crew could hear. "I'll not hear them. Those of you who stay, stay for a reason. Doesn't the *Eschaton* deserve the finest crew in all the skies to sail her?"

"No," said Moonhart, speaking low. She blinked at him, taken aback. "Captain, we'll not argue. But—be careful. Come back to us safe."

"Oh," she said. "Oh. Thank you. Thank you, Moonhart."

"See to it, miss," said her father, coming up and wagging his finger at her. "Your dear ma's not best pleased with me as it is. If you get yourself killed I'll never hear the end of it, bless me!"

"Dad," said Drake, shaking her head. "Of course I won't get killed. I'm the main character." She leaned over and kissed his cheek.

"You only say that, miss, because you know full well there's no such thing." Cid gave her shoulders a final squeeze, then let her go.

No more valedictions—the time was come to act. The six pirates piled into the boat, and Captain Drake raised her arm, ready to give the signal to lower away.

The arm dropped, and the pulleys squeaked as the boat swayed down, down, down alongside the colossal stone, its shadow flickering near and far, near and far, until at last the *Eschaton* was a walnut-shell high overhead, and the boat landed with a splash in the ash-colored water between the gateposts.

"Well, hush my puppies," said Dallon Moral, peering underneath the brim of his sodden, wilted hat.

Lilly Bones womanning the oars, the boat slid into the darkness between the stones.

Light returned gradually, fading in from black to charcoal to fuzzy grey—but such dead, colorless light gave no comfort to the seven in the boat. Only Lilly Bones, whose stoic, square-jawed countenance could have watched a ballet or a beheading with equal equanimity, betrayed no disquiet as the world between the two pillars faded into view.

It was a cave, a cavern so vast its ceiling was shadowed and blurred with distance. Stalactites hung from that dim roof, forming with the stalagmites that grew from the ground pillars so mighty a dragon could have hidden behind one and never been seen. The dingy water through which the boat glided lapped against distant, rocky shores—and more than one of the buccaneers swallowed hard and made a warding gesture at the sight of the moldering bones that rested there.

"This is a place of death," said Dead-Eye Duvay, his loud rasp muffled instantly by the shadowed silence of the cave.

Toggle, seated in the bows next to his captain, whimpered. Drake patted him on the head.

The boat skimmed forward, propelled (it seemed) as much by its own will as Lilly's powerful arms. The channel through the center of the cavern was broad and deep enough that even one of the Royal Navy's massive first-rates, with three decks and a deep draught, could have sailed with ease, and the current swift enough that even that same first-rate would have been swept inexorably forward, forward, towards whatever waited at the back of the cave.

"Be ready, wizard," Drake murmured in Dallon's ear.

The wizard nodded, his odd, colorless eyes watchful.

And now the hulks of rotting ships began to be visible through the darkness—here, the top of a mast breaking through the water, there, a shattered hull lying on the rocks, its bowsprit pointing fruitlessly at nothing, like the broken horn of a long-dead narwhal washed up on the beach. Drake read their names as the boat passed by: Charon, Clymenus, Lachesis...

"Cap'n," said Luna Shee, even her normally exuberant voice hushed. "Over there's the Lobster, lost in 'seventy-five. I'd recognize that ugly figurehead anywhere."

A wooden lobster, its red paint flaking and faded to grey, passed by overhead.

"Who captained the Lobster?" Drake asked.

"Phineas Prosper."

"God rest his soul," murmured Rangle.

"Amen," Moral said.

On and on through the gloom, the wet smell of rot, the chill of the tomb. Drake's wet clothes clung to her skin like the clammy touch of dead fingers, and she shivered.

"Cold?" Moral asked, leaning forward and touching her shoulder.

Scowling, she shook his hand off—and found that with his touch her clothes had dried. She hunched her shoulders inside her now-warm coat, resisting the urge to turn around and smile at him.

Because that, you know, would just never do.

Darkness, cold, despair. Skeletons on the shore. Wrecked ships on wet stone, black water lapping. A grey dusty smell like the tomb. Monotony.

"They were awfully eager to have us here before," Drake muttered. "Where has their hospitality gone?"

"Captain…" said Dallon Moral in a warning voice.

Because now, rising up out of the grey-green water, the back of the cave was coming into view. The swift-moving channel widened to a slow, still lagoon (the coldest and most unwelcoming lagoon you could imagine—no native beauties or coconut grog here). A beach of jagged stones, littered with rusted bits of iron and fragments of bone, ran away from the water's edge a short distance to the cavern wall—and planted on that hostile shore, right at the place where water met stone, was a mighty slab of rock, fashioned into a crude chair. But such a chair—on such a monumental scale—could only be the seat of a giant. The farm where he grew up, barn and cow-pastures and winter wheat and all, Moral reflected, could have fit on the seat with room for the neighbors.

Dangling from the cavern ceiling around this mighty throne were cages—dozens, hundreds of iron cages such as a fisherman might use to trap lobster, but such giant lobsters as would feed the fisherman who sat in that enormous chair. And in those cages—

Drake looked away, shutting her eyes. She had seen men hanged, impaled on sword and harpoon, shot with rifles and dismembered by cannon fire, but she could not look at the horrible, pathetic creatures locked in those cages. Again she felt Moral's touch on her arm, a comforting grip. He gave her shoulder a gentle squeeze and then released her, and she opened her eyes.

There was someone sitting on the throne.

He was huge and terrible, his hair wreathing his head like storm clouds, his lowering frown like lightning. Around his temples was bound a circlet made of rusted iron—anchors and fishhooks and the broken heads of harpoons, detritus such as one would find rotting at the bottom of the sea. His nose was a slab as solid as the stone on which he sat, and his beard was rank and matted with kelp and anemones and other things (tiny snails, and starfish), and he wore a coat made of the skins of dead whales and walruses and walleyes, clumsily sewn with stitches like the gash in the side of a ship when the cannon ball has ripped through. But worst of all were his eyes, deep pits in his hollow face, each one a black abyss that could drown a man and leave not even his bones for his widow to mourn.

"Welcome, mortals," said this titan in a voice like howling wind and crashing wave, "to the home of the Fisher of Souls."

At the sound of the Fisherman's voice, Zeal raised his head off the bars of his cage. Below him, far below, was a boat, and in the boat seven people sat—far enough distant that he would not have recognized his own mother if she had been seated in the bows.

He closed his eyes. He was tired, as weak as if he had been bled, and in his soul was only a flicker of energy, enough for him to think, And now they are trapped, too. God have mercy.

In another cage, not far away, young Peter Goodheart-Smythe watched his captain slump against the rusted bars of his prison and slide downwards to settle halfway between wall and floor. Around him, the rest of the *Circe*'s crew were similarly sprawled in attitudes of death.

He wrapped his hands around the bars of his cage, peering down at the people in the boat. One of them, a slim figure in a brilliant red coat, was standing in the bows and speaking. He leaned closer, the better to hear.

"You are the one they call the Fisherman?" said Drake, standing up to address the gigantic, gloomy figure.

"I am he. Why do you come here?"

Let her answer wisely! prayed Dallon Moral, seated just astern of his captain.

Drake tossed back her shining black hair and replied, "You have something of mine, Fisherman! I've come to get it back."

Moral buried his head in his hands and groaned.

"Something of yours?" With a creaking sound like a ship's mast groaning in a gale, the Fisherman leaned forward. "I can smell your living soul. There is nothing for you here." He grinned, showing his barnacled teeth. "But you may stay, if you like—I have cages enough for you and your crew."

"I know you have him!" Drake cried. "Random Chance—you've trapped him in one of your cages! Give him to me!"

"Random Chance?" the Fisherman said. "There is no such thing. There is only Fate, and Doom, and Necessity."

"I never would've taken the Fisher of Souls for a punster," whispered Luna Shee in her sister's ear.

"You know we've all been thinking it," Lilly Bones returned.

"Random Chance!" Drake repeated, and she would have stamped her foot if she hadn't been standing in the bows of a rocking boat. "A sailor who died and whose body was lost at sea, without even a single prayer spoken for his soul. I know the stories! You claim such souls for your own, and keep them in your cages until nothing remains. Well, not this soul! I've come for him—give him to me!"

"She always was a fiery one," said a voice near at hand. Peter gasped, turning round and round for the source of the voice. The cage on his left held the comatose form of his captain, and the one on the right was empty. There was no one else nearby.

"Back when I was alive," said the voice, "I was a little less transparent."

Peter looked again—and saw that the starboard cage was not empty at all. It held a little wisp of living light, which pulsed and shifted and wavered, now looking almost human, now dimming to a tiny spark. Peter shuffled to the other side of his swaying cage for a better look.

"Are you…" he said, "Random Chance?"

"I was," said the ghost. "But now I'm dead, and though I'm grateful to the lass for trying, it's too little, too late. He'll never release a soul once he's trapped it in his cage, not for the end of the world."

"Never?" said Peter.

"Never!" roared the Fisher of Souls, quivering the cavern with his wrath. The boat in which the seven pirates rode bucked like a fractious horse. "His soul is mine—all these souls are mine, by my ancient right! Who are you to demand anything of me? Even Leviathan himself cannot take what I have caught in my cages.

"However," he continued, his anger (and the water of the cove) calming, "I am always willing to bargain."

"Bargain?" echoed Drake, who had somehow retained her balance in the swaying boat (Dead-Eye had Moral by the scruff of the neck, as otherwise the wizard would have pitched headfirst into the seething waters). "What sort of bargain?"

The Fisher paused, and it seemed the entire cavern leaned in close to listen, the stone pillars bowing near, the better to hear his words.

"A soul for a soul," he said. "That is a good bargain."

"Fine," said Captain Drake, and Dallon Moral wrenched himself out of Duvay's grip (Duvay yelling in surprise and protest), crying, "No!"

His hand closed on his captain's elbow, and she jerked away, shouting something—and all the movement upset the balance of the boat, which pitched, yawed, shipped water, and promptly capsized.

"Wonderful," said Captain Drake. "Thank you, wizard."

Dallon Moral, whose cage hung not far from his captain's, wrung water from his hat, his eyes downcast. "I'm sorry, Captain," he murmured to the sodden, amorphous mass of fabric. "I tried—"

Then a hollow voice, like someone calling from the distant end of a long tunnel, interrupted him in mid-self-reproaching-stream. "Ah, lass," it sighed, "you always had more enthusiasm than sense, didn't you?"

Drake's head jerked around as though hooked, and she lunged against the side of her cage, setting it swaying and shuddering and shrieking on its rusted chain, gripping the bars as she cried out, "Random! Random, is that you?"

But there was no one in the cage adjacent to hers … no, wait. There was something … a flickering light, a translucent wisp of what might once have been a human being with wide shoulders and a square, stubbled jaw, an easy grin and a broken nose, strong, sunburned arms, large, callused hands, a broad chest against which she had often rested her head...

"Random?" she said again, not daring to believe. "But … we had a bargain..."

"And did you expect him to keep it?" asked Random Chance's shade, wavering before her eyes. "My fine, foolish lass … what a bargain you struck. No doubt the ghost of some other proud pirate is blessing you in Heaven even now—but Random Chance still swings in an outsized lobster cage, and now so does Franceline Drake and all her crew, because she was too hasty to be specific."

"Random…" said Drake, taken aback, "aren't you pleased that I'm here?"

"You would have done better to stay away." The image of Random Chance flickered as he spoke. "I'm grateful that you tried—but there's no helping someone caught in the Fisherman's trap." He looked to the side. "Aye," he said, almost to himself, "you'd have done better to stay away."

"But—" Drake clutched the cage bars until they cut her hands. "You called me here! You asked me to help you!"

"Never in life—nor in death, neither!" The ghost's voice grew stronger, almost that of a living man. "Knowing you still lived, free and safe, was enough for me, even if my soul was writhing in the fiery pit. Francie, my girl, my sweetheart—I never would have wished this on you." He reached towards her with one diaphanous hand, as though to brush her cheek; she closed her eyes as though to accept the caress, but neither one felt any contact at all.

And then she said, "But if that wasn't you in my dreams—who was it?"

Dallon Moral sat with his back against the bars of his cage, his eyes closed. He had looked around the mass of cages, seen the corrupted creatures, once men, inside of them. He had heard his captain speak with the spirit of her dead lover. He could see that the situation was hopeless.

It was my pride that brought us to this, he thought, wringing his ruined hat through his hands. I'm a wizard, I know best. Ha! He opened his eyes. In a cage below him and off to the left, a figure was beating its head against its prison's bars. Dallon watched it, nausea and pity welling in his throat.

What exactly was wrong with it, he couldn't have said. Perhaps it was the greyish cast to the skin, or the clayey look of the flesh, as though it were on the verge of sloughing off the bones. Perhaps it was the blind, awkward, bumbling motion of the body as it heaved against the bars, as though the spirit that animated it was long, long gone, and had left behind only the memory of the desire to escape imprinted in those slack muscles and flabby bones. But it gave off the impression that it was melting, dissolving, that soon it would be a soft pile of corrupted flesh, and even that would melt away, leaving another sad skeleton in a cage.

Dallon swallowed hard, nausea overcoming pity. Soon, he thought, I'll be just like that poor fellow: a shambling body without a soul, while that Fisherman sits at his ease and drinks his wine. With one clenched fist he smote the bars of his cage. "Dammit! What is the use of wizardry, if it can't get us out of a fix like this?"

But his magic lay dormant within him like a fox curled in its den, tail covering its nose, while the snow sifts onto ground overhead. Clearly, it wasn't worried about the situation.

With a sigh, Dallon slouched against the bars, resting his chin on his knees and closing his eyes again. A wizard without magic is just a scholar, and very little use unless you need an obscure passage in an ancient tongue translated, or the scientific name of a rare plant.

"Excuse me, sir?"

Dallon's head jerked up. The voice that addressed him had been young and hopeful—and alive. A quick look about revealed the face of a young boy pressed against the bars of a nearby cage, his small hands wrapped around the bars.

"Do I know you?" Dallon said, blinking at him. He was a handsome youth—his hair fine and blond, his eyes large and blue, his skin not yet roughened by exposure to the elements. He looked about ten years old. He also looked familiar.

The boy shook his head. "I don't think so, sir," he said. "I didn't mean to eavesdrop, but did you say you were a wizard?"

"Uhhh," said Dallon. He hadn't realized he'd been speaking out loud. "I suppose I must have."

The boy pressed forward, setting his cage a-swing. "Can you help us? Can you get us out?"

Dallon looked from that young, hopeful face down, down to where the Fisherman sat on his granite throne, a wine cup the size of a moderate volcano's crater in his hand. "You saw what happened," he said. "He's willing to bargain, but only to his own advantage. And he's ancient—even if I had something he wanted, I'd never be able to outsmart him."

"What is he?" the boy whispered, following the wizard's gaze.

For the second time, Dallon Moral told the story of the Fisherman, of his ancient curse and his imprisonment, of the wine he drank distilled from the souls of the dead—or the living, if he could get them.

"It sounds lonely," said the boy, when the story was finished.

Dallon's eyebrow twitched. "I … suppose so," he said.

"Is there no way, sir, to get us out of here, no way at all?" continued the boy. He looked off into the middle distance, where another yellow-haired figure, this one in the blue coat and golden epaulettes of a captain of the Royal Navy, sprawled—and then beyond Moral's left shoulder, where Captain Drake and the ghost of Random Chance still conferred in desperate whispers. And then he looked down at his own small, pale hands and said, "This … this is a terrible way for it to end, sir—for my captain, and for that lady there. She's very brave."

"Aye," said Dallon Moral. "That she is." It was becoming difficult to focus on anything for very long—his thoughts fluttered about in his head like a net full of butterflies set free—he remembered once going to a wedding where the couple had released butterflies, but by the time the nets were opened the butterflies had died, and instead of a shimmer of wings there came a rain of dead bugs. He shook his head, feeling he'd missed the point somewhere.

"What sort of bargain," said the boy, looking down at the brooding giant on the throne, "would the Fisherman honor, do you think?"

Dallon followed his gaze, head lolling. "A measure of wheat for a penny," he murmured, remembering the words as he spoke, "and three measures of barley for a penny, but hurt not the oil or the wine..."

"The wine…" echoed the boy (or perhaps it was the echo of the cave). "The wine!" The cage whined as he shifted his weight. Whine, whine, wine...

"What's your name?" asked the boy, his voice only slowly reaching Dallon's ears, his words only slowly making sense in Dallon's brain. Once, when he was young, he had caught the fever, and his mother (or Mrs Moral, anyway) had held his hand and sung him lullabies. Who would sing to him now, he wondered—and when his soul was sucked from his body, would his mother even remember he had ever existed?

"Dallon…" he said. "Dallon … Moral..."

The boy was moving—the boy was getting to his feet, supporting himself with a hand on the cage bars. He was standing up, a keen look in his blue eyes.

"I'm Peter Goodheart-Smythe," he said.

Ah, thought Dallon as consciousness ebbed away, away. Smythe. That explains it...

"Fisherman!"

Peter Goodheart-Smythe's young, clear voice rang out through the cavern, and those living souls still awake and aware of their surroundings turned to see who had spoken. Franceline Drake, her fingers woven with those of her intangible love, whispered, "What's he doing?"

Random shook his head (or, the shimmer where his head would have been shimmered a little bit more). "There's more than one fool in this cave, I see."

"Fisherman!" Peter shouted again. "I wish to bargain!"

The Fisherman turned his head. It took an age, as though a monument of stone had decided to move. When he saw who had spoken, he rose, creaking and groaning, to his feet, and placed his vast, black eye against the bars of Peter's cage.

"A bargain?" he said. "What could you offer that might interest me?"

The head of the Fisherman filled his vision, but the young midshipman stood his ground—or rather, his rusted iron slats. "A drinking companion," he said.

The Fisherman paused, and all the cavern paused with him. The dead black pools of his eyes held a spark of something new: curiosity.

"Explain," said he, in the voice of the hurricane.

"Sir," said Mr Midshipman Goodheart-Smythe, "everyone knows the tale of how the Lord of the Deep trapped you here, and how you drink your liquor of souls on your solitary throne. But has anyone ever come to share a glass with you, or to ask you how you've been? In all the thousands of years since then?"

The Fisherman glowered, his brows massing over his eyes like thunderheads.

Said Peter, dropping his voice and his gaze, "It must be very lonely, sir."

"No one," rumbled the Fisher of Souls, "has ever presumed to comment. Tell me your bargain, boy, before I drain your spirit and leave your empty husk for the worms."

Peter swallowed hard. The scrutiny of those empty eyes left him cold and shivering inside—and he could almost feel, already, the carrion worms crawling over his skin. But when he spoke, it was boldly, in a voice that would have made his father proud.

"Let me drink with you," he said. "Let me taste the wine of the Fisher of

Souls."

"The draught would destroy you," the Fisher said. "No mortal is strong enough to bear it. And why should I let you drink with me? What do I gain?"

"Company," said Peter, without hesitation. "A break in the monotony of a life that began before the stars were born, and will continue on after they've turned to blackened coals in the sky. Oh, sir, let me drink with you, and give you something new to remember."

"And what," said the Fisherman, "do you want in return? For the lure of the Fisherman's company is not, I'm certain, all that you seek."

"For every drink I take," said Peter, praying, praying as he spoke for a chance—just the barest chink of a chance—that his mad plan would work, "for every sip of your wine that does not kill me, let a soul of my choosing go free."

At first he thought that the Fisherman would refuse, that his words were spoken in vain—and he could feel the same lassitude that had overcome the others creeping through his blood. But the spark of curiosity in the Fisher's depthless eyes remained, and at last he said in a voice like thunder, "Done! Let us drink!" And he clapped his hands.

No one in the Fisherman's cages was conscious to watch what happened. Well, Drake was conscious, more or less, but she had no eyes for anything or anyone but Random's ghost, and they spoke together in low, urgent tones, his voice crackling and fading in and out of hearing like an imperfect radio signal. Random watched the proceedings below with half his gaze, but since he flickered from a pinprick spark to a transparent image of his living self, it was impossible to tell what he thought of them.

Peter sat on the arm of the Fisherman's throne—a vast armrest the size of a moderate ballroom or gymnasium. Before him was a clay bottle as tall as a water tower, the Fisherman's vast chalice, and a normal human-sized cup which the Fisherman had dug out of the detritus in his beard.

The wine he poured was a silvery wisp, like fog turned liquid, and it shimmered with strange and beautiful lights as it splashed into the bottom of the cup. Peter watched in fascination the rippling rainbow colors shivering through the liquid, seeming independent of the wine's own motions—and he realized, as he watched, that he was seeing the light of the souls that the Fisherman had drained for his drink.

"Do you really drink souls?" he asked, feeling small and young. His parents might have been Knights of St George, but he was only ten years old, and still wore the midshipman's white patches on his collar.

"I find," the other replied, taking his cup in one massive hand, "that the draught brings comfort to my own damned spirit."

"Oh," said Peter, and picked up his own drinking vessel. Watching the souls swirling within, he felt his gorge rise, and swallowed it back down.

"You will match me drink for drink," the Fisherman said, lifting his glass as if in toast. "For each drink you take, I will release a soul from my cages."

"And the body too, if it still lives," Peter said quickly, remembering Mr Moral's remarks on the literal-mindedness of ancient spirits.

The Fisherman inclined his craggy head, a wry smile twisting the grave, grey lips. "I drink my pledge to you," he said, "that it shall be done."

He raised the cup to his lips and drank.

Peter, too, closing his eyes and whispering a quick, internal prayer, drank his first draught of the wine of souls.

In later years, many great and valiant deeds to his name, Captain Peter Goodheart-Smythe would cast his thoughts back to the grey cave, the stones, the creaking cages overhead, and try to fit words to his memories. His pen wavering over the page, he would hesitate long, and at last write only, "The Fisherman's wine is not for mortal men to drink. Even now, I cannot say how I felt when I tasted it, or what it did to me."

It was terrible and sublime, burning and freezing as it slid down his throat, kicking through his veins with unbelievable potency. If you were to distill all of human experience, with its dizzying joys and crushing sorrows, its anger and fear, love and hate, sweet contentment and bitter regret and all the near-infinite range of emotion subtle and bright, and then infuse it with the burning power of a thousand suns, put it in a cup and drink it down, you might have some idea of what poor Peter felt as the liquor blazed down his throat and into his stomach and through his veins like lightning.

He gasped, and choked, and began to cough, tears running down his face from the fiery, freezing pain of the draught and the welter of emotions now seething in his heart.

The Fisherman gave a secret smile. "That is one," he said, some dark satisfaction lurking in his voice. "Who would you have freed?"

"Cap—Captain Zeal," managed the boy through his sputters.

The Fisherman bowed his head. "It is done." And he took another drink.

It was true that no mortal was strong enough to withstand the potion's power for long—for who among us, with our own hopes and dreams, our own griefs and regrets weighing on our hearts, can bear as well the weight of others'? Young Peter Goodheart-Smythe, however, did have one advantage that the Fisherman, having never been young, could not have anticipated: that is, his very youth. He was a midshipman on his first voyage, and the white patches on his collar could well have been symbolic not just of his rank, but of his innocence. He had experienced little of life, knew little of its vicissitudes, could not say how he would react in the adventures that doubtless awaited over the horizon. With each sip of the Fisherman's wine, he felt all the longings housed in other souls, all the desires, all the fears—and he felt them all for the first time.

He was weeping as he drank again from the cup, in his breast the pressure of a thousand conflicting sensibilities. Marie would never love him—he was sure to be hanged—oh, watch the fish flying 'round the ship!—ought to push that bleeding bosun down the hatchway—she had written, she had said yes!—oh the joy, the pity, the shame, the rage, oh the hate and the terrible love—!

He wept, but he drank it down, he swallowed the cup's contents and felt them lighting his insides until he was certain that, if he opened his mouth, you could see the glow.

"Who would you set free?" the Fisherman asked.

"Free Mr Morrow," said Peter, wiping his face with his sleeve. The tears kept flowing—the floodgates had been opened.

"It is done," the Fisherman said.

Peter bowed his head and wept.

Pouring the wine a third time, the Fisherman unexpectedly spoke. "I used to be an angel," he said, his gloomy voice low.

Rank fibers of kelp and seaweed hung from his beard, starfish and shells and driftwood washed up among the strands. His coat was made of carrion, his crown of rusted iron. His black eyes stared like the whirlpool's sucking mouth. He looked little like an angel.

But Peter had been well brought up, and made a polite noise, through his tears, that might have indicated agreement.

"We all were," continued the Fisherman, low and gloomy, "those of us who fell. I was not the brightest of them—but how I shone! That was long, long ago."

Peter raised his head. "What happened?" he asked, his natural curiosity overwhelming, for a moment, the bedlam of other voices in his head.

The Fisherman regarded him with a strange look, an expression that could almost have been called a smile, though tainted with ancient bitterness. "You are not so young," he said, "that you do not know the story. It is the oldest story, how certain angels, jealous of God's power, jealous of God's newest creation, chose to oppose him rather than submit to the tyranny of man. Our leader was the brightest of us all—he blazed like the sun at midday, and we were blinded by his beauty. Blinded, too," he said, "by our own jealousy. We dared to rebel against our rightful lord, and we fell, arcing across the sky like comets, like shooting stars. We could not stand against his might. We were fools to think we could." His voice filled the vast cavern like fog, like the low, clinging mist that obscures the lee shore by night, luring the hapless ship onto the deadly rocks that tear her hull and spill her cargo and all her men into the uncaring sea.

Peter sat quietly for a moment, wrapped in the fog of the Fisherman's voice, before he shook himself and regarded the ancient, terrible being before him. "The wine is poured, sir," he said. "Will you not drink?"

Again, it seemed almost that the Fisherman smiled. "I will drink," he said, raising his cup. "Will you?"

"I will," said Peter.

They drank.

Is this how the ocean feels? Peter thought, his spirit fluttering upwards towards hazy consciousness. Receding from him, pulling away surge after surge—like the tide, like a ship on the tide, like a whole squadron, a flotilla of ships dwindling from the shores of his mind—a brightly colored host of memories not his own. Such joy he had tasted, as filled his being with light—and such hatred as to shrivel his spirit to a cinder within him—and sorrow too, bright and bitter … oh, the things he had known … had known … had known, but now forgot as he drifted up into light and life and sound again, a second birth.

"Praise be to God," said an unfamiliar voice. "He's waking."

He was awake, opening eyes that blurred and wept to see the circle of concerned faces that surrounded him—wept from relief, though he could not have said why.

"Peter!"

That face he knew, and he smiled as Captain Zeal fell to his knees at his bedside and took his hand. "Thank God!" he said, beaming relief and joy, squeezing his midshipman's hand. "Thank God you're awake, lad! How do you feel?"

"Captain?" said Peter, blinking. "You're alive!"

Zeal exchanged glances with the others in the cabin (for they were in a cabin—the captain's cabin, in fact, on board the *Circe*, and from the heave and sway of the wooden world around them, at sea)—the surgeon and his mate, Mr Morrow, and there in the corner Mr Duffy, the captain's steward, trying not to be seen. He smiled—but it was an uneasy smile, such as one might wear in the presence of an invalid or a madman.

"Aye, lad," he said. "Alive and free, every one of us. Thanks … thanks to you."

Peter saw the captain's discomfiture—saw it echoed on the faces of the medicos, though they hid it better—but he didn't understand it. "Captain," he said after some thought, "I don't remember anything. I mean, sir, I remember a cave, and a cage, and a strange man … but maybe it was all a dream?"

Zeal's false smile dropped from his face, landing somewhere on the deck (Duffy would sweep it up later, no doubt). "You don't remember at all?" he asked.

Peter shook his head.

Turning to Dr Foxglove and his assistant, Zeal stood and said formally, "Gentlemen, if I could have a word alone with your patient…?"

"Certainly, sir." The surgeon, a small man with a white face and a black expression, bowed. He and his assistant filed out of the room.

When they had gone, Zeal sighed and sat in the chair beside the bed. And then he told Peter everything that had happened—everything that he remembered, anyway, and he finished with, "We all woke here, on the ship, and there was a terrible voice ringing in my head—in everyone's head; we all heard it, though some will deny it now. It said…" he frowned, trying to recall. "It said that even the damned could be moved by compassion and courage. I think … I think he meant you, Peter."

Peter said, "Then why is everyone afraid?"

Under the circumstances, I think he can be forgiven for forgetting the "sir."

Instead of responding, Zeal stood up and crossed the cabin, returning a moment later with a flat sheet of silvered glass in his hand. This he gave to his midshipman, saying, "Look."

Peter grasped the mirror in both hands and peered into it.

Then he glanced back at his captain and said, "But, sir—"

"Look again, Peter," said Zeal.

So Peter did. It was the same face he'd always seen in the glass, the face that owed some to his father (the fine, blond hair, the wide eyes) and some to his mother (the delicacy of chin and cheekbones, still part-hidden by the chubbiness of youth), nothing special about it, just a face... And then he paused, and looked closer.

He couldn't have said what was different, but something was, something subtle and strange. Perhaps his skin was a shade whiter, or perhaps some of that baby fat had melted away. Perhaps it was his eyes—still the same blue as his father's, but subtly changed. They had a different look in them now. He looked … he looked older, although he was still the same age.

"What happened to me?" he whispered.

Zeal coughed.

"What happened?" Peter insisted. "Did—did the wine do this? I'm different—I've changed!"

"No, lad!" Zeal cried. "No, not a bit! You're not different—you're still you, still Peter!"

Peter regarded the mirror. His own face gazed back at him, and frowned at the changes it saw.

Still Peter.

But not the same.

Dallon Moral sat in his cramped cabin, leaning over his writing desk. He wasn't writing, though—he was thinking. More to the point, he was brooding. There was a pen in his hand and a page before him, but the page was blank.

That boy saved us all, he thought. But at what cost! I would not have asked it of him.

His conscience pricked its ears at the thought. Dummy, it said. It wouldn't have been necessary if you hadn't dragged everyone into it in the first place.

Dallon sighed. Good point. But, in my defense, I was just trying to help the captain.

"Help the captain what?" said that selfsame individual from his doorway.

Dallon winced. Oops. Guess I was talking out loud.

"Guess what, wizard," said Drake, stepping inside and closing the door, "you still are."

"C-captain," Dallon said, turning in his chair and forcing his face into a less guilty expression, "I didn't hear you knock."

"That's because I didn't," Drake returned. "Your door was open."

Oops.

"Do you usually talk to yourself?" she continued, taking another step nearer. Her hip twitched as she walked. Dallon twitched, too.

"Only," he said, forcing himself to focus on the conversation, not on the closed door or the proximity of the captain to himself, "when I'm consumed with guilt, Cap'n."

"And why are you consumed with guilt, wizard?"

"Uhhh..." said Dallon, with the sort of mental agility that had earned him top marks at the Schlagsahne University of Magickal Arts.

"Is there something you wanted to tell me?" She leaned over as she spoke, examining the spines of the books visible in the open chest beside him. He examined her spine, and its long, sensuous, catlike curve, enhanced by the graceful drape of her bright red coat. She turned and quirked an eyebrow at him, and he swallowed hard.

Yes! hissed his conscience, jabbing its elbow into his ribs. Tell her!

No, no, no! he thought at it. I can't!

"Can't what?" Drake asked.

Damn!

"Someone needs to teach you how to internalize your dialogue, wizard," she said, moving closer still. It was getting hard to think, what with her standing close to him and all. And then her eye caught a glint of something on his desk, the gleam of lamplight on metal, and she reached across him to pick it up.

Her eyes narrowed.

"Why," she demanded, brandishing it at him, "do you have this?"

"Oh," said Dallon, trying not to look at it. "Well, er—"

It was a fishhook.

"I'm intensely curious," she purred.

"Ahhh…" said Dallon.

His salvation came in the form of a strangled shout, just as Captain Drake was about to shove the fishhook up his nose and demonstrate the ancient embalming technique of removing a person's brains through his nasal passage. "Stowawaaaaaaaay!" someone hollered, and Drake whipped around.

"This isn't over," she said, stalking towards the door. "I will have an explanation, wizard." And she flung the fishhook at him. It missed his head by inches, embedding itself in the bulkhead beyond his ear.

"God help me," Dallon Moral said, "she'll flay me alive." Leaving the hook where it was, he followed his captain above.

The man crouched in the bows, hemmed in by a pair of the for'ard guns. He'd gotten a boarding axe from somewhere, and he used it to keep the *Eschaton*s at bay, snarling and brandishing it whenever anyone came near.

"What's going on?" Drake demanded, arriving on deck.

"He won't let us get close to him, Cap'n," said Luna Shee. "Not sure where he came from—must've snuck on board at the cave..." She fell silent.

The cave.

Random's words came back to her: No doubt the ghost of some other proud pirate is blessing you in Heaven even now—

Oh, thought Drake. Maybe not in Heaven after all. "Pass the word for the wizard!" she shouted.

"I'm here," said Moral, behind her. "What is it, Captain?"

"One more soul from the cages," Drake said, "unless I miss my guess."

Dallon crept forward, humming a hymn under his breath. When he was close enough, he reached out his hand, releasing the spell. The stowaway at once grew calm, and Moral said, "Here. Wherever you've been, you're safe now. You're safe."

"S-safe?" said the stranger, and tottered to his feet.

He was a tall man, and broad, with a shadow of stubble across his squarish chin.

Drake bit back a little gasp. "Random?"

But no. This man was shorter than Random, and his long hair hung in lank, gnarled strands, too filthy to guess at its color. He wore a shabby, dirty jacket and equally squalid pants almost fifty years out of fashion. He kept his hat in his hand, but it, too, had seen better days.

"Wh-where..." said the man, staring around him. Then, stronger, "Where the devil am I?"

By this time the *Eschaton*'s crew had ceased even pretending to work; everyone gathered around, staring at the stranger.

"Looks familiar," grunted Lilly Bones.

Luna Shee shook her head. "I ain't never seen him before," she said.

"What is this?" roared the stranger. "Some new trickery? I'm ready—I've seen all your devilish deceits before! Well, bring it on—you'll not have my soul, that you won't!" And then he froze in mid-rant, staring at a face in the crowd. "By the powers..." The boarding axe dropped from his hand, and he took a staggering step forward.

The crowd of pirates scattered, leaving one of their number standing alone.

"Dad?" said Drake.

"Cid?" said the stranger. "Cornelius Cid—by all that's holy, can it be you?"

The *Eschaton*'s inventor and engineer stood alone—stood frozen, paralyzed by amazement. But the sound of this squalid stranger speaking his name broke the spell, and he started forward, reaching out his hands, saying, "I don't believe it! We thought you'd been lost years ago! But look at you—you haven't aged a day!"

"It is you!" cried the stowaway, falling forward, tears streaking his dirty face. He stumbled and would have fallen, but Cid caught him in his outstretched arms. At once the stowaway's hands came up, patting Cid's face as though assuring himself of his reality, comparing it to his memories. "But," he muttered, as though to himself, "you're old … and your beard…! What's happened here?" he cried out, and burst into noisy tears.

"Flynn Freeborn," said Cornelius Cid, patting the sobbing stranger's back. "Bless my soul! We thought you was dead!"

CHAPTER 5

A Musical Evening with the Captain

Overture

Captain Zeal sat at his writing desk aboard the *Circe*, nibbling on the end of his pen and contemplating the nearly-blank page before him with something like dread. From the open stern windows came shouts and cries, the bosun's howling, the stamp of bare feet on scraped-white planking and the thousand other sounds of a busy ship. *Circe* had run into some dirty weather coming south from Mordghre and Rjomaskyr (following, ever following, the path of the *Eschaton*), but now sea and sky were clear, and Captain Zeal was writing letters.

His official report to the Admiralty had come first—that was finished, signed and sealed, and then sealed again into a lead-weighted sailcloth packet, so that if *Circe* were captured, the confidential documents could be thrown into the sea, where they would sink without a trace (there was no one these days who could or would capture the *Circe*, or even think about doing so, but the Royal Navy had a great love of tradition, and so such habits persisted long past the point of usefulness. But then again, he thought hopefully, perhaps someday the tradition would become useful again). Then the letter to his parents, which had scarcely been easier than the official report. How did you go about telling your mother that you and your entire crew had been captured by an ancient being, some kind of demi-god or demon or fallen angel or whatever you want to call it, and your soul nearly sucked from your body? Not an easy task, I assure you. His mother would have a fit, and his father would stalk around the breakfast room going, "Hrm, hrm" into a lace handkerchief. Zeal sighed. Perhaps it would be best to delay the letter to the parents a little bit.

Setting aside the page that had "Dear Mother and Father" written on it, Zeal contemplated a fresh sheet. Midshipman Peter Goodheart-Smythe had recovered from their adventure in the Fisher's cave (as far as the lad was going to recover, at any rate) and was back to skylarking in the rigging with the other mids, but Zeal felt he owed Sir and Lady Smythe an explanation of their son's … condition.

Dipping his pen, Zeal (a little frown between his eyebrows) wrote, Dear Sir and Madame, and paused. The frown deepened. Sighing, giving the quill-end a ruminative nibble or two, he dipped again and wrote, It is with great honor and deep gratitude that I write to inform you of your son's actions, and from there it was easy (or at least not impossible) to tell them what had transpired in the cave of the Fisher of Souls.

It was your son's courage and compassion that saved us all, Zeal wrote, his pen by now whizzing across the page. He took pity on the Fisherman, and in return, the Fisherman took pity on us. "Come in," he called.

Second Lieutenant Richard Patrick Blake, whose hesitant knock on the cabin door had interrupted his captain's prosing, poked his head in. "Beg your pardon, sir," he said, "but the flagship is signalling our number. Admiral requesting your presence at once, sir."

"Indeed." Zeal, who had been awaiting the order for the last hour and more with an equanimity that ebbed away with the sands in the glass, rose, tugged at his jacket, and turned and preceded Mr Blake out onto the deck and into the blazing sun, where he could see the squadron lying off the coast of Parmigiana, protecting her Majesty's allies' ports from the rash of suddenly fashionable pirating infecting the seas (inspired, no doubt, by that blackguard in the red coat, the captain of the *Eschaton*).

As the captain's barge was lowering away, Mr Blake leaned forward and said in a confidential voice that was nevertheless audible to every man present, "Begging your pardon, sir, but it would be wise to be cautious. They say the Admiral is in high dudgeon—something about his wife and an adventuring seafarer..." He would have gone on, but at Zeal's cold glare the words gurgled to a halt somewhere around his larynx, causing a traffic jam all the way back to his diaphragm (which made it difficult for him to enjoy his meals all that day and into the next).

The great man was indeed in high dudgeon, pacing about his cabin with his hands folded behind his back, a leonine look of displeasure on his broad, fierce countenance. Admiral Oberon Trowbridge, newly assigned to the Parmigiana fleet, was a proud man, and like all proud men, cuckoldry (rumored or otherwise) did not suit him (which is not to say, of course, that cuckoldry suits any man, but a proud man wears his pride like armor, and such a blow is like the poisoned dirk that drives through the gaps: it drains the life from him, and moreover makes him moody, irascible and altogether impossible to live with, especially in the cramped quarters of a man-of-war, even one so large and glorious as the first-rate Hornblower), and he greeted Zeal's appearance with a snarl just this side of civility.

"My lord," said Zeal, taking off his hat and bowing.

Admiral Trowbridge grunted and inclined his head. "Zeal." Pacing to his desk, he took up a sheaf of papers, cocked one eyebrow at them, and said, "Ned tells me you are quite a firebrand, Zeal. Something of a glory-seeker."

Ned, my lord? Zeal almost said, before he remembered that Edwin was the given name of Admiral Crandall, who had ordered Zeal to hunt down the *Eschaton*, an old friend of Admiral Trowbridge, and, not incidentally, the Admiral of the Fleet. They had been mids together, had married a pair of beauteous sisters, and affectionately referred to each other as "Ned" and "Ron." Zeal swallowed his ignorance in the nick of time and said, "Yes, my lord. He told me that as well," and winced.

The raised eyebrow went higher still; with a subvocal harrumph the Admiral continued, "He also says that you are a damn fine sailor and a most promising officer, and he places a great deal of confidence in your abilities." The hand holding the papers dropped down to his side, and now Zeal could see Admiral Crandall's signature across the bottom, a broad, bold flourish. Having said his piece, Trowbridge nodded, paced a few steps away, and turned. "Do you like the opera, Zeal?"

Startled by the sudden change of tack, Zeal blinked and blurted, "The opera, my lord?"

"Aye, the opera, Zeal. Singing and dancing and bombast and spectacle, fat tenors caterwauling on the stage, young women prancing about in revealing costumes! The opera! Are you a devotee?"

"I fear, my lord," said Zeal, at last remembering to choose his words with care, "that I have never had the opportunity..."

"My wife," said Trowbridge, and coughed. Looking rueful, he started again. "My wife has a box at the Porta Bella opera, but I have no interest in it myself. You will be several days in port, I expect?"

Zeal nodded. "Aye, my lord. *Circe* took rather a beating from the most recent storm, and I have need of fresh water and victuals as well."

"Very good." There was a gleam of satisfaction in the older man's tawny eyes. "Then you certainly would not object to escorting my wife to the opera this evening while your premier oversees the necessary repairs."

Zeal could not have been more speechless if the Admiral had suddenly lurched forward and punched him in the throat. He opened his mouth, and instead of words, emitted a low, hoarse creaking noise while Trowbridge looked on in disapproval. At last, when the initial shock had receded, he managed to say, "At what o'clock, my lord, should I call?"

The disapproving glower melted away like storm clouds before the sun, although the Admiral could not quite be said to smile. "Seven o'clock, if you please, Captain Zeal."

Zeal bowed, and Admiral Trowbridge said, "I place a great deal of trust in

Ned's judgment of your character. I am certain you are a young man of quality, integrity and, most importantly, honor." And such a dire emphasis did he place on that final word that a man much more obtuse than Acheron Zeal could not have failed to take his meaning, and, the interview being concluded, his leave.

"But what in God's holy name," he wondered as the barge rowed him back to *Circe* and safety, "am I going to wear?"

"He can't stay," said Captain Drake.

If any pirate ship could be said to have officers, then all of the *Eschaton*'s were gathered in Drake's cabin: Moonhart and Cid, Lilly crouching in her chair to avoid scraping her head on the overhead beams, Luna, Dallon Moral. This last stood apart from the others, his hands shoved deep in his pockets, his shoulders hunched—as though by making himself small he could hope to avoid his captain's notice. His captain, of course, had noticed, but thus far had limited her reaction to a narrowing of her eyes and a pursing of her lips at her wizard in disgrace.

Disgraced or no, however, his was the voice raised in protest at the captain's words: "Cap'n!" he cried. "He's a sick man—he needs our help! You can't just—"

Drake rounded on him. "Can I not?" she said. "Who is the captain of this vessel, wizard? Is it you?" Her eyes flashed, and Moral eased himself back against the bulkhead, even more sheepish and shrimp-like than before.

"Bless me, lass," said Cid. "You can't mean to maroon him!"

"I still say he should be here for this," Luna said, jabbing her sister in the ribs.

Lilly grunted agreement, an uncharacteristic smile on her scarred and rough-hewn countenance.

The object of all this debate and dissent slumbered in a cabin below. Indeed, save for a few brief interludes, mostly spent shrieking and raving, sleep was all he'd done since appearing on the *Eschaton*'s deck. "And you'd think," Drake had remarked, after watching Moral cast another one of his "go to sleep" spells, "he'd be tired of sleeping, after all this time."

"Who knows?" the wizard replied. "After where he's been, it may be a mercy."

Wherever that was. Drake had waved the question aside, incurious, and she waved away her father's remark in similar fashion. "Maroon him?" she said. "With pistol and single shot on one of those desolate islands below? No, I'll not do that. But I'll not keep him on my ship, either. Whatever business he has back in the world again, he can get about it without my help."

Moral shoved himself away from the wall. "So," he said (and this time she did notice that his hayseed accent was nowhere in evidence), "you'll abandon a fellow man in his time of need, simply because he's an inconvenience to you?"

Drake rounded on him, her mouth twisting with disgust. "Wizard," she said, "was there a time when you didn't realize what I am? You'll turn a blind eye on murder, theft, and destruction of property, but harangue me for abandoning a filthy lunatic? This is me being merciful, here. This is me going out of my way. If I wanted to avoid inconvenience, I'd put a bullet through his brain. If you dislike it, I suggest you find some other berth." Their gazes met with a nearly audible clash, and the wizard looked away first.

"Very well, Captain," he said, drawing his gangly body upright into some semblance of dignity. "Since that is the case, you've no need of my presence for the rest of this discussion."

Brushing past her, he went to the door and let himself out.

Drake glowered round at the circle of faces remaining. "Any other opinions?"

After a pause, Luna raised her hand. "If you ain't maroonin him, Cap'n, what will you be doing with him?"

Drake folded her hands behind her back and smiled. "I've laid in a course for Porta Bella," she said. "We've a hold stuffed with treasure just waiting to be spent. We'll drop our uninvited guest off at the same time."

"That ain't kind in you, Francie," said Captain Cid.

"Dad." Drake's eyes did not precisely soften, but the look she bent on him was almost gentle. "If you want to help him, I won't stop you. But he'll get no aid from me. If you can't stand on your own, you don't deserve to stand at all." With a parting glare round the cabin, she strode towards the door. Her hand on the knob, she paused. "If there are no more questions," she said, "I suggest you all return to your duties."

Outside the stowaway's door, Cid and Moral conferred in low voices.

"He'll be waking soon. Will you—"

"Aye, laddie." Cid's broad hand engulfed the wizard's stooped shoulder. "I'll speak to 'im. Bless me—to think of Flynn Freeborn himself, a-sleepin on this very ship!" He shook his head; his curly beard wagged. "Boggles the mind, it does. I wonder what it might portend."

Moral reached within his jacket, pulled out a tiny flask. "I've mixed this draught; it should steady him, for a while. Long enough for him to ... find his sea-legs, I suppose." He smiled crookedly.

The phial vanished into one of Cid's capacious pockets. "It's a long talk I'll be having with him, I can see."

"How long until we reach Porta Bella?"

Cid scratched his head beneath the strap of his goggles. "Long enough, I'm hoping." He patted Dallon's shoulder one more time. "Get on with you, laddie. Cross the cap'n one more time, and it's you she'll be marooning."

"Don't I know it." Moral hunched his shoulders and drew in his neck, rather like a long, awkwardly-shaped tortoise. "I have to keep trying, though."

Cid's laugh was almost entirely devoid of humor. "Bless me, laddie! I've been trying to rein her in for nineteen years, and I ain't succeeded yet! Her mother might've done it, but—" He broke off. "Eh, well. What's done can't be undone, can it?"

"I suppose not." He watched as the older man vanished into the stowaway's cabin. His eyes were fixed on the smooth-grained door, but he didn't really see it. "It can be atoned for, however."

The *Eschaton* tore the miles off swiftly, mountains, plains, forests, seas all a blue blur below, white clouds like towers racing by on either side. Drake sat curled by her stern windows, fingers curved round the cold stem of her pipe, watching the cloudscapes recede. The lofty clouds made the sky seem larger, somehow, as though showing, through their colossal scale, how vaster still was the sky. Such days inevitably reminded her of her earliest childhood, growing up amongst the white roads and graceful columns of Stratocumulopolis, the dragon city. She had hated it there, begged a place aboard her father's ships as soon as she was able. And yet on these high-flying days, the sky a blue so faultless it pierced straight through the eye and struck like a needle in the heart, she felt not anger or impatience or dismay, but a kind of ache. You, too, could stretch out your wings and fly, those soaring clouds, that pure blue, seemed to say.

"But they lie," she whispered, and cast her pipe aside. Restlessness seized her; before she knew what she was about, she was rising and leaving her shadowed cabin aside, and taking the after hatchway down below, to her father's cabin, where the stowaway was, for the moment, stowed away.

The door was shut, and no more light showed beneath it than one might expect on a clear day with the inhabitant sleeping inside. Drake tapped once, waited, and tapped again. She began to feel ridiculous, and to repent of the impulse that had led her down here, when a voice within called, "Come in."

He was sitting up, propped by cushions, in the cot along the aftermost bulkhead, his head turned to gaze out the little round porthole in the hull of the ship. A white cloudscape stretched to the horizon, blazing in the sun, white ridges and blue valleys, deep clefts washed in shadow. "In all my days," he said softly, "never did I think I'd see such a thing. Here's wealth indeed; here's glory."

"Don't get used to it," Drake said, swallowing around a certain tightness in her throat. "We'll be putting you ashore as soon as we make port."

"Putting me aground, don't you mean?" he said. "Aye, they told me." Only now did he turn his head to look at her; the ironic smile he'd put on faltered as his eyes grew wide, then steadied into something decidedly male, deep and appreciative. "'Tis kind in you to be telling me in person, however, Cap'n."

She snorted, unimpressed. He was a good-looking man himself (though nothing on Random, her heart insisted loyally), especially now the worst of his filth had been washed away. His eyes, in his deep-tanned face, were very bright, his long hair a sort of auburn color. No doubt, if she had been a gently-reared maiden of the sort one normally finds in pirate romances, she would have found his open admiration unnerving, but (except for a brief stint in a ladies' seminary in Chai, quickly escaped from) she had lived among sailors since her girlhood, and was used to the looks they gave her. Indeed, she would have been the more surprised if he had not admired her.

"It's nothing of the sort," she said. "I don't want any hard feelings between us, that's all—especially if you are who you say you are."

He grinned. "I've said nothing on that score," he said. "Who do you say that I am?"

"I've only the words of others to go by," she replied, "but I suppose you do look a bit like the paintings."

He shifted in the cot, making room. Suddenly she was aware of the smallness of the cabin, aware of him as a living man, not just a nuisance or a curiosity or a problem, aware of the bulk of him beneath the woven blanket. He smiled sweetly at her, and said, "And will you sit beside me, lass, and tell me of these paintings?"

"I certainly will not," she said. "You look like the sort to take advantage."

"What, and me as weak as a newborn kitten?" he cried. "You wrong me, lass, so you do!" He struck his chest, right across the heart, with an open hand, and gazed piteously at her. "You're a cruel one, you are."

"That's right," she told him. "Best not forget it."

"How can I hope to remember," he said, "and you've not even told me your name?"

"It's only fair," she retorted. "You haven't told me yours, either."

For a moment his eyes remained locked on her face; then his brow furrowed and his gaze wandered, and his mouth tightened, as though he were searching his brain for a memory that escaped him. He shuddered then, strongly, and Drake's mouth opened to shout for assistance, in case he was having a fit. Then he regained control of himself with a wrench, fixing the charming, roguish smile firmly on his face. "Flynn Freeborn your da named me," he said, "and I never knew him to speak false. Though to be sure, when last I saw him he was much tinier than he is today, and now here he is, father to a fine young full-grown lass."

"Do you really not know who you are?" she asked, curious in spite of herself.

He laughed. "Do you know who you are?" he replied, "or must I name you now?" In his eyes she glimpsed something bleak and hollow, a flash of wherever he'd been when he vanished from the face of the earth. Then it was gone, and he was simply a handsome sailor again, flirting with her.

"I name myself," she said. "Franceline Drake." Absurdly, she felt the impulse to put out her hand. She suppressed it, keeping them both folded behind her.

"Ah," he said. "And you're sure you'll not sit beside me, Miss Francie, for a little spell? Tell me stories of all the years I've missed?"

"I don't think I could trust you to keep your hands to yourself."

He grinned and actually wiggled his eyebrows at her. "Are you sure you'd be wanting me to?"

She rolled her eyes. "You knew my dad when he was a kid. You've been gone for almost sixty years. That makes you what—four times my age? No, thank you."

"Nay, lass!" he cried. "I'm as young and spry as ever I've been. You'd see for yourself, if you'd care to try me."

She was almost tempted. He'd reminded of her Random when first she saw him on the deck of her ship, filthy and crazed though he'd been. Something about his build, the shape of the broad shoulders she could see beneath the borrowed shirt; something in his air, perhaps something common to his kind, the cheerful casualness of the lifelong sailor. She could imagine his large, sun-browned hands tight on her shoulders, his stubbled cheek scratching hers ... she tossed her head, clearing it of the image. "You'll be going ashore in a day or two," she said, arching her eyebrows. "Let's not complicate matters."

He sighed and shook his head. "Ah, lass, you don't know what you're missing."

She smirked. "Don't flatter yourself, *Captain Flynn.* I've known many a better man than you."

"You cut me to the heart, so you do, Miss Drake." There was no hurt or sorrow in his manner, though; suddenly she was angry, tired of fencing with him, sorry she'd come.

"*Captain* Drake," she snapped. As she turned for the door, she added, "You'd better rest and recover your strength. You'll need it. After tomorrow, you're on your own."

"Ah, lass," he said quietly—the closing of the door behind her masked the sound, "when I have ever been anything else?"

Act the First

In years gone by, Porta Bella had been, to quote the noted scholar Benjamin K. Nobey, "a wretched hive of scum and villainy," teeming with pirates and corsairs and freebooters, gentlemen of fortune and ladies of the night, thieves and cutpurses and drunkards and gamblers and Mafia bosses—all the sorts of people undesirable in a good, law-abiding town (which Porta Bella, at the time, assuredly was not). With the decline of piracy, the influx of plundered gold and treasure also declined; so, too, did such wholesome family values as murder, theft, drunkenness and all their many fruits, and Porta Bella became a much quieter place to live. The Doge of Parmigiana, Lorenzo di Capellini, as shrewd a businessman as he was vicious a backstabber, had capitalized on the town's reputation as a former haven for buccaneers and transformed it into a popular vacation spot where bored nobles from as far away as the Republic of Chai could pretend to be pirates, shop at the Buccaneers' Boutique, sup at the Corsair's Kitchen, and end the day by taking in a performance by the Porta Bella Opera Company, who specialized in nautical themes.

Captain Flynn Freeborn cut a sad and strange figure on those gaudy streets, his shabby blue coat and uncouth hat out of place among the gaily-dressed ladies and pompous gentlemen, the bright facades of the shops and the merry signs of many a quaint and adorable pub. He had hoped to find that Cid had spoken false, that fifty-five years had not passed since Flynn Freeborn last walked upon the earth, that nothing, in fact, had changed. But The Bad Halibut, where he and his mates had raised many a glass and sung many a drunken ditty, was now The Pirates Cove, and much cleaner and brighter and more wholesome did it look than any cove where Flynn and his mates had ever sheltered. A hand-lettered sign hung in the window: "Piercings: A Buck An Ear!" He shook his head, and stared through the glass at rows of cheap trinkets at exorbitant fares: compasses that didn't work, silver spoons with Porta Bella inscribed on the handles, little glass sextants and kaleidoscopes that looked like spyglasses. One of the shop attendants, as small and cute as the shop itself, saw him lingering outside and gave him a welcoming glance; with regret he shook his head and turned away. "Nay, Flynn Freeborn," he said to himself, "'tis homeless you are now, and cast upon the shore with never a friend to your name."

Hands in his pockets, he shuffled down to the wharves and sat on the end of a pier, watching the swarms of vessels that plied the harbor. All shapes and sizes they were, flying flags of all the nations of the Quadra Terrarum. He saw fishing skiffs and formal barges, catamarans and xebecs and frigates, Cilantroan galleons and Eclairesian snows, even a felucca from Feta. Further out in the bay, the Eagle of Camembert distinguishable even from this distance, a squadron of Her Majesty's ships stood off and on, practicing their manouevres for the Admiral's delight.

It was a poignant sight, and as he watched the distant clouds of sails he sang to himself in a soft baritone, "Did you ever see the wild goose sailin on the ocean, Ranzo me boys, O Ranzo Ray..." It was supposed to be a rowdy drinking song, but he sang it mournful and low, and the rollicking tune transformed itself into something infinitely more moving than those far-off sails, and as he sang the tears ran down his face—first one trickling from the corner of his eye to nestle in the stubble of his unrazored chin, then more and more until his cheeks were salty rivers that would never carry him home to the sea. He had sailed aboard a *Wild Goose* once, long ago—Captain Cornelius Cid's first ship it was, back when Flynn had borne another name and been another person entirely. "O Ranzo, you'll rue the day," he sang, "when the wild goose sails away..."

His power of speech dissolved entirely before the flood of tears, and he took off his hat and bawled into the crown, howled and hiccupped and hollered, and you would have thought, to hear him, that a foghorn and a herd of mad cows were loose upon the wharves.

"Is there anything so pathetic, any creature so low, any man so deserving of our pity and compassion, as a sailor caught ashore?" said a voice at his side. "A farmer without lands or job or money is still a man, but a sailor without a ship is hardly anything at all."

The one-sided discourse, dry and academic, stemmed the lachrymose tide as nothing else might have done. Flynn raised his head out of the hatful of tears (which he emptied into the bay) and looked up at the man who had addressed him so.

"You must be a sailor yourself, mate," he said cautiously, "to recognize one of your own kind, so you must."

Although to tell you the truth, despite the woolen pea coat and knit watchman's cap he wore (these despite the relative warmth of the day), the fellow who stood beside him on the pier looked little enough like a sailor. He had smooth, unlined, beardless cheeks, but he did not appear young. Nor did he appear old, for that matter. What hair could be seen peeking from beneath the cap was an indeterminate shade somewhere between blond and brown and grey, and his age was similarly impossible to judge. He might have been thirty years old, or fifty—he might have been an immortal dragon, nine hundred years old.

And yet, Flynn reflected, my own appearance don't reflect my true age either, so who am I to judge?

"I have been a sailor," said the stranger, "and a scholar, and any number of other things. At present, I am an opera critic." He reached out his hand. "Crispin S Teague, at your service."

"Flynn Freeborn." The two men shook hands. "What's the 'S' stand for, then?"

Crispin S Teague grinned. His teeth were very white in his tanned, windburned face. "I'll leave that to you to discern." He had not relinquished his grip on the erstwhile pirate captain's hand, and now he heaved Flynn to his feet, saying, "Flynn

Freeborn, eh? I've heard of you. You caused quite a stir among the mercantile ships of the area about … oh, sixty years ago." He raised a sandy eyebrow.

"Adventurin' has kept me young!" Flynn declared, fists to hips.

"I read a monograph," said Teague, turning away from the glistering bay and sauntering down the pier. Flynn cast one last longing glance at the ships and the sea and the distant blurred line of the horizon before following.

"Oh, aye?" he said, trying to sound interested. Monograph … wasn't that one of those eyepieces that fancy gents favored, wore 'em on a chain?

"The monograph," Teague continued, "was written almost thirty years ago by a scholar named … what was his name? … Alamo, I think. Or perhaps Albino. Ataraxes? Well, it doesn't signify. He had a theory about the origins and disappearance of Captain Flynn Freeborn that I'm sure you would find intriguing."

"I like a good theory as much as the next cove, that I do," said Flynn, his eyes narrowing. If Crispin Teague noticed the unfriendly look, however, he chose not to acknowledge it.

"I have a box reserved at the opera this evening," he said instead. "I find that nothing refreshes my spirit so much as a good opera. Perhaps you would care to join me? The company is performing *Frisante's La Sirena e Il Marinaio.*"

"The Siren and the Sailor," murmured Flynn, who, thanks to a certain lady pirate, spoke Parmigianese as well as he did Camembertian (better, you might have said, since his Parmigianese was almost free of the sailor's cant that salted his native tongue). "Opera now," he said, "would that be those overstuffed women caterwauling and shrieking and swooning, at all?"

Crispin Teague smiled and patted the pirate on the shoulder. "You'll need some nicer clothes," he said. "I'll see you there at eight of the clock. Box nine."

With that, tucking his hands into his pockets and whistling a jaunty tune, he sauntered away, soon losing himself in the crowd that teemed in the streets … the crowd which parted without notice around Captain Flynn, who stood stock still in the center of the road, frowning in thought.

Gradually, though, the frown grew lighter and lighter, as the rising sun will lighten the layer of clouds hanging in the upper air from indigo to blue-grey to pink. "New togs, eh?" he said, plucking at his worn blue jacket (and hadn't it been to hell with him and back, the poor faithful thing?). "A fancy party-going rig? Sounds fine, it does, sounds grand!" And he laughed out loud (earning himself a sideways glance from a passing young lady in a violet gown). "It may be the glass is rising—we'll have better weather soon!"

Had the good people of Porta Bella, her leading citizens and her Chamber of Commerce, realized the sheer number of bona fide, genuine pirates now gracing her streets and shops, her bordellos and bars, no doubt they would have thrown a parade, complete with drum major and seventy-six trombones, or held a festival in the bucanneers' honor, or at the very least put a banner in the town square. The *Eschaton* having discreetly anchored in a hidden cove, however, the pirates setting forth in small groups to enjoy their shore leave, the Porta Bellini were none the wiser. What were a few more holiday-makers in her midst? And what if those jubilant tourists were a bit rowdier than most? Porta Bella remained, despite her upscale appearance, a port town, and ports—and sailors—are much the same the world over.

Most of the *Eschaton*s, their pockets full of plunder, had made straight for the seediest wharfside taverns and pleasure-houses they could find, and were squandering money as fast as it would spend. Captain Cid had found the home of an old crony and fellow inventor, and the two were closeted deep together in technical talk. Dallon Moral was wading through the dust and must of the back room of a used bookseller, greedily caressing the worn bindings and tattered pages of many an obscure tome—and continuing to hide from the captain, who was certain never to enter such a boring place. Toggle, the mute young foretopman, had found a playground in the town center, and was happily swinging from the monkey bars.

"Come along of us, Cap'n!" cried Luna Shee, her arm linked through Lilly Bones'. "We know a place—the finest in town!"

"Aye," said Lilly, one of her strides equalling five of her sister-in-spirit's. "Come along."

Drake waved them on. "I've plans of my own," she said, "but I wish you all the joy of your afternoon."

A young lady, unescorted, was sure to raise eyebrows in even such a free and easy town as Porta Bella, but such an escort as she could have found aboard the *Eschaton* would have raised them still further, at least in the district to which Drake now turned her steps. Wealth, however, affords its owner a myriad of things, the right to be eccentric not least among them.

Consequently, though her staff murmured behind their hands, Madame de Trousseau, the première couturière in Porta Bella, was happy—delighted, ecstatic—to assist such an exquisite new patron with the enhancement of her wardrobe.

"No doubt mademoiselle's maman has stepped across the street, to view the shops there," Madame suggested around a mouth full of pins. She stepped back to survey her handiwork, frowned, stabbed a judicious pin, then retreated once more to the edge of the platform. "There!" she cried, clapping her hands. "Mademoiselle is exquisite—très jolie! Do you not agree?"

"Mmm," Drake said, craning to view of the back of the dress. The fashions coming out of Eclaire were much more daring than those of Camembert: no modest Camembertian maiden would wear a gown of scarlet satin, cut low across the front and even lower across the back, exposing not only her smooth white shoulders, but a generous expanse of her curving spine as well. Drake admired the warm glow of the fabric against her skin—but suddenly frowned. Peeping out from the dress's backline, a tendril of black ink curled up along the ridge of her shoulder blade. Her breath caught for a moment in memory—Random's hands, holding her gently down, and Random's voice saying, "Here, lass, steady—won't hurt a bit, and won't you look fine when it's done?"—and then she sighed. It would never do for certain persons to see! Lowering her eyelashes in a reasonable facsimile of maidenly shame, she murmured, "Indeed, it is beautiful—but do not you think it a bit immodest? It would never do to be thought fast!"

Madame bowed. "But of course. We shall inflame the hearts of the young gentlemen, but not too far, n'est-çe pas?" She hesitated. "But ... the color? It is acceptable?"

"Oh, yes," said Drake, stroking the radiant cloth. "It's perfect."

As Madame snapped orders to her underlings, Drake returned to admiring herself in the tall gilt mirror. It was not vanity—or not vanity alone—that drew her. She was, without conceit or exaggeration, a striking young woman. If her eyes bore a flinty look, their shape and color were exceedingly fine, their lashes coal-black against flawless white skin. If her black hair was cut too short for fashion, still its curls framed her delicate features to perfection. Her figure, in the tight-laced red dress, truly was perfect, just the right degree of creamy white décolleté showing above the bodice. She sighed as she ran her hands down the front of the gown. It would not do for her current schemes, but it was lovely, with subtle rose-vines woven into the cloth.

Well, and who said she could buy only one gown today? Her purse was heavy with plundered gold, useless if unspent. She let herself smile, and waited for Madame de Trousseau's return.

The succeeding interval can be interesting, perhaps, only to the parties involved; that it was deeply satisfying to Madame could be seen by that worthy's broad smile as she thanked her client, assuring her that the ordered dresses (a dozen of them! all as lovely and distinct as roses) would be ready that very evening. Drake's satisfaction was of a quieter kind, with a hint of the cat whose whiskers are wet with cream. She curtsied to Madame, and turned towards the shop entrance ... but there she was forced to pause, for another woman was entering—this one a tall, regal lady with marble skin and a glorious profusion of sunset-colored curls. Drake stepped aside, her face a careful blank, and the lady smiled.

"Why, there you are, darling!" she cried. "And are you finished at last? I had only stepped across the street, you know, to look in the shops there."

"Aha!" said Madame de Trousseau. "I knew it!"

"Hello, Mother," said Drake.

"I was in the mood for a cappuccino," said Lady Espera Amica of House Phinoparos, stirring her drink, in its dainty white cup, with a tiny tiny spoon. Her autumn-colored eyebrows arched conspiratorially, as though inviting her daughter to join in her amusement.

"And you couldn't get one at home?" Drake, narrow-eyed, did not touch her own beverage, though it enticed her with its artistic sprinkle of cinnamon on top of frothy whipped cream.

"My darling," Lady Amica set down her cup with a dainty clink, "everyone knows that Porta Bella is the place for delicious espresso beverages. Besides, the people of Chai are all very friendly, and they will tie themselves in knots to be accommodating, but they simply cannot make a decent cup of coffee. They have not learnt the knack." She smiled. "Perhaps in a hundred years or so there will be training academies for coffee artists like there are for chefs and fools and wizards, but for now we shall simply have to make do."

"Why didn't you just wait a hundred years, then?" Drake was not to be lulled by her mother's banter. "You have time."

"Yes, true." Lady Amica smiled and sighed. "But I have been living among humans too long. I fear their impatience has rubbed off on me."

"I find it difficult to believe that anything could rub off on you unless you wanted it to," Drake muttered into her cappuccino's disintegrating foam. And then, as her mother raised one perfect eyebrow, she said more loudly (but in not much friendlier a tone), "I suppose your impulse visit to this side of the world had nothing to do with my presence here."

"Dear one," said Lady Amica in the sweet and reasonable voice that had always, always made Drake's teeth hurt, "can you blame a mother for being concerned about her daughter? It has been months and months since I've heard anything of you but what I read in the press."

"Is that how you knew where I was?" Drake said. "The press?"

Amica's perfect lips formed a deprecating moue. "Indeed. Follow the reports of mayhem, death, and piracy, and there my daughter will be. That," she added, before Drake could do more than sniff, "and your father does write to me, from time to time." One of Amica's long nails tapped the table. The hint was too obvious to be ignored.

"I've been busy," said Drake, looking away. The little café in which they sat was full of people in elegant dress, laughing, gossiping, paying no attention to the two women by the window—except, perhaps, to acknowledge their beauty. Drake's mouth twisted.

The Lady Amica reached into her reticule, producing a thick sheaf of papers, bound with a deep-blue ribbon. Her smug, devious expression made Drake long for the simplicity of a roaring broadside. Amica said, "Other busy people find plenty of time for correspondence, my dear," and passed the papers to Drake.

They were letters. At least half a dozen of them, written on thick, creamy paper, her name across the fronts in a fine, bold hand: Miss Franceline Drake.

Drake looked from this unexpected bounty to her mother, her mouth shaping a questioning O.

"Captain Zeal," said Lady Amica, tilting her chin towards the letters, "has a beautiful hand, don't you think? Bold, but with a surprising delicacy. Look at the flourish on the F."

Captain Zeal? Too stunned to make a sound, Drake closed her fingers hard around the letters, twisting the paper in her grip.

Lady Espera Amica appeared to be enjoying her daughter's discomfiture. Her eyes full of silent, elusive draconic laughter, she said, "The good captain is a polite and well-spoken young man. I think he means to propose … if he could be assured that it would be received favoraby. Really, darling, I don't know why you said he might write, if you didn't intend to answer him. Or, indeed, read his correspondence at all."

Her mother's meaning trickled down through Drake's ears into her brain—and as understanding blossomed, suddenly the letters became not objects of revulsion, but inviolably precious—hers. She flipped them over, just to be certain—and the broken wax seals stared up at her, mute and self-satisfied. "Mother!" she cried. "You didn't read them, did you?"

"And why not, dear?" Amica sipped her coffee with studied indifference.

"Someone ought to, and you were hardly going to come home to pick up your post."

"So you brought it to me instead—after perusing the contents. How thoughtful."

Amica inclined her head.

Drake scowled, clenching the letters in her fist. "If you had any idea how much I loathe, revile, abhor and despise that man," she hissed, "you wouldn't play these games with me!"

"I understand perfectly well." Amica put down her cup. Meeting her daughter's eyes for the first time since the conversation began, she said, "He sank your ship, slaughtered your crew, and murdered your beloved Odd Job or whatever his name was."

"Random Chance," Drake snarled.

Amica waved away the correction and continued, "And for these crimes he can never be forgiven, even though he is young, handsome, amiable, energetic and intelligent, all characteristics you look for in choosing a man—except for the last one, of course. Lack of brains has never bothered you—perhaps because you lack them yourself."

Drake's mouth fell open, but no sound came out.

"Close your mouth, darling, you look a simpleton." Amica leaned across the tiny table. "Has it never occurred to you, my sweet child, that if you wish to wound the good captain, there is no better way to do so than allow him to court you—to wed you, even? Husbands and wives have more opportunity for cruelty than any other people in the world."

"You should know, Mother." Drake sneered. "And what makes you think it hadn't occurred to me? You raised me, after all. I may be a simpleton, but my lessons in cruelty started early."

The Lady Amica's eyelashes flickered.

"You have your methods, Mother—and I have mine. I'll deal with Captain Zeal my own way." Drake got to her feet and gathered up her things. Turning towards the door, she said, "Thank you for the cappuccino."

Lady Amica Espera remained seated as her daughter stalked away. The tiny bells on the café door jangled as Drake yanked it open; the draconic woman smiled and took another sip of her drink, waiting. A second jingle of bells, which would have indicated that the door had closed, did not occur. Amica's smile widened.

Drake turned from the door and stomped back to the table, yanking out a chair and thumping into it. "Fine," she snarled. "What exactly do you have in mind, Mother?"

Savoring her beverage, Lady Amica took a moment to respond. And then, with the look of a cat who has got not only the canary and the cream, but also a nice piece of fish, a catnip mouse for dessert and a good belly-rub, she said, "How do you feel about the opera?"

Act the Second

While his captain was off gallivanting through Porta Bella searching for an appropriate opera-going rig, Lieutenant Morrow was haggling with Navy shipwrights over *Circe*'s necessary repairs. "Only the best for her, Tom," Captain Zeal had said, clapping his first officer on the shoulder (Morrow's eyes bulged) before departing for said gallivant. "Don't let them shortchange you, either. They'll gouge out your eyeballs and feed them to their cats if you give them half a chance."

"Aye, sir," Morrow agreed. Never mind that he knew naval ways better than the queer customs of the shore, never mind that he had been at sea so long he was practically a merman, never mind that he had been speaking shipboard slang before Acheron Zeal, that pup, could more than gurgle—when the Captain spoke, his subordinate agreed.

Lucky for Lieutenant Morrow, the *Circe*, though in need of a good scraping, was not in bad shape overall (not half so bad as the poor old *Kraken* after that pirate ship exploded her, thanks be). The Parmagianese shipyard workers showed a distressing inclination to lounge about beneath trees drinking coffee and smoking, but their supervisor was a brisk fellow from Camembert, and between them Morrow and Mr Chips, the *Circe*'s carpenter, were making headway at last. Morrow watched with satisfaction as the supervisor harried his people back to work, and soon the sounds of banging and hammering and sawing filled the air.

"Ahoy there—Tom Morrow!"

Lieutenant Morrow turned, and on his grey, gloomy face was such an uncharacteristic look of pleasure that everyone present stopped and stared at the transfiguration. His eyebrow (he had but the one, like a mutant furry caterpillar crawling across his forehead) leaped up—and was that?—no, surely not!—but it was, it was: a smile, a smile on the face of Thomas Morrow!

"Crispin!" he cried, stretching out his arms. "Crispin Teague, or my eyes deceive me!" The two men embraced, pounding each other's shoulders and laughing. When they broke apart, Morrow said, "But what are you doing here? We all thought you'd drowned off Schlagsahne in 'seventy-three! Where have you been all these years?"

Teague's weathered face was bland and smiling, but his tone when he said, "I've been finding things to keep me busy," did not invite further questions.

Circe's crew, assisting with the repairs, leaned as close as they could to listen. "What did 'e say, mate?" they asked Jug-Ear Jim, who had earned his name from the large (and amazingly receptive) satellite dishes sticking off each side of his head.

"I think," said Jim, squinting in concentration, "he said his hair … is really … frizzy."

"Which he's wearing a hat," said someone else, "so how can you tell?"

"But come," said Crispin S Teague, taking Morrow's arm. "Is there a shop hereabouts where one can obtain a roborative beverage? And you can tell me what you've been doing with yourself, Tom."

"Aye, a capital idea." He turned to Second Lieutenant Blake, who closed his mouth in the nick of time. "I'll not be gone long, Blake. You're in charge here while I'm away."

"A-aye aye, sir!" Blake stammered.

The seamen of the *Circe* watched in slack-jawed amazement as their First Lieutenant wandered off, arm-in-arm with a strange sailor. "Right," said Richard Blake, still staring. "Back—back to work, men."

"You know what I like, Lilly?" said Luna Shee.

"Yup," said Lilly Bones, friend, sister, constant companion.

Such a rejoinder would have stopped any reasonable human being in her tracks—but not Luna Shee, who never let such conversational stumbling blocks trip her up for long. Grabbing Lilly's hand and swinging her arm, Luna said, "I like a day like today, when the sun is grinning down on you and twenty gold doubloons are a-jingling in your pocket just waiting to be spent. Aaaah!" She sighed, stretching one hand towards the sky. "Say, Dead-Eye and a couple of others were going down to the Smoking Bishop later on. Wanna meet up with them?"

Lilly smiled down at her. "You can go," she said. "I've got work."

"Graaah," said Luna, "all work 'n no play, that's you!"

"Mmm," Lilly agreed, reaching up touch a crinkling packet tucked into her waistcoat. Chapter seventeen wanted only a few more pages before its completion.

"You know what you need, Lilly?"

A quiet room, a pot of ink, and a sharpened quill, Lilly thought.

"You need a fine gent to keep you company for an hour or two, relax you, like. Aye, a fine, amiable gent to put a smile on your face and a song in your heart." And while Luna expatiated on the virtues of amiable gents of all shapes and sizes (although the bigger the better, naturally), Lilly pondered how to find such a person, whom she could leave her sister with.

Just as the idea occurred to her, smiling Good Fortune (or her sister, Blind Chance) deposited just such a gent right in their path.

Happily, it was Luna, and not Lilly, who plowed into the poor man. Lilly, who topped seven feet and was built like a linebacker, would have ground the fellow into the dust and kept right on walking, perhaps pausing to wonder why the ground had gotten so squishy. Luna being a tiny person, however, the collision caused a loud thump, a pair of oofs, a rising cloud of dust as the fellow landed on his rump in the middle of the street, and then a sheepish grin as Luna cried,

"Begging your pardon, sir! I was so caught up in my own thoughts I didn't see you walking there!" And she reached out her hand to help him to his feet.

The man, a tallish, well-built fellow in a bottle-green coat and shiny black boots (something of a dandy, then, Luna thought with a sniff), replied, "Nay, I was criminally negligent myself, that I was..." His face, which had been hidden by the brim of his tricorne hat, came into view, and Luna shrieked and released his hand, dropping him into the dust a second time.

"What?" said Lilly, in her hand appearing a large, vicious knife.

"C-C-Cap'n Flynn!" cried Luna. "I hardly recognized you!"

Once Flynn Freeborn resolved to do something, it was as good as done—and so it was with his determination to find a decent suit of clothes and join that Teague fellow at the opera. Never mind that he had no money, no friends in town, and no assets to speak of. Never mind that he'd never seen Teague in his life, and the whole thing might be some sort of bizarre, elaborate set-up (for what, though, Flynn had no idea). Where there was a will, Flynn firmly believed, there was a way.

The way soon presented itself in the form of a noisy mob of young so-called gentlemen carousing through the center of the street (never mind that the hour for luncheon had scarcely passed). Flexing his fingers, choosing his mark with care, affecting a drunken stagger, Flynn made for the center of the crew, his shoulder knocking into that of the loudest and fanciest of the young men.

"Watch where you're going, ruffian!" cried the youth, his face an ugly purple.

"Sorry 'bout that, mate," said Flynn, flashing a charming smile and swaying on his feet. "Terribl' sorry..." And he hiccupped.

"I'll make you sorry!" the angry young "gentleman" snarled, readying a fist.

"Here, now, Toby!" said one of his companions, soberer in dress and demeanor than the others. "The man's obviously drunk. You don't want to cause a scene, do you? Think what your father would say!"

The dire reminder of the paterfamilias was enough to quiet the young man's rage. Lowering his fist and raising his nose, he said, "Yes, of course. It wouldn't do to scuffle with a low ruffian like this, anyway." To the low ruffian he said, "Be more careful when you cross the path of your betters, fellow!"

"Aye, sir," grovelled Flynn, tugging at his forelock, pitching his voice to grate just this side of bearable, "thank'ee, sir, thank'ee!"

The gentleman's lip curled. "Oh, stop that! And get away from me, you dog!" The shove he gave sent Flynn sprawling, and he watched from a seat in the dirt as the mob pranced away, more pompous and self-important than before.

"Aye," he murmured, smiling to himself. "Aye, I'll watch out for me betters, that I will." The purse in his hand gave a satisfying clink; its heft was the familiar, comforting weight of gold. "Aye, that I will!" he repeated, and laughed out loud.

The gold in the young man's purse bought him a fancy new rig, from a fine coat of green velvet to shiny black knee-high boots. His waistcoat was creamy silk, laced with more gold than an Admiral's, and his breeches were softest doeskin. Topped with a new tricorne hat, his long hair cleaned and combed and then braided with beads and coins that jingled as he walked, he fit the bill of gentleman as well as any man in town.

Taking off his hat, regarding his reflection, he shook his head and sighed. Who are you joking, Flynn? he asked himself. You never was a gentleman, and you never will be.

But he paid the shopkeeper and proceeded into the street, the shadow of melancholy fading away under the bright afternoon sun. Was he not alive and in the world again, given a chance to make amends after all those years of sinning? And was he not Captain Flynn Freeborn, the resourcefullest pirate in the southern seas? Why, life was brief, and you never knew when a vengeful ghost would appear to drag your spirit back down to hell, so no time for moping, my lad, no time for melancholy or gloom—best make the most of the time you're given, and if you can atone for past ills in the bargain, why, all the better!

So he determined, and was stepping with swinging strides down the center of the street when he collided with a person he had not seen and fell backwards onto his arse in the dust of the road.

"Begging your pardon, sir! I was so caught up in my own thoughts I didn't see you walking there!" cried a young, female voice, and a slim, brown hand was thrust into his face, forcibly hauling him to his feet.

"Nay, I was criminally negligent myself, that I was..." began Flynn, tilting his head up to look at her around the brim of his hat.

But the moment his face was revealed, she let out a horrible shriek and dropped his hand—and for his own part, he was too stunned to make a move to save himself, and landed for the third time that day in the dusty road. The young woman was speaking, but her words held no meaning for his stupefied brain; his eyes, wide and wondering, traced the familiar lines of her face, and his lips shaped a name he had not spoken in half a century:

"Lu … Lucenza?"

For a moment he did see, laid over the reality before him, an image of a face he'd not seen for fifty years, the proud, flashing eyes and the curving lips of the Queen of Pirates. Reaching out to her he said, "Ah, so you've come for me again, lass—I knew my time above the earth would be brief. Well, I'll not be stopping you dragging me down to hell..."

Then a voice that was not Lucenza's said, "Cap'n, what the hell are you talking about?" And another voice, much deeper, said, "He got the first syllable right, anyway." Flynn blinked, and saw that the woman before him was indeed as small and dark as Lucenza di Ladro, but there the resemblance ended. Her pointed face was more catlike, her eyes not darkest brown, but a pale, pale green—and Lucenza had never let the tattooist's needle touch her long, slender arms.

"You all right?" this stranger asked him, and he felt a pang of disappointment. Not that he wanted to face Lucenza's angry spirit a second time, but … well, a familiar face would have been a comfort. He continued to gaze at her, stupidly, and she said, "Cap'n Flynn?"

His eyes re-focused; shaking himself, he said, "Do I know you, then?"

"Aye, we've met." Her teeth flashed in a wide, white grin. "Aboard the *Eschaton*. You remember: Get away from me, you devils! You'll not have my soul!" She hunched her shoulders and gesticulated, doing a credible imitation of an earlier Flynn, his hair hanging in lank, filthy strands before his face, his eyes glazed with madness, laying about him with a boarding axe and roaring. And then she straightened and shrugged, "Or words to that effect."

Red rose to Flynn's face, and he said, "Aye, well, you know..."

"Glad to see you're feeling better," she said, cutting off his embarrassed stammers.

"And looking cleaner," added the woman next to her—more woman, Flynn thought appreciatively, than he had ever seen in all his days.

Rallying his scattered and beleaguered brain cells, Flynn said, "You've the advantage of me, ladies, that you do. You know me, but I can't swear to having ever seen you in my life. So perhaps a proper introduction would ease the transition between hopeless confusion and the certain friendship to come." He smiled.

No woman could have looked on the smile of Flynn Freeborn and remained un-charmed, and the small, dark pirate was certainly a woman. Grinning in return, mischief sparking in her pale green eyes, she said, "Why, Cap'n, you flatter us. Well, I'm called Luna Shee, and this is my sister here, Lilly Bones." The giantess inclined her head.

"Charmed, ladies," said Flynn, removing his hat and making a handsome leg. "And I be Flynn Freeborn, as well you know."

Luna giggled and dropped a curtsey (a ridiculous gesture from someone wearing nothing but the baggy, striped pants of a sailor and a tight leather vest). "Care to join us for some afternoon entertainment, Cap'n?"

Captain Flynn Freeborn may not have been the keenest cutlass in the weapons chest (so to speak), but it would have taken a man denser than Sunday pudding to miss the pirate lass's meaning. And he was tempted—Lord, was he tempted!—but the shadow of Lucenza di Ladro still wavered in the air before him, and with a vague sense of guilt he shook his head and said he must decline. "But some other time, perhaps," he said.

"Some other time, then, Cap'n," she said, and stood on tip-toe to kiss him on the cheek. And she waved him all the way down the end of the street and out of sight, calling, "Good-bye, Cap'n! Good-bye, good-bye!"

"I like him," Lilly Bones said unexpectedly, as Flynn turned the corner and disappeared.

Luna looked up at her sister. "Aye," she said. "I do too."

"Too bad about him 'n the Cap'n."

Luna gave her a sharp look. "Him 'n the Cap'n what?" she said.

Lilly snorted.

"Him 'n the Cap'n ain't anything!" Luna cried, jabbing her sister in the ribs. Lilly grunted.

"Well, no," she said. "Not yet."

Luna's voice drifted after him—*Good-bye, Cap'n! Good-bye, good-bye!*—as he turned the corner, and he half-turned to wave back at her—

—And smacked right into the person walking the other way.

Ow! was his first thought, followed hard by *I need to start looking where I'm going,* and, as he raised his gaze to the fellow he'd just collided with, *Oh, bloody hell and red death,* for the other man was wearing the uniform jacket (almost unchanged this last half-century and more) of a captain in her Majesty's Royal Navy.

"I beg your pardon, sir!" cried Captain Flynn, taking off his hat.

"And I yours," replied the other, a tall fellow with long, blond hair and a tiny stripe of a goatee down the middle of his chin. His eyes narrowed. "Do I know you, sir? I feel as though I've seen you before."

Maybe on an antique wanted poster, Flynn thought. Out loud, "No, sir, no, I don't believe so, sir," he said. "Fine day, ain't it, sir?"

"Yes..." said the blond-haired captain. "Very fine."

"Thank'ee, sir, I think so too, sir," said Flynn, not at all suspicious in his manner, backing away as quickly as he could go, leaving the navy dog far behind.

The navy dog watched the odd fellow scurry away and frowned, suspicion brewing in his brain. He'd seen that face before, he could swear to it ... and hadn't he heard a voice, just before they collided, calling, "Good-bye, Cap'n! Good-bye"?

The frown deepened, ploughing a furrow in his forehead. "Cap'n," eh?

Dear reader, I hope it is not stretching the bounds of credulity too much to imply that the voice that had shouted valediction rang a bell of familiarity in Captain Zeal's head—a bell that sounded not unlike the gentle chime of the young captain's chronometer, which a certain pirate wench had once lifted from him.

Two and two added to a glorious and terrible four; Zeal's frown disappeared as his eyes widened in shock. Turning on his heel, he cried, "I say—you, there! Wait!"

But the street was empty. The man (the pirate, Zeal supposed, and perhaps his quarry of these many long months) had gone.

"Damn," said Zeal.

"Well, but what's wrong with him?"

The question gave Thomas Morrow pause. The lieutenant had been enlarging to his old friend Crispin Teague his captain's many flaws, a discourse made more free by the several bottles of wine that now stood empty on the table between them. Most of the wine was by now inside Lieutenant Morrow, but enough of his natural reserve and respect for rank remained to check his bilious ranting that poor Crispin had absolutely no idea what his friend was talking about.

"Well," said Morrow, accepting more wine, "take this pirate-hunt, for example. A fool's chase if ever there was one. Any reasonable man could see it's preposterous for a sailing ship to try to catch a sky-sailer—in fact, it's totally unbelievable! And yet he wears us all to shadows trying. The thought of failure never crosses his mind." Moodily, he drank his wine. "And he calls me Tom," he muttered.

"I call you Tom," Teague pointed out.

"Yes," said Morrow, "but I *like* you."

"He sounds," said Teague judiciously, pouring more wine, "like a good man, and a good captain. Ambitious, active … zealous." Morrow winced. "All of his flaws sound more like virtues to me. Should we not admire the man undaunted by adversity? The man willing to sacrifice all for the good of his country?"

"And his career," Morrow added, but under his breath. Teague's eyebrows raised, and Thomas burst out, "Aye, it's true! Catching this pirate will make his career! Look at him—twenty-five years old and a junior post captain still, no hope of a prime command unless he does something spectacular. Aye, he'll move up the list all right, but he'll be sailing a desk if he ain't lucky, and the only fleet he'll command is a gaggle of paper-pushing bureaucrats." The bitterness in his tone threatened to sour the rest of the wine. Teague's eyebrows threatened to merge with his hairline.

"And," said he, leaning forward, "let me guess. No hope of advancement for his officers, either, unless said pirate swings."

Morrow's Adam's apple worked up and down, but he made no sound other than a sort of ghng, gnhhhg.

"How long have you been a lieutenant, Tom," asked Crispin Teague, "with no command of your own?" He leaned back and took a long draught of wine.

Tom's long, grey, gloomy face grew longer and gloomier still, his lone eyebrow drawing down over his deep-set, dingy eyes. He uttered a long, lugubrious sigh (not unlike the hooting call of the melancholy stipe, a large white bird of the Chai islands), and for a moment Crispin feared he would begin to weep into his wine. It was a good wine, a rich and spicy red from Schlagsahne, and Crispin would have been sad to see it spoilt by bitter salt.

But Lieutenant Thomas Morrow of her Majesty's Royal Navy, though a bit tipsy (soused, even, you might say) was still master of his own emotions, and he swallowed his tears as though drinking the sea, while other conversations swirled around him.

Then, as Crispin was fishing for something comforting to say, the other conversations ceased. The room fell silent. Crispin raised his head and looked to the doorway, where two tall men in black uniforms were standing in a rectangle of afternoon light.

"I say, Crispin," said Tom into the tense silence, as the door closed and the rectangle vanished, leaving the wineshop in sepia-colored dimness once again, "you never did tell me where you've been all these years."

The two black-uniformed men, one tall and one short, both identical in their expressions of grim efficiency, began to move through the crowd. The wineshop's patrons shrank away as they passed, each endeavoring to make himself small and insignificant, utterly beneath notice. Teague's eyes flicked to the doorway (no way out there, with the men in black filling the narrow pathway between tables) and then to the back of the shop, where the proprietor was cowering behind the bar, only the shiny top of his bald head visible above the polished wood. No way out there, either—no second exit of any kind. No windows, either. He supposed he could climb into the fireplace and out through the chimney, but the Parmigianese favored those long, narrow pipes for their stoves, and though Crispin Teague was not a burly man, neither could he slither like a snake through a six-inch tube.

"Crispin?" said Morrow.

"Crispin Teague?" said the uniformed man now on Crispin's left.

Teague closed his eyes. When he opened them again, the two uniformed men were still there, flanking his seat. He nodded.

"You know who we are?" said the man on the right (shorter than the other, with a little bristly moustache).

Teague nodded again.

"Crispin," said Morrow, eyes widening with alarm, "what's going on here?"

"It's all right, Tom," Crispin said. "You'd better sit down, or they'll probably arrest you, too."

Confusion and concern on his face, Morrow did as he was told.

"Will you come with us quietly?" asked the man on the left.

"Yes, I'll come," said Teague.

"Then there is no need to bind you." He nodded to his companion, who took the cue and said, "By order of his Highness the Doge of Parmigiana, we hereby place you under arrest, to remain in custody until such time as you come to trial." There was a ripple of reaction through the room, quickly suppressed as people paid elaborate attention to their drinks.

Crispin sighed and got to his feet. "Right," he said. "Lead the way."

Tom Morrow watched in befuddlement as the men in black escorted his old friend away. Teague, a bitter smile twisting his mouth, was as good as his word and put up no resistance. When the door had closed behind them, the wineshop burst into nervous and relieved conversation. Morrow hunched in his chair and listened to the words around him (those words of Parmigianese he could understand): amazing … the Carbonara, here! … poor man, what were they going to do with him … just be thankful it's not you, that's all … what do you suppose he'd done…?

Sighing, eyes half-closed, Morrow reached for the wine.

Act the Third

Lady Clarissa Trowbridge was a fine, well-made woman in her early thirties, much younger than her husband the Admiral, and her ready smile and ringing laugh made her seem younger still. She giggled when Zeal kissed her hand, and covered her mouth with that same hand and blushed when he complemented her hair or dress or jewels, he couldn't remember which. Admiral Trowbridge gave them both a stern glower (more like a father sending his daughter on her first date with an unknown quantity than a husband giving his wife into the care of a trusted subordinate), and then he was handing her up into the carriage, which set off at a brisk trot through the darkening streets of Porta Bella.

The horses' hooves made a fine ringing clatter against the paving stones—not so fine a clamor as the crash of a well-timed broadside, he thought, and when he said as much to Lady Trowbridge (more for the sake of having something to say than any hope of engaging her interest) she uttered her melodious, chiming laugh and said, "You navy men are all alike. I cannot speak to the admiral on any topic, however mundane, without he must relate it back to seas or ships or sailing or somesuch. I had thought it was a quirk of his, but now I find that you are much the same."

"We sailors have salt water for blood, it's true," Zeal said with a smile, "and like the kappa of Chai, we cannot long survive out of our native element."

"Oh," cried Lady Trowbridge, "have you ever seen a kappa? I have always longed to."

"Once," Zeal replied, "bathing in a hot spring on the north island. It fled as we approached."

"Marvelous," said she, clapping her hands.

The rest of the carriage ride (not a long one) was spent in amiable conversation: strange creatures seen, when and under what circumstances, the relative scarcity of encounters these days. When the carriage had rolled to a stop in front of the opera house and Zeal handed the lady down, she linked her arm through his, still chatting away as though she had known him since she was a girl. They joined the stream of people trickling through the doors of the tall building with its grand marble façade, and their passage caused little ripples and eddies of conversation to spring up in their wake. After all, it was not every day that the intelligentsia and the glitterati of Porta Bella saw the wife of an admiral on the arm of a mere post captain—and so openly, too, right in front of everybody!

"I adore the opera," said Lady Trowbridge as they passed through the portals. "I'd come every night if I could."

"Mmm," said Zeal, who was a little dubious about all the flash and the dazzle and the color that surrounded them, here in the foyer. The walls were adorned with a bas-relief, quite lifelike, of various opera singers performing their craft, wearing all manner of fantastic costumes. Overhead, in the trompe l'oeil style popular in Eclaire, the Nine Muses descended from a golden Heaven, bearing the tools of their various trades (lyres and quill pens and whatnot), surrounded by flocks of little chubby half-naked baby angels who appeared, from their expressions, either to be singing, or about to be ill. The extravagant artwork would have been quite enough on its own, but the foyer was stuffed to the seams with overdressed, overfed rich people laughing and gesticulating and flaunting their wealth. Zeal himself was not a rich man (although the full dress uniform of a captain in the Royal Navy was quite splendid), nor especially concerned with becoming one (although a little extra money for fending off the creditors would have been nice), but the air of complacent self-congratulation in the room made him feel queasy. Or perhaps that was just the mingling of expensive perfumes, cloyingly sweet in the overwarm air.

"Shall we go up to my box?" asked Lady Trowbridge, cocking her head up at him. "I'll have wine sent up, and we can relax before the performance."

"A capital plan," said Zeal, no little relieved to escape the press, the noise and the reek. Give him a cannonade and an enemy ship any day!

But wine and congenial company soon revived his flagging spirits—and he was soon to have reason to revive still further, as, reader, you shall soon see.

"Eight of the clock," said Captain Flynn, consulting his new pocket watch (an unintentional gift of a fancy cove Flynn had bumped into only a few minutes before) and striding down the street, tall boots clomping. "Box nine."

The colonnaded façade of the Porta Bella Opera House loomed before him, not so large as the opera house in Schlagsahne's capital city, Erdbeere (for the Schlagsahnich had enthusiastically adopted opera, originally a Parmigianese art form, and many an acclaimed composer hailed from that country), nor as grand as the one in Parmigiana City—but it was a charming jewel box of a building in an area of town dedicated to playhouses and little coffee shops and one marvelous café that would sell you a parfait bedecked with sprinkles and heart-shaped cookies and chocolate sauce for a literal song. Flynn cast a wistful glance towards the café, which served sandwiches and spicy fried potatoes as well, then pocketed his watch and approached the doors of the opera house.

"Ticket?" said the doorkeeper, a thin little playhouse creature dressed all in black.

"No ticket, love," replied Flynn, smiling down at her. "I'm meeting a friend of mine here—Crispin Teague's his name. Box nine."

It was reassuring, the effect his smile still had on the ladies. She melted into a puddle at his feet, and her dull eyes grew soft and warm. "Of course," she cooed. "Go right on in. To your right."

"Much obliged," he said, and dropped a kiss on her unresisting hand. He was rewarded with another gooey, eloquent look—and then he was inside, in the midst of the throng, and he drew a deep breath and grinned. "Right. Box nine."

He found the box right enough, a little curtained alcove overlooking the stage, where the box owners could relax and watch the show in relative privacy (without having to rub elbows with the unwashed masses already filling the seats below). He did not, however, find any sign of his host. Box nine featured several chairs and an attendant number of little, low, highly-polished tables, but it did not feature the lean, weathered figure of Crispin S Teague. On one of the tables, however, leather covers glossy in the light of a glass oil lamp, was a stack of books, and on top of the books was a note.

"Hmm," said Flynn, and picked it up and read:

Friend,

I regret that I will be unable to join you for tonight's performance; I have been unalterably detained by circumstances beyond my control. I have, however, had sent up a number of texts that will aid you in 'brushing up', as it were, on recent historical events.

In addition, as it appears you are in need of a ship, I have the following advice. Go tomorrow to the Frigid Insect, an inn by the wharves. There you will find a merchant captain named Tom True, of the Rhymer. He is in need of a sailing master, his own having been devoured by giant sea turtles off the coast of Garam Masala. Tell him I recommended you to him, and you will have no problem getting aboard.

Your most humble and obedient servant,

Crispin S Teague

"Merchant captain…" Flynn muttered. "Sailing master..." He shrugged. "And why not, at all? Any ship is better than this purgatory the lubbers call dry land." And he flopped into the chair next to the table-load of books, to flip through them until the show began.

Taking up the top book, a thin little leather-bound volume, "Well, bless my soul…" he murmured. Turning it over, he read the title again: *An Humble Proposal Regarding the Mysterious Disappearance and Even More Mysterious Origins of the Famed Pirate Captain Flynn Freeborn,* by Leon Ampersand, Scholar of Elhard.

"Famed, am I?" he said. Grinning, he settled back into the chair and began to read.

The opera itself began without much notice from Flynn, absorbed as he was in a lively account of his adventure with Prince Remington (later crowned Alexander Remington VII, called "Remy One-Eye" by his affectionate people) and the female raiders of Erris. Lively, and not wholly inaccurate, though its language was moderated in deference to the sensibilities of the reading public. How had the scholar known? Perhaps young Remy had kept a journal. While sailors and sirens and one great, large lass with a monumental bosom (Flynn took a moment from his book to appreciate the bosom) cavorted and caterwauled onstage below, he wandered the pages of scholar Leon Ampersand's modest little book (a book which had brought him equally modest fame among his own kind), and relived memories of distant times, seldom contemplated, but well remembered. Catrionaugh Adaire, now, she had been a hell of a woman, even if she had tried to kill him on any number of occasions. "Can't hardly blame the lass, though, now, can we?" he murmured. How odd it was to see her name in print! "Anyone would've done the same. And I was trying to escape." He grinned at the memory.

And if other parts of Scholar Ampersand's book suffered from inaccuracy and rank speculation, so much the better. Let the world keep guessing about Flynn Freeborn, if it wished.

There can be no doubt, the scholar wrote, *that Captain Flynn was the son of a nobleman; for, although there are no "Freeborns" enrolled in the scrolls of nobility, it is surely no difficult proposition for a man to change his name and go a-pirating. Perhaps his family had fallen upon difficult times, or perhaps he wished to avenge some wrong perpetrated upon his name. Scholar Selwyn Humpernickle suggests, in his book...* Here the author sailed off into a meditation upon some of Scholar Humpernickle's more recondite ideas on the nobility, especially where the subsets of impoverished noblemen and pirates intersected, but Flynn's eyes had ceased to focus on the page.

To avenge some wrong? After a fashion.

He remembered his father's death as though it were yesterday and not the sixteen years it seemed to be and the seventy-one it was in fact—and he remembered that black-hearted d'Urstwhil as well, fat and satisfied in a hideous waistcoat that had probably been cannibalized from some granny's sofa. He remembered his mother's dark-circled eyes like hopeless pits in her pale, drawn face—made paler by contrast to the subfusc mourning gown she wore, even on her wedding day, in defiance of her new husband's railing.

And he remembered (closing his eyes while the memories, and the rich, dark voice of the baritone, swelled up around him) the long, horrible fall, and the cold shock at the end. Death, he had thought, and the hands that plucked him out of the sea and hauled him up into life-giving air once more, rebirth.

Rebirth, he thought. Ah. And this, then, would be re-rebirth, I suppose. Well, here's to it.

He raised his glass of brandy, really capital brandy left on the table with the books, in silent salute.

Sometime in between the first act and the last (or between the first glass of wine and the one he was currently drinking, however many might lie in between), Lady Trowbridge migrated from her little chair a discreet and proper distance away to a seat on the couch beside Captain Zeal, although there was hardly enough room for both of them there. Blushing, Zeal tried to scoot farther away, to give the lady more space, and when that would not answer, he got to his feet and walked across the room—or he would have, if the lady's slim little hand had not grabbed his wrist and pulled him, with surprising strength, back down.

"Now, Captain," said Lady Trowbridge, and the way her long lashes lowered over her eyes gave her a singularly sinister look, "you can't pretend you don't understand what I'm about here. If this were a naval battle you would be taking every advantage. Can you not do the same with a woman who is, shall we say, ready to be boarded?"

His face a wonderful shade of scarlet, "My lady—" Zeal began—but his protest was cut short by Lady Trowbridge's lips, her red, ripe, fruity lips, smashing against his, and he was unable to say much of anything. Then, with a gasp, he broke away, this time successfully reeling to the other side of the box, his heart thudding in his chest, while Lady Trowbridge looked on in disapproval and disappointment.

"My lady," said Zeal, standing up very straight to cover his discomfiture, sternly addressing her right shoulder—no, not her right shoulder, smooth and white and round and left bare by the low neckline of her dress, which plunged downward to reveal other smooth, white, round portions of her anatomy…! His gaze flicked up to the striped wallpaper behind her, and color rose to his cheeks once more. "This—it—it is not proper! You—you are a married woman, and your husband my superior officer! It will not do!" He was proud of the firmness of his tone, the erectness of his posture … which lasted until he looked at her again, and then he crumpled.

Her lips were trembling, her quivering eyelashes eloquent. "Am I not beautiful, Captain Zeal?" she asked.

His mouth was dry. "Very beautiful," he said.

She rose to her feet. "Am I not desirable, Captain Zeal?"

He swallowed hard. "Very … very desirable, my lady."

"Then why," she asked, stepping nearer and nearer, "can you not forget about your 'duty' and your 'honor' and 'propriety' for just a moment … and oblige a lady?" Her lips yearned towards his, and he found his hands (of their own accord, it seemed) reaching down to encircle her waist, while her own hands came up and tangled in the thick hair at the nape of his neck, pulling him down to her.

Zeal closed his eyes, tasting on her lips the wine she had drunk, the sweetness of her own unique flavor. His hands knew what they were doing, even if he did not, and pulled her closer, to press against his chest (oh, the sweet softness of her body against his) while that delicious, lingering kiss went on and on.

"Acheron," she murmured against his mouth, and if his eyes had not been closed already he would have closed them then. As it was, he breathed for a moment and opened them, gently removing her to an arm's length away.

"So," she said, and even her good breeding could not disguise the bitterness in her eyes, or in her voice.

"I would if I could," he said, and meant it.

"But why can't you?"

Duty, he could have said. Honor. Propriety, even. But also, and importantly, "You're the Admiral's wife," he began.

It was answer enough. She turned away from him, settling herself back on the couch, taking great care in spreading her rustling skirts just so. His eyes were drawn to the motion of her smooth, white hands against the deep burgundy of her dress, and he cleared his throat.

Her eyes flicked up to his face, regarded him with studied disinterest for a moment, then dropped back to contemplation of her hands' work.

"Your husband," said Zeal, "already thinks you've been unfaithful..."

"Damn my husband!" cried Clarissa Trowbridge, raising her head with fierce passion. Zeal, startled, fell back a step from the blaze of fury in her eyes.

Fortunately for everyone at the opera house, not to mention her own reputation, Lady Trowbridge's outburst had coincided with the lead soprano's passionate crescendo. And now she repeated in a quieter voice, no less fierce, "Damn and rot him!" Zeal blinked at her, and she continued, "He suspected me of infidelity almost before the wedding vows were spoken. Perhaps he fears that a younger woman could never be faithful to an older man. I don't know. He has always been proud … and now that horrible rumor..." She looked at him. "Understand, Captain Zeal, I have never given him any reason to doubt my fidelity."

"Until today," Zeal added before he thought, and regretted the words before they left his mouth.

A quiver ran through her; the look in her eyes could have struck a man dead. "Well, yes," she said. "Until today." She looked away, fidgeting with her skirt. "It's all very fine if you're a man," she said. "You can do anything, go anywhere. Fight wars, write books, sail the seas, discover a cure for some disease. And fidelity lasts until you leave your home port, and then becomes just a word in the language you spoke back there. What recourse does a woman have, if she will not—if she cannot—just stay at home and knit doilies?"

On impulse, Zeal came to her and knelt on the carpet at her feet. Taking her hands (soft as silk against his own sea-roughened palms) he said, "But a woman has other recourse. Why—why, the Queen's own chief bodyguard is a woman, and a Knight of St George! And—and there have been other famous women, important women—physicians, scholars, wizards. Remember Fairrylyn the White!"

"You are kind, Captain Zeal," she murmured, turning her face away. "But those women had the spark of greatness that I lack. I only . . . I only wanted a bit of adventure, before I lost my chance to age and resignation and despair."

"Your chance?" He was going to reach up and touch her cheek; with a sharp mental reprimand he told his hand to avast that nonsense and stay where it was.

The smile she turned on him was bright and brittle. "If my husband is going to suspect me no matter what I do, I should at least give him a reason, shouldn't I?"

Zeal closed his eyes. "Oh, my lady..."

"Clarissa," she said, and he looked up. "Please. Even my own husband calls me Lady Trowbridge. Please, call me Clarissa."

"Clarissa, then." He smiled.

"And I shall call you Acheron."

"Even my own family," he said, "don't call me Acheron anymore."

"Then I shall be pleased to be the only person in the world who does." She smiled—a truer smile this time, though bitter sorrow still lurked around its edges—and patted the cushion next to her. "Come up here, Acheron," she said, "and sit beside me until the play is over."

"Gladly," he said, and did as he was told.

"I," said Captain Drake, as she and her mother exited their box, "hate the opera."

"Come now, darling, you hardly gave it a chance." Lady Amica took her daughter's arm. "Recall, please, that it is not one of your low, piratical entertainments. People of culture and breeding come to the opera."

"Ladies," a new voice interrupted, and a tall figure in a bright green jacket bowed before them, sweeping off his hat. When he rose, Drake bit her lip in surprise, and Lady Amica raised her eyebrow. "What a pleasure it is," this newcomer continued, "to be seeing you at such a place as this. And what a surprise, I might add. And don't you just look the very picture of beauty and gentility?"

"Appearances can be deceiving," Lady Amica murmured.

Whether he heard her or not, he made no sign, but continued, "I hope I find you well this eve, Miss Drake?"

"None the better for the seeing of you, Flynn Freeborn," replied Drake, her eyes narrowed. "I didn't know you were a fan of the opera."

"Well, now," said Flynn (for of course it was he), "and I could be saying the same of you, that I could—but friends and shipmates—or even ladies and gentlemen, as indeed we are—don't question each other's doings, even by implication." And he raised his pierced left eyebrow. "And who's this, then?" he continued, turning to the Lady Amica. "A friend of yours, Lady Drake? Or perchance a younger cousin?"

"Flynn," said Drake through her teeth, "this is my mother, the Lady Espera Amica of House Phinoparos. She's a dragon. Mother, meet Captain Flynn Freeborn."

"Charmed," said Amica, in the voice of winter.

"A dragon, now!" exclaimed Flynn, bowing and kissing her hand. "And here I was thinking all along that dragons were vast, great, scaly lizardlike creatures with enormous wings! If all dragons are as beautiful as you, lady, I'll be a devotee of dragons for the rest of my days." He made as though to kiss her hand again, but Amica, her eyes narrowed, snatched it from his grip.

"Darling," she said, "you meet such interesting people in your line of work."

Drake bared her teeth in something that no one in his right mind would ever describe as a smile.

"Now, don't be insulting the lass," said Flynn. "She rescued me from hell, she did! Saved me from an eternity of torment. Gave me a second lease on life and all that."

"Flynn," hissed Drake, "kindly stay out of this!"

"That I won't!" Flynn declared. "I've no wish to be disrespectful, that I don't, ma'am, especially not to a lady as beauteous as yourself. But I'd have to be a fool and blind to miss the animosity betwixt the two of you. And it seems to me that if a fellow—or a lady, as it were—can't depend upon his family for love and support, why, then he may as well hang himself from the highest yardarm, for there's no one in the world he can depend on." He looked from Lady Amica, whose face was white and pinched, to Drake, who simply looked appalled, and said, "But I'll not be troubling you with me presence any longer, that I won't. If you'll excuse me, I must see to the disposition of some rare and valuable volumes." He bowed once more, and then, resettling his hat on his head, took his leave.

Drake watched him, her eyes lingering (without her knowledge or approval) on the motion of his shoulder blades beneath his coat, the swishing of his long hair behind him. The beginnings of a smile crooked the corners of her mouth.

"Franceline," said Lady Amica, "I don't believe I approve of that young man."

Drake looked up at her mother and rolled her eyes. "You don't approve of anyone, Mother," she said. She caught one last glimpse of Flynn's back before he disappeared into the crowd. "As for myself, I believe he may have potential."

To see to the disposition of some rare and valuable volumes, Flynn had said, and that was what he did. Finding a porter in the atrium of the opera house, he inquired, could the gentleman direct him to the finest inn in town, and could he further aid him in transporting some old, rare books thither? The gentleman could, and vowed he would see to the delivery of the books himself; Flynn, with a bow and a smile, pressed the porter's hand (and pressed a large coin into that hand), and was about to go on his way when a loud and angry voice cried, "You there! Stop!"

It was with shock and horror that Captain Zeal recognized the same pirate he had seen before, deep in conversation with one of the porters who hung about the opera house. Bringing Clarissa's hand to his lips, he kissed it and murmured, "Forgive me," before dropping it and shouldering his way through the crowd, closer to where his adversary stood.

His adversary! After so many long months of searching, to think they stood now in the same building—in the very same room! His heartbeat quickened, and the starched swath of his cravat around his neck tightened like a noose. But no—it would be the pirate who would wear the noose! Drawing a deep breath, he let loose a shout that would have done the opera singers proud: "You there! Stop!"

The green-jacketed figure was in sight—he was hurrying away—but Zeal reached forward and grabbed him by the shoulder. "Stop, I say!"

The man turned, a cold look in his eyes. "I don't think you want to be doing that, mate," he said, very low.

"Oh," returned Zeal, just as coldly, just as softly, "I think I do. Pirate."

The pirate's gaze flicked to the left, then to the right—the crowd of opera-goers had paused in their egress to take in the post-show entertainment. In a deceptively gentle voice, the pirate said, "I came here to be watching scenes, mate, not causing 'em. You'd be well advised to let me go."

"I think not." Zeal bared his teeth. "I know who you are, devil, and I won't let you get away this time!"

"This time?" The pirate seemed genuinely baffled, and Doubt's broad, black shadow passed over Zeal's head. But no—this was the pirate, and this the chance he had awaited! And, indeed, the pirate shrugged, a philosophical look on his face. "Well, if it's a scrap you want, 'tis a scrap you'll have."

Zeal never even saw him move—but suddenly there was a fist colliding with his face, an explosion of white pain, and he was careening backwards, one hand held to his cheek. He grinned.

Somewhere, a lady screamed. Somewhere, people raised their voices in shock, in amusement, in speculation. But Zeal's field of vision had narrowed to a tunnel: and at the end of it, his foe. Roaring, he charged, and felt with satisfaction the shock as his fist smashed into the other's face.

Now, brawling is all well and good for a Sunday's entertainment, but gentlemen with a quarrel usually meet in a discreet location on a misty morning to kill each other like civilized beings, and the two fighters soon collected a crowd of gawking, gaping, shouting, pointing, cheering, gambling onlookers. Not that either noticed, each being too engrossed in the occupation of beating the stuffing out of his opponent to pay attention to his surroundings.

Among the crowd were three ladies … well, of course, dear reader, you understand that there were far more than three, but it is with three that we are chiefly concerned. The first, of course, was Lady Clarissa Trowbridge, who watched, horrified, as her escort made an ass of himself in front of Porta Bella's high society. Indeed, she had covered her face with her fan, and only watched the goings-on in short peeks snatched over its lacy edge.

The other two were Drake and her mother, who were engaged in another of their bitter wrangles as they approached, and so did not, at first, see what was going on. And then the crowd before them parted for a moment, and the situation was made clear.

"Well," said Drake, fluttering her own fan. "Isn't that interesting?"

Lady Amica's face was white to her nostrils. "Well indeed," she said, only the quiver of her eyelashes betraying her wrath.

But Drake smiled to herself, a cold, feline grin. "I shall write a letter first thing tomorrow," she murmured behind her fan. "Oh, such a letter!"

Meanwhile the tide of battle was turning. You would think that Captain Flynn, being the broader and heavier of the two, the veteran of many a barroom brawl, would have a distinct advantage in this kind of combat—and it first seemed that he would emerge victorious, covered in glory. The only thing covering him at present, however, was bruises, and with each well-timed, vigorous blow of Acheron's fists, more sprouted up on his skin like fungus covering an old tree trunk. Zeal had a cool, strategic mind, and each punch he threw was as devastating as a shot from the *Circe*'s cannons—and now those who had bet on the chap in the green coat were wishing they had thrown in their lot with the Navy captain instead.

Howling like a fiend possessed, Zeal fetched his foe a blow so fierce that it knocked the hat right off his head and knocked his feet out from under him, and with a resounding thud like the sound of a mighty oak crashing in the forest, Flynn fell.

Cheers erupted from the encircling crowd. Zeal, coming back to himself, looked round and saw a sea of unfamiliar faces—no, there was one he recognized, against all hope or probability—and he gasped, "Miss Drake?"

Then Flynn swept out with his feet and kicked Zeal's legs out from under him, landing him on the floor next to the winded pirate.

"Lord love you, Captain," said he, pulling his silver flask out of his coat pocket, "you fetched me quite a turn there, that you did." He swigged from the flask, and then, grinning at Zeal out of his bruised and purpling face, said, "Drink?"

Zeal glared at the fellow with cold dislike. The audience, seeing the show concluded, began to disperse, coins and bank notes changing hands, and Zeal closed his eyes, feeling, now that the battle was over, the quiver of reaction in his stomach. He opened his eyes again. "Yes," he said. "Thank you."

The pirate passed the silver flask, and Zeal took it and drank. Brandy washed down his throat, its cleansing fire burning down into his belly. He coughed a little, while the pirate grinned. "That's good," he said, returning the flask.

"Figured you could use it, mate, after such a tearing brawl." Propping himself up on one elbow, the pirate (who really did look worse for wear, like a mere sloop after a pounding from a frigate) said, "Now … no hard feelings, eh, mate? Can't have you taking me off and hanging me, and me as innocent as a newborn babe."

"Eh…?" said Zeal, suddenly feeling very stupid.

The flask descended in a blaze of silver and struck against his temple, and the world went black.

"And then didn't Cap'n Flynn just clock that navy dog across the forehead and knock him out cold?" Luna Shee concluded, joining the rest of the *Eschaton*s in raucous laughter and cheers. "And then he ran like hell, on account of being a sensible fellow, not wishing to wear the hempen necktie."

"Aye, I'll drink to that!" called Dead-Eye Duvay (who had twice been caught, and nearly hanged, by the Royal Navy), and raised his mug in salute.

When the shouting and cheering and spilling of frothy brew had died down, Dallon Moral leaned across the rough table. "But how do you know all this?" he asked.

Luna shrugged. "Got it from the cap'n."

"The captain?" Moral felt an unpleasant twinge in his belly. Guilt, his ma would've called it. "Our captain?"

"Who else?"

"And … where is he now, do you know?" For the wizard had some questions he would dearly have loved to put to Captain Flynn.

"With her, I reckon," the tattooed pirate replied. "Wouldn't you say, Lilly?"

Lilly Bones, voluble as ever, grunted assent.

"With … the captain?"

Luna gave another of her fluid, dismissive shrugs. "Who else?" she said again, twisting the knife in Dallon's heart.

But Flynn and Drake were not engaged as you would expect … not at the moment, anyway.

"Come back to bed, sweetheart," called Flynn, propped up among the pillows of his fine bed in the finest inn in Porta Bella.

Drake, quite gloriously bare, sat at the room's writing desk, pen scratching away. "I will," she replied, "in a moment. Let me finish this first."

"Very well," said he, watching her. "Take your time."

At last she finished, signed her name and sealed the letter, then glanced around as though looking for something.

"And what might you be seeking, my fine lass?"

Drake closed her eyes against a momentary twinge. Random had called her that, before.... She opened her eyes. "A dressing gown, if you have such a thing."

"And why," said Flynn, leaning across to her, "would you want to be covering up this…" He searched for the right word, spreading his hands in a wide, encompassing gesture. "This glory?"

"To send a letter." She flapped the missive in question at him. "Have a little patience, Captain. We've been up all night already." There was no dressing gown, so she took a sheet and wrapped it around herself, tugging the bell-rope and waiting until the servant arrived. And then she gave the man (who swallowed hard at the sight of that carelessly covered body) the letter and said, "See that this is delivered at once. It is of vital importance."

With a wrench, the servant raised his gaze to meet her eyes. "Yes, my lady," he said.

"Very good." She dropped a coin into his hand with the note and turned away, closing the door behind her.

"And have you no other pressing business this morning?" said Flynn, rising from the bed and going to her, putting his large, broad hands on her slender shoulders.

"Look at you," she said, reaching up and touching his bruised face (the sheet sliding to the floor as she released it). "What a beating he gave you."

"I've hardly felt it all night," he replied. And then he kissed her, and as they kissed, picked her up and carried her to the bed, where he laid her gently on the rumpled sheets.

Once, when Zeal was a lad, he and a friend had sneaked into a neighbor's orchard and gorged themselves on stolen apples. It was an escapade such as boys will have, nothing out of the ordinary, but when he got home with the juice of his ill-gotten gains still sticky on his cheeks, his father gave him such a dressing-down, you'd have thought he'd been caught stealing the Crown Jewels instead. His backside had smarted for days, and his infant pride much longer than that.

But the wrath of a father is nothing to the wrath of an Admiral.

For the better part of an hour Oberon Trowbridge stormed about his great cabin like a hurricane ill-contained, and poor Zeal stood as best he could before the tempest's blast. He heard every word of it, miserable and downcast: disgraceful business, really, shameful! A disgrace to his name, disgrace to his family, disgrace to the service! He was lucky he wasn't stripped of his command, stripped of his rank, set ashore without even a bumboat to call his own!

"As it is, Zeal," said Admiral Trowbridge, "you had best hope for a god-damned *miracle* to erase the stain from your name. A god-damned miracle," he repeated, shaking his head.

"I did think I had him, my lord," Zeal ventured.

"Oh, aye, I'm sure you did, lad. You're lucky Lady Trowbridge spoke up for you, or I'd have keel-hauled you myself. Shameful business!" He subsided into a thunderous muttering, of which only the odd "shameful" or "disgraceful" were at all intelligible. And then at last, feeling his subordinate had been chastised enough, he said, "I hope to see your *Circe* ready to set sail within the next two days, Zeal, to return to your mission. Any further delay could prove disastrous." And then he turned his back on the unhappy Zeal, clearly considering the subject closed.

It was a miserable and nauseated Zeal who rowed back to shore, and though he could not have known it, further misery awaited him at his lodgings.

"Letter for you, sir," said the landlord. Dizzy from his head injury, dispirited from his dressing-down, Zeal took it in silence and went at once to his room.

It was from Miss Drake.

There is no need to quote the text of the letter in full, but the final words made poor Zeal waver on his feet, then sink, unbelieving, to sit upon the bed.

After last night's abominable and distasteful display, it said, I must say plainly that I hope never to see you again. Stop your letters, for they will not be read.

"Franceline Drake." He breathed her name like a prayer, then crushed the letter in his hand and fell back onto the bed, shutting his eyes and pressing the crumpled paper against them. So many opportunities, gone, gone, never to arise again. The letter disintegrated under a wave of tears.

That evening, under the rose and vermilion streaks of a glorious sunset, as the evening tide was making, the merchant ship *Rhymer* put out to sea with a full complement of men and a brand-new sailing master on the books. Captain Drake stood on the wharf, watching it go, a contemplative frown on her face. She watched until it was hull-down on the horizon, and its sails were dark blurs, indistinguishable from clouds, against the peach-colored eastern sky.

And then she turned and walked through the darkening streets to the Smoking Bishop, where her crew was drinking, entering so suddenly that Dallon Moral (still living in fear of her wrath) barely had time to yelp, spill his beer, and duck under the table before she was seated across from him, regarding him with an amused little grin.

"Don't worry, wizard," she said, "I'm not going to keel-haul you."

"Or maroon me on a desert island with nothing but a giant sea tortoise and an aged marmoset for company?" Watching her, he held his body at the ready; he was a lean, gangly fellow, and he reckoned he could run pretty far and fast before she caught up with him.

"Or that, either." She nodded her thanks as the serving wench brought her a mug of frothy brew. "I've decided that you did me a favor, and though I don't appreciate being tricked, I think the outcome was positive enough that I'm willing to forgive."

"Oh..." said Dallon. "Well … that's a relief." In spite of himself, he thought of Flynn and the captain in bed together, and to hide his sudden blush he took a deep draught of beer, nearly drowning himself in his haste to swallow it down.

"There, there, mate," said Luna, thumping his back as he coughed. "Don't die, now."

"Thanks," he choked.

Drake was still gazing at him with amusement in her deep green eyes. "Still," she said, "though I'm willing to let bygones be bygones this time, if you ever do it again, I will keel-haul you, and without a moment's hesitation." Her grin was sharp and feral. "Now, unless you like being dangled underneath a sky-sailer's hull when she's hundreds of miles up..."

"You make your point abundantly clear, Cap'n," said Moral, looking down at his beer. "I am heartily sorry, and will never trick you into doin' something ever again. Even if it's for your own good," he added in an undertone.

"So glad that's settled," she said, and he knew by her smile that she'd heard every word he'd spoken. But she raised her hand and her voice and yelled, "Barkeep! Another round for me and my mates!" and further conversation was made impossible by the ensuing cheers.

Over the next two days Zeal drove his men hard, very hard, to finish the *Circe*'s refitting before the Admiral's deadline—and he scarcely drove himself any easier. If he gave himself no time to eat or rest, well, then he had no time to think, either, and the numb silence of exhaustion was better than the thoughts that would have haunted him, if he'd had the energy to think them.

The tide was making as *Circe* proceeded to sea, and since there was no doubt in anyone's mind that the Admiral was watching with a keen and critical eye (news travels fast on a man-of-war, and rumor travels even faster; the men knew full well what had transpired at the opera house, even if some of the details were a bit inaccurate), the *Circe*s made a show of warping out, setting the sails and wearing away that not even God Himself could have found fault with.

"What course shall I set, sir?" asked Lieutenant Morrow.

Zeal, whose gaze had been fixed on the receding rooftops of town, did not at once answer, and Morrow bit back a sigh and prompted, "Sir?"

With a jolt, Zeal returned to himself, to the deck of the *Circe*, the fresh smell of the sea air, the myriad tiny sounds of a working ship—and the disapproving frown of his first officer.

Zeal sighed. "We'll make for the Chai Republic, Mr Morrow. Kindly make it so."

"Aye, sir." Morrow hesitated. "The Chai Empire, you mean, sir?" All Porta Bella was a-buzz with the news, how a minor bureaucrat had beheaded most of Chai's parliamentary body (as it were) and crowned himself the first Emperor of Chai in over a thousand years. Morrow disliked to correct his captain, but facts are facts, and it doesn't do to get them wrong.

He needn't have worried. His captain gave him a long, indifferent stare, and said at last, in a dead voice, "Indeed. Right you are, Mr Morrow. Well, I don't suppose it's changed location as well," and then turned and disappeared into his cabin, there to read and re-read a certain letter, as though to read it again were to change the words it bore. But rereading brought no change, and at last he took the paper (already much-crumpled, its ink blotched and running) between his hands and shredded it, letting the scraps rain down on the deck like confetti on a dolorous parade.

"If love brings me no satisfaction," said he to himself, "very well, I will ask no satisfaction of love. I will ask nothing of love! I am done with it!" He surged to his feet as he said so, though he was hardly aware of it. Dusting the last scraps of Miss Drake's missive from his hands, he said, "I have my duty, and my duty is clear! I shall hunt down that blasted pirate, and I shall see him hanged." Looking down at the scraps of paper that littered the deck (and his steward, Duffy, was already fuming about the mess to clean up) he added, as though to himself, "I shall at least have that satisfaction."

CHAPTER 6

The Wreck of the Rhymer

"Women," said Captain Flynn Freeborn. "It's true, what they say about 'em. You can't live with 'em, and you might just die because of 'em."

Sighing, he settled back, trying to find a more comfortable position on his lonely chunk of rock. All around him, from horizon to horizon, sea and sky were clear and faultless blue and utterly empty. No ... no, not utterly: to windward, perhaps a cable's length away, floated the broken bits of mast and few shattered planks that were all that remained of his ship. And far to leeward, receding rapidly into the distance, the seething black clouds and howling winds that had deposited him here, on this solitary chunk of coral in the middle of the Shiraz Sea.

"Well, this is a fine mess you've gotten yourself into this time, Flynn Freeborn," he said to himself. "Sure, you should never have shipped out with Captain True."

Golden evening descended on Porta Bella, painting the western sky the delicate pastel shades of Easter eggs, dyeing the sea a deep purple-red. The merchant ship *Rhymer* rode at single-anchor, awaiting the last members of her crew. On the docks, a tall sailing man was bidding farewell to his love.

"Don't cry, sweetheart," he said, brushing her cheek with his callused thumb. "We'll meet again, that we will."

"Idiot," she said, turning her face away. "I'm not crying. And I don't give a damn whether we meet again or not."

He grinned. "You say that now, lass, but wait 'til a thousand miles of sea come between us. You'll find your thoughts turning to me, whether you will it or no. 'Ah,' you'll say to yourself, 'if only I hadn't spoken so cruelly to him then—I wonder if he thinks of me now!'"

"Idiot," she said again, though there was less rancor in her voice. "I've things to keep me busy while you're gone."

"Oh, I've no doubt of that, love," he said, and winked. "And when you tire of him, you know where to find me."

"Don't you have somewhere to go?" she demanded coldly. "'Lysander *Peregrine*'?"

"That's me name, so it is," he said. And, bending, he planted a kiss on her unwilling lips. "Until we meet again, me darling, fickle Lady Drake."

He turned away from her scowl, running lightly up the side of the ship. Already the crew was at work, preparing the ship for her departure. Her holds were stuffed with gold and gems, silks and lace, perfumes and wine—luxury items from Parmigiana, sure to fetch a high price in Chai.

I should go find my crew, thought Drake. *A prize like this would set us up for life.*

Yet she lingered on the docks, watching with a keen and professional eye as the *Rhymer* made ready and the evening tide began to ebb. The shadow of the sky deepened, and if she had not been watching the ship with particular attention, she would have missed the dark-cloaked figure that descended its side and began to hurry away.

Franceline Drake, however, had not become the most successful pirate of the modern era by being inattentive to her surroundings. She stepped into the cloaked figure's path—

—and groaned. "I might have known!"

"Why, darling!" cried her mother, throwing back her hood. "What a surprise, meeting you here! I thought for certain you'd be ... occupied."

"'In the mood for a cappuccino', eh?" said Drake sourly, raising her left eyebrow. "God knows there's plenty of cappuccino to be found on sorry old merchant tubs like that."

The Lady Espera Amica, of the ancient House Phinoparos, raised one sunset-colored eyebrow of her own and sniffed. "I don't believe I am obliged to explain myself to you, darling," she said. "If I want to deliver illicit goods to the captain of that ship, in secret, at night, without shouting it out to the entire world, that is certainly my business." She gave a delicious little smile. "Oops," she said.

Disgusted, Drake rolled her eyes. "Mother," she said, "that ship is going to Chai."

"Yes," Amica agreed. "And?"

"*You're* going to Chai. And you'll probably get there faster than that poor fat old slug."

"Yes," Amica agreed. "I really fail to see your point, my dear. Do they not teach logic on the high seas?"

"I don't know why I even bother talking to you," Drake said.

"Well," said Amica, looking down at her perfect fingernails. "Generally, you don't." For a moment, veiled by thick lashes, her eyes met those of her daughter. She bit her lower lip, appeared to come to a decision, and said, "Listen, my dear. I know you are the product of your unfortunate upbringing, and that you very rarely listen to me, but can you do me a very great favor?"

"What favor?" asked Drake, cool and noncommittal, one hundred per cent the product of her unfortunate upbringing.

Amica looked neither left nor right, but continued in a lower tone, "I know that the *Rhymer* makes a tempting prize for someone of your profession (if one can call it that). But I beg you, leave her alone! It is vital that she reach her destination unharmed."

"Why?" Drake's eyes narrowed.

Amica shook her head. "I cannot say. Cannot you trust me, just this once?"

"Don't be so melodramatic, Mother," said Drake. "I only trust you as far as you trust me. Why should I do as you say?"

She had never seen her mother so agitated. She wrung her long, elegant fingers, gnawing on her lower lip as her eyes searched the ground, as though the answer might be written there. At last, she met her daughter's gaze again and said, "Well, if you cannot trust me, you cannot. Why should you, indeed? I should be very sad, however, to see anything unpleasant happen to that handsome young man of yours." Tugging her hood up over her bright hair, she turned and walked away, leaving her daughter alone on the docks.

"He's not my young man!" Drake shouted after her.

There was a tower in the city of Parmigiana, where the Doge, Lorenzo di Capellini, found it expedient to keep dangerous criminals, malcontents, members of the Gelati family, and any other person likely to make his rule less peaceful. At the top of this tower was a room accessible by means known only to the Doge and his most trusted men, where the most dangerous criminals of all were contained until such time as they could be disposed of.

The room had been empty for decades, ever since the death of the infamous madman Leonardo da Gelati, who had claimed (among other fabulous stories) that Lorenzo di Capellini had been responsible for the wholesale slaughter of his entire family during holy services one Sunday morning. Oh, the wild fancies of the mentally deranged! In his insanity, he had even attempted to assassinate Parmigiana's beloved Doge—and he had ended his life in that narrow tower room, his mad harangues abruptly stilled when he choked to death on a bone in his soup.

But now the room had an occupant once more.

"Who is he?" asked the youngest guard, new to his job and yet unaware of its strange etiquette.

"Better you don't know," his cohorts replied. "He crossed the will of the Doge."

They came at night to fetch him, two black-clad members of the Doge's personal guard, tying a sack over his head and shoving him into a dark carriage with muffled wheels. It sped through the shadowed city streets in silence, to some destination unknown. An unmarked grave outside the city walls, no doubt.

The tower guards shook their heads. Thus to all who crossed the will of the Doge.

Two days out from Porta Bella, Captain Zeal broke the seal on his secret orders. In substance they were nearly identical to his public orders, commanding him to continue his fruitless bloody chase for that elusive bloody pirate, apprising him that the merchant ship *Rhymer* had just set out from Porta Bella, loaded with gems and silks and all manner of precious goods, a ripe target for a greedy pirate ship.

His eyes skimmed on to the middle paragraph:

Among the Rhymer's cargo is a certain item, a gift from Her Majesty to the newly crowned Emperor of Chai. You will protect this item at all costs. It must not fall into the hands of the enemies of the realm.

Fail to comply with these orders at your peril.

Zeal folded the orders and stared out the stern windows, where the *Circe*'s wake frothed white against the cerulean sea. A faint smile twisted his lips. "Well," he said, "that's fairly straightforward."

Odd, though, that a gift from Queen Miranda of Camembert should be on board a merchant ship out of Parmigiana. Unless.... He tapped the paper against the side of his face, thinking. He already knew that the *Eschaton* was in the area; if her captain found out about a valuable trinket aboard a lone merchantman in the middle of the Shiraz Sea, he would not hesitate to snap it up.

And Zeal would be there when he tried.

A broad grin split his features. "Thank you, my lord!" he breathed, clutching his orders to his breast.

The Doge was drinking espresso out of a tiny cup worth more than the gross national product of Garam Masala when the first of his visitors arrived. "Ah," he said, as two black-clad Carbonare propelled the first guest between them, "Welcome, my friend, welcome!" And to his men he added, "You may as well remove the bag from his head."

They did as he bade them (unthinking, automatic obedience being one of the first lessons taught at Carbonara school), and at the Doge's nod, left the man revealed alone with their prince.

"Spyridon, my friend," said the Doge, advancing with open arms. "I am so sorry about the accommodations. Thank you for your understanding."

"My lord," replied the other man, warily. He didn't look like the sort of fellow that Lorenzo di Capellini would call 'friend.' He looked, with his unshaven cheeks and his cable-knit sweater, more like an out-of-work playwright. Flynn Freeborn would have recognized him as the itinerant opera critic and sometime sailor, Crispin S Teague. "I'm honored to stand once more in your presence."

"Now, now," said the Doge. "There's no need to stand on ceremony. In fact, there's no need to stand at all. Have a seat." His eyes narrowed with amusement at his little joke. When Crispin had taken a chair, he said, "Cappuccino?"

"No. Thank you."

Di Capellini raised one pencil-thin eyebrow. "Spyridon, my friend. You seem tense. What have I done to warrant your distrust?"

"Well," said the man called Spyridon, clearing his throat and looking to the side, "you did have me arrested, beaten, and locked in the Tower."

"Piffle." The Doge waved a dismissive hand. "What are such things among friends?" He smiled, inviting Spyridon to join in his amusement—but Spyridon's solemn face did not so much as splinter. "My friend," said the Doge. "To the world, you appear but a mendicant historian—"

"Because I am a mendicant historian," Spyridon interrupted under his breath.

"But to me, you are a trusted ally and a source of valuable information."

"A spy, you mean," muttered Spyridon.

Di Capellini heard him perfectly (it was his excellent hearing that had saved him from Leonardo da Gelati's frenzied attack), but did not reply. "It were best if the world in general knew nothing of our arrangements. You understand that, of course."

Spyridon kept his expression under control. "Of course, my lord. I understand."

"Wonderful." The Doge's grim look broke into a dazzling smile. "Now—" he began, but a knock at the door killed his fulsome speechifying almost before it began. "Ah!" he cried. "That must be our other guest! What marvelous timing!" He rose and went to the door, and Crispin Teague's mistrustful gaze followed. The Prince of Parmigiana was a small man, slight of build and narrow of frame, but he did an admirable job of blocking the doorway, and it was not until he stepped aside that Crispin got a view of the Doge's other guest.

She was tall and slim, with an improbable shock of multi-colored hair that stuck in a tail straight out from her head before cascading down past her waist. She wore a pair of tiny spectacles perched on the end of her nose: the right lens was blue, and the left one red. By her outré appearance, Crispin guessed her either a pirate or a singing telegram.

"Spyridon," said the Doge, and Crispin got to his feet. "May I present to you February Valentine, captain of the flying ship *Pandora*?"

"I've heard of you," he said, ignoring her outstretched hand. "You pick over ancient ruins, hunting for rare and valuable artifacts, which you auction off to the highest bidder. You're not above a bit of smuggling, either, I hear."

"I prefer to think of it as 'treasure hunting' and 'creative resource redistribution'," said Valentine, grinning at him over the rims of her parti-colored glasses. Her eyes were yellow. He drew back, startled, and her grin widened. "A grateful alchemist in Eclaire gave me these," she said, "in exchange for a magical gauntlet. Neat, huh?" She winked.

"The knowledge of the ancients should not be put to such petty uses," he said, his voice very low.

"Hey," she replied, "if we can, why shouldn't we?"

"A fascinating question for the philosophers," said Lorenzo di Capellini, shepherding them to their seats. "And if we were all philosophers, no doubt we could spend hours—nay, years!—debating it. But as we are not philosophers, but men and women of business, perhaps we should turn to the matter at hand."

"Which is what, exactly?" asked February, flopping into the nearest chair. "I was just about to close a sweet deal with a black monk when I got your message. My lord," she added.

Crispin's ears perked up. "A Black Monk of Mordghre?" he said. "I thought they were all wiped out in the war."

She shrugged. "You find a couple of 'em here and there, now and then," she said.

"Perhaps it were best if you gave your report first, Spyridon, my friend," said the Doge. There was an icy edge to his voice. He was patient with them because they were useful—but he would not abide many more distractions. Crispin schooled his face to impassivity.

"I met the draconic envoy to Chai in Porta Bella, as you suggested, my lord. She was receptive to the plan, and agreed to give Captain Thomas True, of the merchant vessel *Rhymer*, the artifact we discussed. It is to be presented to Emperor Katsukare as a gift from Queen Miranda of Camembert, to honor his coronation."

The Doge nodded. None of this information was new to him—but he was pleased that his instructions had been carried out so efficiently.

February Valentine, whose eyebrows had quirked at the word "artifact," leaned forward in her chair. "What sort of gift?" she asked, voice full of feigned unconcern.

Crispin glanced at the Doge. Di Capellini nodded, and Teague answered her. "I didn't see it myself. Some sort of magical gewgaw from Stratocumulopolis, I imagine. Camembert seeks to flaunt her alliance with the dragons, impressing Chai with her power and wealth."

But February's brain had obviously stopped processing his words—she was stuck back at "magical gewgaw." "Pretty valuable, I suppose?" she asked, still with that elaborate lack of interest.

Lorenzo di Capellini leaned back in his chair and sipped at his now-cool espresso. A faint smile tugged at the corners of his mouth. "I hear it is extraordinarily rare," he said. "One of a kind, in fact. Unique." And he watched the naked greed blaze in her golden eyes.

"It is yours," he said. "All you have to do is obtain it."

The acquisitive joy at his first words gave way to consternation at his last, and she frowned.

"I'm not sure I like this bargain," she said. "I'm no thief. I take things that other people have forgotten or lost, that's all. And I'm sure this Captain Whatever-his-name-is won't just turn over a priceless artifact on my say-so."

Displeasure tugged the line of the Doge's mouth straight. "The captain of the *Rhymer* will be in no position to dispute the ownership of the item," he said. "All you have to do is acquire it. Do we have an accord?"

"I'm no pirate," said February, "and I won't kill."

"No one is asking you to." The Doge's patience was about to run out.

But the treasure hunter grinned, her teeth a blaze of white against her golden skin. "I know," she said. "I just needed to say it out loud, is all." She stuck out her hand. "We have an accord."

They shook hands (the Doge barely brushing her hand with the tips of his fingers before withdrawing), and she got to her feet. "I'll show myself out, thanks," she said—but when she reached the door she paused, turning back to look at the Prince of Parmigiana. "You won't want to see it, once I've got it, will you?"

"No." The Doge waved his hand. "No. In fact, the less I see of you, ever again, the better for everyone."

She grinned. "Just making sure." She turned to Crispin, tipping her first two fingers to him in a mocking salute. "Catchya later, 'Spyridon'." She winked over the rims of her strange glasses, and was gone.

Crispin's stomach turned to lead within him. "She knows," he murmured, sinking back in his chair. "She knows I'm more than I claim to be."

"My dear Spyridon," said the Doge, arching an eyebrow at him, "everyone knows that."

"They do?" How much did di Capellini know? There was a pellet of swift-acting poison sewn into his cuff—he would kill himself before he allowed himself to be captured—his secrets wrung from him by the Doge's expert torturers....

But di Capellini simply laughed. "You don't expect anyone to believe you're nothing more than an itinerant opera critic, do you? Honestly, Spyridon, have sense. You are a man who has seen many things—your experience shows plainly on your face. I'm sure any woman would be intrigued to know your secrets." He smirked, eyes crinkling at the corners (the eyes themselves remained hard and bright and watchful), and slowly, Crispin relaxed. Di Capellini knew nothing. He forced his mouth into a smile, heard the mechanical sound of his own laughter. He was safe enough.

"I'll have my guards show you out," the Doge was saying. "Would you prefer to escape again, or would you rather be rescued? Or I could arrange for a false suicide..."

"Ah," said Crispin, faintly. "Nothing too complicated. Simple plans are the best plans." Would that he had remembered his own advice, long ago.

Yes, he was still safe.

But for how long?

The cry originated on the quarterdeck: "Pass the word for Mr *Peregrine*! Pass the word for Mr *Peregrine*!" It grew louder and more raucous until, at last, the man himself was found up in the maintop, singing to himself in a melodious baritone and smoking a pipe.

"Oy, Peggy, what're you at?" said the mariner who found him, a yellow-faced man called Walleyed Felipe. "Cap'n's been hollering for you this last glass and more."

Even on a ship like the *Rhymer* it was a bad idea to annoy the skipper—and Captain Thomas True was not known for his sweet temper. By the time *Peregrine* had extinguished his pipe, slid down a backstay, and approached the holy quarterdeck, Tom True was literally hopping mad.

"Damn your eyes, *Peregrine*!" he greeted, jumping up and down. "What the hell are you playing at? Are you not an officer on my ship?"

"Aye, sir," said *Peregrine*.

"And are not the officers on my ship subject to my command?"

"Aye, sir," said *Peregrine*, "that they are."

And now Captain True detected a whiff of alcohol about his subordinate—a whiff, did I say? Nay, a reek! Mr *Peregrine* stank of spirits—a cloud of fumes surrounded him—like being downwind of a distillery. Leaning forward and flaring his broad nostrils, Captain True said, "Mr *Peregrine* … are you drunk?"

"Aye, sir," said *Peregrine*, wavering a little, "just a touch." And he hiccuped, as if for punctuation.

Now, Tom True was no teetotaller—liked his grog as much as the next man—but you can't have your officers setting a bad example. Next thing you knew, the whole crew'd be drinking and carousing and carrying on, none of them competent to so much as heave the lead or shake out a reef in the main t'gallant sail. His bushy grey eyebrows lowered on his brow and met at the bridge of his nose in a look of thunderous displeasure.

"By God!" he cried. "By God! This is a rum do, indeed it is!"

"Lit'rally," said *Peregrine*, narrowing his eyes with amusement. "Drink?"

But Captain True shoved the proffered bottle aside, earning a hurt look from his sailing master. "Mr Corby!" he said in a loud voice.

"Aye, sir!" said the first mate, appearing beside his captain with amazing rapidity and a sharp click of his heels.

"Mr Corby," said the captain, "what do we do with a drunken sailor?"

"Feed him enchiladas?" suggested *Peregrine*, swaying a little and looking winsome.

"Well, sir," said Corby, clasping his hands behind his back and considering, "generally we put him in the longboat 'til he's sober."

"Make it so, Mr Corby."

"Aye, sir." And, taking the befuddled *Peregrine*'s arm, "Come along, then, mate. You'll be sleeping cold and wet tonight."

Cold and wet indeed, and it was with a pitying look back at the longboat, hauling aft, that Langer Corby rejoined his captain on the quarterdeck. A conciliating remark was on his lips, but Captain True was in no mood for conciliation. Indeed, he took no note of the mate at all, but stomped back and forth along the sacred windward side of the quarterdeck, grousing in a tone that hardly qualified as "under", the burden of his complaint being, when a dear old friend of yours sends you a sailing master to replace the one you lost—a dear, old, well-trusted friend, yet—you expect the replacement to be at the very least competent, and not a witless, shiftless, good-for-nothing, rum-soaked layabout who couldn't steer a ship straight across a flat sea!

Corby hid a smile as the captain turned on his heel and approached. "All squared away, sir," he said.

"Very good, Corby. The deck is yours."

"Aye, sir." And Corby watched as Captain True went below.

Yes, Thomas True had been ill-used indeed by his old friend Crispin Teague.

He had been eating an early dinner or a late breakfast in his favorite inn in Porta Bella, the Frigid Insect, pondering (to the best of his abilities) several things at once: the bales of silk and strongboxes of jewels even now being loaded into his ship; the need to sail on the next tide; the mysterious noblewoman who had approached him earlier in the day; and the problem of what to do about replacing his sailing master, the unfortunate Jonas Svein, who had been devoured by giant sea turtles when the *Rhymer* put in for water off the coast of Garam Masala. A bad business all around, that, bad in that the shrieks of poor Jonas had unnerved the men as they filled the water barrels, making them hard to handle for the last leg of the cruise; worse in that he now had no sailing master, no one to navigate the ship through the shoals and reefs that outlay the coast of Chai, the destination of the above-mentioned silk and jewels.

Let it be said that Tom True was not a cheerful man to begin with, that these unhappy thoughts had brought his spirits even lower, and that his unsatisfactory late breakfast (or early dinner) was doing little to raise them. Thus, he was disinclined to be friendly when a long shadow fell across his plate of scrambled eggs and hash, and he looked up with a sharp and unwelcoming scowl.

"What do you want?" he asked.

"Be you Cap'n True, of the *Rhymer*?" replied the stranger. The strong light from the windows and the inn's open door cast his face into shadow, but he had a pleasant voice, and the accent of a sailing man, and True thawed a little.

"Aye," he said. "Who's asking?"

"A mate of mine tells me you're in need of a sailing master. I hope he hasn't led me astray."

"Depends," said True. "Who's this mate of yours?"

"Crispin Teague's his name, and here's his letter to me, if you're needing proof."

True took the note, but the well-known name dissolved any last doubts he might have held. "Aye, I know Crispin, and if he says you're capable, then capable you must be. How soon can you ship out?"

"How soon do you need me?"

"We sail with the evening tide."

"Then I'm yours from here on." The sailor stuck out his hand, grinning.

But True had one last question. "What name will I be entering on my ship's books?" he asked.

If the stranger hesitated, it was for less than an instant, less than an eyelash-flicker of time, and then he said, "*Peregrine*'s my name. Lysander *Peregrine*."

"Well, then, pleased to make your acquaintance, *Peregrine*," said Tom True, and the two men shook hands.

And now Flynn Freeborn (and he had been Flynn Freeborn long enough that Lysander *Peregrine* felt like the alias, and Captain Flynn the true identity) lay in the *Rhymer*'s longboat as it towed astern of the merchant ship, his flask in his hand. Closing his eyes, he tipped the mouth of the bottle towards his own mouth, waiting for the bright, amber-colored stream of liquid forgetfulness. It did not come, however, and with a sigh he opened his eyes, sat up, and ascertained that his flask was, in fact, empty.

"Damn," he said mildly, tucking the empty bottle into his breast pocket and lying back down. Shifting his length into a comfortable position, he closed his eyes once more and waited for sleep.

He crooned to himself a lullaby his mother used to sing him (long ago, far away), and the cool night pressed against his eyelids, the phosphorescence of the *Rhymer*'s wake rising up around him, the starlight beaming down. Peace, it said to him, peace. And sleep came, but it was not the peaceful roborative oblivion that heals man of his waking wounds, nor yet the blank unconsciousness of the grape, but a restless torment broken by periodic flashes of memory: faces he had known, words he had said, things he had done, and through it all running like the slow drone of the bass violin beneath the convolutions of the string quartet a rising pressure in his chest, in his throat, that would surely break if he could only scream, but his mouth remained closed, his vocal cords slack, and he writhed in silent agony on his hard wooden bed.

There are things the soul of man is not meant to remember, places from which it is not meant to return—but he had returned from them, and he remembered them still, if only in the nightly torment of his dreams. He no longer woke up screaming—the dreams would not loosen their grip so far—but it was a haggard, red-eyed *Peregrine* who was hauled on board the next morning, and he looked to have aged twenty years in the night.

"Storm's a-brewin', mate," whispered Walleyed Felipe, his starboard eye winking at *Peregrine*, his portside one goggling out to sea.

"Oh, aye?" said *Peregrine*, but without much interest. A tot of grog would set him right—aye, just a wee nip...

"Mr *Peregrine*, the captain wants to see you in his cabin," said First Mate Corby, approaching him.

"Oh, aye?" said *Peregrine*, rasping his hand over the three-days' growth on his chin. "Does he want me to be presentable, at all? Or is it a thing of urgency?"

"You've time for a shave and a change of shirt, at least," Corby replied, with a look of concern. "Are you all right, *Peregrine*? You look." But just how Mr *Peregrine* looked escaped him, and he finished with, "I'll tell the captain you're on your way."

"Aye. Thank'ee, sir."

A dash of water on his face made him feel more human, and down in his berth he stropped his razor and contemplated that face in the glass. "How far have you come, Flynn Freeborn?" he asked himself. "Or have you made any progress at all?" The razor had a wicked edge; he held it to his throat and contemplated the line it made there, then shook his head with a weary grin. "And even if the dear Lord hadn't made a sin of self-slaughter," he said, "there's always hope." The eyes of the man in the glass lacked conviction, and he repeated the words, as though repetition would make them ring true: "Aye, there's always hope."

Clean and shaved, he waited on Captain True in his cabin, a cabin as sparse and unwelcoming as the captain himself.

"Sit down, Mr *Peregrine*," said Captain True.

Peregrine, removing his hat, did as he was told.

"How long have you been at sea, Mr *Peregrine*?"

Flynn thought about it. He'd been twenty-eight years old when the angry ghost of Lucenza di Ladro, called by some the Queen of Pirates, dragged his spirit down to hell—and that had been fifty-five years ago. "Oh," he said at last, the actual figures escaping him, "long and long, sir. Since I was a wee little sprout." And I've been me own master for most of the years since then, he thought, with a weary look at True. Not a bad man, to be sure, but by no means a captain after Flynn's own heart.

"Hmm," said True. "And how long have you known Crispin Teague?"

"Why, as to that, sir," said Flynn before he thought, "he's but a recent acquaintance, he is, a generous man who lent some aid to a stranger in need."

"Hmm," said True, the words Just as I thought all but forming a scrolling marquee over his grizzled head. He got to his feet, swaying with the motion of the ship. "I tell you how it is, Mr *Peregrine*," he said. "Crispin is an old mate of mine; we sailed together many years ago, and I'll not hesitate to tell you he saved my life on a number of occasions. He's a good man, and I've never had cause to doubt his judgment."

Until today, thought Flynn bleakly, seeing in his mind the path the conversation must take, like the arc of a cannon ball before it struck a fine ship's hull.

"Understand me," said Captain True. "I've no doubt in my mind that, under different circumstances, you'd be a fine sailing master, a fine sailor." He cleared his throat. "But I can't be having your drunken antics endangering my ship or my crew, Mr *Peregrine*. It don't answer, not a bit."

"Nossir," said Flynn, looking down at his hands.

True paced back towards his desk. "I'm a generous man, and I owe Crispin a great deal," he said. "I'll give you until we make landfall to reform your ways. But mark me, Mr *Peregrine*—" and he wagged one thick finger at *Peregrine*'s nose, "—if I see you cutting up, or neglecting your duties, or God forbid drunk on your watch, I'll clap you in irons and set you ashore at the first island I find, for I cannot have it on my ship, no, I will not abide it. Am I clear?"

"Clear as daylight, sir," said Flynn, head still bent. "Clear as the sea on which we sail."

"Very good." True jerked his head. "Back to work, then."

"Aye-aye, sir." Flynn touched his knuckles to his brow and heaved himself up out of the chair, feeling every one of his eighty-three years as he made his way from the cabin and out into the sun.

"Get some rest, *Peregrine*," said Langer Corby as he walked past. "It's not your watch for hours yet; you've time for some sleep. In fact," he added, now that the sun was full on *Peregrine*'s face, and he could see the unhealthy pallor beneath the sailor's tan, the deep purple circles beneath the sailor's eyes, "perhaps you should report to the sick bay. Perhaps the surgeon can give you a draught to help you."

"Aye, sir," said *Peregrine*, barely pausing in his shamble down to his berth. "Thank'ee, sir."

And as he swung into his hammock, he thought, Bloody merchants, anyway. Back in the day I'd've taken this ship before they could blink, that I would, and been halfway to the other side of the world before they'd noticed anything was amiss. Oh, aye, back in the day I'd not submit to their infamous tyranny.

And then, as sleep wrapped its arms around him and began dragging him down, he thought, So why do I now?

He slept.

Captain Drake leant against the taffrail, watching the shadow of the *Eschaton* flicker across the waves below. It was a fine day, a bright day, a clear day, but there was an edge to the air she little liked, a feeling.... You got the sense for it, once you'd been sailing awhile, and Drake had been sailing sea and sky alike since she was old enough to walk.

She sighed, one hand caressing the silky wood of the *Eschaton*'s rail. Without looking at the plunging mercury in the barometer, she could feel the storm's approach. She should give the orders, prepare the ship. Sky-sailers were handy craft, could sail right into the teeth of a wind, but they couldn't bear a blow any better than the smallest sloop; she should wear away, find a sheltered cove to wait out the storm. From the tingling of her skin, it was going to be a bad one.

"Captain."

She had heard no one's approach. "Wizard," she said, without turning.

Dallon Moral settled beside her, leaning his scrawny elbows against the rail.

"You know," she said, "just because I've forgiven you doesn't mean you can make bold to approach me whenever you want. There are certain rules of behavior aboard a ship."

"Yup," said the wizard, but made no move to go. His colorless eyes scanned the ocean—the lookouts should be sighting the *Rhymer* any moment now. The merchant had almost a week's head start, but an awkward little tub like that could never out-sail the *Eschaton*.

"Did you want something?"

"Nope." He continued gazing out into the distance. "Reckon we'll catch up with her soon?"

She bit back a sigh. "I reckon we might," she replied, putting a mocking twist on the words.

"Hm." He turned around, resting his back against the rail and tipping his face up into the afternoon sun, closing his eyes. She frowned at him. He was an ugly fellow—had his nose been broken at some point, or had it grown that way naturally? Reluctantly, she compared him to Captain Flynn: a handsome devil, and he knew it too. She scowled.

"Don't you have somewhere to go?"

"Me?" The wizard didn't even open his eyes. "No. No, not in particular."

"Perhaps you should find someplace." Count to ten, her mother had always advised her when she was angry. She'd never gotten past four.

Moral turned his head and looked at her. His eyes were clear as quartz crystal. Only pride kept her from stepping back.

"Maybe we all should," he said, and waited.

She blinked. "What?"

He sighed. "Sail away?" he prompted her. "Find another prize? Somewhere not here?"

For a moment, she almost considered it. Her mother had been sincere, earnest in her plea. And there was a storm coming....

No. She shook her head. When had Amica ever done anything for her? Never, that was when. Captain Drake made her own way in the world.

"Your mother loves you," said Moral, still pinning her with that disconcerting gaze.

Drake scowled at him. "Get out of my sight," she said. "Go help Cid in the engine room. Or scrape barnacles off the hull. Go peel potatoes! Anything! Just leave me alone!"

His gaze lingered on her a moment longer. Then, "Aye-aye, Cap'n," he said, and walked away.

"What's he playing at?" demanded Luna Shee, her bare arms wrapped around the ship's wheel, watching the wizard as he walked by.

Lilly did not look up from her whittling. "Being a nuisance," she said.

Luna snorted. "Cap'n Flynn, now," she said. "There's a man."

"Aye," agreed Lilly Bones, a little smile on her massive, scarred face. "That he is."

All that long day, the level of mercury in the glass dropped, dropped steadily, dropped farther than anyone had ever seen it drop before, portending dirty weather of epic proportions.

"I've taken in sail, sir," said Lieutenant Thomas Morrow, standing some little distance from Captain Zeal on the *Circe*'s quarterdeck. When the captain did not reply, Morrow cleared his throat, shuffled his feet, and repeated his report, adding, "Perhaps we should retrieve the boats as well, sir?"

Zeal's back was to his lieutenant. He didn't even bother to turn as he said, "Oh, yes. A capital idea, Tom. Make it so."

Ye-e-es... Lieutenant Morrow gritted his teeth and soldiered on (or perhaps it would be more accurate to say he sailored on, since as a rule he had little use for soldiers, they being a pack of filthy drunkards in general, and sad ignorant landlubbers besides). "Sir," he said. "Do you have a plan, for when we encounter the *Eschaton*?"

And then Zeal did turn, fixing his premier with the gaze of a man who, through sleepless nights, pain, anger and adversity, was no longer quite sane. Not, Morrow thought bitterly, that Captain Zeal had been all that sane to begin with.

"The storm," said Captain Zeal, never blinking his bugged-out eyes. "The storm will finish him, Tom, and then he'll be ours!"

"Er..." began Morrow, but his poor mad captain was already turning away from him. "See to the boats, Mr Morrow," he said.

"Aye, sir," said Morrow, and went.

When the promised storm came, it came all at once, blowing up with a shriek, turning the blue sky to purple-black in an instant, pouring down rain by the bucket and whipping up the sea to such a feverish mass of seething water that sea and sky were all but indistinguishable, and men had to cover their faces to breathe, it was as though forty days and forty nights of rain had been condensed into forty hours. It was touch-and-go for the first twenty-four, snatch a bite and a wink while you had a chance, the wind howling in from all points of the compass and not a man knowing up from down and right from wrong, but at the end of the first day the rain broke for a moment, and a shaft of golden light fell upon the main topmast, limning it in a brief blaze of glory.

"Look," breathed Zeal, his eyes on the sky overhead. "There he is."

Then the clouds slammed back in, blacker than before, and the wind let out a redoubled shriek, and the world dissolved back into chaos.

The *Pandora* was unique among airships, a trim little sky-sailer of her captain's own design based on carvings she had found in an ancient ruin deep in the Ironback Mountains, early in her treasure-hunting days. From the outside she looked a little like a bubble, or a strange bird-fish-insect hybrid. She was small, only big enough to fit half a dozen people, if they weren't too particular about personal space, and instead of the open-air maindeck of most sky-sailers (based, as they were, on the designs of a former ocean-going pirate, made practicable only by a huge expenditure of magic), her decks were completely enclosed. She had a cockpit (her forward end was a single pane of diamond-hard glass, affording the pilot a dazzling view), was steered by means of an array of pedals and levers, rather than the traditional wheel, and could (if necessary) be operated entirely by a single person.

Convenient, since February Valentine preferred to work alone.

She was contemplating a means of propulsion that didn't depend on magic at all—a fragment of an ancient scroll, found in yet another ruin (possibly the site of the famous Library of Finitia, which had burned to the ground over two thousand years before), had suggested steam power. How would it work, though? It would be an unwieldy system, certainly, requiring both large quantities of water and the means of heating it. Still, it'd be worth it, to avoid the tyranny of wizards and their tedious morality.

A dial on the panel before her whirred, and a warning bell dinged, and February frowned, leaning forward to tap the glass. Damn thing had been malfunctioning for days ... she'd have to give the old boat an overhaul, after....

Some strange motion caught the tail of her eye, and she looked up.

A wall of cloud the color of bruises, pulsing with green and purple lightning, was boiling up before her, filling her field of view. On her current course, the *Pandora* would fly right into its heart.

"Oh, hell, no," said February Valentine. She stomped one pedal, yanked on the starboard lever and thrust forward on the port.

Pandora banked and turned back the way she had come, fleeing the storm.

"Lord, *Peregrine*," said Corby, dripping and wiping his sodden face as he ducked into the wardroom, "it's like the Great Flood come again. If we survive, I'll light a candle at every church I come to for the rest of my days."

"Aye, indeed?" said Flynn, raising his head off his arms. He was too tired to rest, too numb to eat: he had nibbled the corner of the biscuit in front of him, but had been unable to summon the energy to finish it. "I hadn't taken you for a religious man, so I hadn't."

"Well," said Corby with a little laugh, "I never have been, you know. But how I love my life! And how grateful I'll be if God lets me keep it." He gripped the edge of the table as he spoke, and as the ship gave a mighty lee-lurch, and Flynn's biscuit went flying, he caught the hard chunk of bread and said, "Were you eating this?"

Flynn shook his head. "Have at it, mate. It's almost my turn back on deck anyway."

Corby bolted the dry biscuit gratefully.

"How're the men holding up, then?" Flynn asked the question idly, but he watched Corby as the mate considered.

"Well enough," Corby said at last. "Knotting and splicing like madmen, pumping like fiends. I thought we were all lost, when the foresail split..."

Flynn nodded. True was mad to carry so much sail in a blow like this. The *Rhymer* was a crank old tub to begin with, and carrying such a press of sail drove her deeper into the trough of each massive green wave, while the water rose high on either side of her and the wind died for half an instant, threatening to swamp her. Each time she rose to the crest of the next wave, the crew breathed a prayer of thanksgiving—but each time she rose, she wallowed more heavily than the last, and everyone knew there'd come a time she'd rise no more.

"Well," he said, "it's back into it for me." He heaved himself to his feet, plucking his sodden oilskin off the bench beside him and throwing it over his shoulders. In the doorway he paused, hesitated, and then said, "Mayhap I'll be lighting candles right alongside you, if we survive."

But Corby had laid his head down on the table and was already fast asleep.

"Hell" is a word we use casually, without thinking, rarely grasping its true implications. "She has plunged me into hell!" might the rejected suitor groan (as Acheron Zeal had groaned every night since leaving Porta Bella), without understanding the import of his words, little realizing that in time the sting of her cruelty will fade, leaving him free to pursue a woman more worthy of his ardent affections. "Go to hell!" a sailor might wish his tyrannical bosun after his shoulders have felt the sting of the rattan cane. But would even the most dissolute rating consign his officers to the abyss, did he understand the awful fate awaiting the human soul in the depths of the world? Doubtful. "Go stub your little toe against a doorjamb," he might say, or, "May every beer you drink from now on taste like piss," but not, "Go to hell!" And who among us has not exclaimed, "Oh, hell!" on one occasion or another? Indeed, the favorite curse of Franceline Drake she learnt from her father: "Bloody hell and red death!"

Yes, we are natural-born exaggerators, one and all prone to say not just what we mean, but moreso, as though inflating the truth will make it truer. Thus, when in a rare free moment a sailor aboard the *Circe* said, "By God, it's hell come to earth!" there was not a man on any of the rain-lashed ships converging in the Shiraz Sea who would have disagreed with him.

Well, actually, I exaggerate.

Actually, there were two.

And one of them was a boy.

And this story isn't really about him.

Do not misunderstand, gentle reader. Peter Goodheart-Smythe's story must be told, and shall be told, but as a lowly midshipman in Her Majesty's Royal Navy, currently soaked to the bone and dazed with weariness, he has little enough to do in this tale. Although it shouldn't interrupt the narrative flow too much to note that, as he struggled aft, small hands clinging to the lifelines while the howling sea pounded the *Circe*'s fragile hull, he paused to speak to his captain.

"It's all right, sir," he said, his eyes shining through the murk and the rain and the flying spray, literally shining, like the lighthouse's glim, "we're going to survive this."

"Aye?" Captain Zeal managed a weary smile for the lad. "Thank you, Peter," he said, before returning to the real and present difficulty of keeping his ship afloat.

Strange how men speak of hell as a place they could find on a map, but fail to see the working of the supernatural even when it's right in front of them.

The other man who knew what hell was really like, and knew that a little bit of a hurricane couldn't begin to compare, was up in the rigging of the *Rhymer*, his eyes squinted almost shut against the gale. His hands worked almost of their own accord, for hadn't he been sailing since he was a wee sprout, until knotting and splicing were easier than breathing? As he worked, he sang.

It was impossible to tell what he was singing, as the wind tore the words away, shredding them as soon as they were uttered, but it was probably something with lots of "weigh-hey"s or "yo-heave-ho"s in it, possibly having to do with grog. He finished his knot and his song at the same time (cursing Captain True for a stingy bastard who wouldn't spend the money to buy decent cordage) and began his descent to the deck.

The sky turned white for an instant, and the stinging smell of lightning overwhelmed the salt stench of the spray. There was a crash that shook the *Rhymer*'s boards, and Captain Flynn was flung from the rigging and out into black space.

Something hard caught him across the small of the back; he somersaulted, hands flailing for a grip on something, anything. His fingers touched solid, and he scrabbled for purchase, willing himself not to fall.

"Oh, blessed backstay!" he cried, wrapping his arms and legs around the thick cable. "Never again will I curse your name! Never again will I tell my men to make sure that goddam backstay is taut! Never again—Oh my God."

The foremast was burning.

Despite the driving rain, despite the wind that kicked up the spray until sea and sky were one homogeneous unbreathable froth, the flames roared up red-gold and angry. Already, far below, men were heaving buckets at the blaze—too late, Flynn thought, too late, too late. We really are going to die.

He raised his eyes to the heavens. To beg forgiveness, or mercy? He'd already been to hell once, and little relished the prospect of going back so soon. But whatever his intention, it was forgotten as he gazed up into the swirling eye of the storm.

Lightning blazed and crackled, illuminating a familiar red-painted hull. The *Eschaton*, here? He smiled to himself. He'd known she wouldn't be able to stay away for long.

Several things happened at once, then. The red airship began to boom and spit, raining flaming death on the merchant below. The *Rhymer*'s hissing foremast, still sullenly burning, gave a horrible groan that rose above the white noise of the storm and slowly, awfully, began to fall.

"Bloody hell!" swore Flynn. "Axes!" he roared before he thought, sliding down the backstay towards the deck. "Axes! Clear away that wreckage before it sinks us!" His own axe was in his hand before his feet touched the deck, and he rushed forward, chopping at the tangle of ropes that bound the *Rhymer* to her broken mast.

Aboard the *Eschaton*, "What in God's holy name do you think you're doing?" yelled Dallon Moral.

"I'm bombarding the *Rhymer*," Drake replied. And, raising her voice above the wind and rain, "Steady there!" she shouted. "Keep her steady, or I'll strip your hide from your back!"

"If you sink her, you'll kill every man aboard!" Dallon cried.

She shrugged. "Fewer men to oppose us."

He tried a different tack. "What about the plunder? If you sink it, you'll get none of it."

"Shouldn't be too hard to recover." The smile she turned on him was bright and feral. "What do you say, wizard? Can't your kind breathe under water?"

He stared at her for a moment, too shocked to speak. Then, "Sorry, Cap'n," he said. "I can't let you do this."

Her eyes mocked him. "How are you going to stop me?"

Perhaps she expected further moralizing (so to speak), or possibly a spell. She was certainly surprised when his fist crashed into her temple. Her eyes rolled back into her head, and she said in a shocked voice, "Well—!" before she collapsed.

He caught her in his arms and lifted her up. She weighed no more than a wet kitten. The sailor at the helm gave him an odd look as he passed.

"Change of plans," he heard himself say. "We're getting out of here."

The pirate blinked at him. "Aye-aye, sir," he said.

Moral carried the captain to her cabin, laid her on her bed, and stood contemplating her for a moment. At the sight of the bruise already purpling her face, he winced. She's gonna kill me this time for sure, he thought. She really, really is.

Well, he'd deal with that when the time came.

He turned and left the room, locking the door behind him. The air was clear, the *Eschaton* already leaving the storm behind.

The broken mast slid over the side; the *Rhymer* groaned and began to right herself. She still heeled far to larboard, her deck slanting like the roof of a church, but the immediate danger was past. Someone was shaking his shoulder and shouting, "*Peregrine*! *Peregrine*!"

"We'll have to jury-rig a mast," he heard himself saying. "Just needs a scrap of sail on her, something to give her steerage-way...."

"It's being seen to," said the person gripping his shoulder. Corby. That was his name. The first mate. "Come on. I need to talk to you."

Inside the captain's cabin, the mate took off his hat. "Captain True is dead."

Dead? Flynn tried to find a meaning to hang on the word. Dead.

"So are Dollet and Graham," Corby continued.

Dollet. Graham. The second and third mates. A question occurred to him, and he asked it: "How?"

Corby sat on the edge of the captain's desk, bowing his head. "Captain True died when the mast fell. It landed right on him. Dollet went overboard. Graham broke his neck falling down a hatchway." His long pigtail was dripping on the captain's desk. "We're the only officers left."

Flynn said nothing. His brain was working, but slowly, slowly. Corby was still speaking; through the haze in his mind, he could hear it:

"There's more. The ship's taking on water, more than she ought, even in this sea. The carpenter's looking for leaks, and I've got men at the pumps, but...." Corby shook his head. "Worst of all, I don't know where we are."

That broke through. Flynn looked up sharply. "Don't know?" he repeated. "How can you not know?"

Taken aback, Corby said, "We haven't seen the sky for three days. Dead reckoning's useless in winds like these, coming from all directions at once, and without the sun to take our bearings, or better yet a good lunar, we're at sea." He seemed to realize his pun, for he added with a bitter half-smile, "So to speak."

"You've at least got a compass, though," said Flynn. "We at least know which way we're going."

A strange pressure was building in his chest, an emotion he could not name. Lost. Lost at sea. The *Rhymer* was lost in a storm, and of her officers, only Langer Corby and Flynn Freeborn survived. The *Rhymer* was an unwieldy tub, but there was enough treasure in her hold to buy a new ship, a better ship. Maybe a flying ship. Aye, ever since he'd seen the *Eschaton* he'd been coveting one of those beauties.

His hand crept up to the haft of the axe stuck in his belt. Corby'd never fall in—he was a decent cove, not the sort to turn pirate. But anything could happen in a storm like this. Tragedy could strike before you knew it.

"*Peregrine*?"

"Aye, sir." Flynn dropped his hand. Time enough for that sort of thing later.

"You can read a chart?"

"Aye, sir." No more than that. He waited.

"Stay here, then. See if you can't work out our position."

"Aye, sir. And what will you be doing, sir?"

Corby gave a wan little smile. "I'll be making sure we don't die."

"Good idea, sir."

They smirked at each other for a moment. Then Corby let himself out, back into the howling gale, leaving Flynn alone in the captain's cabin.

Captain Flynn Freeborn, once the most fearsome pirate in the southern seas, alone in the cabin of a merchant vessel. He laughed aloud. Then he got to work.

The captain's desk yielded nothing out of the ordinary: maps and charts, pens and inks, a pouch of coin which Flynn put into his left pocket. A rather nice compass, the four elemental poles represented by four different-colored gemstones. He tucked that into his right pocket, then went on to search the rest of the cabin.

He had plundered many a merchant vessel in his day, and he knew the lengths to which merchant captains went to hide their valuables from buccaneers. Many's the man who had spat at Flynn Freeborn's feet and declared, "I'd rather see it at the bottom of the ocean than in the hands of a pirate!" Flynn chuckled. In the end, their efforts were always vain. He had a knack for this sort of thing, a nose that smelt treasure, and so, when he pressed a certain panel on the starboard bulkhead and a little box tumbled out of the wall, he was not particularly surprised.

"Well, what have we here, me beauty?" he said, prising open the lid.

Inside the box was a jumble of items—more coins, a necklace of pearls and rubies (into the pockets went those), and a bag of purple velvet, heavy with embroidery.

Flynn tugged open the drawstrings and peeked inside.

"Mr *Peregrine*?"

Damn! He hadn't even heard the door open! He sprang to his feet, shoving the purple bag inside his shirt.

"Aye, sir?"

Langer Corby gave him a puzzled glance. "Any idea of our position?"

Flynn shook his head. "Not yet, sir. No, sir. Still no better idea than when I started. Sir."

Corby peered at him. "What were you doing, *Peregrine*?"

Flynn licked his lips. Here it was: truth or consequences. He gripped his boarding axe and opened his mouth.

And the *Rhymer* ran herself aground, tearing her side open on the hidden rocks, her remaining masts tumbling like dominoes.

"Oh, God!" cried Langer Corby, and turned and ran out on deck.

Releasing his axe, Flynn Freeborn followed.

The passing of the storm brought silence like a benediction. The sun's last bronze-colored beams broke through the flying clouds, touching the upturned faces of the weary sailors aboard the *Circe*. They had come through, they had survived. The sea still heaved and surged, but it had regained its sanity, and the waves no longer threatened to swamp them. The wind relaxed, returning to order, blowing from just the one direction again.

Captain Zeal turned to his first lieutenant. "By God, Mr Morrow!" he cried. "We made it!"

For one horrible moment, Morrow thought the captain was going to try to hug him, and prepared to duck out of the way—but Zeal only clapped him on the shoulder, laughing in relief.

They had survived, but the circle of water around them was clear from one horizon to the other. The *Rhymer* was gone.

Gasping, Flynn hoisted himself up onto the rock and collapsed. He was ragged, salt-soaked and barefoot. He was also alone.

The cruel waves had battered poor *Rhymer* to pieces; half the crew had drowned before they could even launch the boats. Then, in the rush and panic, the first boat had swamped itself, dumping its burden into the sea. Those who couldn't swim (and that was most of them) were lost.

The second boat had fared little better. They managed to launch it without mishap, Langer Corby gripping Flynn's arm in farewell as he climbed aboard—but a freak of the wind had caught the little cutter's scrap of sail and dashed it into one of the nearby rocks. No one survived.

And I only am escaped alone to tell thee, thought Flynn, closing his eyes.

He had dived off the side of the ship, hoping to escape the inevitable suction as the *Rhymer* sank. He had kicked off his boots and writhed out of his coat, he had abandoned his hat. He still had his shirt, and in his pockets were the things he had stolen from Captain True's cabin. It was a hollow victory to survive a shipwreck, only to perish of hunger and thirst with your pockets stuffed full of a dead man's treasures.

"What are you doing?"

Flynn opened his eyes, but saw no one. Another ghost, surfacing from the depths of his mind to haunt him? You'd think he'd be used to it by now. "Dying," he said. "Go away."

"Why?" asked the voice. "You do not appear to be injured, and you have adequate air. Unless the tales I have heard of your kind are untrue."

No ghost at all, but a living voice. Flynn sat up. Sitting in the water beside his rock, her bare arms hugging the edge, was a young woman with wispy green hair like fine kelp, and pale blue skin. She smiled at him. "Hello."

He found himself smiling back. "Hello. What did you mean by 'my kind,' then?"

"Oh, you know," she said. "Your kind. Air-breathers. Humans. I have heard many tales, but never seen one up close before today."

"And what are you, then?" he asked, but he already knew the answer. Below the pellucid surface of the water, he could see the curving, golden fish's tail.

The siren heaved herself a little further out of the water, revealing her slim and maidenly and (Flynn swallowed) quite naked torso. So it wasn't true, what they said, that mer-maidens wore seashells to cover their bosoms. Her eyes were like drops of ink, black and arresting. "Would you like to kiss me?" she asked.

His throat was suddenly very dry. "I wouldn't mind it," he confessed.

Her smile widened. "Come here, then," she said.

Flynn leaned forward, closing his eyes and pursing his lips.

Her arms came up and wrapped around the back of his neck. Her mouth opened, revealing a double-row of sharp, serrated teeth.

Flynn's eyes flew open. He gasped and tried to jerk away—but it was too late, and those slender arms were like steel. She dove, her arms still around his neck, pulling him down.

"I am really going to kill you," said Franceline Drake.

Moral looked at his shoes. "I know it."

"What were you thinking? That was mutiny, is what it was, and I won't have it on my ship! I ought to peel your skin off in little strips, roast it and feed it to you!"

Moral shuddered.

"When I took you aboard," Drake continued, "I asked you, Will it be a problem that you're a white wizard and I'm a pirate? And you shuffled your clod-hoppers and said No, ma'am, No ma'am, it won't be no problem, and I—I was such an ever-loving, god-damned bleeding innocent fool that I believed you! There's a reason, Dallon Moral, that there's only one captain on board a ship!"

"Yes, ma'am," Moral said, peering up at her through his hair. Her green eyes snapped with anger. He cringed. That bruise was really awful.

"Now," she said, reining in her temper with an effort. "I'm going to lock you in the cable tier. And I'm going to let you sit there, thinking about all the things I could do to you, for a little while. And then I'll deal with you. Understand me?"

"Yes, ma'am."

Leaning forward, she seized a hank of his hair and pulled his head up. "If I were you, wizard, I'd start praying," she said.

He averted his eyes. "Yes, ma'am."

"Do you really think she'll kill him?" asked Luna Shee.

Lilly Bones, taking her turn at the helm, shrugged her massive shoulders. "Don't know," she said. "I would."

For the second time that day, Flynn Freeborn gasped for air and dragged himself out of the ocean's briny embrace. In one hand, he gripped a broken spar. In the other, his boarding axe. He heaved himself up onto his rock, dropped the axe, and took off his shirt. His arms and shoulders were covered with bite marks and bruises.

The shirt had seen better days, poor thing. Yesterday, for example, when it had been clean (well, kind of), fresh and not covered with thin blood and fish scales. And yet, it was still the closest thing to white he owned. He threaded the broken spar through the sleeves, making them fast as best he could. When he had made a crude flag, he looked for a hole in the coral in which to plant it. Perhaps someone would see his signal and rescue him.

He sat down on his rock, put his back against the makeshift flagpole, and fell asleep.

"So." Someone was laughing at him. "Here you are, the famous Flynn Freeborn, stuck on a rock in the middle of the ocean."

He opened his eyes. "Ah, Francie!" he cried. "I knew you'd come!" He raised his hand to her.

She laughed. "Come?" she said. "Yes, I've come! For this!" And she dangled the purple velvet bag at him, just out of reach.

Puzzled, he said, "Then you won't be rescuing me?"

"No, I won't be rescuing you," said Franceline Drake. "I've got what I wanted. As for you, stay here and rot for all I care. I told you I didn't give a damn if we met again, and I meant it. But I thank you for saving at least some of the treasure for me." She tugged on the rope she held, and at once began to lift up into the air.

With his eyes, he followed her progress. Ah, so that's why he was sitting in the shade—the *Eschaton*'s great red hull was blocking the sun.

"Are you sure you won't reconsider, Francie?" he called after her. "Think of the good times we could have!"

"There's only room for one captain on a ship, Flynn," she replied. "I wish you the best of luck, but I never want to see you again!"

She dwindled as she spoke, until she was a tiny figure being helped over the *Eschaton*'s side. With a roar and a rush of wings, the pirate ship was gone, leaving Flynn Freeborn alone once more, on a rock, in the middle of the vast blue sea.

"Women," he said, closing his eyes and leaning back against his flagpole. "It's true what they say about 'em. You can't live with 'em, and you might just die because of 'em."

After awhile, he fell asleep.

"On deck! On deck, there!"

"What do you see, Mr Paisley?"

"Looks like a signal flag, Cap'n," the lookout replied. "Two points to larboard, in among those rocks."

"We may as well investigate," said the captain. "Helmsman, alter course. Two points south by southwest, and a half south."

"Aye-aye, Cap'n!"

Her Majesty's Ship *Boadicea* headed toward the distant flag.

CHAPTER 7

World Enough and Time

I. Paroxysms of loyalty—A family reunion—Etymology discussed—The merits of low-rent housing—A buyer's market

The city of Umeboshi was a miracle of light. The dim mountains sloping gently down towards the bay were aglow, each of the city's many streets and stairways and temples lit by a thousand lamps, flickering a thousand faeryland shades of gold and pink and green. The dim waters of the bay were alight, throwing a shifting dance of rippling reflections back to the night sky, rivalling the bright spray of stars overhead. Seen from a distance, the city shimmered and glowed, surrounded by a shivering halo of light, golden against the blackness of the surrounding countryside.

But to be in the midst of the city was no less impressive: to see the faces of friends and shipmates illumined by soft colored lights, to smell the cooking exotic foods, most of all to hear the pulsing sounds of celebration, the throbbing of the deep drums, the shrill wail of flutes and the hooting of instruments more outlandish, the stamp and clash and shout of the gaily-dressed celebrants themselves.

"They're coming this way," said Peter, a certain apprehension in his luminous blue eyes (and whether his eyes were luminous all on their own, or merely as a side-effect of the colored paper lanterns that hung from every available surface, I will leave to your imagination). "Do you suppose we should move back?"

"Don't be such a baby, Petey," said Vaughn, from his vast advantage (three whole years!) of age—not to mention his at least nominal advantage in rank, Peter Goodheart-Smythe being the fifth midshipman on Her Majesty's frigate *Circe*, whereas Dalziel Vaughn was the second. As representatives of Her Majesty Queen Miranda in a foreign land, both boys were somewhat lacking at the moment. Peter had proven his bravery over and again, in many a sticky situation—but now he was half-hiding behind a squid-seller's stall, his eyes threatening to engulf his face. As for Vaughn, not much of a credit to the ship in the first place, half a day of shore leave had almost undone him entirely. His blue midshipman's jacket with the white collar patches had disappeared sometime around mid-afternoon, and had been replaced by a garment such as the natives of Chai wore, patterned with pink and green fish and belted round the middle with an orange sash. In one hand he held the glazed and grilled remains of a moderate cephalopod (a delicacy in Chai). His cheeks were flushed (even in the warm light of the festival lanterns, they glowed like beacons), and his eyes had the glassy look indicative of his very first drunken bender.

"Come on," this paragon said. "Let's watch."

The sound of the parade had grown louder and nearer as the two boys talked, and as your narrator paused for ecphrasis, and now it was nearly upon them. The stamping of a multitude of feet quivered the very paving stones, and the pounding of great drums vibrated in the boys' chests, and rising over these sounds and the festival babble surrounding them, the curious ululating cries of the paraders: joyous, but inexpressibly foreign. And now, as Midshipman Vaughn said, "Let's watch," he grabbed Peter's sleeve with his free hand and dragged him out into the middle of the narrow street—right into the path of the oncoming parade.

The acrobats appeared first, leaping and bounding and cart-wheeling and hand-standing down the street, their faces painted white, their eyes outlined with red, their black hair confined by multicolored headbands. Next the dancers, moving with a more subtle grace, their tiny feet bare, swaying and bending like reeds in a gentle wind. Vaughn's eyes widened with appreciation, and he took a bite of his squid.

And then the first dragon appeared.

Peter gasped in wonder.

Not, of course, a real dragon, but a sort of puppet made of cloth and gold and gems, carried by a troupe of twenty dancers who hid beneath its shimmering bulk and gave it the semblance of life. It came writhing up the street, its shining folds rippling, its enormous eyes glowing in the lantern light, its red mouth clacking, while the dancers underneath growled and roared.

"Oh," said Peter, a strange pressure building inside him, his gaze caught and held by the enormous jewel-like creature. The lanterns around him seemed to dim, while the golden-maned dragon grew bright. "Oh," he said again, and felt his knees give way.

"Here, now, you two!" cried a familiar voice, and a hand on his collar dragged him out of the street just as the first of the acrobats tumbled by. Back from the road, in the cool shade behind the food-sellers' booths, he felt his cloudy vision clearing, and he looked up into the round, red, disapproving face of Arin Murray, captain's coxswain, who had also nabbed Vaughn by the scruff of the neck.

"Now, what do you pups think you're about?" Murray cried, shaking them, just as you would shake a disobedient puppy.

"Mr Murray...." was all that Peter could say.

Unfortunately, Vaughn was much more articulate. "What do you think you're about, Murray?" he roared—or tried to. His voice, however, had just begun to change, and it cracked at the worst moment possible, ending on an embarrassing squeak.

Besides, it's difficult to be impressive and commanding when your feet are dangling three feet off the ground (Murray was a big man, and Vaughn still a small boy).

"Cap'n's been looking for you this last glass and more," said Murray, unmoved.

"Shore leave ended at sundown."

"What?!" Vaughn writhed in the seaman's grip. "The hell you say!" And then his eyes narrowed, and he said shrewdly, "What about you, Murray? I don't see you back on the ship."

"Shore leave ended at sundown," Murray repeated, "for little boys who don't know how to hold their liquor. Sir," he added, a scathing afterthought.

Peter dangled from Murray's left hand, trying to remain unnoticed. Vaughn was getting enough attention for the both of them.

Indeed, his shrill cry of "I'll see you court-martialed for disrespect, Murray!", accompanied by much flapping of arms, attracted the attention of the Chailanders around them. In typical Chai fashion, they showed their embarrassment by studiously ignoring its cause.

"Aye, sir," said Murray, beginning to walk. Absently, he set Peter on the ground, allowing the grateful boy to walk instead of being carried. But on the struggling, cursing, wailing Vaughn he kept a firm grip, and it was in this manner that Mr Midshipman Dalziel Vaughn was returned to the *Circe*.

"Very good, Mr Murray," said Lieutenant Blake. "An extra ration of grog for you." Murray grinned at him, and Blake added, "Er ... that is, once we're back at sea."

"Aye, sir. Thank'ee, sir." Murray knuckled his forehead and withdrew.

Lieutenant Richard Patrick Blake had not yet mastered that look of Jovian disapproval worn by the more disciplinarian captains in Her Majesty's navy, but he was a quick learner, and, being only the second lieutenant aboard the *Circe*, had some years yet in which to practice. At any rate, the glower he turned on the two truants was tolerably grim, and both boys quailed.

"All Midshipmen are to be back on board by nightfall," he said. "Captain Zeal's orders. I am not surprised that they slipped Mr Vaughn's mind," he said, "but I am shocked at you, Mr Goodheart-Smythe. You in particular ought to have known better."

"Aye, sir," said the miserable Peter, hanging his head. The queer feeling in his chest had yet to abate; it was all he could do to stand.

"No more shore leave for either of you," Blake said. "And no more grog until we set sail. And—" he stopped, his eyes bulging. "Mr Vaughn," he said, carefully articulating each syllable, "what in God's holy and everlasting name has happened to your uniform?"

Vaughn gathered the pink and green robe about him and tried to look dignified.

"Perhaps you will be better able to contemplate your crimes from the masthead, Mr Vaughn!" said Blake, his face purpling.

"But, sir—!" cried Vaughn. "It's dark!"

"You noticed that, did you?" said Blake. "Perhaps in the future you will behave with a dignity more becoming to an officer of Her Majesty's Navy! Now jump!"

Vaughn jumped.

Peter regarded the officer with wide and trembling eyes. Dragons were singing in his head—if he had to climb to the top of the mast, he'd fall off and die. Dragons, with wide and shimmering wings....

But, "To bed with you, Mr Goodheart-Smythe," said Blake, in a much kindlier voice. "And thank you for keeping Vaughn out of trouble."

"Aye, sir," said Peter, not knowing what else to say. "Good night, sir." And he stumbled blindly down to his berth.

"Good night, Peter."

"An unfortunate business all around, Zeal, I must say," said the Admiral, leaning back in his chair. "Most unfortunate, indeed. More sillery?"

"Thank you, sir." Captain Acheron Zeal had already drunk as much sillery as he could hold, not to mention port wine, brandy and punch, but it would never do to refuse the invitation of an admiral, especially not an admiral as ancient, as venerable, as admirable as Admiral Bayard Rangle, who had been a celebrated adventuring frigate captain before Zeal was even a mote in his father's eye, or however the saying goes.

"Yes, an unfortunate business," Admiral Rangle repeated, pouring the pale wine. A grizzled spaniel, nearly as aged as its master, limped up from underneath the table and placed its head on the admiral's knee, gazing up at him with pleading, its brown eyes actually filling with tears. Chuckling, the admiral poured an extra dish of wine and laid it on the floor. The sound of noisy lapping at once filled the cabin. "And yet," the admiral continued, "one can hardly lay the blame for the weather on you, Zeal. You're no demigod. You can't command the winds."

"No, sir," said Zeal, not drinking his wine. "And we did search for the *Rhymer*, sir—searched every shoal and reef from here to Garam Masala, but not a sign of her we found. Some native fishermen thought they may have seen a ship of her description run aground on some rocks, but they couldn't be certain."

Admiral Rangle waved his hand—a thin and aged hand, it was, spotted and veined. "No matter, Zeal. We can't change the past. And, in truth, the fate of the *Rhymer* is of little concern."

Zeal glanced up, his eyebrows raising.

"What is more worrisome, Captain Zeal, is the fate of the *Eschaton*."

At the very mention of the name, Zeal's stomach gave a little lurch.

"Aye," said the admiral, grinning, and pouring more wine for the whimpering spaniel, "the *Eschaton*. How long, Captain Zeal, have you been pursuing her? And how long has she been evading you?"

Another man might have made excuses. Another man might have protested that a mere sailing frigate would be hard-pressed to sink, destroy or capture a flying ship under the best of circumstances. But that other man would not have been Captain Acheron Zeal.

"Almost nine months now, sir," he said.

Admiral Rangle nodded. "Well," he said. "Well."

Well what, exactly, he was never able to pronounce, for a series of sharp, cracking booms shattered the serenity of the night, and Zeal at once flung himself to the deck, covering his head.

The spaniel, with an inquiring whine, put its damp, cold nose against the back of his neck. Admiral Rangle ignored his subordinate's curious behavior and looked out the stern windows, where blooms of red and green fire were erupting in the night sky, accompanied by more explosions.

"They've been carrying on in this heathenish manner for weeks now," he said. "Ever since that Katsookarry fellow went and lopped off the heads of the heads of the Diet...." He stopped, repeated "the heads of the heads," looked briefly self-conscious, shrugged and went on, "they've been attempting to prove how rapturously loyal they are by throwing a non-stop festival in his honor. The mayor has paroxysms every time you say the word 'Emperor' to him. Rather amusing, really."

Zeal raised his head off the ground. The spaniel licked his cheek. "So ... we're not under attack?"

"Attack?" Rangle raised one fluffy white eyebrow. "No, indeed. At least, not yet."

He did not attempt to clarify that ominous remark, but, in truth, he didn't need to. The alliance between Camembert and the Chai Republic had never been a strong one, based mostly on trade and the consensus that neither wanted to go to the bother of conquering the other, and now that Katsukare I, as he was calling himself, had overthrown the millennia-old republic and instituted a tyranny, the lay of the land was unclear. Would he continue the ally of Camembert, or would he decide that what he really wanted was to expand his empire?

"He's got his hands full rounding up the last dissidents, at any rate," said Admiral Rangle. "The Queen has time to convince him that he likes the status quo." He finally looked down. "What the devil are you doing on the floor, Zeal?" he demanded. "Get up at once! You're an officer of Her Majesty's Royal Navy, not some damned barbarian!"

"Aye, sir." Zeal scrambled to his feet. "Sorry, sir."

"When you get to be my age, you lose all patience for that sort of jiggly-puffery."

"It won't happen again, sir."

"I should certainly hope not. Have some more sillery, Zeal."

There came a knock at the door, and the flag lieutenant poked his head in. "Sorry to bother you, sir...."

"In or out, Mr Ansley. Don't hover. An officer in Her Majesty's Navy is decisive!"

"Aye, sir." The lieutenant opened the door, revealing the two marines behind him, and the struggling man they held between them. "This man assaulted one of our officers, sir. I thought it best to bring him to you directly."

"I just needed a bit of a drink, I did—you can't be arresting a man for that!"

"Silence, you!" The starboard marine gave the prisoner a cuff.

The admiral waved his hand. "Lock him in the brig. I'll deal with him later."

"Aye, sir." As the lieutenant turned to go, the light from the great cabin fell fully on the prisoner's face for just a moment, and Zeal gasped. He knew this man!

But more astonishing was the admiral's reaction. His ruddy face turned white, his broad brow broke out in a sweat, and his hands (firm and steady for the hands of an eighty-seven-year-old man) began to shake. "Belay that, Mr Ansley," he commanded.

"Sir?" The lieutenant turned.

"Leave him here with me."

"Sir?"

"You heard me, Mr Ansley. Leave the prisoner with me, and I shall deal with him." His voice and his hands had steadied, though his face was still pale. To Zeal, he added, "I'm afraid, Mr Zeal, that we will have to continue our conversation at another time."

"Sir!" Zeal protested. "I know this man—he is—"

"That will be all, Captain Zeal!" Admiral Rangle's voice held the whipcrack of command, and the young captain subsided. Saluting, he took himself from the cabin, to be rowed back to his own ship, where the duties of his own command awaited.

But as he made his exit, he paused and looked the prisoner full in the face. This isn't over between us, he promised the man silently. Not by a chalk as long as your arm.

And the haunted eyes of the captain of the *Eschaton* stared back at him. Right you are, mate, they replied. 'Tis far, far from over.

When the door had shut, and Admiral Bayard Rangle was alone with the prisoner, he rose unsteadily to his feet and advanced on the man who stood, head bowed and arms bound, before him.

"Can it be?" he said. "Can it truly be? You look just like him ... but how is it possible?"

The prisoner looked up. "I don't think I know you, mate, so if you'll just be letting me go, I'll be going on my way, and we'll all be the better for it, that we will." He held out his bound hands.

But Admiral Rangle continued his amazed inspection. "Same eyes," he muttered. "Same absurd ring through the same eyebrow. Same hair. Same chin. Same height, same breadth. Same posture, same stance! Amazing!"

"I ain't a prime rib, mate, and you've no beef with me, so stop eyeing me like a cow for market and let me go!" the prisoner cried.

"What is your name, sir?" asked the Admiral, completing his circuit and looking the fellow straight in the eye.

"Thomas True, captain of the merchant ship *Rhymer*," the prisoner declared, his eyes flicking to the side. "An honest man in an honest trade! Now will you be letting me go?"

"You always were a terrible liar," Bayard said. Reaching behind him, he drew a dirk from his desk and slashed the man's bonds—grabbing his right hand and turning it palm-up before he could protest.

"Here now!" the prisoner cried, pulling away.

But Bayard had already seen what he needed to see: a small, round scar on the palm of the prisoner's hand, obscured by calluses and grime, but still visible. His legs trembled, and his knees threatened to give out. "Don't you remember?" he said quietly, holding up his own right hand, palm out, to the man he had not seen for fifty-five years. "They match."

Wide-eyed silence from the dirty prisoner.

"How old were we, when we got these?" Bayard asked. "Eight? Nine?"

"I was seven," said the other, his voice hoarse and shaking. "You were ten."

That confirmation was all the old admiral needed. "Cousin Flynn!" he cried, and "Cousin Bayard!" cried Flynn, and laughing with amazed joy (and I won't assert that no tears were shed), the two men embraced.

"But explain this thing to me," said Bayard, leading his cousin over to the chair Captain Zeal had so recently vacated, "how it is that you're still alive, and not a day older than the last time I saw you?"

"Ah, cous," said Flynn, shaking his head and accepting the glass of wine Bayard offered, "'tis the longest of all long stories, that it is."

"Then you'd best start telling it, hadn't you?"

Three bells in the morning watch, the loneliest time of the night: midnight was long past, but dawn still hours away.

On board the *Circe*, Captain Zeal admitted at last that sleep was spurning him, and padded up on deck in his nightshirt, letting the nighttime breeze cool the sweat of his skin. Hands clasped behind him, he took up his familiar course, pacing the weather side of the quarterdeck, treading the thoughtful path that so many captains had trod before.

"You'll catch your death out here like this," his steward grumbled in an undertone, wrapping a cloak about his shoulders.

"Thank you, Duffy," said Zeal, gathering the heavy folds closer around his neck. But Duffy had already made his obedience and was gone.

Captain Zeal had endured sleepless nights before—as the captain of a sailing ship, it was unthinkable that he should not. Wind and tide do not arrange themselves to suit a nine-to-five schedule; a howling gale will not moderate itself to let the poor men on the beleaguered ship get a few hours' shut-eye. Why, for three days during the recent hurricane Captain Zeal had stayed on deck, limbs numb with fatigue but mind still sharp, directing his men in a time when the least wrong decision could kill them all. And they had survived.

But a woman is not a hurricane, no matter what jilted lovers may say—to deal with her devastation requires resourcefulness of a different sort. Poor Zeal may have been a post captain in Her Majesty's Royal Navy, fully entitled to wear those two heavy gold epaulettes on the shoulders of his blue broadcloth coat, experienced in the ways of leading men at sea, but he was young in the ways of the world, and the cruelty of a young woman had broken his heart, and there was no remedy for it.

"I have hardened my heart," Zeal said, clenching his jaw, as he paced. But it's one thing to say I shall harden my heart and another thing entirely to do it. Zeal had been busy, he had been distracted from his pain, but his heart had remained as soft and malleable as ever.

To see her once more! Aye, that would be the thing! To look once more upon her face, into her sweet green eyes, and ask her straight: "Was there a time when you loved me at all, Franceline Drake?"

Three bells in the morning watch, the loneliest time of the night: but in an upper room in a rat-trap inn in Umeboshi city, a candle lent its golden glow to the scarred face of a large young woman, and the page against which her pen studiously scratched.

Celestine ran through the dim upper halls of the crumbling mansion, her white lace nightgown tangling about her slender legs. As she ran, she continually glanced over her shoulder, gasping in terror lest the beast that pursued her should catch her at last. "O!" she sobbed, "if only I had been more wary! I should have realized at once that the dark and mysterious nobleman who tempted me here as governess of his monstrous children was in fact a beast!"

From behind her came a hideous sound, the slavering roar of a creature enraged, which contained, most horribly, yet elements of humanity in it. As the man-beast pounded up the corridor behind her, Celestine shrank against the wall and screamed—

From the street below came a ragged strain of song. The parades were long over, but the celebrating continued, and now, from the sound, a party of drunken sailors was staggering down the road, bawling out the words of a popular tune:

Farewell and adieu to you Spanish ladies,
Farewell and adieu, you ladies of Spain—

"Oi!" one of the singers broke in. "You know what I've been wondering? Just what the hell is a Spanish lady, anyway?"

"Well," said another, "it's a description, like. You know, a whadyacallit. An adjudicator."

"Adjunct, you bleedin moron."

"An adjective," someone else corrected. He had a fussy sort of voice—the sort of voice that would wear spectacles and a tiny moustache, and save all of its receipts.

"But what's it mean, is what I want to know."

"Maybe it means, you know, sort of wide."

The others took a moment to digest the idea, murmuring amongst themselves. "Ah!" one said. "*Span*-ish!"

The young woman at the battered writing desk shook her head, killed a large insect that had scuttled across her page, and went back to her task:

"Help me! Won't somebody help me?"

But there was, of course, none within fifty miles of the crumbling, ancient manse to hear her frantic pleas.

The door behind her banged open. Without turning or even bothering to look, she tossed a dagger with her free hand and continued writing.

If the girl in the doorway had been someone else, things might have ended rather badly for all involved. But Luna Shee only grinned (showing a number of gold-capped teeth), snatched the missile from mid-air, tumbled forward, and rose to her feet, still grinning, with the dagger in her hand.

"Good one," she said, "but you won't get me that easily."

"Keeps you on your toes, though," replied Lilly Bones. "Nice night?"

Luna rolled her slim shoulders. "Tolerable," she allowed. "You'll never guess who I saw!"

"Probably not."

Luna pouted at her sister—but as it was impossible for her to stay angry (or silent) for more than two seconds at a time, she said, "None other than the illustrious Cap'n Flynn Freeborn himself!"

"Cap'n Flynn?" For the first time Lilly looked up from her page. "So he's alive." The news pleased her; a small, secretive sort of smile curved her lips. "Did he look well?"

"Lilly." Luna perched herself on the end of the desk. "He always looks well." She rolled her eyes with absolute admiration. "But as he was busily engaged with being arrested by a passel of Royal Marines, I didn't stop to inquire about his health." She grinned, shaking her head. "Got a talent for trouble, that one has."

"Aye," Lilly agreed.

"Don't understand why you feel the need to stay in run-down fleabag firetraps like this," Luna said, hopping down from the desk and roaming the tiny room. Contents: a mattress of dubious quality, a rusted basin, and the writing desk. Inhabitants: Luna, Lilly, and countless thousands of extra six-legged guests. A particularly large one ran across the floor, and Luna shuddered. "As much money as we made off that last cruise, you could stay in the richest hotel in the city. And after Cap'n sells that trinket she found—imagine! You could swim in champagne, if you wanted."

"I like the quiet," said Lilly, pointedly.

But it would have taken a hint as broad as the Quadra Terrarum itself for Luna Shee to take her meaning. She was running her fingers along the walls, then removing them and examining the residue that clung to their tips.

"Wizard still alive?" Lilly asked abruptly.

"Aye, as far as I know. Cap'n talks big, but I don't think she'll really kill him. Not until she's got his replacement lined up, anyway."

Lilly grunted. "Mutiny." She almost spat the word. Of all the crimes imaginable to man, it was the only one that was, always and everywhere, unforgivable.

"Aye." Luna sat back down on the edge of the desk. "Wonder what was going through his head?"

"Mmm," Lilly agreed.

Much later than three bells in the morning watch: the last hardcore party-goers were slumped in doorways and in gutters, and even the stars had gone to sleep. A young woman walked the dark streets with a light but steady tread, the hem of her magnificent red coat swaying as she went. She did not skulk in shadows, but strode down the center of the street, and when she reached the puddle of light thrown by one sad and guttering lantern, she paused and turned.

"If it's my money you're after," she called, "then I suggest you seek an easier mark. And if it's my honor..." She paused, smiling. In her hand was a slim and deadly length of steel. "Well, that's long gone, so you might as well save yourself the trouble."

Rapid footsteps pattered off into the darkness.

"Wise choice," she called after them, putting the sword away and continuing down the shadowy street.

When she came to a certain doorway, down a certain alley, past a certain shop, she paused, knocked thrice, and waited.

And waited.

Her foot tapped against the paving stones.

A panel in the door slid open, and a pair of eyes peered out at her. "Well?"

"I have goods for sale. Is Dorobo here?"

The eyes narrowed. "What sort of goods?"

"I'd prefer not to discuss it while standing out here in the street. Is he here, or should I find another buyer?"

Eyebrows knitted (and an impressive pair of eyebrows they were, appearing to have been made out of heavy black wire), the person on the other side of the door considered. And then: "No. No, I don't think so. Dorobo's not in the market right now."

The panel slammed shut.

Closing her eyes, Captain Drake turned and leant against the door, sighing. Dorobo had been the last person she could think of who might take this blasted thing off her hands (she was not so foolish to pull the purple velvet pouch out of her pocket, still less to reveal its shining contents in this dark street, but the image of it was vivid in her mind). "Hell and death," she grumbled.

She considered kicking the door in, but that would only lead to scuffed shoes and stubbed toes. No, she would go back to the ship, there to plan her next move.

"Bloody hell," she remarked, "and red death."

She turned to go.

A tall figure, muffled in black from head to toe, bumped shoulders with her as she exited the alley. From the shadow under his hat came a constant muttering in a language she did not know. He staggered on down the street, apparently unaware of the collision.

Drake rubbed her shoulder, scowling after him. "Ought to've run you through, friend," she said, watching him go. "Tonight's your lucky night, I suppose."

"More wine, cousin?" said the aged admiral, proffering the bottle. But Flynn put his hand over his glass, shaking his head, and Bayard said, not for the first time that long night, "I am amazed, amazed. To think that you are alive, and on earth again, after all these years!"

"Aye, well," said Flynn. His face was grey with weariness, and a new growth of beard showed dark against it. "But tell me, cous, as I've been talking all the long night through, what of things at home? What of Mother? And what..." He hesitated, unsure how to continue, or whether he should. Then draining the dregs from his glass, and finding there the false courage of the grape, he said, "What of Evie?"

Bayard looked away, unable to meet the fear and the hope he saw in his cousin's eyes. His gaze instead on the curly head of the old spaniel, he said, "Your mother died years ago. Grief, many said. But not before she bore a son to her new husband." Flynn nodded, and wished he had accepted the offer of more wine. "That son married, produced children, and I've no doubt one of those children would hold the lands now, if they had not all perished in the war." He looked up, in his glance a question. But Flynn had read about the war, in one of the books given him by the itinerant opera critic Crispin Teague. "Your family lands," Bayard concluded, "stand empty and unclaimed."

"And...?" Flynn could not bring himself to say the name again.

With a wry smile, Admiral Bayard Rangle rose creakingly to his feet, dislodging the spaniel (which gave him a look of complete and total disapprobation). He paced across the great cabin to the stern windows, and stood with his hands clasped behind his back, gazing out across the bay. "The sun will be rising soon," he said. "We've talked all night, cousin."

Flynn half-rose. "Cous..."

But Bayard waved him back down. "Do you remember—it must have been sixty years ago now—you had captured my ship and brought me down to your cabin on the *Peregrine*, and I was certain you were going to kill me. But you showed me that scar on your hand, and I knew that the cousin—the brother, almost, for we were like brothers, do you recall—whom I thought was dead, was alive again. But do you remember what you said to me?"

Flynn's head was bowed over his hands; his long hair fell in lank coils across his face and over his knees. His voice, when he spoke, was harsh and low: "Aye," he said. "I remember. 'Lysander Peregrine is dead,' I said. 'He died on that cliff fifteen years ago. There's only me now, Flynn Freeborn, the fearsomest pirate ever sailed the seas....' " His voice trailed away.

"And you said, that if my sister died you were sorry for it, but there was nothing you could do." Now Bayard turned from the window to face his cousin. Flynn raised his head, and for a long moment the two men regarded one another: the one, white-haired and stooped, but on whom a lifetime of command had left the indelible stamp of confidence and authority; the other, outwardly young and strong yet somehow frail, as though the horrors he had seen had broken something within him.

"Aye," said Flynn. "I remember."

"I want you to do something for me. A favor, if you will."

"Ah, cous," said Flynn.

Bayard raised his hand. "I'm not asking you. You're still a wanted man, dear cous, and if Her Majesty's Navy ever found out you were alive ... well, we would be required and directed to take steps to remedy the situation."

Flynn raised a hand, rubbing his neck. "I've never wanted to wear the hempen necktie," he said. "That I have not."

"If you do this thing for me," said Admiral Rangle, "then you will have your freedom. I could even, if you wanted, beg Her Majesty to pardon you for all your crimes."

"Nay." Flynn shook his head. "That won't be necessary, cous. Tell me this favor of yours and have done."

Smiling, Bayard did so.

It was nearly dawn when Drake returned to the *Eschaton*, moored in a secret place just outside of town. Her people might have their choice of the finest inns of Umeboshi (or the seediest), but the captain must stay with her ship.

It was no great burden, however, to call the *Eschaton* home. A trim little sky-sailer, about as large as an ocean-going sloop, her hull painted glossy red, her brightwork all gleaming brass, her broad white wings folded alongside her, as the wings of a swan asleep: who would not be proud to return to a home such as this?

She nodded a greeting to the sleepy pirate who straightened at her approach (she would no more leave her beloved ship unguarded than she would leave the door to her home unlocked—she knew all too well what sort of unscrupulous people walked the earth) and made her way aft, to her cabin, boot heels ringing strong and proud against the deck. Once inside, she threw off her fine red coat (it landed across the bed) and threw herself into a chair with a sound half groan, half sigh. With her eyes closed, the room revolved sickeningly around her; she forced them back open and, with the careful, slow movements of the ill or the bitterly tired, pulled a purple velvet bag from her inner vest pocket, picked open the cords that bound it, and removed the object it held.

It was a ... well, to be honest she had no idea what it was. It was egg-shaped and egg-sized, but if it was the offspring of any hen that ever clucked or pecked in the Quadra Terrarum, then she was (she smirked) an honest woman. She lit her pipe as she regarded it, and soon the cabin was full of blue, fragrant smoke.

It was made of gold and gems, and when you pressed a certain ruby on its side, a little mechanism whirred, and out fanned wings made of ivory, revealing a crystal dome. Inside the dome, picked out in gleaming enamel, was a tiny, perfect map of the Quadra Terrarum, every land, every sea, every city in its place. And if you pressed a certain emerald, the miniature came to life: little ships sailed on the glossy blue seas, little airships sailed above, caravans rode the trade routes, wisps of cloud floated overhead, sometimes bringing showers of rain or snow, and over all floated Stratocumulopolis, the dragon city.

"But what," Drake demanded in immense frustration, exhaling smoke, "is it for?"

The device, wreathed in a cloud of blue, gave no answer.

When her pipe had gone out and her weariness was too much to bear, just as the sun was beginning to stretch its arms over the eastern horizon, Drake gave up in disgust and went to bed. She was soon fast asleep.

Far below, in the *Eschaton*'s hold, one other was awake to greet the dawn—although no hint of the sun's rays could penetrate his prison. The wizard Dallon Moral opened his eyes on darkness, and knew instant disappointment. He had been dreaming of home, his own bed in his parents' house, dreaming so vividly he could smell the clean linen and the tantalizing waft of baking apple pie. His mother called to him, telling him to hurry, get his lazy bones out of bed before he missed breakfast. And he had responded before he was awake, sitting up and opening his eyes—

To darkness.

"Well," he said to himself. "Look on the bright side. At least you ain't dead."

Not yet, anyway.

II. Mrs Emelie Hartdegen—Invitations are delivered—The beauty of sailing vessels contemplated—A hard bargain—Proclamations of doom

Under the morning sun's first amber-colored beams, the city of Umeboshi was a much different place. Those who loved the darkness fled Sol's rising, unwilling to bare their souls to his scrutiny. And those honest, polite and generally good people who throve by day began to venture forth.

One of those people was Mrs Emelie Hartdegen, who ran a ladies' seminary in town—one of those schools where young women of good breeding learn to sit up straight, to take or serve tea, to speak gently and learnedly on a number of topics, to crochet doilies, and so on. Mrs Hartdegen was the wife of Mr Alexis Hartdegen, an itinerant inventor who had come to Chai at the behest of one of his more wealthy patrons, and whose plans for a horseless carriage would have revolutionized intra-national travel in much the same way as the sky-sailer (the invention of Mr Hartdegen's old friend Cornelius Cid II) had international, save that, the first time he threw the switch, both creator and creation had disappeared in a pulse of blue-white light, never to be seen again.

Left to her own devices in a foreign land, Mrs Emelie Hartdegen was, however, undaunted. Once it became apparent that her husband was not going to re-materialize any time soon, she determined that she would have to shift for herself. This she did, and over the years Mrs Emelie's Ladies' Seminary grew in fame and popularity, until parents from as far away as Schlagsahne and Camembert sent their daughters to her, confident that she would return them in much better condition than she had found them.

On this particular day in late spring, drifting cherry blossoms filling the air like rain, as Mrs Emelie walked down the street, her parasol held at just the right angle (but not a right angle, which would not have been right at all!), people waved and wished her good day, and she smiled and wished them the same. At the market she bought a tin of tea, a number of small seed cakes, six eggs, and a handful of brightly colored ribbons, put them in her basket and returned home. In her kitchen, she put the kettle on while she made breakfast, humming to herself a tune from her childhood in Eclaire. She was not thinking of her missing husband (she had thought of him often over the last ten years, usually with fond exasperation and, sometimes, wistful loneliness), or her past students, or anything else in particular, and so, when the doorbell jangled she was completely unprepared for it, and she gave a little scream and dropped an egg on the floor.

"Splat!" went the egg, and "Bother!" exclaimed Mrs Emelie.

Well, the past was done; there was nothing for it but to answer the door. She gave the broken egg a look of extreme disapprobation and went off to do so—

And gave another little scream, this one of delight, upon seeing the figure revealed.

"Why, Mrs Emelie!" cried the tall young woman on the other side of the door. "Don't you look marvelous!"

"And you as well, my dear," Mrs Emelie replied. "Navy blue suits you, I find."

"Do you like it?" The young woman twirled, displaying her fine blue coat with the twin gold epaulettes on her shoulders.

"Indeed I do." Mrs Emelie stood aside. "Won't you come in, and tell me how you've been, Captain?"

"Well," she said, when they were ensconced in her parlor, teacups in hand, before them the remains of a lovely quiche quickly (but daintily, of course) devoured,

"I am certainly happy to hear you have been prospering, my dear. However," she sipped her tea, "I am sorry to see that you have cut your lovely hair."

"Oh!" The young captain gave a little laugh, fingering her shoulder-length curls. "Well. More practical for shipboard life, you know."

"Ah, of course." Mrs Emelie took another dainty sip. "Listen, my dear," she said. "The envoy from Stratocumulopolis is throwing a party two days hence. I will be taking my current crop of young ladies as a sort of graduation exercise. Perhaps you could come along?" She raised her eyes but not her head, regarding her former pupil from beneath delicately arching brows.

The young sailor laughed out loud. "Why, Mrs E!" she cried. "I should love to!"

"A party?" said Captain Zeal, regarding the black-suited messenger with some confusion (sleepless nights did that to him).

"When her Excellency learnt that you were in town, she was most eager for you to attend, sir." The messenger bowed, still presenting the creamy white envelope with both hands.

"Ah," said Zeal, recovering his wits and accepting, at last, the gilded invitation. "Well. Tell her Excellency I should be most happy."

"Very good, sir." The messenger bowed and took his leave.

"A party?" exclaimed Admiral Rangle. "Tell her Excellency I should be most happy to attend, most happy indeed!"

"Very good, sir. Her Excellency will be prostrate with joy. As you know, her love of the Royal Navy nearly equals her love of her own land." The messenger bowed and took his leave.

"And you shall go with me, cous," said the Admiral.

Flynn raised his head off his hands. His face was haggard. "Will I?" he said.

"Oh, indeed you shall. I will send one of my lieutenants into town to obtain what you'll need." The Admiral rubbed his hands and grinned. "A party! How marvelous!"

"A party?" cried Captain Drake. "I'll be damned first."

"Her Excellency in her wisdom foresaw your response, my lady," said the messenger, "and bids me reply, in her own words, 'You'll be damned if you don't'. She also bids me remind your ladyship of a certain item, now in your possession, and respectfully requests that you bring said object to the fete with you, lest you, and I quote, 'suffer her wrath.'"

"Damn her!" snarled Drake, kicking a nearby unoffending ringbolt.

"Calmly now, Captain," cautioned Albius Moonhart, her first mate.

The messenger waited in stiff and formal silence, his face unutterably smug. Drake longed to hit him.

"I will not be calm!" she shouted. "And I will not go to her be-damned infernal bloody party! Tell her I had rather hang from a gibbet than smile and simper and curtsey and play the dutiful daughter in front of a pack of greasy, overfed nobles! Aye, I'd rather my soul rot in the Fisherman's cages than bow one more time to her whims!" And here she stopped, realizing (too late), that to speak so was to court the wrath of Fate—more implacable and inexorable than the wrath of a mother, even a mother like Lady Amica. With one shaking hand, she reached out and touched wood.

The messenger's smirk widened, but before he could speak, a new contender entered the fray.

"Here, now!" cried Cornelius Cid II, stumping up the deck, "what's all this about damnation and death? Bless me!"

"Cid," said Moonhart, relief palpable on his thin face. "Thank God. Perhaps you can talk reason into her."

"What's all this to-do, my Francie?" asked Cid, regarding his daughter. He was rather wider than he was tall, and it was unclear how such an odd, trollish little man could have produced such an elegant child—but produce her he had, and though it remained inexplicable to him, he took it as a sign of Heaven's grace.

"Dad," said Drake. "Please stay out of this."

But Cornelius Cid had not become one of the most famous privateers of the previous age by staying out of things. He had not befriended the Queen of Camembert by staying out of things. And, by God and all His angels and saints, he had not invented the flying ship and thereby saved the world by staying out things! No! And he would not stay out of things now!

Thus, when the situation had been explained to him (by the anxious Moonhart and the smirking messenger), he said, "Why, bless me, Francie! 'Tis been long and long since you've seen your dear mother!" ("Not long enough," muttered Drake.) "Of course you must go! Bless me! And here I thought the world was ending, from all the hooting and hollering and carrying on!" ("It may as well be," groaned Drake.) Turning to the messenger, he said, "Of course she's going. And I'll be going too! Bless me! For indeed, it has been long and long since I've seen my sweet bride!"

"God help us all," said Drake.

"Amen," Moonhart agreed.

There is no more beautiful creation of man's devising than the wooden sailing ship. The three towering masts, blooming with white sails, give it an otherworldly appearance as it lifts and surges across the waves—the thrill in the breasts of Macbeth's army at Birnham Wood's advance is nothing to the shiver a man feels to see that glorious machine gliding across the open sea. And even the ship at rest, at safe anchorage in a sheltered harbor, has some of the same stark beauty as a forest in winter, bare masts raking the jealous sky. What a marvel of complexity! Of ingenuity! Of beauty! Mere words are inadequate to describe the glory of those lofty sails, that maze of ropes, the gleaming, painted hull and bright brass of the ship of war, wind and water harnessed (but never tamed!) by the ingenious hand of man!

And if a single ship, alone on the glassy sea, be a glory, then how can this poor author begin to convey the grandeur and magnificence of the vast flotilla covering the shining expanse of Umeboshi Bay? For, indeed, it seemed that the entire Royal Navy of Camembert had come to Chai, and the bay was white with sails. The people of Umeboshi lined the wharves, watching the ponderous manoeuvres of the mighty three-deckers, the swift grace of the frigates and sloops, the darting motion of the single-masted tenders—and pointing with wonder at the fleet shadows of the sky-sailers overhead.

Even Flynn Freeborn, who had no cause to love the Royal Navy, was moved by the sight, and the salt tears rolled down his cheeks.

"Ah, Flynn Freeborn," he said to himself, scrubbing his streaming eyes with an execrable pocket handkerchief, "you always was a sentimental fool, that you were. But, indeed," he added, even softer still, watching the moving sails just beyond the window pane, "if there is a Heaven at all, up beyond the dome of the sky, then perhaps it is a little like this." Reaching up with one unsteady hand, he touched the glass—and, "Oh, you buggering fool!" he roared, starting from his seat. "Don't you handle her like that! She'll miss stays, you bleeding incompetent!"

Odysseus, attempting to go about, succeeded only in floundering awkwardly in the water, nearly taking off the bowsprit of the nearby *Siren*, who, in trying to get out of the way, almost dismasted the smaller *Dido*. Shaking his head, Flynn subsided back into his chair.

"Feeling better, cous?" said Admiral Rangle, entering.

"I'll be better after this god-damned travesty is concluded," Flynn returned, not bothering either to stand or to turn around. "Really, cous, what the devil are you thinking? That you can pass me off as a gentleman after all this time? Are you planning to introduce me as your long-lost great-great-nephew?" Sulking, he slouched lower in his seat. "And just what the hell are they doing out there? It looks like a bleeding armada."

Bayard only smiled. Going to his cabinet, "Drink, cousin?" he said.

"God, yes," said Flynn, dropping his head into his hands. "God, yes."

For the next two days, the city was abuzz with preparations for the envoy's fete; the excitement managed to eclipse even the people's rapturous adulation of the new Emperor, and all through the town the envoy's servants hurried and scurried, fetching flowers, bearing bouquets, carrying candles hither, thither and yon. The tailors and seamstresses of the city also saw an upsurge in emergency commissions, for everyone who was anyone would be attending this monumomentous soiree, and nobody wanted to be under-dressed.

Captain Zeal was abroad, with Midshipman Peter Goodheart-Smythe, who would also be attending the party, since, as Zeal himself said, "I did promise your parents I would see to your education," although goodness knows if attending fancy parties in foreign lands was what Sir and Lady Smythe had meant by their directive.

Captain Drake was also abroad, having determined when she became one of the most successful pirates of the age that she would never wear the same gown twice, and therefore in need of a new one. Blue, she was thinking. Something to emphasize the blackness of her hair and the whiteness of her skin, and bring out the sapphire highlights in her eyes.

"And diamonds," she added to herself, touching the hollow of her throat. "Something to draw the eye."

She would have continued musing about her attire, complaisant if not precisely happy, if something across the lane had not caught her eye. She paused, cocking her head, wondering what it had been.

It was a woman, a tall young woman with an incredible waterfall of multi-colored hair, leaning over a stall and haggling. It was the hair, in a million violent shades, that had caught Drake's attention. She frowned, a memory tugging at the corner of her mind.

The young woman turned, looked up, caught Drake's scrutiny, and straightened. She wore a pair of curious round spectacles, one lens red, the other blue. The eyes behind them were tawny gold. They widened when they caught sight of Drake, and a puzzled frown came over herface. She shook her head as though to clear it, and returned to her bargaining.

Drake, also frowning, continued on her way.

Not long after, she heard rapid footsteps following her down the street. She put one hand to her dagger as the self-same tawny young woman came pounding up beside her.

"Hey," said the stranger, "I know you, don't I?"

"I don't think so." Drake could be cold if she chose; now, the chill in her voice would have frozen Old Man Winter himself.

Her interlocutor was, however, undeterred. "No, I'm sure of it," she said, tapping her lips with one finger. And then her eyes widened. "Yeah!" she said. "That's it! You're Franceline Drake, aren't you? Of the *Eschaton*." She grinned. "Heard you're looking to sell something."

Drake stopped. "Who the hell are you?" she demanded.

The stranger also stopped. "My name's February," she said. "February Valentine, captain of the *Pandora*. I—"

"You." Drake's mouth twisted with scorn. "I've heard of you. You're a scavenger, a hyena. You prey on others' leavings, like a vulture feeding on rotting flesh."

February's eyes narrowed. "That's pretty fancy talk, coming from a murdering pirate," she said. "Now I'm not sure I wanna do business with you after all." She turned to go.

"Wait," Drake said, and she paused. "What business?"

February grinned, flashing her very white teeth. "You may have found, dear Captain Drake, that the market for fancy trinkets plundered from unsuspecting merchant ships is pretty depressed right now." Drake scowled, and February waved one finger. "However," she said, "there is one person in town who'd be willing to take it off your hands ... for the right price." And she grinned. "Shall we go discuss the possibility of trade?"

"Yes," said Drake through gritted teeth. "Do let's."

It was after the two ladies (and here it must be understood, gentle reader, that we use the term "ladies" in the loosest sense possible, and that furthermore both young women would chuckle and snort to hear themselves so described) had concluded their business to their mutual satisfaction that they rounded a corner and came face-to-face with Captain Zeal and young Peter Goodheart-Smythe.

Peter's eyes grew very wide.

Drake's mouth opened, as though to speak, but no words emerged.

Captain Zeal's face grew hard, and with a brief nod (barely a jerk of his head), he continued on his way, leaving poor young Peter scurrying to catch up.

"Ex-boyfriend?" asked February, her voice an amused drawl.

"It's none of your business," said Drake.

"Captain Zeal ... sir?" said Peter, after perhaps five blocks of scrambling to keep up with his death-marching captain. "Sir, who was that lady?"

"No one, Peter," Zeal replied, his face still grim and set. "No one at all."

But Peter, though admittedly young, had not been born the previous morning, and the tone of his captain's voice bespoke a lie. He was no prophet, though sometimes it seemed he could see the many strands of destiny coiling before him, and could, with a little effort, discern the individual threads and where they led—but it didn't take someone with supernatural vision to see that the captain was troubled. The lady meant something to Captain Zeal, and what she meant was—

"Doom!" cried a nearby voice, and Peter had jumped halfway to the moon before he had discerned the voice's source.

"Death!" the voice cried. "Despair!"

"Pay him no mind, lad," said Captain Zeal, laying a hand on his shoulder. "He's just a doom-sayer."

The speaker was an old man, wild-eyed and wild-haired, dressed in a rough garment of some coarse material, barefoot, dirty, clutching a placard that had written on it (in many different languages) Doom! Peter couldn't help it. He stared.

"Disaster!" cried the doom-sayer, brandishing his placard. He looked straight past Peter, giving no indication that he saw him at all. "Death!"

"Peter..." said Captain Zeal.

"The days of darkness are coming!" the doom-sayer cried. His teeth were rotting, and his breath was rank. "These days of peace are but an illusion, a trick to lull the unwary! Be not lulled! Be not unwary! For the dark times are at hand, and they will engulf the innocent and guilty alike in a wave of blood! None shall be spared! The cataclysm that will shatter the world—"

"Come, Peter," said Captain Zeal, taking a firm grip on the midshipman's arm and hauling him away. "Let's leave the gibbering maniac in peace." But Peter turned and watched the maniac recede into the distance, still gibbering. Only when the pronouncements of doom were no longer audible did Captain Zeal release him, and only then did Peter's attention return to the present.

"Oh, Captain!" he said, flushing. "I'm sorry, sir. I don't know what came over me."

Captain Zeal smiled and shook his head. "Quite all right, lad. To tell you the truth, I had much the same reaction the first time I saw one. Why, I remember it was back in the year..."

But Peter had ceased paying attention. Doom. The threads of destiny coiled out before him, tangled and impenetrable.

The evening came. The house of the draconic envoy, situated on a tall hill just outside the city (dragons are perfectly willing to fraternize with human beings, but they cannot abide living on the ground, their own city being built on a floating mountain, and will therefore, when in human lands, choose the highest point available for their dwelling places), was a perfect blaze of light. The coaches and carriages and other conveyances of the city's wealthy and important, hung with lanterns, clattered along the roads; if seen from above, it would appear as though the city were made of living light, pulsing like blood in a vein, making its way to the magnificent, glowing heart.

"Come now, ladies, come!" cried Mrs Emelie, clapping her white-gloved hands, and at once her pupils broke off their primping and turned to face their mistress.

Mrs Emelie surveyed them with satisfaction. They were, perhaps, the best group of students she had ever taught, all of them meek and courteous, decorous (that is not to say decorative, although they were lovely girls) and polite. Six young faces turned toward hers, and she smiled.

"It is time," Mrs Emelie said. "Tie your ribbons, fasten your earrings, put on your shoes, my dears—the coaches have arrived, and we must away."

"Oh, Mrs Emelie!" cried one, a young lady with golden ringlets, "Will not Verity be joining us?"

"She will meet us there, my dear, I am sure," replied Mrs Emelie. "Come now. Let us away."

Captain Flynn clean, sober and well-dressed was a different creature entirely from the squalid wretch they had hauled aboard H.M.S. *Boadicea*, believing him to be a shipwrecked merchant captain (it helped that he had Captain True's papers on his person), completely different from the haggard, unshaven, hollow-eyed quivering ruin he had appeared when the Royal Marines arrested him for assaulting the captain of the flagship (the treasures he had taken from Captain True's cabin had been spent more quickly than he could have expected; having been ashore for several weeks, he had been growing desperate, and it's hard to pick a pocket when your hands are shaking). But now, standing before the mirror in Bayard's stateroom, knotting his cravat, his hands hardly trembled at all. He regarded his face in the glass, the face of a handsome grey-eyed rogue, and gave himself a smile just for practice. It looked, to his own eyes at least, a little forced, and a little sickly.

"And what's to be done with you now, Flynn Freeborn?" he asked himself, rubbing his freshly-shaved chin. "Is there peace in this life for an old sinner like you?"

"After you've fulfilled your obligation to me," said Bayard, entering as quietly as a vampire, the aged spaniel at his heels, "you are free to do what you will." He stopped beside Flynn in the mirror. "Don't you look natty, cous?"

"You're none too shabby yourself," Flynn returned. The Admiral's uniform was ablaze with gold, its front adorned with medals.

"Shall we go, then?"

"All right." Flynn took a deep breath, drawing himself up straight, and turned away from the face in the glass. "Let's."

III. Meetings and greetings—All the comforts of home—Cupid's arrow strikes hard and deep—The potential of the Chai navy discussed—All manner of startling revelations revealed

Who was there?

Everyone!

Officers of Her Majesty's Navy, and her Army, were there, the former in deep blue, the latter in red. Camembertian expatriates—diplomats, nobles, their wives, clad in an array of colours, from lavender to bottle-green. Local officials, dressed in their usual somber black. The city's intelligentsia, bespectacled and awkward in coats with corduroy patches on the elbows and too-short sleeves. So too were all the marriageable young ladies Umeboshi could produce, all of them glittering so with gold and gemstones that to look at them directly were to look at the very sun.

Of the envoy from Stratocumulopolis, there was yet no sign.

It was rumored that Emperor Katsukare himself might later be in attendance.

Who else was there?

Captain Franceline Drake, resplendent in sapphire-blue velvet, a collar of diamonds at her throat. Her eyes sparked with malice, and her smile was predatory.

Captain Acheron Zeal, in his most beautiful formal uniform, ablaze with gold lace, young Peter Goodheart-Smythe beside him. "Stay close, lad," said he. "This sort of place can be dangerous."

"Dangerous, sir?" said Peter, his eyes very wide.

"Yes," Zeal said, and put a hand over his heart, but said no more.

Captain Flynn Freeborn, tall and dashing in a coat of amber-gold and new black boots. With one glance he took in the hosts of eligible young women, vying for the attentions of the eligible men. With the next, the legions of serving-men, circulating through the crowd with trays of drinks on their shoulders. Rubbing his chin, he gave a long, slow smile.

"Behave yourself, cous," said Admiral Rangle.

Flynn turned on him a look of wide-eyed, wounded innocence. "Ah, cous!" he said. "When have I not?"

Mrs Emelie kept her charges close to her, as a shepherdess keeps watch over her flock.

"Oh, Mrs Emelie, shall we not be able to dance?" said one young lady, with a sigh.

"Certainly you shall," Mrs Emelie replied, "when the dancing has begun. For the time, however, you must stay near me."

No sooner had she spoken than golden-haired Lethe let out an unladylike shriek and pelted across the room, flinging herself into the arms of a startled young man in a post-captain's uniform. "Brother!" she cried.

"Why, Lethe!" exclaimed Acheron Zeal, catching her and twirling her through the air. "I had no idea you would be here!" He set her on the floor, examining her. "You are looking very well indeed. May I present to you Mr Peter Goodheart-Smythe? Peter, my sister, Lethe."

"Charmed, ma'am," said wide-eyed Peter, making a leg.

"Indeed, Mr Goodheart-Smythe," said Lethe, giggling, "the pleasure is mine." And tucking her hand through Zeal's arm, she said, "Shall I introduce you to the others?"

"Who is that handsome young man on Lethe's arm, Mrs Emelie?"

"That, I am quite certain," Mrs Emelie replied, "is her brother, Captain

Acheron Zeal. But we shall find out in a moment, I think."

Indeed. Lethe—rosy-cheeked, bright-eyed, laughing—dragged the handsome young man towards the waiting circle of women (waiting, Zeal thought uneasily, like a gaggle of gorgons eager to devour their hapless prey) and made the appropriate introductions. To Mrs Emelie he bowed; to the twins, Cantaloupé and Envelopé Avoirdupois, daughters of an Eclairesian diplomat, he gave each a brief kiss on the hand (blushes, giggles from the twins); to sweet-faced Lola Leitmotif, of Schlagsahne, the same. When Lethe reached the last member of the group, a young woman whose lively face was framed by short auburn curls, whose blue gown was cut after the fashion of a naval uniform, she gave a little pause and then said, "And this is Captain Verity Tannin. Captain Tannin, meet Captain Zeal."

"Captain?" repeated Zeal, blinking.

"Oh, indeed." There was laughter in her eyes. "The *Boadicea* is mine."

"Ah," said he, and then bowed as he would to a fellow officer of the Navy.

"But, Captain," said Verity, laughing, "have you no kiss for me?"

"I believe there's an injunction in the Articles against officers kissing," replied Zeal, with a smile. "But I would offer you a dance, if you would have it."

"Gladly," said she, and he led her away.

Lethe, watching, gave a smile of immense satisfaction.

Peter, left to his own devices, wandered toward one of the edges of the room, where he could watch from a position of relative safety. He found the presence of so many people a little overwhelming. Here they all were, dancing, flirting, conniving, making alliances or breaking them, the sound of their laughter diamond-bright, diamond-hard, diamond-sharp. He shrank against the wall, using a marble column for support.

"Don't like parties, lad?"

At the voice he gasped and jerked away from the wall, whirling to accost his accoster—

And at once felt a total sense of relief.

The full ceremonial armor of the Knights of St George was seldom seen these days; many people considered it old-fashioned, not to say passé. But what did the Knights care for the passing fashions of the world? They were sworn to serve God, and they served Him best in their beautiful burnished plate-mail, their white surcoats, and their blood-red cloaks, clasped at the throat with the silver badge of their order. The antique armor may have been out of place at such a fashionable gathering as this, but to Peter it spoke of comfort, familiarity and home. Though the man who wore it was unfamiliar, the armor was not, and it put him immediately at ease.

"Thibault Hawthorne, at your service," said the Knight, placing his hand over his heart and bowing. Peter did the same. When they had straightened, Sir Thibault said, "And you, young sir? I can't speak to having met you before, but I know your face."

"Peter Goodheart-Smythe," said Peter, and the Knight's clouded face cleared.

"Ah, of course," he said. "Your father's stamp is plain upon you." He smiled. "And your mother's, too."

"You know my parents, sir?" Like any youngster in a foreign land, Peter was eager for news of hearth and home.

Sir Thibault smiled. "I had the honor of serving beside them both, in the war."

"Will you tell me about it, sir?" Neither Sir Gregory nor Lady Althea had ever seen fit to tell their children about their experiences during the war. Even Sir Ryan Effervens, his father's best friend, on other topics garrulous, even verbose, grew close-mouthed when the subject came up.

And it seemed Peter would be frustrated once again. "It's no fit subject for a place like this," said Sir Thibault. "And if your parents haven't told you the stories, then it's certainly not my place to do so." Peter opened his mouth to protest, and the old Knight's eyes flashed. "Leave it, young Smythe," he said.

Peter hung his head. "Yes, sir."

"Good lad."

Peter sighed and went back to watching the people. Here was a woman with pink and lavender hair, dressed in a garish gown of purple and gold, looking like the Queen's own fool. And there, a man in a whiskey-colored coat, his auburn pigtail falling halfway down his back. There was Captain Zeal, dancing with a lady in navy blue. She was very pretty, he thought, and she was laughing as he whirled her through the measures. Surely, surely that was a good thing?

"Now, tell me honestly, Captain," said Verity Tannin, her hand warm on his shoulder even through the dense layers of broadcloth, "you're not just being humble? Because I've heard great things about you, and I'd hate to think I'd been deceived."

"When evaluating the truth of what you hear, Captain," Zeal returned, "it's best to consider the honesty of the messenger."

"Oh," said she, "I've never had reason to think this messenger anything but honest." Her eyes flicked over his shoulder, and he turned to follow her glance. Lethe, partnered with a stocky military man, smiled cheerfully at him.

He turned back to his own partner. "Honest, maybe," he said, "but a little given to hyperbole."

She grinned. "Perhaps. But she told me her older brother was the handsomest and most charming man she knew, and so far I've had no reason to doubt her word." And then, perhaps surprised by her own boldness, she looked away from him, her cheeks (almost as sun-browned as his own) turning a dusky rose. And, to his surprise, Zeal found his own face warming, his heart beating a little faster. He cleared his throat and said,

"But tell me. I heard rumors of a Captain Tannin who duelled the pirate Benten to a stand-still on her own quarterdeck. Was that you?"

Verity gave a little nod.

Zeal stared in admiration. "I had always assumed that Captain Tannin was a man," he admitted.

"Most people do," she replied, with a sly little grin, "until they meet me."

"At which point," he said, "they can't help but be disabused of their erroneous notion."

Her smile widened. "You flatter me, Captain Zeal."

"You will find," he answered, "that, unlike my sister, I am not prone to hyperbole." He was rewarded with another radiant smile, and he smiled to himself. If he wasn't careful, he might find himself addicted to those smiles—might find himself doing all manner of imprudent things to earn them.

So when she looked over his shoulder and gave a little start, he was prepared to be pleased if she were pleased, or to comfort if she were unhappy. "Oh, look!" she said. "There's Captain True."

Captain True? Zeal turned, to see what she saw.

And there, just behind him, was the vile wretch, the nefarious ne'er-do-well, the wicked dog he had pursued cross half the world and more—bold as brass, in the middle of a room full of naval officers:

The captain of the *Eschaton*!

And he was dancing with Zeal's sister!

Captain Flynn was having a marvelous time. Here was all the grog he could drink, and surrounding him was charming womanhood in all its delightful variety. He danced and flirted and drank, and drank and danced and flirted, and if there was a lady present whose heart had not fluttered, whose breath had not come quicker, at the attentions of the handsome Captain Flynn, it was only because he hadn't got to her yet. Here and there he caught glimpses of people he knew—Miss Francie, looking as beautiful as spring and as venomous as a serpent, moving across the floor with graceful purpose and leaving no doubt a chain of broken hearts in her wake—the blond post-captain from the opera, dancing with Captain Verity, his beauteous rescuer—Cousin Bayard, hobnobbing with the rich, the famous and the powerful.

There came, while he was standing by a refreshment table, pouring himself a drink, one of those universal pauses that sometimes occur at parties, when the entire room holds its breath for an instant to allow the Fates to do their work. The crowd before him parted (images of the Red Sea), and he saw—oh, he saw, for the briefest of instants—a vision of heaven, of beauty so sublime he felt his heart grow light, grow winged, and fly to land itself at her feet.

"Oh," said he, his glass dropping unnoticed from a hand grown slack, an acquisitive leer lighting his face. "Oh, I must have her."

Of such tangles are our destinies made.

Through the crowd he forced himself, following his heart's beacon, like a lighthouse guiding him past wicked shoals to safe harbor and home. Perhaps, he thought as he searched, perhaps it was an illusion, some nefarious trick played on him by the ghosts in his head. Perhaps he hadn't seen her at all, perhaps she wasn't real—

He found her.

"Begging your pardon, mate," he said, tapping her partner. "I'm cutting in, so I am."

"Here, now, you—!" cried the fellow, but the measures of the dance had already whirled on without him. Her hands were in his now, she was in his arms, slim and perfect, so perfect...

"I don't believe I know you, sir," she said, not glancing aside as maidenly decorum would require, but boldly meeting his eyes. His pulse quickened.

"No more you do, damsel," he replied, "but we have world enough, and time."

"Will you not give me your name?"

Blue eyes, blue as summer, blue as a southern sea. Golden hair, like sunlight on the sails. Roses on the porcelain of her cheeks. Oh, but she was a vision—no, no vision at all, for here he was, holding her living hand, leading her through the dance.

"And what name should I give you?" he asked. "What name would you accept from someone like me?"

"Are you such a terrible person? Should I fear you?"

"Oh, aye," he told her. "Oh, I'm a rogue and a sinner, and there is no virtue in my soul. I can see nothing beautiful but I want to corrupt it, and I'd sell out me own mother if the price was right. You should be fleeing me, so you should, fleeing as far and as fast as you can, and never letting me find you again." Her eyes widened, and she trembled in his arms. "Don't flee from me," he said, suddenly pleading.

"Tell me your name," she said.

My name, he thought. It was difficult to think. My name. My name is Forever, and my parents christened me I-Love-You. I'm the child of a tempest and a devil, and if you trust me with that sublime beauty of yours, I will surely ruin you, tarnish you, betray you—Oh, run from me—Oh, stay!

"Flynn," he said. "Flynn is my name."

"I am Lethe," she said.

She dropped his hand and walked away.

He thought his heart would stop.

"I think, sir," said an icy voice behind him, "that you had best explain yourself now."

"Trouble?" said Sir Thibault.

"My captain," said Peter. "He's short-tempered and impetuous."

"Ah." Sir Thibault folded his arms and leaned against the wall. "Then we may as well watch the show."

The rogue turned slowly, and on his face was a strange mixture of resignation and despair, still lit with a last disappearing ray of hope.

"What were you doing with my sister?" Zeal demanded.

"Dancing," the pirate replied. "As you saw."

"Upon your honor, you swear you didn't—" He was unable to continue.

"Honor, now," said the pirate, with a slow, bitter grin. "That's a tricksy word, so it is. And what's it to do with the likes of me? But your sister—" and the bitter look faded, to be replaced by something not unlike regret, "she's got more sense than to let a rogue like me despoil her, that she does, and so I reckon she's safe enough."

Zeal's face, which had purpled at *despoil*, slowly resumed its more natural hue. "Perhaps so. However, it was foolish of you to come here. You must have known I would find you."

"Why, Cap'n, if I'd known you was looking for me, I'd have saved you the trouble. Though in truth, 'tis sorry I am about our little misunderstanding at the opera house. I hope you didn't bruise too badly?" He managed to look both solicitous and smug.

Verity, standing all but forgotten at his side, watched the exchange with interest.

"You know perfectly well," said Zeal, "that that's not what I'm talking about. Pirate. You're a wanted man, and in the morning you'll face the hangman's noose. You've despoiled Her Majesty's trade long enough." He took a certain pleasure in throwing the pirate's word back in his face.

"I've despoiled..." repeated the pirate, then stopped. Slow comprehension dawned, and he laughed out loud, clapping Zeal on the shoulder. "Oh!" he chortled. "Oho-ho-ho! Ohhhhh!" He bent double, wheezing with laughter.

"I really don't see what's so funny about your imminent demise," Zeal said.

"Hoo-hoo-hoo!" Wiping his eyes, the pirate straightened. "Oh, mate," he said. "You're laboring under a terrible misconception, that you are. If it's the captain of the *Eschaton* you're seeking, then you're not looking for me." He stuck out his hand. "Cap'n Thomas True, late of the merchant ship *Rhymer*."

Confused, and feeling not a little bit foolish, Zeal took the man's hand and shook it. "Then you're not...?"

"Nay, I'm not." Captain True shook his head. "Sorry to be disappointing you, mate."

"See?" said Verity. "I told you."

Captain True bowed and took her hand. "And what a pleasure it is to be seeing you again, Captain dear."

She smiled. "I'm happy to see that you have recovered from your misfortunes."

"'Tis all thanks to your sweet help, my lady." He kissed her hand.

Zeal's head was reeling. "I'm very sorry about all the confusion, sir," he said. "I really thought—I truly thought—"

"'Tis no trouble at all, mate. No trouble at all." Captain True, now that he was not being accosted by an irrational, gibbering Navy officer bent on sending him to the gallows, was chuckly and expansive. "And may I wish you the best in finding your actual prey, Cap'n...?"

"Zeal," he said faintly. "Acheron Zeal."

"Cap'n Zeal." Tipping an imaginary hat, still chortling to himself, Captain True took himself away, and was soon lost to sight.

"Lethe Zeal," said Flynn to himself as he walked away, testing the sound of the name. He found it sweet in his mouth, melodious to his ears, and he gave a little smile as he went in search of her once more.

"Well," said Verity, watching the merchant captain swagger away. "I'm happy that's resolved." She cast Zeal a curious glance. "But did you really think he was the captain of the *Eschaton*?"

"I really did," Zeal said.

"Hmm." She bit her lip, hesitating. "But, then...."

Catching her mood, "What?" he said.

"No. Nothing." She shook her head, smiled brightly at him. "Shall we dance?"

Relieved, Peter resumed holding up his pillar. Sir Thibault looked down at the boy. "Situation normal?" he asked.

"For now," Peter replied, narrowing his eyes. He could feel, like the fluttery feeling of dread you get in your stomach when you're about to go to the dentist's, the approach of something, something awful and irrevocable, but here in this room, where so many destinies coiled and tangled, it was impossible to tell from what quarter it might come. He shook his head. "I can't see." And then his eyes focussed, and he jumped. "Oh!" he said.

Sir Thibault chuckled.

The wall of grey that had blocked his vision resolved itself into a rough grey coat, its hem long enough almost to brush the ground, which adorned the man before him—a swarthy fellow with cold eyes, who was bowing to Sir Thibault, his gloved hand over his heart.

Standing a pace or two behind the man was a boy, about Peter's own age, dressed also in grey. He had dark hair and fair skin and pale blue eyes. It was the eyes that caught Peter's attention ... and drew it down in, deeper and deeper.... "I know you," Peter whispered in confusion.

"Peter," said Sir Thibault, and Peter jerked back to the present. "May I present Sir Aldreas Zindel?"

"Honored, sir," said Peter, bowing. The man gave a little jerk of his head, his black eyes never blinking. "What sort of Knight are you, sir?" he asked, when he had straightened, curiosity overcoming good breeding. "I've never seen that sort of coat before."

It was rather a fantastic garment. Its sleeves stopped at the man's elbows, and bright-colored beads were sewn along them and along the hem. Where an embroidered trim might adorn an ordinary coat (or, at least, might have done several centuries before), there were very small, very detailed pictures of people with bright, alert eyes.

The Knight gave a harsh chuckle. "Like it, boy? Keeps the demons off. They don't like the sound." He moved his arm, and the colored beads clashed and jangled.

Demons? In some confusion, Peter looked up at Sir Thibault.

"Sir Aldreas is a Knight of Lazarus," Sir Thibault explained.

"More Knights in this world than just you pansy-ass Georgians," Sir Aldreas said with a terrifying, bleak grin. "We keep the world safe for the rest of you."

"Meanwhile running it from your secret hide-out under the Basilica," said Sir Thibault.

"Somebody's got to keep the conspiracy theorists happy."

"I'm Peter Goodheart-Smythe," said Peter, to the boy hiding behind Sir Aldreas's coat.

The boy's eyes flicked up to his master—but the strange Knight was still busy trading barbs with Sir Thibault. Creeping forward a little, he said, "Leonides. Eberhard Leonides," and held out his hand. Peter reached out and took it.

A strange thing happened then, when the two boys' hands clasped. Peter could see, as a scroll unrolling before him, Fate's woven tapestry—could see his own thread, bound closely with this other boy's—and then, in a flash, the vision was gone, and Peter shivered.

"I do know you," he said, staring.

"Not yet," said the other boy, eyes equally wide. "But you will."

"Leonides." The harsh voice of Sir Aldreas made him drop Peter's hand with a jerk. "Come on. We've got work to do."

"Yes, sir." Sir Aldreas turned and strode away, heavy boots thudding against the marble floor. After a moment, Leonides turned and followed. Peter watched them go, feeling weak and confused, as you will after waking up from a strange dream, feeling as well that something unspeakably important had just happened, although he couldn't have told you what it was.

"Lazarites," said Sir Thibault, shaking his head. "Odd bunch. Comes of skulking through the shadows, chasing vampires all the time, I suppose. Still, that was interesting and edifying, eh, young Smythe?"

"Yes, sir," said Peter, still watching the grey Knight and his squire, although they were long since lost in the crowd. "It was."

"Nice party," said February Valentine, she of the purple hair and the purple-and-yellow dress, gazing around her through her red-and-blue spectacles. Never one to limit her color palette, was February Valentine. "Thanks for the invite."

Drake shrugged, indifferent. In truth, she had scarcely heard a word of the treasure-hunter's prattle all evening; her jealous gaze was fixed on one figure, a certain blond-haired post captain who had shown a distressing disinclination to pay attention to her—had shown, in fact, a distressing disinclination to pay attention to anyone besides the woman with the auburn curls, whose side he had not left all evening.

"It is too much," she said to herself, tapping her folded fan against the palm of her hand. "It cannot be borne."

"Uh-huh," said February. "Listen. I'm gonna go get a drink. You want anything?"

"No." Drake bared her teeth. It was one thing to do business with such a loud-mouthed raparee, quite another to associate with her after-hours, as it were. "Go have fun. Someplace far away, preferably. I hear Schlagsahne is lovely this time of year." She returned her attention to Acheron Zeal, who was still focused on that red-headed creature, as though she were the only female in the room, or perhaps the entire world!

A nudge in the ribs recalled her to her companion. "What, still here?" she asked.

"Francie." February had leant very close, near enough to whisper in Drake's ear. "You know everybody. Who is that?" She pointed with her elbow.

Drake looked ... and then smiled. "Well, well," she said. "So he survived. He has the devil's luck, that one, and more lives than a cat."

"Great," said February. "But who is he?" She bore no small resemblance to a cat herself—a cat who has seen a large, plump and tempting prey item on the other side of the window pane. She was practically licking her lips.

Still smiling, Drake gave the other woman a little push. "Why don't you go and find out?" she said. "Introduce yourself."

"Yeah." February drew herself erect, smoothing her violent-colored hair. "Yeah. Good idea." And off she marched, on a path that would soon intersect with that of her quarry.

Drake breathed a sigh of profound relief. "Finally." She had prey of her own to hunt.

Nor was she the only one. But the game that Flynn Freeborn hunted was elusive, fleet as the bounding doe who leads the hunter cross swift-running streams, through sun-dappled glades, and every time he thought he had cornered her at last, he found that she had evaded him once more. Glimpses he caught of her, a glimmer of golden hair, a gleam of summer-blue eyes, a strain of her drifting laughter—and when he turned to follow them, they disappeared, leaving him alone again in a sea of strangers.

He found her at last, dancing with a soldier in a coat as red as his face. She looked up and saw him, and he could not read the emotion he saw in her sweet summer eyes: did she welcome his approach, or rather fear it? Only one way to find out, he thought, tugging at his coat, starting towards her—

Only to find someone else standing in his way.

"Hi, there," said the woman before him. She was not unlovely, in her way—but as soon compare the beauty of mortal Briseis to the pristine, chaste pulchritude of Diana, as compare this woman with the one he sought.

"Aye, good evening to you," Flynn replied, trying to inch around her. "If you'll just be excusing me—"

She blocked his way. "My name's February," she said. "What's yours?"

"Begging your pardon, Miss February," said Flynn. Red-coat was leading Lethe away. She glanced back once, then turned her face away from him. As soon deprive him of the sun's sweet light! "But I'm in a terrible great hurry, so I am—"

"Too much hurry to give a lady your name?" she asked.

He paused and regarded her. Her skin was golden-bronze, her hair the colors that might result if a cake-decorator's shop exploded. She grinned at him.

If you're a lady, he thought, his gaze travelling downwards to the generous expanse of bosom that her costume revealed, then I'm the King of Cilantro, so I am. His eyes sought Lethe one more time—but she was going, she was going....

"Gone," he sighed. "She's gone."

Face it, Flynn, he said to himself. She would never have been yours, never in a thousand ages of humankind.

It was with a brittle feeling of despair that he turned back towards the young woman with the fantastic hair. "Nay," he said, switching on his smile (and false it felt, as false as his clothes, his hair, his damned foolish accent, as everything about him), "never in life, sweet lady."

"Good." She saw that his attention was hers, and she revelled in her triumph. "What do you say we find someplace a little more private, where we can chat?"

"Aye," he found himself saying, helplessly. What else was there to say? "Aye, that sounds fine, it does. It sounds grand."

He let himself be led away.

Lethe Zeal looked back over her shoulder one last time. The man from earlier, who had been approaching her with such purpose, she had thought, had turned away again, was leaving on the arm of a woman of dubious quality. And whether the feeling that rose up in her breast was relief or disappointment, she could not have said, and didn't try.

"I must confess," said Captain Zeal, "I've never had much of an opinion of the Chai-landers' naval capabilities."

"Of course not," said Verity. "But do consider, Captain—they are an island nation, and although they've never shown much interest in the larger world, they still must trade, and fish, and protect their shores from the threat of foreign invasion. They've been sailing far longer than we have, actually."

The two were sitting in the envoy's garden, enjoying the cool breeze that came off the distant bay, enjoying, too, the relative peace and quiet after the din of the ballroom. The envoy to Chai had arranged the grounds of her great house to mimic the famous hanging gardens of Stratocumulopolis, where graceful vines and sweet-smelling blossoms and slender trees harmonize with marble fountains and exquisite statues and elegant architecture to create a symphony of beauty. Zeal and Verity had found a marble bench under an arbor of roses and night-blooming jasmine, near enough the manor to hear, faintly, the music and laughter within, and see the golden lights of its myriad windows, but far enough that these reminders of the presence of others did not disturb their sense of privacy. They sat near each other, though not near enough to touch (although, if Zeal had wanted and dared, he could have reached out and taken her salt-roughened, sun-browned hand), each revelling in the novel, by no means unpleasant sense of having found a thoroughly amiable, not unhandsome, charming, intelligent and completely like-minded person.

"Fishermen," said Zeal. "No match for the full might of Her Majesty's Navy."

"Don't be so quick to dismiss them, Captain," said Verity, smiling. "Those fishermen gave me a tense moment or two. You know, of course, that the pirate Benten was from Chai?"

Zeal nodded. "Sort of a pirate queen in these parts, wasn't she?"

"Oh, yes. It's practically a national pastime, piracy, and an old family business of hers. She'd called in all her old family debts and assembled a vast squadron of those little bluff doggers they're so partial to. They made themselves quite a nuisance, playing Old Harry with trade, and eventually I was sent to put a stop to their capers." She gave him a keen glance. "This was when you were on the other side of the world, chasing after the *Eschaton*."

"I did hear about it," Zeal said, "but only at second- or third-hand. Will you tell me the story?"

"I will," she said, and she did, describing the relative might of the two squadrons, how the Chai pirates had scattered, concealing themselves in small inlets and hidden coves, only to pop out and pepper the men-of-war, then scurry away again before the squadron could react.

"Frustrating business, it was," Verity said, "but I had several fast frigates with me, and with the squadron spread out as far as it would go, every ship just within signalling distance of the next, I was able to net the lot of them at last." The pirates' two-masted doggers were no match for a squadron of the Royal Navy, and only a few managed to escape—one of those few, however, was the pirate Benten, in her ship *Good Fortune*.

The squadron gave chase (in the cadences of her voice, Zeal could hear the rush of the salt spray, the white crash of the sea rising up to meet the warships' bows, the taut hum of lines and sails as the captains bent all their wiles to urging their ships to just one more knot of speed), cornering the pirates at last in the sheltered bay of an island just south of Garam Masala.

"Here," said Verity, scooting away from him on the marble bench. "This pebble is *Boadicea*, and these are the frigates, *Bedivere, Aeneas* and *Ramage*. Now..." she said, scouting around her, "I need two pirate ships..."

"This rose petal?" said Zeal, offering it to her. "And..." fishing through his pockets, "this coin?"

"Perfect. And this pistachio shell that someone has discarded here can be the *Good Fortune*." She positioned the markers, shook her head, nudged the *Aeneas* pebble slightly to the right, and then smiled. "Well," she said, and gave him the lay of the land, the direction of the wind, the choppiness of the water, the squadron close-hauled on the starboard tack as they beat up into the bay, the pirates, smug and waiting with the weather gage, allowing the warships to tire themselves out before they descended like hawks. And then the smoke and the thunder, as battle was joined! The glorious din!

The pirates determined to carry the day by boarding, being outmanned and outgunned, "but we turned the tables on them," said Verity, a fierce grin lighting her face, "and we drubbed them on board just as we drubbed them a-sea. I led my party to the quarterdeck of the *Good Fortune* itself, and there I fought that pirate to a stand-still. The others soon surrendered, preferring to lay down their arms rather than see their leader killed. And that," she said, "was how it was done."

"Brilliant!" said Zeal, gazing at her with admiration ... and, to be honest, a touch of unease. It was very well for women to captain ships, even to lead them into battle, he supposed (there had been one or two other female captains in the history of the Royal Navy), and if a man had told him the story, he would have had nothing but respect for his deeds ... but was it not a stain on a woman, to have her hands bloodied by the filthy work of war? It was the task of men to go to war, that the souls of womankind might remain unsullied by its squalor. And yet, he thought of Lady Althea Goodheart-Smythe, the Queen's Champion, whom he had once met. No one could say that her bright soul was sullied by the work of war—its darkness could not touch her.

"Captain?" said Verity, her hand brushing his, concern in her eyes. "Are you all right?"

"No doubt," said a new voice, from behind him, "he is struck dumb with awe at your mighty deeds, Captain Tannin. He is speechless to think that a mere woman has done what he could not."

"I don't believe I know you, sir," said Zeal coolly, rising to his feet and turning to face the newcomer. He was a man of below-average height and above-average girth, his dark curly hair and enormous great sideburns framing a round-cheeked, olive-skinned face. His mouth was wide, like that of a toad. His eyes were murky brown.

"Captain Acheron Zeal," said Verity, also standing, "meet Captain Pfillip Pflugelhorn, lately of Her Majesty's frigate *Aeneas*."

"And currently of Her Majesty's flying ship *Boreas*," said Pflugelhorn, puffing out his chest, the better to show off the sky-blue sash encircling it, the mark of a flying captain of Her Majesty's Navy.

"Ah," said Verity, "and have you attained that ultimate felicity? I congratulate you, sir. It doesn't hurt, I'm sure, to have friends in ... ah ... high places."

"I hope you are not implying, Captain Tannin," said Pflugelhorn, sniffing, "that my promotion is the result of anything but my own consummate seamanship and my leadership abilities nonpareil."

"I implied nothing, sir," Captain Tannin replied coolly.

Zeal couldn't help it. He snorted.

Captain Pflugelhorn shot him a hard look. "I've heard of your exploits, Captain Zeal," he said. "You were sent to capture a single pirate, and instead managed only to sink your own ship. Given a new ship and a second chance by the Lords of the Admiralty—passing generous of them—you've done nothing but squander opportunity after opportunity, and the *Eschaton* remains a constant irritant to Her Majesty's trade."

"I suppose you believe, Captain," said Zeal in a clenched voice, "that you could do better?"

"I hope, Captain Zeal, that I have not offended you," said Pflugelhorn in grating tones of false conciliation.

Zeal counted to ten. Ten seemed inadequate, so he counted to fifty. Then he counted fifty more, just to be safe—although a count of a trillion would have been inadequate to cool down his temper, once roused. "Not at all, Captain," he gritted. Verity laid a hand on his arm, and it was a cool balm against the heat of his anger.

Here let us insert a few words about Captain Pfillip Pflugelhorn: son of a minor lord, with considerable interest in the government, his career thus far had been as undistinguished as his rise through the ranks remarkable. His father, Lord Pfrederick Pflugelhorn, was known to predict at his club, when the sherry and the punch had been flowing freely, that if Pfillip was not an Admiral and wed to a peeress, by the age of forty, it was no fault of his, Lord Pfrederick's, own, despite any of Captain Pflugelhorn's defects of person or personality.

That being said, he was also notable duellist, and had been out more than fifty times—despite, he protested, being as peaceful and amicable a man as anyone could possibly wish.

"Still," said Pflugelhorn, examining his fingernails, "one does wonder, doesn't one? Why would the Admiralty send an ocean-crawler after a sky-sailing pirate? And why send an unknown, untried young frigate captain against the most famous pirate of the age? If one were inclined to question his betters, one might wonder what they were thinking."

Verity's grip on his arm tightened. "Easy," she hissed into his ear.

"Yes of course," Zeal growled, but he subsided, manfully not smacking Pflugelhorn a good one.

"I know!" said Pflugelhorn, striking his palm as though struck by a bolt of inspiration from Heaven. "Perhaps they should send Captain Tannin here. She has a certain skill in hunting down lady pirates. Like calls to like, I suppose."

Verity gave him a look of horror. Captain Zeal shook off her hand and started forward. "Listen to me, Captain. You can insult me until the sun rises and the stars go home, and I'll bear it without a murmur, but don't sully Captain Tannin's name with your filthy mouth, or by God and all the saints I will see you bleed for it!"

Something in Zeal's face—his bared teeth, perhaps, or his blazing eyes—must have impressed Captain Pflugelhorn, for he raised his hands in the universal gesture of peaceful intent and took a step backwards. "I meant no offense, Captain Zeal," he said, still backing away. "Sometimes I don't know what I'm saying—you understand—"

"No offense taken," Zeal spat.

Verity sighed with relief.

And then something Pflugelhorn had said trickled down the passageway of Captain Zeal's ear and penetrated his brain. He frowned. "What exactly do you mean, lady pirates?" he asked.

Verity covered her face with her hands.

From her seat not very far away, Franceline Drake had been listening to the exchange with interest. She had recognized the woman at last: a fellow inmate, or escapee, from that horrid finishing school that was her parents' compromise when she grew too wild (Amica's adjective) under Cid's exclusive care. The fat man was wholly unfamiliar, however; she wondered how he'd guessed her secret, or what had given her away. Certainly her identity was not widely known, else artists' renderings would be decorating those Wanted For Piracy posters by now. Upon Captain Zeal's frustrated question, she decided it was time to interrupt.

"You mean you don't know?" said Captain Pflugelhorn, oblivious to her graceful approach. "Why, I thought that everybody knew!"

"Knew what?" demanded Zeal.

"Why—" began Pflugelhorn, when Drake drew her rapier and ran him through, dropping him to the ground in an instant, spraying his blood all over the woman who had been monopolizing Captain Zeal. The woman screamed, and Zeal turned to her with a mixture of wonder and terror in his eyes. She—

—Actually did none of those things, but laid a hand on Captain Zeal's shoulder, and at once he fell silent. "Forgive me for interrupting," she murmured sweetly. "But it sounded as though the conversation were growing heated, and I so hate the thought of disharmony, especially here in my mother's own house."

The looks on their faces were gratifying. The woman regarded her with horror. Captain Zeal held his expression under tight rein, lest it run away from him. Captain Pflugelhorn's jaw dropped.

"Miss—Miss Drake," he stammered. "We—we were just discussing you!"

"We were?" Zeal said.

"We certainly were not," the woman said desperately, firmly.

"Oh, thank God," said Zeal.

"Indeed we were!" cried Pfillip Pflugelhorn. "Indeed we were, Captain Tannin, and I'll thank you not to prevaricate! And it's a marvelous coincidence, is it not, that the subject of our conversation should approach just as I was about to utter her name! Speak of the devil, and she shall appear!"

She glared at him with flat hatred.

A sort of chilly calm had washed over Captain Zeal. "Captain Pflugelhorn," he said. "You have insulted me, you have insulted Captain Tannin, and now you insult Miss Drake. I told you I would not lift a finger in my own defense, but now you have impugned two ladies' honor, and I will not have it. My seconds shall call on yours, to arrange a time of mutual convenience."

Excellent Captain Zeal! Drake could have cheered. She could not have arranged things better had she given them a script in advance!

Pflugelhorn's face purpled. "Are you calling me out, sir?"

"I believe I just did, sir."

"You're a fool," Pflugelhorn spat. "A fool who defends the honor of strumpets and whores!"

"I can only kill you once, Captain," Zeal said mildly. "You'd do better to save your words."

"Indeed." Puffing himself up, tugging straight his sky-blue sash, Pfillip Pflugelhorn turned and stomped away. "I am staying at the Nelson Arms. Your seconds may find me there."

Verity Tannin regarded Zeal with a look of disappointment and dismay, but said only, "I'll stand as your second if you wish it, Captain."

"That won't be necessary. Thank you, Captain Tannin."

Shaking her head, she took herself away, favoring Drake with a vicious stiletto of a glare as she brushed past. But Drake had been glared at by centuries-old dragons until she was seven years old, and let the other woman's enmity slide past, unacknowledged and un-felt.

And now she was alone, in the moonlight, in a bower of roses, with Acheron Zeal.

"Who will stand as your second, Captain Zeal?" she asked.

"I don't believe, Miss Drake," said he coldly, "that is any concern of yours." He turned as though to walk away.

"Wait." She stopped him with a hand on his sleeve. "Are you not fighting this duel for my sake?"

He paused, meeting her eyes for the first time since she entered the garden, and she was startled at the anger and the cold hatred in his gaze. "Miss Drake," he said. "I am fighting him because I think you are a lady. If I thought there were any truth in his words, I'd hang you with my own two hands. You made your feelings for me abundantly clear in that charming letter you wrote. If I live past tomorrow, I'll thank you very kindly to stay out of my life. Good night."

He turned and stalked away.

"Wait!" she cried. He did not turn. "Captain Zeal," she said. "Wait. Please."

"What?" he demanded. "What more do you want? Would you like to run me through yourself? I'm sure if you batted your eyelashes at Captain Pflugelhorn he'd be more than happy to let you!"

Two minutes ago—thirty seconds ago—she would have said Yes, that was what she wanted more than anything in the Quadra Terrarum: to kill Captain Acheron Zeal with her own two hands, to avenge the death of her love and the destruction of her ship, to watch that pretty face of his working with agony, to kick him in the kidneys and say, "Guess what, sailor? I am the captain of the *Eschaton*," and laugh as he died slow.

But now her conscience—her conscience? She hadn't known she even had such a thing! —stung her. She ran to him and put her hand on his arm, and turned him round to face her. "Captain Zeal," she said. And then boldly, sweetly, surprising herself, "Acheron. Can you forgive me?"

If he felt it, the shock of his name in the air between them, spoken for the first time from her lips, he gave no sign. He looked aside, his mouth a hard line. "I don't know."

"Not—" Her courage failed her. Her conscience, awakened now, stabbed her with needles of guilt and remorse. "Not for the letter." She hesitated. Jab-jab-jab went her conscience. It was like being shut up in an iron maiden! No wonder she'd never had any use for the damned thing before! He was regarding her now with consternation. She swallowed hard, swallowed her pride right down, and a cold hard lump it made in the pit of her stomach, and said, "No. Forgive me, because I lied to you. He was telling the truth: I am the captain of the *Eschaton*." She drew herself up straight, waiting for what would come.

Captain Zeal only stared.

She reached out toward him. "Ash—" she began.

He retreated. "No," he said. "Don't touch me. Don't say my name. Don't—" His hands came up, as if to ward her off. He backed away, slowly at first, and then whirled and fled, leaving her alone in the garden, alone under the wheeling stars.

In a private room in the envoy's manor, a man and a woman sat before a comfortable fire, drinking tea. She was tall and statuesque, with a glorious mane of autumn-colored curls piled atop her head. He was small, with the characteristic black hair and black eyes of the people of the Chai islands, and he was simply, though richly, dressed in robes of black silk.

"Well, Lady Amica," said the man, "I have greatly enjoyed this little chat. But should we not go down and mingle with your guests?"

The woman smiled. "Indeed we should, my lord," she said. "But not yet." She picked up the teapot—a marvelous little artifact carved from a single chunk of jade. "More tea?"

Zeal fled blindly at first, not knowing which way he went, only that it must be away, away, and in this manner he stumbled back into the middle of a party still going strong, as though no one knew that the world was ending, and he might have kept running all the way through the seething throng and out the other side and all the way down to the sea, if his sister had not stepped in his way.

"Brother!" she cried, and then, "Whatever has happened?"

His eyes focused, his vision cleared, and shame and rue fell over him in a cold cascade. He shook his head, forcing his lips into a watery smile. "Nothing," he said. "Nothing's wrong. Everything's ... fine?" But as sense returned, he saw that the carefree revel was anything but: laughter too tense and shrill, lights too glinting, smiles too wide, more grimace than grin. The musicians had abandoned their alcove, and no more servants circulated with crystal drinks. He took Lethe by the shoulders. "What's going on?"

"I don't know. A man in black livery came and talked with Admiral Rangle, and then they both went away." Her eyes were huge. "I thought you did, and that's why you were..." she waved her hands, "distraught."

"No." He searched the crowd. Most of the men in Navy blue had disappeared. Of Admiral Rangle there was no sign, but here was Peter Goodheart-Smythe, parting the crowd like a cutter in a choppy sea.

"Sir, what's happening?" he asked.

"I don't know, lad. But whatever it is, it can't possibly be good."

At the far end of the ballroom was a balcony. In the wall behind the balcony was a door—its only point of access. Now the door opened. The the party-goers hushed as two figures stepped out onto the balcony: one, a tall woman with brilliant copper hair, the other, a small man in black silk robes.

Lethe gasped. "Oh, my gracious, it's the Emperor."

"And Lady Amica," Zeal muttered, frowning.

Peter made a strangled sound, and his knees threatened to buckle. With a curse, Zeal caught him and held him upright. "Steady, lad," he said.

Emperor Katsukare I, Beloved of the Gods, raised his hands for silence—a thoroughly superfluous gesture, since no one in the whole vast ballroom dared even breathe.

"My children," he said in Camembertian, "and my friends from foreign lands. It is with deepest sorrow that I stand here to inform you that my beloved sister monarch, Queen Miranda Regina Allegra Felicity Cardamom of Camembert, is dead."

IV. The Navy motto discussed—The utility of archaisms—A Moral decision—The Amazing Plahtt Device—A dastardly innovation

Long before dawn, Flynn Freeborn awoke, rolled over in bed, and regarded the woman beside him. She was smiling faintly (this he could see from the dim light that entered through the room's single window), a catlike look of satisfaction on her golden face. Her arms were wrapped around one pillow, her face nuzzled into another.

Kicking off the blankets, he got out of the bed and began to put on his clothes. He cast one last glance at her before leaving the room, then shut the door softly behind him and took himself away. By the wry looks the inn staff gave him, they were not unaccustomed to strange men exiting that lady's chambers in the dead of night.

Once out in the cool darkness, it took him some time to get his bearings. By the stars, it was still hours 'til sunrise, and the harbor was in that direction. He began to walk.

Behind him, detaching itself from a cluster of deeper shadows, a dark figure also began to walk. It kept pace with him, pausing when he paused, speeding up when he quickened his steps. At last, in the middle of a little park-like area between buildings, where giant goldfish splashed in an ornamental fountain, he stopped.

"All right, mate," he said, turning, "I know you're there, so avast your lurking and your skulking and come out and face me man to man."

He waited.

His stalker stepped out of the shadows.

Flynn groaned. "I might have known! Did Bayard send you?"

The young naval officer nodded. "Aye, sir. Sorry, sir. Didn't want to let you out of his sight, sir."

Flynn shook his head. "Does he not know me well enough to know I'd not go back on me word to him?"

"I think that's the problem, sir," the youth offered. "His exact orders were, 'Follow that scalawag cousin of mine and make sure he doesn't go back on his word,' sir."

"Were they, now?" said Flynn, rubbing his chin.

"Aye, sir." The young officer (a lieutenant, probably a minor one, by the cut of his jib) bobbed his head.

"And was you waiting outside yon hotel all night?"

"Aye, sir."

Flynn thought some more, still rubbing. "Right, then," he said, coming to a decision. "No point in forcing you to skulk along behind me like some blessed cutpurse, young laddie, that there ain't. Just walk along beside me, and we'll go on back to the ship together."

"Aye, sir." The young man looked dubious about the arrangement.

"What's your name, then?" Flynn asked, beginning to walk.

"Nimble, sir," said the young man, perforce following. "Jonathon Bartholomew Nimble, fifth lieutenant of the *Aubrey*."

"Well, Jack," said Flynn, "(you don't mind if I'm calling you Jack, do you?), we'll just be hieing ourselves back to the *Aubrey*, we will, and you can be returning to your duties, and I to mine, eh?"

"Aye, sir," said young Nimble, with palpable relief.

They walked for a space in silence, neither having anything in particular to say to the other one, passing through ill-lit side-streets, beneath dark bridges, and through narrow rows of buildings that leaned in close, their blank eyes staring. It was outside one of these corridors that Flynn paused, cocking his head.

"Did you hear that?" he asked.

Jonathon Nimble shook his head.

"I did." Flynn reached for the boarding axe he kept at his belt—but of course, it was gone, Cousin Bayard not trusting him with weapons any more than he trusted him with women. "Damn."

"What is it, sir?" Nimble turned towards him a face filled with anxiety, not to say stark, staring terror (he was very young).

"We're being followed," said Flynn.

Which was when the vampire leapt out of the shadows and attacked them.

The reader must not conclude that vampire attacks were commonplace in that day and age in the Quadra Terrarum. The defeat of Baron von Death and his vast armies of doom some quarter-century earlier had left the forces of darkness diminished and demoralized, and although you might hear now and again of a werewolf terrorizing sheep in northern Eclaire, or a shaman of the Paprika Desert raising armies of brain-eating undead, such incidents were by no means as common as they had been in the years before the war. And, for the most part, such creatures of the night did not stray from their native climes—a vampire might be seen haunting remote villages in Schlagsahne, but a major port city in Chai? Unheard of!

It would do little good, however, to tell that to the indisputable vampire leaping onto poor Jonathon Nimble. Its mouth opened in a hiss, revealing the unnaturally pointed fangs; its eyes glowed red, as though the flames of hell were trapped therein; its skin, even in the scanty light of the stars, was corpse-pale; and its hands, crooked into claws for the attack, bore black fingernails of inhuman length and sharpness.

"Aaaargh!" screamed Jonathon Nimble.

"Holy water!" cried Flynn. "Have you any holy water, lad?"

"What?" retorted Nimble (somewhat muffled by the vampire sitting on his chest). "No!"

"What?! Isn't your motto Semper paratis?"

"That's the Coast Guard—arrrrrrgh!"

"Here, now, you!" cried Flynn, dashing up and kicking the vampire, whose teeth had latched onto poor Nimble's throat, in the head. "Get off of him, you hear?" It was a solid blow, and the vampire went flying, blood spraying off its teeth. Nimble was still screaming.

"Hush up, lad." Flynn swiftly untied his cravat. "Press this against the wound."

The vampire was getting to its feet, eyes ablaze with infernal light, blood dripping from its mouth. It grinned at him, wiping its hand across its chin and succeeding only in smearing the blood further. Flynn gulped. How did one fight a vampire? Fisticuffs? He hoped so, as he hadn't any holy water, and his last Latin lesson had been almost seventy years past.

"Er—evil creature, begone!" cried he, gesticulating. "Back—back to the darkness from which you came! Aroint thee! Aye! Aroint thee, I say!"

A look of horrified shock came over the vampire's face; it clutched at its chest, its eyes bulging, blood trickling from the corners of its mouth. A cry, terrible to hear, ripped from its unbreathing lungs, its jaws stretching, tendons straining, to utter such an unholy shriek. Flynn dropped to his knees and covered his ears.

The cry ended, cut off abruptly, and he looked up.

"Well," said he, dusting off his breeches and getting to his feet. "I didn't expect that to work. Here, young Nimble. Are you all right?"

"S—sir..." Nimble was pointing beyond Flynn's left shoulder.

"Eh?" Flynn turned and looked.

The vampire lay in a heap on the ground, its head several feet away from its body, the path it had taken demarcated by a wide spray of blood. "Lost its head, did it?" said Flynn with a chuckle. "Who would've thought 'Aroint thee' would be so effective?" He struck a pose. "Aroint thee!"

"S—sir..." said Nimble, still pointing. The cravat he held to his neck was soaked red.

"Eh?" said Flynn.

Because now, kneeling beside the vampire's corpse, was a bleak-faced man in grey, leaning on a crimson-smeared sword and doing something with his free hand. He did not look up from his work when, curious, Flynn stepped closer.

He held a crystal phial, the contents of which he sprinkled over the vampire's body, producing a hissing steam. Grunting with satisfaction, he capped the phial, made a few obscure (though doubtless meaningful) gestures, and got to his feet—the entire operation being performed without ever acknowledging Flynn's presence.

"Got that head, boy?" he called over his shoulder.

"Here, sir," said a lad of about ten years old, running up, carrying the vampire's head by its lank black hair.

The man in grey grunted. "We'll have to burn it, just to be sure," he said, "but that's done at last."

"Yes, sir," said the boy, eyes downcast.

"Ahoy there, mates," said Flynn.

"The Abbot will be pleased," said the man in grey.

"Yes, sir," said the boy.

"'Tis grateful I am for your saving me life," Flynn said, "and the life of me companion there, though he was sorely mauled about the throat by yon creature of darkness."

The man and the boy, who had been cleaning up the mess with the grim efficiency of long practice, at last paused and looked at him, the boy with a wide-eyed expression that could only be described as fear, the man with exasperation.

"Figures," said he. "Leonides. Finish clearing this stuff up, while I go look at the victim."

The boy bowed his head. "Yes, sir."

Nimble still lived, but barely, and his skin was ghastly pale. He wobbled his head and groaned when Flynn knelt beside him, and his eyes fluttered when the man in grey moved the blood-soaked cravat aside to look at the awful wound in his neck.

"We can save him," said the man, "but we'll have to hurry. Can you carry him?"

"Aye," said Flynn.

"Good. Come on." He got to his feet. "Leonides. Have you got everything?"

"Yes, sir," said the boy. Now, instead of a severed head, he held a canvas sack. Instead of a decapitated corpse on the ground, there was now a lump of canvas.

"Good. Let's go." With a practiced heave, he slung the shrouded vampire's body over his shoulder and started off down the street, boots clomping against the paving stones. The young boy hurried after.

"Aye, well," said Flynn, bending down to pick up the now-comatose Nimble, "best do as he says, eh, Jack?" And off he went, following the men in grey.

After the Emperor made his announcement, the revellers drifted away in stunned silence, in knots of people grieving or plotting or confused, according to their natures. Drake made her way back to her ship, ascending the side in a fog. Her father had not returned with her. He was, she assumed, still at her mother's house.

She descended the companionway, flinging the diamond collar away as though it were paste, brutally stripping off the blue velvet dress and hurling it to the deck. Then she dressed again in her everyday clothes, drawing her coat on last of all (it was not the magnificent coat she wore ashore, though like that garment it was both well-tailored and red, but her workaday coat, more suitable for daily life on a ship), but leaving off her boots. Barefoot, she left her cabin and went forward, to the main hatchway.

Down into the depths of the ship she went, making her way in the dark. She knew the *Eschaton* well, knew every inch of her—she needed no light.

She reached the cable tier. She knocked.

"Wizard," she said. "Are you awake?"

"I am now," came his voice from the other side of the door. "Are you here to kill me, Cap'n?"

"No." She reached into her coat and drew out a key. The key fit into the lock on the door, turning with a satisfying clunk. Replacing the key, she opened the door. "I'm letting you go."

"Oh, good," said Dallon Moral. "Did you open the door, or just make a door-opening sound effect? I can't see a dag-burn thing."

"No," she said. "It's open."

"Oh, good," he said again. "Hold on." He muttered something, and a tiny flame sprang to life, hovering just over his right hand. Drake winced away from the light ... and then, when her eyes had adjusted, she winced away from the sight of him.

He'd always been thin, but now he was gaunt, skin and bones hung with a scarecrow's rags. His hollow cheeks were covered with a lank growth of beard, and his colorless eyes were sunken pits. She took a step back.

"Well, what did you expect?" he asked her. "This ain't exactly the local health spa."

"Come up to my cabin," she said. "I'll get you some clean clothes, and a proper meal."

He gave her a long, long considering look. Perhaps it was the beard, or the dancing shadows cast by the tiny, flickering flame, but she could not read what his expression might portend. She waited.

"All right," he said at last. "Lead the way."

Washed, shaved, clean, he felt like a human being again. He made his way to Captain Drake's cabin, wondering what reception he might find there—knocked, entered, and found out.

She was sitting by the stern windows, her bare feet drawn up onto the seat before her, her arms around her knees. On the table beside her was a magnificent, steaming spread: fresh bread, creamy butter, corn on the cob, baked beans, roast beef, mashed potatoes, apple pie ... just such a meal as he would have chosen for himself, if he'd been given the option.

He regarded her with suspicion. "What's all this about, Cap'n?"

She had been gazing out the stern window, watching the reflections of the city lights rippling in the bay; now she turned her head and returned his stare. "Sit down, wizard," she said. "I have a proposition for you."

"I bet you do," he muttered, but the savory rich smell of the roast beef and the warm yeasty aroma of the bread (fresh bread, by the holy name of God! How long had it been?) overwhelmed him, and he sank into the chair and began helping himself, barely remembering to pray (O God, thanks for the grub) before digging in. For a long interval the only sound in the cabin was his desperate eating. The captain had turned her face away, and was once more staring out the window. He paused in mid-bite, watching her, suddenly more hungry for conversation with another human being than he could ever have been for mere food.

"So," he said, "about this proposition."

The smile she turned on him was brittle and bitter. "I'm giving you a choice," she said. "You may stay with the *Eschaton*, on the condition that you swear never more to interfere with my orders, or you may go ashore here. Either way, your life is yours to keep."

"That's mighty generous of you," he said. He couldn't keep the sarcasm out of his voice.

Her eyes flashed. "I could still kill you, if you'd rather. Lilly offered to tear you limb from limb. She has strong feelings about mutiny."

He looked down at his plate. "That won't be necessary," he said.

"I rather thought you'd say that." He could feel the weight of her gaze pressing against the top of his head. "Well, what's it to be, wizard? Obedience, or exile?"

He thought about it. "If I leave?" he asked.

There was a studied casualness about the shrug she gave him. "I'll find another wizard. One who can obey my orders."

"Hmm," he said, and looked back down.

Silence in the cabin.

"Would you really leave me?" she asked, in a small voice.

Dallon's head jerked up. As cruel and world-weary as she was, it was easy to forget that she was still young. But there she was, curled up in her big chair, and the look on her smooth and perfect face, the vulnerability of those small bare feet, cut him to the bone.

Rising from his seat, he went and knelt on the deck before her. "Would you mend your ways, if I stayed?" he asked. "Would you give up your callous piracy, your casual murder, your…." He trailed off. "Would you? Could you?"

She looked away from his searching gaze. "How can you ask that?" she said. "I am what the world has made me. I'll not change for the sake of one expendable man."

"Ah." He got to his feet. "In that case, Captain," he said, "I'll trouble you no longer. Thank you for the meal."

He walked away.

His hand was touching the door-handle when she caught up with him. "Please," she said. "Please, don't go. Everyone is leaving me."

She was in his arms, filling them with soft sweetness, and his hands were tangled in her rich black hair, his mouth was on hers, or hers was on his—he was kissing her, kissing her, his senses full of the lush, dusky fragrance of her, and he thought perhaps he might die.

Gently, and with regret, he disentangled her, putting her safely at arm's reach. Her face was wet, and tears sparkled in her eyelashes.

"Moral," she said.

"I'm sorry," he said. His voice was rough. He tried again. "I can't do this. I can't help you. And anyway, I'm not the one you want."

Her smooth brow furrowed, and it would have been easy then (desperately easy) to take her back in his arms, to pick up that kiss where it had left off, and Lord have mercy but how he wanted to!

But no.

"You're really leaving," she said, as he turned away. Hurt, in her voice. Disbelief. And the beginnings of a cold, murderous rage.

"Yeah," he said. "Goodbye, Cap'n. God bless."

He shut the door gently behind him, and walked away.

Alone in her cabin, Drake sank to the floor and cried.

Flynn had expected the demon-hunters to lead him to a hospital, or a physician, perhaps a wizard of their order, some wizened old man with a grey beard and the knowing spark of wisdom in his eyes. Instead, after running through the maze-like streets of Umeboshi town for what might have been hours, years, or only a turn of the glass, the burden of Jack Nimble growing increasingly heavy across his shoulders, the elder of the two vampire slayers led the small party down a narrow alley that smelled, incongruously, of roses, and out into a cobbled square, up a flight of marble steps, and through a pair of wide, carved doors, and into—

"A church?" said Flynn, hesitating in the doorway, Nimble joggling against his shoulders.

"Where else?" The grim-faced man in grey was already striding up the center aisle, boots thudding in the hollow silence. "Come on."

Long and long it had been since he'd entered a church, aye, many and many a year, but even now the cool incense-scented darkness, softly lit by golden candles on the distant altar, recalled to his mind ancient pieties, rituals he'd thought long since forgotten. Crossing the threshold, he dipped his fingers into the font of holy water, raising his hand before his eyes to regard the water clinging there....

...And flicked the drops into the comatose Nimble's face.

The unfortunate lieutenant stirred and groaned.

"Still alive, then?" said Flynn. "Good." And he hurried up the aisle after the man in grey, who waited with the stolid patience of a petrified oak tree beside the massive marble slab of the altar. At Flynn's approach, he reached out with his free hand (that is, the hand not keeping hold of the shrouded vampire slung over his shoulder) and grasped one of the candlesticks, giving it a mighty tug.

The altar shuddered, let out a groan almost human in tone and timbre, and began to roll aside, revealing a hole in the floor and a ladder that descended down into darkness.

"Amazing!" breathed Flynn. And, looking up at the grim-faced vampire hunter, "Do all churches have these, then?"

"Only the ones built by our order," the man replied.

"And what order is that?" asked Flynn. "Alphabetical?"

"The Knights of Lazarus." And he jumped down the hole into blackness. Flynn waited for the awful splat that was sure to follow, the crunch of splintering bones.

After a moment, the vampire hunter's voice drifted up. "Pass your friend down to me, and follow, quickly."

Flynn gritted his teeth. "Er ... right. But I think I'll be using the ladder, so I will."

"Hurry, sir!" said the young boy beside him. "It doesn't stay open for very long."

"Right then." And Flynn eased the unconscious, bloody, battered dead weight of Nimble off his shoulders and down the narrow shaft. One of Nimble's feet (amazingly large and floppy feet they were, too, like the shoes of a clown) caught on a rung, and he had a devil of a time jogging it free, but at last he heard the Knight say, "All right. I've got him," and he released his burden with a sigh of relief.

"Go, sir!" whispered the little boy.

"Aye, of course." Flynn turned about and shinnied down the ladder, the child diving in just behind him, just as the altar stone gave a second shudder and began to grind shut. He watched, as he descended, the slow and inexorable eclipse of their only light source, and just as his feet were touching solid ground, it gave a last, hollow boom, and all the light disappeared.

It was all Flynn could do to keep from screaming. Even at sea, on the darkest of nights, there was light—even on a cloudy night in the black of the moon, the ship's lanterns provided anchors to reality—but here in this tunnel there was not a glow, not a glim, and it brought back to him an atavistic terror that his deepest soul remembered, even if his waking mind had forgot.

A firm hand gripped his shoulder. "Peace," said the elder Knight's harsh voice. "There will be light soon."

Sure enough, even as he spoke, Flynn's straining eyes caught the barest hint of a glow, a dim radiance that gradually grew, until there was enough of the pale, sourceless light to see by.

"But where's it coming from?" Flynn asked, only grunting a little as the Knight laid Nimble back across his shoulders.

"Who knows?" said the Knight, shouldering his own burden. "Some holy magic, no doubt. I've never inquired." He started down the corridor, Flynn perforce hurrying after.

After they had walked for a little while, Flynn began to notice something curious about the architecture of the hallway.

It was made of bones.

Old bones and new bones, big bones and small bones, interlaced tibiae and fibulae forming the curving walls, the ribs that supported the vaulted ceiling (for vaulted it was) made of, well, ribs. Large ribs, some of them. Huge ribs. Flynn had no desire to learn what sort of creature had provided them, that he did not. Here and there, intended no doubt as some sort of ghastly decorative element, whole skeletons were attached to the walls, encircled by florets made of patellae and carpal bones. Bone lanterns hung from the ceiling (even the chains that suspended them were bone), and here, at last, the mystery of the sourceless light was explained: it emanated from the open mouths and empty eye sockets of the skull lamps.

"Why, isn't that clever, then?" cried Flynn, shrinking away from a grinning lantern. "Decorative and functional, too!"

"Not much farther," grunted the Knight.

"They're made from the bones of our brother Knights who have died," the young boy whispered, "and the monsters that they killed."

"The monsters that killed 'em, you mean," Flynn muttered.

"Sometimes," the lad agreed.

"Must be an awful bloody lot of you," Flynn observed, shuddering as they passed another grim mosaic. This skeleton was holding his skull in his left hand, and a balance (made, of course, from bones) in his right. He was not too displeased about his situation, however, from his bony grin. "Must've been around for an awful span of years."

"Since the beginning," the boy agreed eagerly. Flynn got the impression that he didn't get to speak much, not around his laconic mentor. "When the first demon slithered out of a steaming, stinking, sulphurous crack in the earth, we were there. We are mankind's unseen protectors, daring to face the shadows of which he is unaware. We—"

"Leonides!" the elder Knight barked, and the boy fell silent.

The Knight had stopped before a low, narrow door of ancient, dry and dusty wood. "We're here," he said, tugging it open (Flynn was relieved to see that it had an ordinary metal handle, instead of one made of clavicles, or some such) and stepping through. Flynn and the boy followed.

When the door had closed behind them, the light of the skulls went out.

Zeal spent the night putting his affairs in order When he had written all the necessary and appropriate letters, he sealed them in an oilcloth packet and went up on deck.

"Evening, sir," said Thomas Morrow, touching his hat.

"Tom," said Zeal, and paused. "Listen. Should things go badly tomorrow, I hope you'll do me the honor of delivering these papers. If things go well—" and he tried to smile, "well, you can give them back to me, and no harm done."

"Aye, sir." Taking the papers, Morrow tucked them inside his jacket.

"Very good. Thank you, Tom." The captain turned to walk away.

"Sir?" said Morrow.

"Yes, Tom?"

Thomas Morrow was a lean and grey and gloomy man, a man who had no great love for his captain, but now he said, "Sir—that Pflugelhorn. He's a coattail-dragging scrub, if you want my opinion, picking fights and then bleating about his damaged honor. You shouldn't have to fight him, sir."

Zeal smiled, though it was a bitter smile with little humor in it. "As it happens," he said, "I agree with you. But I am a gentleman, even if he is not, and I intend to see it through to the end."

"The bitter end, I fear, sir," said Morrow.

"Well," said Zeal, "who knows what the morning will bring?"

The morning brought, among other things, an anxious and weary Flynn Freeborn, perched on the arm of an uncomfortable chair, keeping watch over Jonathon Nimble, who lay waxy-pale and unmoving in a bed in the hidden safe house of the Knights of Lazarus, past the secret chapel, beyond the hallway of bones.

"He'll live." Sir Aldreas had finally introduced himself, after anointing, praying over, and doctoring the awful wound in Nimble's neck.

"Praise be," said Flynn.

"Of course, if he doesn't, we'll have to chop off his head and burn his body to make sure he doesn't rise again as one of the ravening undead."

Flynn shot him a look.

Sir Aldreas shrugged. "It's good to be prepared for all contingencies."

Now Flynn sat in vigil and in thought, hands clasped before him, regarding the slack face of the young man who hovered on the brink of death, because he'd been sent to keep Flynn Freeborn on the straight and narrow.

He heard a heavy tread behind him, and without turning he said, "I've always been a sinner, and a proud and unrepentant one at that. I've been to hell, and I've come back, and have I taken advantage of this second chance, or tried to atone for my many crimes? No, I have not. It's right back into the wayward, aberrant, deviant behavior with me. Who knows? I haven't tried to change, and maybe I can't. Maybe it's impossible." He stared gloomily down at Jonathon Nimble's face.

"To hell, you say?" said the voice of Sir Aldreas, behind him.

"To hell itself," said Flynn. "To the very pit of the inferno."

Sir Aldreas grunted. "The sun is up," he said. "You should take him back to his ship. It should be safe now. Leonides will lead you out."

"Aye." And Flynn rose painfully to his feet. He may have looked like a young man, but there were times when he felt every minute of his eighty-three years. "Come on, then, Jack," he said, easing Nimble upright. "Let's get you home."

Morning also saw February Valentine awaken to the sun's first gleams through the open window, stretch, catlike, from top to toes, and roll over to regard the empty space in the bed beside her. No great surprise there; she had hardly expected him to stick around for waffles and hot chocolate. If she felt a twinge of disappointment she quashed it ruthlessly and without remorse, and, stretching again, got out of bed.

She dressed for the day, pulling her clothes from the various heaps where she had tossed them, splashed her face with water from the basin, and regarded her reflection. You cutie, you, she told herself, and blew herself a kiss.

And then her gaze fell at last on the vanity before the mirror.

Its surface had been cluttered with a fair degree of detritus, expected and understandable; after all, she had been in town for many days engineering the return of her item, and she was never what one would call a tidy individual in the first place. However, she had a keen eye for detail (it came, perhaps, from digging through ancient tombs, and ancient tomes, for treasure), and she noticed at once that something was missing.

The purple velvet bag.

If Flynn Freeborn's absence had come as no surprise, it was only that she might exhaust her full supply of amazement, shock, consternation and wrath in her reaction to this—this perfidious calamity. "Where is it?" she cried, in tones of operatic dismay. "Where the hell is it?" She swept the various scent bottles, make-up cases, coins, beads, earrings, candies and ancient scrolls aside (crashes and smashes as they struck the floor, and a rising odor of commingled perfumes), snarling and growling like a beast.

There was only one conclusion she could draw. Flynn Freeborn was gone—and so was the marvelous gadget, the golden egg, her rightful payment for a job done for the Doge of Parmigiana. Coincidence?

"Oh, I'm gonna kill him!" she snarled, snatching up her spectacles and thrusting them into place. "I'm gonna make him wish he'd never been born!"

"I wish I'd never been born," said Flynn Freeborn.

"Oh, come now, cous!" said Bayard. "Surely it's not as bad as all that!"

He had returned to H.M.S. *Aubrey*, seen poor Nimble down to the sickbay (Sir Aldreas' mumbling and gesturing and aspergating were all very well, but when a man had been mauled by a terrible monster, what he really needed was a good dose of physic), and then sought out his cousin in his stateroom. Would that he had stayed with the Knights! He'd look mighty fine, he reckoned, in one of them grey jackets.

"Couldn't you just give me a ship?" he asked. "You'd never rue placing your trust in me, I swear it, for I'd be treating her like she was my very own!"

"That's what I'm afraid of," said Bayard. "But no. I'd take you myself, but ... well, with the situation as it is now, I must remain here until I am ordered otherwise." His face darkened. Then, placing his hand on his cousin's shoulder, he said, "Don't worry, cous. The *Prometheus* has a most comfortable hold, I hear." He glanced at his pocket watch. "Now, if you'll excuse me, I must go witness a duel. I do hope young Zeal doesn't get himself killed—a most promising young officer—hoist his flag at the main someday, I shouldn't doubt. That is, if he lives past this morning." Leaning down, he patted his faithful old spaniel on the head, then took himself away.

Flynn sank down into a chair. "Just you and me now, old fellow," he told the dog, and sighed.

The spaniel whined. Bayard poked his head back into the room. "Come on, there, boy," he said, patting his leg. Wagging its tail, the spaniel trotted after its master.

"Damn," said Flynn.

In a private room in the house of the envoy to Chai from Stratocumulopolis, the dragon city, in a chair with a striped silk cushion, before a newly-kindled fire, sat the envoy herself, Lady Espera Amica, of the ancient House Phinoparos. There was a pot of tea and two cups on the table before her, as well as biscuits, mini quiches, strawberries and the like. Just beyond the table, in another chair with a striped silk cushion, sat her husband, the privateer, inventor and engineer Cornelius Cid II.

Take a moment, Reader, to contemplate this scene: a little sitting room, elegant, of course, but also clearly decorated by a feminine hand. In the sitting room, a woman of surpassing beauty and grace, tall and statuesque, her neck like a slender column, her hair a glorious sunset profusion of curls. Her posture is impeccable. In her left hand she holds a little china saucer, and her right serenely raises a cup to her lips. And in this environment, in such company, a short and dumpy little man dressed in hobnailed boots and coveralls, a greasy wrench sticking out of his breast pocket, his beard bristling, an absurd pair of goggles shoved up onto his balding pate, showing the pale circles around his eyes where wind and weather have not reached. In his large, broad hand, the china teacup appears ridiculous, small and fragile—and in such a genteel setting, he appears large and clumsy and out of place. Contemplate this image, friends, for you will never find a more perfect study in contrast.

The servant who had brought the tea and the breakfast things had been gone for almost a quarter of an hour before either one of them spoke.

"I am glad you came," said Lady Amica, regarding her spouse with a look that might have been termed "shy"—but surely was not, not from someone as poised and self-possessed as the elegant Lady Amica!

The look Cid gave in return was pure affection. "Aye, well, my fine lass," said he, "how could I be staying away? Bless me! 'Tis many and many-a since last I've seen thee." Setting down his diminutive tea cup, he reached out and took her hand. "Can you be forgiving me, I wonder?" he asked. "'Tis purely my doing that's brought us to this pass."

"Never think it, love," Amica said. Her lips twisted into a rueful smile. "We are neither of us ideal parents, I fear."

"Nay," agreed Cid. "That's God's own truth, it is." He contemplated their joined hands for a moment. "And how go your plans, then? Is everything falling out accordingly?" When she did not immediately answer, he said, "'Tis sorry I am to hear of poor young Mira, God rest her dear soul. I dandled her on my knee, I did, when she was the tiniest little thing you ever did see. Bless her! What a fine girl, indeed she was! Never in life did I think I'd outlive her." He raised his eyes to those of his wife.

Amica looked away, withdrawing her hand. "It was ... unexpected," she said.

"Unexpected?" asked Cid, and waited. Twenty-five years of marriage was no great span of time to a dragon, who count their ages in millennia (the Consul and his wife had just celebrated their three thousandth anniversary), but to a mortal man it was a prodigious stretch, plenty of time in which to learn another person's ways, and how to manage them, even if the couple in question spent months of each year apart. Thus, he waited.

"It was none of my doing," Amica said at last, each word drawn reluctantly from her, like a miser counting coins into the collection box. "Of course it was not! I am capable of many things, but murder is not one of them!" Amber fires flashed in her eyes, but Cid sat stoic and calm, and the flames died. "I pray it was nature that killed her, and not the hand of man." She picked up her cup, sipped. Twenty-five years was time enough to learn another person's ways, time enough to learn the difference between the appearance of composure and composure itself. "If I learn that di Capellini has done it," she said, placing her cup very gently back on its saucer, "I will destroy him."

"Di Capellini?" echoed Cid, in some surprise. "But why in the good and holy name of Heaven would he be doing such a thing?"

"He is playing a very deep game," said Amica, her eyes not on her present surroundings, but fixed on some imaginary diagram that only she could see, covered, no doubt, with circles and arrows and exclamation points. "Even I do not yet understand everything he plans. Be assured, however, that I will stop him. I will end him, if it comes to that." Her marble-smooth countenance was fierce, an echo of her draconic nature in her flawless female features.

"Is he so very bad?" asked Cid.

"My darling," she said, raising her gaze, "he could destroy the world."

A conveniently-timed knock broke the tension of the scene. "Ah," said Amica, rising to her feet. "How conveniently timed." She went, not to the door, but to the window; thrusting aside the heavy drapes and the lacy curtains, undoing the latch, and opening the glass—which was tall and broad enough to be a second door. "Please," she said, to the person who clung to the side of the house with his toes and fingertips, "come in."

"Thank you, my lady." With a grunt, the newcomer heaved himself up through the window and into the room, where he sat on the floor for a little while, recovering his breath. Behind him, Lady Amica locked the window and replaced the drapes.

Meanwhile, Cid stared in frank astonishment. The man was dressed from head to foot in black—black shirt, black trousers, black socks, soft little black shoes, black webbed gloves, a black hood covering his head, a black mask concealing his face. Such an outlandish get-up, Cid felt certain, would be not at all conspicuous in the middle of the day in a cosmopolitan city like Umeboshi.

"And have you brought it?" she asked, when the fellow had recovered sufficiently to stand.

"I have, my lady," he replied, with a questioning glance first at Lady Amica, and then at Cid. When she nodded, he pulled off his head-covering and stuffed it in a pocket, at the same time slinging a knapsack round to his front and beginning to rummage.

Cid stared in complete and utter amazement. "Why, bless my soul!" cried he. "If it isn't Crispin Teague! It's been an age! And here you are, running errands for me own dear wife!"

Crispin paused in his rummaging to give Cid a wry look. "Ah," he said at last. "Here it is. Easy enough to obtain, my lady—would you believe she actually sleeps with her window open?—but I was obliged to take rather a circuitous route to get here, since the Emperor's men were out last night in force, and I saw at least two of di Capellini's other spies in the streets."

"I am not surprised," Amica murmured, holding out her hand. Into it Crispin placed (what else?) a heavy purple velvet bag, thick with embroidery. Amica smiled. "Come have some tea, dear Crispin," she said, loosening the cords that fastened the bag as she led the way to the little table. "What other news do you have for me?"

The object she placed on the table, amongst the little scones and the pots of jam, the reader will recognize at once, for it has already been described in these very pages. The reader, moreover, will not be the only one who recognizes it.

"Why, bless my soul!" cried Captain Cid. "If it isn't the Amazing Device of

Benjamin Plahtt!" He poked a ruby on its side, and the little ivory wings unfurled, revealing the miniature Quadra Terrarum within. He poked the emerald, and tiny ships began to ply the enamel waves, tiny airships to fly beneath the crystal dome. "Proud as Lucifer he was, when he showed it to me, and rightly so, bless me, for 'tis a marvel, indeed. But what in the blessed name of God," he said, "is he doing with it, when I gave it to you?" He raised his eyebrows at his wife.

She had the grace to look embarrassed. "It may be starting a war," she said. "Or preventing one."

"Aye, well, that's cryptic enough," muttered Cid, and returned to watching the workings of the Amazing Plahtt Device.

"There is one other thing," said Crispin Teague. "The whole city is buzzing with it. Captain Pfillip Pflugelhorn is to fight a duel this very morning, in the grove beyond the ruined temple by the beach."

"What of it?" said Amica. "You may as well say, 'Captain Pfillip Pflugelhorn is breathing'."

"With all due respect," said Teague, "it's his opponent that is of interest to you."

"And who is that?"

"Captain Acheron Zeal."

The grove beyond the ruined temple by the beach was full of people. Most of them stood back among the trees, keeping the center space clear. Captain Verity Tannin was there, as was Lethe Zeal—they held each other's hands, and it was difficult to say which one looked the more anxious. Admiral Rangle was there, in his workaday clothes, his faithful old spaniel sitting at heel. The Admiral had brought with him his ship's surgeon, and her wizard; the physician of the *Circe*, Everett Foxglove, was also in attendance. Various other officers of the Royal Navy were present as well, their expressions as varied as their persons. A group of men in sky-blue sashes stood at one end of the grove, all of them glaring with unconcealed animosity at Captain Acheron Zeal.

The two combatants stood apart, one at either end of the little space between the trees. The sun had not yet risen high enough to dispel the shadows there, and the air was cool and blue.

The seconds stood in the center of the grove, their heads together, speaking in soft, agitated tones. Captain Zeal's second was Captain Kermit Feldspar of the *Prometheus*. Captain Pflugelhorn's second was Colonel Brock O. Lee, a marine.

"What could be happening?" Verity asked. "They should have agreed to everything already."

Lethe shook her head, clinging more tightly to Verity's hand.

Colonel Lee raised his hands for attention. Since everyone was already watching the discussion with keenest interest, the gesture came off as unnecessarily theatrical. "As the challenged party," he announced, "Captain Pflugelhorn insists that the duel be fought with pistols."

A ripple of amazement ran through the watching crowd.

"A damned innovation," growled Admiral Bayard. "No good will come of it." The spaniel at his feet also growled.

"Oh, that blackguard!" said Verity, very low. "That damned odious scrub!"

Captain Pflugelhorn puffed out his chest and smirked.

Captain Feldspar looked at his friend, who made a weary gesture of assent. He had suggested smallswords, as the traditional weapon, but if Captain Pflugelhorn preferred to fight with pistols, it was, as he said, his prerogative, and there was nothing Captain Zeal could do. Captain Feldspar nodded glumly.

"The combatants will stand back-to-back, where I am standing now," he said. "They will take ten paces, and at my word, turn and fire. Are we agreed?" And when all parties involved had indicated their agreement, he said, "For God's sake, gentlemen, cannot you put this disagreement behind you and part as friends?"

"If Captain Pflugelhorn will apologize for his words, I will be perfectly happy," said Zeal.

"As I am the insulted party," said Pflugelhorn, "I have nothing for which to apologize."

With a sorrowful countenance Feldspar said, "Very well." There was relative silence in the grove, then, as the pistols were produced, examined, and loaded.

Captain Zeal took off his jacket, folded it carefully, and lay it on the ground.

"For God's sake, be careful, Ash," said Kermit, handing him his pistol.

Zeal gave a whimsical little grin. "There's this to be said for it," he said. "At least it won't take long."

Kermit shook his head.

With the two captains standing back-to-back, the watchers could easily observe their physical disparity: Captain Zeal tall and handsome, his blond hair bound in a flowing queue at the nape of his neck; Captain Pflugelhorn squat and toad-like, his already unlovely features in no way ameliorated by the expression of settled self-adoration that he wore. And is it possible that the naval officers in the audience saw the duel as more than merely an argument between two proud and willful men, saw the difference between the two captains as somehow symbolic? Symbolic of what? Of the clash between tradition and innovation, between the familiar and the modern, the old and the new? Who can say? Those who ply the waves or fly the air are prone to strange and whimsical notions, and of necessity look for meaning where, perhaps, there is none.

Verity and Lethe held each other close. "I can't bear it!" Lethe whispered.

Colonel Lee began the count. "One." And they took a step. "Two." And another. And so on to ten, when the two men stood at opposite ends of the grove once more, backs to one another, pistols held up before them.

There was a pause. Silence in the grove, save for the singing of birds, and the distant sound of the sea.

"On my word..." said Kermit Feldspar. A sickening pause. Lethe closed her eyes and turned her face away. "FIRE!"

Zeal whipped around, bringing his pistol to bear, pulling hard on the trigger. In that moment, between the firing and the gun's discharge, he thought, I will shoot him in the arm, only; it would be low and lubberly for me to kill him, poor fool.

Twin flashes of the powder igniting, twin cracks as the pistols discharged, twin plumes of smoke from the two guns' barrels.

Silence, utter and absolute.

For a moment no one moved—it might have been a painting of a duel, save for the eddying powder smoke. Captain Pflugelhorn wavered on his feet, then straightened, smiling.

Captain Zeal looked down. On his breast, small enough that his fingertip could cover it, a hole.

He fell.

"No!" Verity cried.

Dr Foxglove was already racing forward. He knelt at Zeal's side, turning him gently. There was the hole, and now the creamy white of his waistcoat was stained with red. The physician bent over the supine young man, listening. Verity's face was white and strained. Lethe's eyes were burning.

"I think that settles it, eh, Brock?" said Pfillip Pflugelhorn, with satisfaction. Zeal's shot had scored a shallow wound across the fleshy part of his upper arm; absently, he covered it with a handkerchief.

"Indeed so," the colonel agreed.

Dr Foxglove raised his head. His face was grim.

"Well, Doctor?" said the Admiral, impatiently.

Dr Foxglove shook his head. "I'm sorry, sir. He's dead."

The Dead March

Part the First: The House of the Dead

Like a beautiful woman whose husband has died, who cuts off her long, shining hair, who lays aside her beautiful garments for rough sackcloth, who rubs ashes on her lovely face, Her Majesty's frigate *Circe* was in mourning. Her yards, which should have been squared to the masts at neat and precise ninety-degree angles, were all a-cockbill, slanting here and there and every which way; rope ends dangled; sails hung slack and puffy; the Eagle Crest of Camembert, which should have flown proudly at the mizzen, dangled at half-mast, twitching now and then in the listless breeze. In short, she gave the impression that her officers and the men who sailed her were so distracted by grief that they no longer knew up from down, right from wrong, or north from south, and couldn't have so much as flemished a line or catted the best bower if their lives depended on it.

To be sure, the other ships in the great fleet that dotted Umeboshi Bay were similarly dishevelled—the flagship, the great first-rate *Aubrey*, was so covered in black crape she appeared to have been attacked by a giant spider (a giant spider, it might be added, with no clear idea of how to build a web)—for Queen Miranda, wise and just ruler of Camembert for thirty years, was dead. But the *Circe*'s state of ceremonial mourning was somehow greater, more intense, more forceful and more honest, for she had lost something of infinitely more value than a mere queen.

Her captain, Acheron Zeal.

How could it come to pass that such a promising young officer, active, vital—zealous, even, one might say—should be cut down in the very flower of his youth? Was there no justice under Heaven, that one such as he should feed the worms in cold and moldering eternity, while other, lesser men still walked and laughed and breathed under the sun? What lawless fiend had slaughtered our young paragon—or was it Nature's pitiless hand that felled him?

No, for Nature herself would have wept to see those strong, proud features stilled in the repose of Death, to see those once-warm hands folded across a breast that no longer rose and fell with the rhythm of his breathing. Old age had not stolen him from the world, nor the withering suspiration of disease, nor yet lightning strike or act of God—nothing but the casual arrogance of the duellist's bullet had murdered the young captain, leaving him stock, stone, cold dead.

Dead.

How could it be?

"How?" cried Franceline Drake, pacing as though to wear a hole in the floor with her feet, and gesticulating as she paced. "How can this have happened?" She rounded on the room's other occupant, a tall woman with sunset-colored curls. "How can you have let this happen?"

"I?" said her mother, blinking. "I wonder at you, my dear, indeed I do. What could I have done to prevent it? He was of a rash and hasty temperament. Could I have prevented him from fighting his absurd duel? No, I could not. It was out of my hands entirely."

"Don't talk about him like that!" cried Drake, wringing her hands. "In the past tense! Like he's—like he's—"

"Defunct?" said Amica, raising her left eyebrow. "Deceased? Expired? Exanimate? Late? Lifeless? Dead?" Drake's expression grew angrier, more enraged, and far more mutinous, with each synonym. "My darling, he is all of those things. He is 'pushing up daisies,' to use that charming human phrase. He has 'kicked the bucket,' so to speak. I only wonder that you are so ... agitated by the fact."

Indeed, it is ridiculous to rage, rage against the dying of a man whom you'd have been more than happy to run through yourself, the author of all your misery, the symbol of everything you hate in the Quadra Terrarum. Ridiculous, self-contradictory, pathetic. Drake hated herself more with every word she spoke.

"I..." she said, looking aside. Her fists curled into tight little balls, and she raised her head, shouting, "It's not bloody fair! It wasn't his time! Can't you—can't you do something, work some kind of magic and bring him back?"

"Darling." Amica unfurled herself from her place by the hearth, coming forward and taking her daughter's hand, leading her into a nearby chair. "Listen to yourself. It is not my place to interfere. Mortals die. It is the way of things. Accept it and move on."

"I can't!" Amica was startled to see tears in her daughter's eyes. "He wasn't finished yet—it wasn't his time to die, I know it! If you're so concerned about the proper order of the universe, then bring him back!"

Amica seated herself in the chair opposite her daughter, folding her hands in her lap. "I cannot," she said, with real regret. "I would if I could, but I cannot interfere. It is not my place to say who dies and who lives, and if I did resurrect your young man, then my own life, perhaps my soul, would be forfeit." She paused, and in the brief silence Drake mumbled sullenly, "He's not my young man." Amica continued, forcing a brightness she did not feel, "Besides. If word got out that I made a practice of raising the dead, I'd never have a moment's peace. Every bereaved sister, aunt, mother, uncle, brother in the Quadra Terrarum would come to me demanding that I bring back poor Jimmy, untimely deceased."

Drake's head was bowed over her hands. Amica sighed to herself. She should know better, by now, than to try levity with her singularly humorless daughter.

"It's just not fair," said Drake.

"Dearest," Amica replied, "you cannot expect me to believe that an experienced old sea-dog like yourself has any illusions about the fairness of life. Random, unpredictable, sometimes beautiful, yes. But fair? Rarely, if at all."

Drake caught her lower lip between her perfect white teeth—and then asked, unexpectedly, "But what about all your great schemes? Doesn't this throw them into just a tiny bit of chaos?" There was a shrewd look on her face. "Weren't you planning on wedding bells for the two of us? That can't very well happen if he's dead. But bring him back, and I promise I'll do what you want. I'll marry him." There, said her expression. There are my cards, spread out on the table, and aren't you amazed at the hand I've played?

Amazed, yes, but outwardly serene. "Plans change," Amica said, though she was—for just an instant—tempted. "I cannot help you. If you really want him that badly, I suggest you go get him yourself."

She rose to her feet, even that simple motion (as always) so graceful it would have made a dancer weep with envy. "Come. I'll show you out." She took her daughter's elbow, helping her to stand.

On Franceline's face was a look of stupefaction. She allowed herself to be guided from the room. "You won't help me," she said. Already, rising beneath the stunned amazement, was the white fury of thwarted will.

"I will do what I can," Amica said, keeping her grip firm. Franceline turned on her a look of wonder. "I will pray for his soul." Drake drew in a breath to respond. "Here is the door, my darling," said Amica, opening it. "A very good day to you."

She had not slept since she heard the news, had not slept, before that, since Moral left, could not have slept, she suspected, if she tried. She had lain in her bed that night, the night after her mother's wretched party, the night the world fell apart, inert and aching, and the empty space beside her was not half as empty as the space inside.

The name she had whispered to herself as she lay in the empty bed was not that of Acheron Zeal, for what cause had she to whisper his name, except in hate? Random, she thought, and although she was sick of weeping, twin tears had squeezed from beneath her eyelids and slid down her cheeks, tickling her nose. It did no good to imagine him there with her, his strong arm snug around her, his beard prickly against her ear, the warm weight of him pressing against her back. He was dead, and there was no power in the world that could bring him back.

But she lay awake that night, and she wished...

The next morning, almost before the sun was properly up, her bosun and her coxs'n had come skipping up the side, smiles on their faces. "Ahoy there, Cap'n!" hailed Luna Shee, all but dancing as she approached. "We come bearing the best news it's possible to bring."

"Oh, aye?" said Drake, too listless to care. "What might that be?"

Luna's teeth flashed in her dark face. "It might be that Lilly here's found herself a rich and handsome beau, and she's going off to be the new Queen of Camembert." Lilly snorted. "It might be that I've discovered my own latent magical talents, and am applying for the job of ship's wizard." She danced an impromptu little hornpipe, whirling about to spread her arms towards her captain. "But it ain't."

"Luna." Drake's supply of patience, far from inexhaustible under the best of circumstances, had quite run out.

"Aye, Cap'n." Luna drew herself to her full five feet, touching an imaginary hat. "Seems that your arch-nemesis got himself into a bit of trouble with an expert duellist; word is he shot him through the heart not—" she checked her watch, "—half an hour since."

If Luna Shee's antecedents were unclear, her meaning was not. The *Eschaton*'s solid, warm deck plummeted away from her feet, and Drake reached out a hand toward the rail to steady herself.

"Dead?" she heard herself whisper.

"Aye." Luna beamed like Christmas come early. "Dead as a doornail." And then she frowned. "Funny saying, that. Why a doornail? What makes a doornail any deader than any other nail, d'ya suppose?"

"Dead as a coffin nail," Lilly Bones suggested.

"Aye, that sounds about right!" Luna turned back to Captain Drake. "Anyhoo—ain't that the best thing you've heard all day?"

But the space where Captain Drake had stood was empty.

"Huh," said Luna. "Thought she'd be happier."

"Hmm," said Lilly, a frown creasing her broad, scarred brow.

How indeed to explain her current unhappiness, the bitter taste in her mouth as she hurried down the steps of her mother's house, away from that unequivocally closed door, the hem of her fine red coat swinging with her swift, purposeful stride? She settled her plumed red hat on her head and, reaching the bottom step, nodded at the footman who held the carriage door for her. As the whip cracked and the matched bay horses stepped out, their hooves ringing on the paving stones, she settled back and closed her eyes. Anger was the taste in her mouth; frustration, too, that her mother would thus thwart her desires (although she should never have expected otherwise); and what was that hint of ... something, something so unfamiliar she could not name it. Disappointment? Sorrow? Regret, God forbid?

She took her hat off again and laid it in her lap, dragging her hands through her thick, black hair. This would not do. She was never at a loss for a plan of action (not until Random died, her newfound conscience needled her); if she decided that Acheron Zeal should return from the dead, then by God and by Heaven (her conscience: or by darker powers if necessary, eh?) she would find a way.

Closing her eyes, she leant her head back on the cushioned bench, listening to the rhythmic rattle of the horses' hooves. Was it the simple perversity of human nature, to want most what is least attainable? And, the converse, to value at nothing the heart's desire attained? Hadn't she dreamt daily of Acheron Zeal's death?

"That's different," she muttered, sitting up and drawing back the carriage curtain. Blue daylight lanced in, and she winced away from it, letting the curtain swing back into place, shuttering her in darkness once again.

Get him yourself, Amica had said, if you want him. But do I? Drake wondered. *Do I?*

She imagined him cold and dead, his lean, sun-browned hands folded across his breast, his mobile features frozen for ever. And then the worms came, and the bugs, and stripped him to ragged cloth and moldering bones. Bile rose up in her throat, and she pressed her hands against her mouth to keep from being sick.

Drake passed a trembling hand across her eyes, ran shaking fingers through her sweat-dampened hair. For long moments she focussed on breathing, just breathing, swallowing great gulps of blessed air.

If you want him, go get him yourself.

"Fine," said Drake. "But how?"

Another evening in Umeboshi, no different from any other, save for the air of uneasiness, as though the city held its breath, waiting. Good citizens hurried indoors early, and locked their doors and shuttered their windows, now and then peering through the cracks at the dim streets outside. Waiting, but for what? There was a sense, indefinable but undeniable, that the world had gone wrong somehow, a sense almost tangible, and the people of Umeboshi waited for it to be set right again.

But in the breathless hush of evening, in the tension of waiting for something undefined, life continued.

With the making tide, the blue flag that signified departure broke out at the main of H.M.S. *Prometheus*, emphasized with a gun. With such a taut captain and expert crew, she was soon far out to sea, white topsails mere blurs in the gloaming. She made for Camembert and home, and she carried an unusual cargo: a prisoner, locked in irons, deep in the reeking darkness of her hold. No one knew what he had done, but it must've been right awful, mates, the wickedest, brutallest, terriblest crime you could think of, and rumor said he was bound to be hanged. (The prisoner himself knew better, but he was in no position to disabuse the common seamen aboard the *Prometheus* of their wild notions, and had been sworn to secrecy besides.)

A young woman, face red and blotched from weeping (none of your discreet, genteel, behind-the-handkerchief sniffling, either, but the real sobbing and wailing of perfect grief), sat at a writing desk with pen in hand, though the page before her was blank. She hesitated, dipped the pen, wrote *Dear Mama*, and stopped. Fresh tears slid down her cheeks, and she buried her face in her hands to muffle the sound of her sobs.

In a narrow alleyway behind a wine shop (red lantern hanging under the eaves, the Chai symbol for booze painted in black), Captain Pfillip Pflugelhorn was attacked by a gang of men, masked, but with the long pigtails and swinging strides of sailors. They beat him and left him for dead—which, indeed, he might have been, had he not been found in the early hours of the morning by a compassionate passer-by, who took him and nursed him back to health.

Waiting. For what? For inspiration, epiphany? For some glorious apotheosis that would never come? The world was the way it was, and if there was some sense that something, somewhere, had gone wrong—well, how was that different from any other evening in any other town?

In the second-seediest inn in Umeboshi (the seediest inn, the Canopic Jar, was full up, mostly with pirates who liked its proximity to the town's bawdy houses), a man sat on the edge of a rickety bedstead, tuning a guitar. Although he was a youngish man, he was not particularly handsome, his nose being too large, his chin too square, his face in general too asymmetrical for good looks, and his eyes, as colorless as water in a brook, most people found off-putting. But if his hands were too big at the ends of his bony wrists, the fingers on the guitar's strings were sure and graceful, and when they had wrung out the last twangs and plongs, and given one last twist to the last tuning peg, they coaxed from the instrument a melody more euphonious, filling the low, dirty room with rippling sound. His father had been a handsome man, but no musician (his blood father, that was: Pa Moral had often come in from the fields singing "Ye Banks and Braes" or "Jolly Plowmen" or the one that began St George was a soldier); in the son, the traits were reversed. He would never win any prizes, but he could hit a note true in the middle, and his voice was pleasant enough. After a decent interval, he began to sing.

"*O*," he sang,

midway on life's journey
I found myself alone
All in a deep and darkling wood,
In solitude I roamed.

The wolf, the lion, the leopard
My steps they did impede.
At their rav'ning jaws I quailed,
And I was sore afraid.

'Fear not!' the poet told me,
'For I shall be thy guide—

A knock on the door shattered his concentration and jangled the guitar to silence. He frowned (who would be visiting him here? The neighbors, objecting to the noise? Seemed a mite hypocritical, what with all their hooting and hollering and carrying on), and the knock repeated itself, hollowly. Grasping the guitar by the neck (he had some thought of using it as a weapon, if it came to it), he went to the door and opened it. The doorknob came off in his hand; he glared at it in disgust.

The figure in the doorway was slim, black-haired, and painfully familiar. And here I thought I'd seen the last of her, he thought (although he had never thought that, not really—he had known better from the moment he walked away), and out loud he said, with a heartiness he did not feel, "Why bless my soul! If it ain't the beauteous Captain Drake!"

"Hello, wizard," said she. "I need your help."

The Sow's Ear was an eating house in the western style: lamplight, polished wood furniture, chairs with embroidered cushions—none of your woven mat floors and kneeling-pads—and an attempt, at least, to serve food adapted to western taste buds, although no plate of squid-ink-and-bean-curd spaghetti had ever yet graced a table in Parmigiana, Dallon Moral was quite sure; it was here they had adjourned, Captain Drake having flat refused to set foot inside his squalid little room, her disdainful gaze raking the ill-lit corridor, the shabby chamber, the wizard himself with equal asperity.

“I ain’t quite sure I understand the problem,” said he, a cup of weak coffee untouched by his elbow. “I thought you wanted....”

“I wish people would stop saying that!” she cried, nearly upsetting her own glass with her quick, angry gesture. And then she checked herself (the first time he had ever seen her rein in her hasty temper), catching her lower lip between her beautiful white teeth. Beautiful. His heart beat faster at the sight of her, the absurd pink flush coloring her cheeks.

“Well, Cap’n,” he said (“well” became “wail”; his accent, as always, coming on more strongly in his agitation, though he thought he hid it wail enough), “if you go around stompin and swearin and shakin your fists and wishin death and the torments of Hail on a feller, and then come over all remorseful when you get your wish, you shouldn’t be upset when folk express a bit of surprise.” He sipped coffee, winced. The hot water and the coffee grounds had been introduced by a well-meaning third party, but nothing had come of the acquaintance but a murky, vaguely brownish, muddy water sort of brew. How he longed for a real cup of coffee, rich and bitter, like life.

“I know that,” said Drake, and now that the blush had faded, she looked unutterably weary. “Of course I know that.” She glanced up at him through her eyelashes. “I didn’t know you were a musician,” she added, almost shyly.

Was this the same woman who had thrown him in the cable tier, threatening torture, disembowelment, defenestration? He regarded her with wonder. She must be a Gemini. “Oh,” he said, with a shrug. “I’m no Orpheus, but I get by.” He fixed her with his clear gaze, noted that she neither flinched nor looked aside, and said, “And I can’t raise the dead, if that’s what you’re askin. There’s no one alive as could do that.” He knew one person who could, actually, but that one had forsworn those powers, was living anonymous and penitent in a lonely abbey with high stone walls.

“Then what good is wizardry?” cried Drake, starting from her chair. “Of what use to man or beast? You can’t raise the dead, can’t make gold from lead, can’t turn stones into bread—what the devil can you do?” The other patrons of the Sow’s Ear were staring at her; she lifted her chin and tossed her rich, black hair, but she did not sit back down.

"There are laws," he explained, but it sounded lame even in his own ears. She was glaring at him with complete and total disapprobation, like gum on the bottom of her shoe. "But I could—"

"No," she said. "No. Forget I came. I'm sorry to have troubled you." She was turning away, dismissing him from her mind; in a moment she would have forgotten his existence entirely.

But something was gnawing at his brain, an idea half-formed, waiting to be born. Something one of them had said.... Orpheus, he thought. "Captain, wait!" he cried, leaping after her. He was lean and gangly, and could practically touch her arm without leaving his seat. She whirled and snarled at him, actually baring her teeth, green eyes flaring with rage. "I said I couldn't raise the dead—I never said I wouldn't help you." She waited, snarl fading. "I think I have an idea," he said.

It was unseemly, everyone agreed, even to think of burying a naval officer on shore, but the mayor of Umeboshi had thrown such a tantrum at the idea of his guests (and they were guests, if uneasy ones) tossing bodies into the bay that the *Circe* had weighed anchor and, with a suitable escort, proceeded to sea, far enough from the Chai islands that no one in that country could object. There she hove to for the burial of the dead.

"And so we commit his body to the deep," intoned the parson, while the ship's company stood by divisions, hats in hands, looking mournful and grave. The acting captain, Josiah Alcuin by name, stood near the binnacle, extremely conscious of being an outsider, an intruder on the *Circe*'s private grief. Beside him were two women: the first a tall, handsome lady in naval uniform, Captain Verity Tannin of the *Boadicea*; the second Captain Zeal's own sister, Lethe, whose tears had spent themselves (for the time being at least), and who stood as straight and erect as any of the officers present, though her face was white, and her eyes red-rimmed. Neither was attending to the parson's words—hope of paradise, angels and martyrs, heavenly city, et cetera—but they saw him clap his prayer book to and give a nod, and the two men stationed beside the flag-draped coffin lifted the board on which it rested. There was a splash, and the fine wooden coffin (the ship's carpenter had been up all night a-building it), weighted with shot, sank into the glinting waters.

Lethe gave a low moan, a broken animal sound deep in her throat, but the threatening tears did not spill over. The watching seamen looked at her and nodded. She was a lady, she was, and a rare plucked 'un, too. They could admire resolute impassivity.

Then Captain Alcuin gave a nod to the waiting gun crews, and one by one the cannons boomed out their solemn salute. When the smoke had cleared, he dismissed the men and gave the orders that would return the *Circe* to Umeboshi Bay, where she could finish her fitting-out before the Admiralty sent her ... wherever they decided she needed to go.

"Come, ladies," he said, taking their arms. "Let us go below. Would you like some tea?"

Drake was standing on the quay when the *Circe*'s boats deposited the last of the mourners ashore. Captain Alcuin leapt out of the boat to assist the ladies himself, bowed and kissed their hands, then stepped back down into the vessel, giving the quiet order to row away. Drake held her breath as the two women approached, walking arm-in-arm, perfect postures, perfectly blank faces, neither looking in her direction. They were abreast of her, they were past her, they were walking away.

And then they paused, the female captain leaning over to murmur in her companion's ear, releasing her arm and striding back down the quay. Drake lifted her chin and waited.

"I hope that you are very well satisfied with what you've done," the woman said, putting her face very close to Drake's and whispering in her ear, "because you have ruined everything, everything, and I will never, never forgive you, you evil, selfish little harlot." She smiled (a singularly sinister look, by the fading light of the sun), patted Drake's shoulders, and turned and walked away.

"Wizard!" Drake cried, banging into his wretched little rented room. At her entrance, he leapt to his feet, gasping (he had been sitting on the floor, surrounded by maps and charts and crumbling, moldy old texts, quite absorbed by his work—he had not even heard her footsteps approaching, although she had sounded like a herd of oliphants thundering up the stairs).

"Thanks for knocking," he said, willing his heart not to explode.

"What's all this?" she said, flapping her hand at the mess. It looked as though a tornado had blown through a cartographer's and an antique book dealer's, depositing its burden squarely in the middle of the wizard's floor.

"Reference materials," he said, a little defensively, kneeling to gather them into something closer to order. "I need to know where we're going, and what to do when we get there."

"Are you not ready yet?"

"What's the rush?" he asked. "He ain't getting any deader."

She flinched, the impatient anger running out of her all at once, and he cursed himself for an idiot and a fool. If you wanted to hurt her, he said to himself, well, good job, 'cause you succeeded. She turned her large, green eyes on him (like a kitten's, huge and deceptively innocent), and he had to master the urge to go to her, to comfort her as best he could.

"I just need one more thing," he said, as close to an apology as he could come. "Then I'll be ready."

"When will you have it?" she asked, though her voice was dull.

"Tomorrow night," he said, hoping it were true. "I'll meet you at your ship."

"Very well," she said, and was gone.

In theory, pirate vessels were far more democratic than their naval counterparts, little mobile commonwealths where every man has his say—but theory and practice were kissing cousins at best with Franceline Drake in command—a more willful, autocratic, headstrong miss you would never meet, by land or by sea. The crew of the *Eschaton* were accustomed to their captain's close-mouthed, tight-lipped, play-'em-close-to-the-chest, follow-me-or-be-damned-to-ye, tolerably whimsical ways, however, and when the wizard came over the side, and shortly thereafter came the order to unmoor and proceed to sea, they obeyed with their usual alacrity, but also with many a raised eyebrow, a rolled eye, a pursed lip and a shaken head. Whatever the skipper was about, it was beyond their ability to comprehend, aye, and though they'd follow her to the very gates of Hades itself, they were none too sure about this current caper.

If only they had known that the gates of Hades were exactly where they were bound.

"Here," said Dallon Moral, stabbing the chart with his finger. "Here's where we're going."

"That's the middle of nowhere—empty ocean—nothing for miles, not even a rock!"

"Yup."

"Here, now, wizard!" Drake cried. "If I find you're making game of me—"

"Never in life, Cap'n," said Moral, tightening his jaw. "I said I'd help you, and help you I shall. What that means, though—" fixing her with a penetrating glare, "—is that you're gonna hafta trust me."

She snapped her mouth shut, clenching her own jaw, and her face went white. "Very well," she said, and strode out on deck, where he could hear her calling orders in clear, ringing tones. The sails sheeted home, the white wings snapped open, and the *Eschaton*, already running swift and free across the water, bow-wave foaming high before her, dripping, freed herself from gravity's embrace and rose into the air, humming with magic. Drake took the wheel herself for this manoeuvre, loving to feel the living tension beneath her hands, and when the Shiraz Sea was a dim blue blur far below, she set a course north and a point west. "Keep her thus," she said, relinquishing the wheel.

"Aye-aye," said Luna Shee, with a puzzled glance as the Captain disappeared once more into her cabin. "Cap'n's gone mad," she opined. "Stark, staring, raving, barking loony. She's not playing with a full load of bricks, or however it goes. Lost her marbles, like."

"Hmm," said Lilly Bones. "Maybe." But, when pressed, refused to elaborate.

Dallon Moral was laying things on her dining table when she re-entered: a book, a scroll, a branch that appeared to be made of solid gold. "Oooh..." she breathed, entranced by this last.

"No," he said, absently smacking her reaching hand. She gave him a wounded look and he said, "It's not for you. It's an offering—a propitiation. It's not booty."

"But think how much it might be worth!" she said.

He knew very well how much it was worth, and his purse and his bandaged right hand still smarted from the expenditure. He chose not to comment, however, saying instead, "How long will it take to get there, do you think?"

"At this rate of sailing" (and the *Eschaton* could sail much, much faster than an ordinary ocean-going vessel) "we'll be there tomorrow morning."

"Perfect," Dallon Moral said. Drake raised her eyebrow, and he shrugged. "I just really, really, really don't want to be doing this in the dark, that's all."

The *Eschaton* was not the only one winging away from Umeboshi that night. Under the light of the emerging stars, the Lady Espera Amica ascended to the roof of her house and stood in the middle of that broad, flat surface, chin pointing skyward. Breathing deeply of the warm night air, she allowed the mortal shape she wore to fall away—just as you or I would slip out of a shirt or a robe. The air around her shimmered as with heat, and now, where a tall and lovely woman had stood, was a creature out of tales and legends and popular fiction: lean and sinuous, but with nothing of the serpent about it, with a proud, maned, leonine head. Eyes that glowed with the sun's own warmth. Scales stronger than the strongest armor, in white and gold and amber and crimson, all the blazing colors of a glorious sunset. Winged, of course, but such wings! Translucent and gossamer, they appeared too fragile to bear that great weight through the air—and indeed, perhaps they were, for dragons are creatures of magic. She coiled herself like a spring (the celestial dragons have no legs, which is why, they say, Lord Bahamut gave them the ability to take on human form, that they might raise up temples to his glory, and make other objects of great beauty) and launched herself into the air, wide wings beating.

In the city below, some saw the dragon take flight, and pointed and gasped with wonder, for to see a dragon (as everyone knew) was a wonderful omen.

West, and slightly north of west, and it was midnight before she reached her destination, cool moonlight pooling silver and blue on high white clouds, on marble streets, on the alabaster steps of the temple itself, where she landed (rush and roar of mighty wings), shimmered, and became human again. Gathering her skirts in her hands, she mounted the stairs.

Cool, silver silence in the temple, moonlight and starlight and the reflected light of the city below shining through the gaps between the enormous columns, her footsteps the only sounds in that vast empty space. A looming shape before her, black and immense, lit only by small braziers (a hint of outstretched, rainbow-colored wings in the darkness), and she knelt at the base of the colossal statue of Bahamut, first dragon, King of Dragons, dragon-god, bowing her head in humble prayer.

"I was told you had been sighted," said a deep voice behind her, "and I am amazed, amazed, to find that it is true. I thought you had more shame, Lady."

Amica's head remained bent, although the voice had sent a familiar thrill (half fascination, half disgust) along her spine; she forced her thoughts to remain focused on the divine, bringing her prayers to their conclusion before she stood, dusting the ashes of incense off her fingertips. She took a moment to compose her features (she could feel his presence, his palpable impatience) before she turned to face him.

The males of House Hiemis were uniformly beautiful, tall, black-haired, graceful; and Noctis Darius was indubitably a male of House Hiemis, although his eyes were not blue or black or grey, but gold, and the beauty of his countenance was somewhat marred by the sneer he wore.

"I hear I am to congratulate you, my lord," she said. "Consul, and at such a young age! Such a coup for your family! But," she added, taking his arm, "we should not sully the sanctity of our Lord's temple with temporal talk. Come. Let us walk in the gardens."

"I'm surprised you would think of such a thing, or care," he said, once they had quit the temple. "You sullied its sanctity the moment you set foot inside."

She raised one eyebrow, but said nothing, steering him along the dim roads (but wide, wide and smooth, all paved with white stone) to the Hanging Gardens, said by some to be the wonder of the world. Her silence encouraged him, and he continued, "Fraternizing with humans—wearing that shape, day after day—it's a wonder you still remember how to fly!"

In among the gardens, now, surrounded by night-blooming flowers, hanging vines, the cool, green scent of growing things. "I note that you wear a human shape yourself, my lord," Amica murmured. "And it would be improper, I'm sure, to bring up certain ... youthful indiscretions."

He wrenched his arm free of her grasp, rounding on her with a ferocious scowl. She smiled, whimsically.

"Damn you, Amica," he said, dropping onto a convenient bench. "You shouldn't have come back. No." He shook his head. "You should never have left. We need you here, not gallivanting down below with mortals." He said the word as though it were a disease.

"The Senate sent me down below," said Amica serenely. "They agreed that the time for isolation was past. You could reverse that decision, if you cared to, Consul. But it would mean dissolving the Senate, returning to the old dictatorship, destroying millennia of progress..." She examined her fingernails.

Darius pounded his knees with his clenched fists. "You're very clever," he growled, that gorgeous deep voice like a distant rumble of thunder. "Too clever by half! Someday that cleverness will catch you out, and you'll wish you'd done as I told you and come back here for good."

She sniffed. "Melodrama runs in your family, my dear," she said. "I am certain I shall wish no such thing." She inclined her head, distantly, and turned to go. "You will excuse me, I'm sure."

"Amica." She paused, turned. Darius had risen to his feet, was holding one hand out toward her. After a hesitation, she went to him, took it. He brushed her fingertips with his lips, his eyes seeking hers. "Our children should never have been born," he said, his voice low, gentle, persuasive. "You know that. Their very existence is an affront to God, and he will punish us for it."

With a hiss, she snatched her hand away. “I love my daughter!” she cried, white with fury. “How dare you speak so?”

“And I my son,” he replied. “Does that change the truth?”

“I’m beginning to agree with you,” she spat. “I should not have come back!”

This time he let her go; she departed with all the haste dignity would allow, and he stayed where he was, watching the sky, until the sunset-colored dragon heaved itself into the air and flew away.

On through the night the *Eschaton* glided, a dimly-lit, self-contained world in the midst of darkness. Down in the captain’s cabin, Dallon Moral bent over his books—but his eyes were beginning to blur: there’s only so many times you can read over the same passage before you give in for the night. Drake was nodding, sprawled catlike in a chair, her mouth opening and closing as she drifted off, then jerked back to semi-consciousness. He watched her for a time, a queer half-smile on his lips.

“I read one time,” he said, “that long, long ago, the first dragon lay down with the first woman, and that’s how wizards came to be.”

Drake’s eyelashes fluttered. “What?” she said. “Oh—I wasn’t asleep.” But her eyes were mere slits, her movements languid. She yawned. “ ‘S nonsense. Lookit me. Got no magic—not a jot, not a whit. Magic-free, tha’s me.” Her voice was trailing off into unintelligibility; he rose, plucking her magnificent red jacket from where she’d thrown it, draping it across her.

“Get some sleep, now, Cap’n,” he said. “You’ve a long day tomorrow.”

“Long day...” She yawned, curling up beneath the coat. “Aye, indeed...” And then she was fast asleep.

Magic-free? he thought, contemplating her, the sweet curve of her cheek, the blackness of her lashes against her white, white skin. “Oh, no, Cap’n,” he said quietly, “I disagree.” More to himself than to her (sometimes one needs the sound of words to put one’s thoughts in order) he spoke of other hybrids, their magical abilities (if any, and how much), their quality of life (short and unhappy, mostly, doomed to end in heartbreak, misery, exile or death—how much to be attributed to upbringing, how much to blood?), their rarity. He prosed away gently, hardly knowing what he said, and the sound of his own voice must have lulled him to sleep, for the next thing he knew it was morning, and someone was shaking him by the shoulder.

"Wizard." Drake's voice, hard and cold—no kittenish sleepiness about her now. "Wizard, wake up. We're here."

Huh? Here? Where here?

"Oh," he said, raising his head off the table (his book had left a red imprint on his left cheek). "Uh ... great. Good. Well—let's get going, then."

"Looks like every other stretch of bare-arse ocean from here to Mordghre," Luna Shee remarked, craning to look. Around and behind her, the other Eschatons shuddered, made cataleptic gestures to ward off the bad luck of that ill-omened name.

"That's what I said!" cried Drake. "But did he listen? Or perhaps explain his plan at all? No, he did not. Be damned to wizards and their need to be mys-teeee-rious!" She wiggled her fingers.

Luna eyed her askance. "Uh, yeah. Cap'n, about that..."

A curious hooting sound interrupted her: Toggle, the mute young foretopman, was bounding about the rigging, gibbering, pointing at something below. All hands (and the cap'n, too) turned to look.

Somehow the wizard had managed to creep to the bows unseen, and was standing with a book in one hand and the golden branch in the other. The first he raised aloft, the second he read from—then he realized he'd gotten it backwards, reversed their positions, and tried again.

The Latin rolled off his tongue in round, golden, sonorous phrases, infinitely satisfying (a brief thought: where did Latin come from, in what country was it spoken? None he'd ever heard of, that was for certain sure), and the sailors clustered around him (but not close enough to touch him, no sir, not if it was ever so—they wouldn't be contaminated by his magicking, not they) gasped with awe. Something was rising, majestic and awful, out of the sea.

"Amen," said Dallon Moral, clapping his book shut. Then, rearing back, with all the might of his skinny arm he heaved the golden branch into the sea.

Gasps, universal groans of dismay. "What the hell did ee do that for, mate?" "Wizards is mad, all of em, I always say." Calmly, he turned to Captain Drake. "We have until sundown," he said. "Have a boat lowered, and let's be on our way."

Drake's eyes were wide. "You heard him, lads," she said. "Moonhart, you're in command 'til I return."

"Aye-aye!" The first mate clicked his heels.

"Might be best not to linger in the area," Moral said. "Come back at sunset. We'll either be here waiting, or—" he shrugged, "—we won't."

The hands exchanged uneasy glances. Was that any way to talk? No, it was not, sure as eggs is eggs. But the boat was ready, and Captain Drake was already going over the side. "Lower away," came her voice, as the wizard hurried to catch up. And then she was disappearing, dwindling, she was gone.

"I feel a certain amount of déjà vu," said Moral, as the little boat swayed down toward the heaving ocean, down toward the strange structure that had risen from the waves. What was that thing? It looked like modern art, the ugliest sculpture of barbed wire and rusty metal the world had ever seen.

"Oh?" said Drake.

"Well," he said, "don't it seem like you make a habit of being lowered down to ominous portals in the middle of nowhere to bargain for the souls of your lovers?" He was gazing astern, his tone was off-hand. He might have been remarking on the weather.

"Zeal," said Drake, clipping off the end of each word, "is Not. My. Lover."

"Just as you say, Cap'n," said Moral, with infuriating calm.

It was a gate. A tall, black, twisted gate—or the frame of one, for there were no doors, no hinges, no walls, and nothing on the other side of that empty, gaping mouth but, well, the other side. The other side of the rock, and beyond it the sea. Surmounting the ruined arch (bent and wracked, as though it had been struck by lightning, not once, or twice, but again and again) were words. Their letters were all familiar, perfectly intelligible, but the words themselves made no sense, none at all.

"What does it say, wizard?" Drake shivered and hunched herself deeper in her red coat. The day was clear and sunny, but the space before the gate was cold. Perhaps it was only their proximity to the Pole of Wind.

The wizard had no idea. They might have said "Do Not Enter," or "Beware of Dog," for all he knew. He smirked. "Beware of Dog," maybe (if the dog had three snarling, fire-breathing mouths and was twenty feet tall), but more likely, "Through me the doleful city," he said softly.

She turned to stare at him. "What?"

"Don't you know this one, Cap'n?" he asked. "It's as old as old can be." And he sang,

THROUGH ME THE DOLEFUL CITY,
Proclaimed that gate of dread.
ABANDON HOPE, WHO ENTER HERE
TH' INFERNAL PATHS TO TREAD.

"Wizard..." Her voice held a warning note. She would not be patient much longer—was, perhaps, incapable of it.

"Well, if you're in such a dag-burned hurry, then step on in," he said. Now that the moment had come, he felt light (light-headed, you might say) and free. He had seen his priest, had delivered his will and most of his books to a wizard he knew, and all that remained was to pass through that ominous threshold and bargain with the King of the Dead for the soul of one Acheron Zeal, post captain, R.N. No problem.

Drake still held back. "If you think—" she began.

"Come on," he said, grabbed her arm, and pulled her through.

"Sir, Madame," a voice was saying—a cultured voice, a proper voice, the voice of the perfect butler, "I bid you welcome. May I take your coats? Your hats? Would you care for a glass of sherry?"

"Whuh?" said Dallon, blinking. Out on the rock it had been cold daylight, and here ... here was ... not what he'd expected. He had been prepared for an alien landscape, bleak stones, bats, stalagmites, dim phosphorescence, that kind of thing. Instead, candles in crystal sconces, warm, polished wood, an opulent rug that might have graced a sultan's palace. And a butler.

"Oh, no thank you," said Drake, with automatic politeness, though her eyes were a little wild. "We won't be staying long, I think. We're here to see the King of the Dead, if he's available."

"Why, yes of course," said the butler, bowing (perfect black tuxedo, shiny bald head). "He is always available to those who call on him. Especially to those who know the old rituals." This last he directed, with a leer, at Moral. The golden branch had appeared in his hand. "They make very handsome candle-holders," he said.

"Oh—uh-huh?" said Moral.

"I will announce you to his Majesty," the butler said. "What names shall I give him?"

"Oh," said Drake. "I'm Franceline Drake. This is my ... um." She paused. "Dallon Moral."

"Very good, miss. If you will follow me?"

He turned and proceeded down the corridor, his pace smooth and stately. The branch in his hand, Dallon saw, was in fact emitting a faint golden glow, not unlike candlelight. With nothing better to do, he shrugged and followed.

"Wizard!"

"Aye?"

"Just what the bloody hell is going on?"

Dallon had been ruminating on the selfsame thing; now, sprawled at his ease in an overstuffed chair in this low, warmly-lit, opulent room, he leaned back, closed his eyes, breathed deeply (no scents, no smells of any kind, in the dry air) and said, "Wail, Cap'n, I reckon—"

"Do not," Drake snapped, "gabble at me in that hideous patois, that wretched cant. Speak like a civilized human being. I know you're capable."

"All right." Dallon drew himself upright and opened his eyes. "You've heard the term 'the house of the dead,' I presume?" Biting her lip, she shook her head. He grimaced. "What did they teach you in school?"

Her teeth flashed white in the gloom. "Knitting, and conversation, and serving tea—until I ran away. And then navigation, and sailing on a bowline, and overhauling a smaller vessel and boarding her in the smoke of my own guns. Are you going to get to the point sometime today, or would you rather crow about your superior education for awhile?"

He felt the heat rise in his cheeks. "Point taken, Captain," he said. "Beg pardon." She waved him on, and he said, "Well, then—it's pretty common in literature: 'the hero fell, and then his spirit went down to the house of the dead,' that sort of thing. But I'd always taken it for a metaphor, you know. And instead, here we are, in the house of the dead, and it's—" He flapped his hands.

"A house," she finished.

He nodded.

"Literally."

"That's it."

"Hmm." Drake sagged forward, leaning her chin on her hand. "Do you suppose this is where Captain Flynn was, before? Before we found him in the cages, I mean."

Dallon grunted. "Could be," he allowed. "We mighta found out, too, if certain people had let me talk to him before chucking him over the side." She opened her mouth to protest, and he finished, with a certain grim satisfaction, "You were cruel to him, you know. Not to mention wildly inconsistent."

Their gazes crossed: his, cool and clear, hers, emerald-green but hard as diamonds. She looked away first, fidgeting with her finger nails. "Yes," she said. "I know."

"His Majesty will see you now."

Good servants are supposed to be silent and unobtrusive, of course, but this infernal butler appeared in the doorway as quietly as if he had appeared, stepping, perhaps, out of a hole in the air, to stand in the doorway of their waiting room. Dallon jolted out of his chair as though struck by lightning, but Drake rose with her usual grace and poise (her mother had taught her well, in this one thing at least) and said, "Well, then. Lead us to him."

More dim, opulent, empty hallways, lined with unimaginable wealth, the air curiously still, as though no living breath had stirred it for ages beyond counting. It was like the air inside a mausoleum.

Or a necropolis, thought Drake, and shivered.

"The Vikings believed that the afterlife was one great big party," remarked Dallon Moral. He stooped as he walked, his hands in his pockets. He might have been a museum curator, giving a tour—all he lacked was corduroy patches on the elbows of his coat. "Worthy souls would eat and drink and wench and fight, and then do it all over again. The Greeks, on the other hand—"

"Vikings?" said Drake. "Greeks?"

"We have arrived," said the butler. "Please." He opened the door and bowed, ushering them inside.

He closed the door behind them.

And then he locked it.

Well, not really, but Drake had half expected something of the sort, and was fully prepared for the sound of massive iron chains binding the door, trapping them for eternity in this dank, cheerless...

...Beautiful, sumptuous, inviting room. A lounge of some kind, or a study. A masculine room: leather chairs, mahogany tables, books lining the walls, their oiled bindings gleaming in the light of the fire in the grate. The smells of tobacco and fine old alcohol and wealth and age. A framed painting above the mantel, its subject somehow obscure—she could make out shadowy shapes, but whether they were human figures, or a landscape, or something else altogether, she could not see. Then something flared in its depths, and she turned away, shuddering.

"There's no one here," said Moral, looking around, wondering. "There's no one—but there should be; I can feel—"

"Can you bind the sweet influence of the Pleiades," said a deep, dark voice, cutting him short, "or loose the bands of Orion? Can you bring forth the morning star in his season?" Dark smoke was pouring out of the fireplace—or perhaps down from that shadowy portrait above the mantel—and it was from this tenebrous cloud that the voice seemed to issue. "Can you guide Arcturus with his sons?" The smoke was coalescing, taking on substance and shape. And then it was a man, dressed in subfusc garments, his deep-set eyes mere shadows in his face. "Do you know the laws of heaven, wizard, and can you establish their dominion on earth?" He smiled, not unkindly. "Or are there more things than are dreamt of in your philosophy?"

They gaped at him, and, for a wonder, Moral was the first to recover his wits. "I stand corrected," he said with a bow. "I hope I gave no offense."

"Of course not." He spoke in a basso rumble, dark but mellifluous, perhaps the most beautiful voice Drake had ever heard. It was hard to say what he looked like, whether young or old, handsome or hideous. That shifting shadow hid his features, with only a stray gleam of light now and then where his eyes should be. "Please," he said. "Be welcome. Sit down."

"You're him, aren't you?" said Drake, sinking into her chair, her legs gone weak and boneless. That hidden face frightened her, more even than the Fisher of Souls, that ancient power. "H-him. The King of the Dead."

"Yes." He spread his hands. "I am Dis."

She shot a look at Moral, who shook his head, baffled. "This? This what?"

"No, no. Dis."

"This what?"

"Dis. Just Dis."

"Justice? As in, 'and justice for all'?"

He smacked his palm against his forehead. "Dis," he said. "My name. Is Dis. D. I. S. Dis."

"Oh." She felt very small, and very, very stupid. "Oh. Of course. I thought maybe it was a sort of metaphysical statement—you are this, you know, everything around us."

He smiled. "Well. That, of course, is also true." And before she could digest that curious statement (Moral looked like he'd just been thwacked in the face with a dead mackerel), he said, "So. You are very welcome in my realm. We have few visitors these days—well, few live ones, anyway. Back in the old days you couldn't turn around without stepping on some hero come to rescue some dead loved one or other." He chuckled—an unsettling sound—and made as though to sit down. Black mist swirled around him, and when it cleared, there was a chair behind him. He sat, and crossed his legs. "What can I do for you?"

Drake looked at Moral. He shrugged one shoulder, then looked away. You're on your own, the gesture said. I got you this far, but now it's your turn.

She gave an inward sigh—then composed herself, drawing herself to sit up straight in her seat, forcing herself to smile. "How strange," she said, "that you should mention dead loved ones." And she told him about Acheron Zeal, late a captain in the Royal Navy of Camembert, who had died in a duel—a duel that she had caused, she did not neglect to mention. Nor did she omit that he had sunk her first ship and killed the only man she'd ever loved, and how she hated him for it.

"Ah," said Dis. "And you are grieved that you didn't kill him yourself? You want revenge, perhaps?" The tone of his deep voice was neutral.

She looked down at her hands. Her cuticles were torn where she had worried at them. "No," she said. Her voice was very small. "No, I want him back. I want him alive."

"Ah," said Dis. He leaned forward, his eyes gleaming. "I would hear this tale, if you would tell it."

She glanced over at Moral, but the wizard was no help at all. His eyes were closed, his head lolled back against the back of the chair, and as she watched, he let out a low snore. Rolling her eyes in disgust, she turned back to the King of the

Dead. "All right," she said, and told him.

Faithful readers already know most of the details of Franceline Drake's tale; those yet unrevealed, the author humbly reserves the right to withhold until a more opportune moment. Besides, Drake did not begin her story with her childhood, divided between the cool pillars of Stratocumulopolis and the vagabond life on her father's ship, or her escape from Mrs Emelie's Ladies' Seminary in the dead of night with the first of her lovers, or even the start of her piratical career (details which are, no doubt, of little or no interest to anyone), but with the sinking of the first *Eschaton* and the death of Random Chance. Having told the tale more particularly elsewhere in this volume, it is hardly necessary to recount her exact words here.

"As for revenge," said Drake, and stopped. "As for revenge..." she repeated. But, uncertain where the sentence was going, she could not find the words to finish it. "If you had seen his face," she said at last. "It would have been kinder to run him through and have done."

"Kindness is not vengeance," the King of the Dead pointed out.

"No," Drake agreed.

Silence, then, in the comfortable room, save for a long, thin snore from Dallon Moral. Even the fire made no sound.

"You get used to it, after a time," said Dis, unexpectedly. The dark voice was almost apologetic. "Not that time, of course, has any meaning here. This place is not the end, but a waystation, a pause along the journey. A place of waiting. That's what they do, in the countless rooms in my house—they wait."

"For what?" Drake asked.

"The end." A flicker on that shadowy face: a smile? "When the last word is written, and the ink is dry, and the book is closed at last. Then my task will be done, and all the souls in my charge will go on to their final destination. I don't know," he admitted, "what will happen then. Fire, or the sword? Perhaps our hearts will all be weighed against the iron feather. But until then, we wait."

"Um," said Drake.

Dallon Moral opened his eyes. "Do all souls come here," he asked, "or just certain ones?"

"Ha!" Drake hissed, a low, triumphant whisper. "I knew you weren't really asleep!" The wizard quirked one eyebrow and shrugged.

"Not all," said Dis. "Some languish in the cages of the Fisherman—as well you know. Some others wander the earth for a time, restless, miserable. Still others, I know, sometimes fall through the cracks in this world, down to the darkest depths—or are dragged. Whose fate would you know, wizard? If he rests inside these walls, you could speak with him." He did not appear to move, but suddenly he was on his feet, and there was a bell in his hand.

"Um," said Moral. "Well..."

"Sir?" The butler had materialized as silently as smoke. "What is your will?"

Dallon blinked.

"Go with him, wizard," said Dis. "The lady and I have things to discuss."

Drake's eyebrows shot up in alarm. She looked at the wizard, who shook his head, helpless. The butler took his arm. "Come, sir," he said. "This way."

"But—" said Drake. No, he can't leave! she wanted to say. I need him here, to bargain for me! But the wizard had turned his face away, he was following the little man in the black suit, the door was closing behind them, she was alone in the room with the King of the Dead.

"Now," said he, resuming his seat. "Let us discuss the return of your beloved."

"Oh, dearie dear," said Dallon Moral to himself, following the silent butler through the silent halls of the silent house. "Ain't no way this is gonna turn out well."

"He's not my beloved," said Drake. "He's—" Just what exactly he was escaped her.

"Oh, no?" said Dis. "How interesting." He did not say, "How interesting that you would venture into the underworld to bargain with the King of the Dead for someone about whom you care nothing." There was no need. The words hung in the air between them, silent but understood.

"Tell me," said Drake, in a desperate attempt at levity (something she was not very good at under the best of circumstances), "what's the going rate these days for a human soul? Gems? Gold? I'm a wealthy woman—I'm sure I can pay whatever price you ask."

The dark figure in the other chair leaned forward; his voice, when he spoke, was amused. "Gems?" he echoed. "Gold? Have you looked around you? The wealth of kings is nothing to me. I have the wealth of the dead."

"Then what?" she asked. "What price?"

Suddenly he was beside her, looming between her and the fire. He knelt down at her side. "I want you to remember," he said, his face very close to hers—and even so, she still could not make out its details, "when all this is done, that you are the one who mentioned price. I might have given him to you for the asking. But now you will never know."

Drake closed her eyes and held her breath.

His hand came up and touched her hair. "The singer, he played for me, and these gloomy halls were filled with music, and I gave the soul of his wife back to him in return." He was stroking her hair. She gritted her teeth. "A soul for a soul?" he asked, his fingers tangled in the hair at the nape of her neck. "Would you take that bargain? Release him to the sunlit lands above while you take his place here, sleeping amongst the forgetful dead?" She drew a breath to answer, but he said, "No. Don't tell me. That is not the price I ask."

He released her abruptly, rising to fold his hands behind his back and pace before the fire. The shadows he cast were living things, crawling and writhing across the floor of their own volition. She shrank back into the chair's embrace. Finding her voice (perhaps it had been hiding among the chair cushions) she said again, "Then what?"

"I'm thinking." She watched him walk away from her (she avoided looking at his shadow). When he turned back towards her, he said, "Tell me. If you do not love this Acheron Zeal, why not rescue your Random Chance instead?"

She reeled back as though he'd slapped her. "Is he here?" she gasped.

He nodded.

She looked down at her hands. "But," she said, "when I freed him from the Fisherman's cages, I thought he was at peace."

"And so he is. He sleeps in one of these rooms, awaiting the final judgment." He looked at her, and she thought she saw him grin. "He was no saint. Did you think he went straight up to Paradise?" He chuckled.

Random. Alive again, teeth flashing white against his black beard as he laughed—that rich, deeply amused laugh she had always loved. What times they had had together! Plundering the ships of Camembert, cutting away before the Royal Navy appeared, the *Eschaton* throwing a fine, high, white bow-wave. Draping each other with ropes of stolen jewels, twining pearls through their hair, spending the wealth of nations like water.

Acheron Zeal had put a stop to that, hadn't he? Sank her ship, slaughtered her crew. Killed Random, a lucky cannon shot cutting him in half before he had the chance to blink.

"I had hoped..." she said, burying her face in her hands to stop the images reeling before her eyes.

"And what had he ever done, in all his life," asked Dis, dark and inexorable, "to deserve the eternal reward of the just?"

"He loved life," she began. And then she stopped. The King of the Dead was gazing at her, his eyes burning sparks in the shadowed pit of his face.

"Yes," he said. "That is certainly true." He turned and walked away, pausing in the shadows beyond the fire. His back was to her; she couldn't see what he was doing.

She pulled her feet up onto the chair, wrapping her arms around her legs. Random. Alive again. How marvelous that would be!

But—

"I came here for Acheron Zeal," she cried, her feet hitting the ground hard as she flung herself out of her chair, "and it's Acheron Zeal I'll have. How dare you try to distract me?"

"Calmly," he said. He was by her side, his hands gripping her wrists. He was smiling. "It's true, I would not have given you Random Chance even if you'd asked me. His time is done. As for Acheron Zeal ... well, one can at least make a case for his return." He turned her hand over and looked at it.

"What are you doing?" she asked.

He knelt at her feet. "What price, you asked me, to return one junior post captain to the world of the living. Now I give you my answer."

And he told her.

She gave him her reply.

Dallon Moral had been waiting, with increasing anxiety, in the foyer, when at last Drake appeared, leaning on the arm of the King of the Dead. He waited for the other figure, the third person who should be with them ... and waited ... but no one else appeared.

"What about—" he began.

Dis met his eyes. "It has been attended to," he said. "That is all you need to know." He turned back to Drake. "Here I leave you," he said. "Farewell."

She nodded. Her face was white and drawn. She looked ill: consumptive, or just queasy.

"Wizard." Dallon raised his head. "Take care of her." Dis leaned down to speak to her, urging her forward. Looking dazed and unhappy, she left his side and went to Dallon.

"Captain," he said, "are you all right?"

"Please," she said, clutching his arm. "Let's just go."

He looked at the King of the Dead. It was impossible to say for certain, but he thought he detected a hint of anxiety in that tenebrous countenance. "Go," said Dis. "Be well."

Putting his arm around Drake's shoulders (she had buried her face in his shirt, and was shuddering, little abrupt jerks, as with extreme cold), he nodded. The door opened at his touch. Leading his weeping captain, he stepped through.

"Cap'n? Cap'n?" A familiar face, a familiar voice, blurred before her. She blinked her watering eyes, and raised her head. I must have fallen asleep, she thought.

"Cap'n?" It was Luna Shee speaking, Luna joggling her shoulder, Luna looking increasingly concerned. "You all right?"

"I'm fine." Drake raised her head, shoving her subordinate away. "I'm fine. I just ... fell asleep, that's all."

"Uh-huh." Biting her lip, the other pirate said, "Well, then what's he doing here?" She pointed.

Dallon Moral lay sprawled on the deck, his mouth open, his limbs all ahoo. He was snoring.

"Him? Oh..." For a moment she stared at him as though she'd never seen him before. "I decided not to kill him after all."

"Uh-huh." Luna was still eyeing her askance. And then her eyes brightened. "Hey!" she said. "Nice ring! Where'd you get it?"

"This?" She looked down at her hand. On the third finger was a silver band, set with a single black pearl. It was simple, but it drew the eye, as though visions swirled in the depths of the stone. She frowned at it, something tugging at her memory. "I don't know. I've had it forever, I suppose."

"Huh," said Luna. "Funny I never noticed it before."

Clapping her other hand over it, Drake said, "What are you doing here, anyway?"

Luna wriggled her shoulders and grinned. "Came to report," she said. "Seems your favorite person's got himself a spot of trouble. About to get himself killed by one Captain Pfillip Pflugelhorn."

Drake jolted out of her chair. "That's now?" Hadn't it happened already? Or maybe she'd dreamt it. She shook her head to clear out the cobwebs. "I have to go!" Leaning down, she lifted Moral's head by the hair. "Wizard!" she shouted. "Wake up!"

"Uh?" he said, sitting up, his eyes wide open but unseeing. "Who? What? I'll obliterate the lot of you! I know a spell—oh, it's you, Cap'n." He rubbed his head, wincing. "Where the blue blazes am I?"

"You're on my ship, and you're about to come with me into town. Come on!" Grabbing his shoulder, she yanked him up onto his feet. "Hurry!" She dashed out of the cabin, swirling the red coat around her shoulders as she ran. Shaking his head, the wizard followed.

"Huh," said Luna Shee, plopping down into a chair. "Well. Ain't that peculiar." And she shrugged.

"For God's sake, gentlemen," said an unfamiliar voice as they skidded to a halt among the trees, "cannot you put this disagreement behind you and part as friends?"

"If Captain Pflugelhorn will apologize for his words, I will be perfectly happy," said Captain Acheron Zeal, from his side of the grove.

"As I am the insulted party," said Pfillip Pflugelhorn, "I have nothing for which to apologize."

"What's happening?" asked Moral.

"They're about to fight." She bit her lip. What to do?

"Can we stop it?"

She shook her head. "It's a matter of honor. They'd both rather die than back down. Idiots." She twisted the ring on her finger, thinking. The seconds were loading the pistols now: powder, shot, ram it home... "Wizard!" she gasped, clutching at his arm. "Can you—do something to that bullet? Make it disappear?"

He looked dubious. "Matter can neither be created nor destroyed," he said. "But I'll see what I can do. Maybe I can send it to Schlagsahne."

The guns were loaded. Captain Zeal took off his jacket, folded it carefully, and lay it on the ground. His second, a small, dark, round-headed man of a type often seen in the Royal Navy, leaned close to him, saying something. Zeal gave a whimsical little grin, then turned and walked toward the center of the space between the trees. Pflugelhorn met him, smirking. They stood back to back, their pistols raised.

Moral let out a breath and shook his head. "Sorry, Cap'n," he said. "Didn't work."

Drake clenched her fingers round his arm. "Dammit, wizard! There must be something—!"

But Pflugelhorn's second, a man in the red coat of a marine officer, was already counting. "One." The combatants stepped forward. "Two." Another step. And so on to ten, when the two men stood at opposite ends of the grove once more, backs to one another, pistols held up before them.

There was a pause. Silence in the grove, save for the singing of birds, and the distant sound of the sea. Drake twisted the ring as though she would wrench her finger off.

"On my word..." said the round-headed naval officer. A sickening pause. Drake bit down on her lip until the blood ran. "FIRE!"

Zeal whipped around, bringing his pistol to bear, pulling hard on the trigger. In that moment, between the firing and the gun's discharge, he felt a strange disconnection, a dislocation. *I've done this before,* he thought, baffled, *but how can that be?*

Twin flashes of the powder igniting, twin cracks as the pistols discharged, twin plumes of smoke from the two guns' barrels.

Silence, utter and absolute.

For a moment no one moved—it might have been a painting of a duel, save for the eddying powder smoke. Captain Pflugelhorn wavered on his feet, then straightened, but his face was dark, and his arm was bleeding.

Captain Zeal looked down, and for a moment he seemed to see a wound in his breast, a tiny hole just beginning to bleed. He raised his hand it touch it—but of course there was nothing there to touch. He was unharmed.

There was a tense pause.

"Captain," whispered Dallon Moral, "let go of my arm before you break it."

"Oh," said Drake, releasing him. "Sorry."

"Well, gentlemen," said the round-headed man. "Is honor satisfied?"

"For my part," said Zeal, tossing his pistol away, "it is."

"Captain Pflugelhorn?"

The airship captain was staring at the gun in his hand. "I missed?" he said. "Impossible! I never miss!"

"Well," said his second, the marine, "there was that time—"

"Shut up, Brock!" Pflugelhorn snarled.

"Captain Feldspar asked you a question," said an old man in an admiral's uniform, stepping forward, a little spaniel at his side. The spaniel looked up at Pflugelhorn and showed its teeth. "Is honor satisfied?"

Pflugelhorn's head jerked up, twisted by an evil scowl.

"Mr Pflugelhorn?" said the admiral.

"Aye, sir," Pflugelhorn spat. "Perfectly satisfied." Sketching a salute, he turned and stomped away. "Brock," he snapped over his shoulder. "Come."

They walked right past Drake and Moral as they left the grove, but neither the angry airship captain nor the pig-faced marine gave them a moment's notice. Drake's heart was thudding hard enough to batter right through her rib cage and burst out of her chest.

Moral looked at her. "Do you want to talk to him?" he asked.

She hesitated. He had gone to speak to the admiral, and to the tall woman in the post captain's uniform, the one he had danced with all night at the ball, and to a blonde girl who could only be his sister. The round-headed captain came up to join them, holding the pistol case under his arm.

"No," she said. "Not right now. Let's go."

"Aye-aye, Cap'n."

Captain Zeal glanced away from the little knot of people, all smiling in relief, all speaking very fast, their words running over each other. He thought he had seen, out of the corner of his eye, a flash of red...

"What price, you asked me," said Dis, kneeling at her feet, holding her hand, "to return one junior post captain to the world of the living. Now I give you my answer." She caught a glimpse of black and silver, gleaming in the firelight, and then he slid the ring onto her finger. It fit perfectly. "Be my bride. When your days on the earth are done, come back to me, lighten my dark days with your brightness. Fill these empty halls with your laughter, until the last day comes and we are parted for eternity." As she watched, the shadows fell away from him, revealing ... just a man, with dark eyes and a hopeful smile. "This place," he said, "could use a woman's touch."

"For Acheron Zeal..." she said.

"For him," he agreed.

"How..." she began, then hesitated. Trying again, she said, "How will it ... work?" She had visions of leading a misty image of Acheron Zeal by the hand out of the house of the dead (oh, the questions her crew would ask then!), or (much worse) dredging the waters of the Shiraz while he, newly revivified, helplessly drowned.

"Would you believe," said Dis, "it's actually easier to alter time than to bring the dead back to life? For me, at any rate. Others have other methods, of course, but as far as you or anyone else is concerned, Acheron Zeal will never have died."

She thought about it, gnawing on her lower lip. He could see an objection growing behind her eyes, and he thought, She will refuse, then, and that's the end of it. Ah, well, in spite of what they say, even the dead can hope.

But when she spoke, she glanced up at him through the dark veil of her eyelashes, and he thought his heart would stop (not, of course, that it was beating in the first place, but in these circumstances, the usual tropes are helpful).

"Will I remember?" she asked. "Any of this?"

"In dreams, perhaps," he said. "My dear. Dare I hope, then, that your answer is yes?"

She swallowed, her throat suddenly dry. And then, closing her eyes, "Yes," she said. "My answer is yes."

"Then it is done." The very foundations of the house shuddered as he spoke. His hand came up, brushing her cheek, wiping her tears away. "Am I so very terrible?" he asked. He sounded wistful.

"I don't know—I don't know!" She was sobbing too hard to stand; he caught her in his arms, lowering her into the nearest chair. He held her, soothing her as you would soothe a child, until her shaking stilled.

"I am not cruel," he said. "And it is not forever. Only until the end of time."

She drew a shuddering breath, and wiped her eyes on her sleeve.

"And who knows?" he added. "Perhaps the world will end soon, rather than late, and you'll only have a century or two in which to put up with me." She stared at him, and he grimaced, ruing his hideously ill-timed attempt at apocalyptic humor. "You should go," he said. From somewhere he produced a handkerchief, which he gave to her. She scrubbed at her face as though to remove the top layer of skin. He watched her, his dark gaze somehow diffident. "I don't suppose," he said, "before you go ... just once...?"

She closed her eyes in assent.

He leant forward, on his face the look of a man who, hardly daring to hope, has seen a green oasis in the midst of the shimmering desert heat. His trembling hand barely touched her cheek. His lips met hers, brushed, then parted.

"I made a very poor bargain once, you see," he said, his mouth still next to hers. "Long ago. Can you forgive me?" His tears mingled with hers. "May you have many long and happy years above the earth," he said, "before I come to claim you." He kissed her again. Her eyes slid shut.

When she opened them, she was alone in her cabin. The *Eschaton* was gliding through the darkness of night, away from Umeboshi, away from Acheron Zeal. The black pearl gleamed softly on her finger. The memory was already fading.

"Will you run from him forever?" she asked herself, rolling over in bed, looking at the ring. "He'll catch you eventually, you know."

And the answer came: would that be so very bad?

But she did not bother to reply, and soon she was asleep.

"On your head be it, Flynn Freeborn," Bayard said.

CHAPTER 9
The Dead March

Part the Second: Memento Mori

She used to imagine what it would be like when he came home to her at last. He would come striding over that hill, a man grown now, with the swinging walk of a sailor, and he'd take her in his arms, and whirling her up through the air he'd say to her, "Well, I've come home at last. Would you do me the honor of marrying me?" And, "Oh, yes, of course!" she would say, and that would be that; they would be together forever, never to be parted again.

There was only one small, crucial problem.

The years went by, and he did not appear.

She was a girl when he went away (she would not say "disappeared," even in the deepest silences of her heart, still yet "died"), and the years went by, and she grew to womanhood and she waited, but he did not appear.

And the years went by, and she waited.

"You should at least eat something," her brother said to her, more times than she could count. And, "I will, later," she always replied. And whether it was the not eating, or the standing out on the cliffs overlooking the sea in all weathers, or some perilous flaw in her blood—or something else entirely—the physicians were unable to say, but in her eighteenth year she fell ill, and there was no one who thought she would survive.

"I will not die," she said, "not until he comes home again."

"He's not coming home, Evelyn!" her brother exploded, his voice full of anger and grief. "He's dead!"

"You don't know that!" she cried. "You didn't see it—no one did! He might be—he must be—" And she doubled over, coughing, and the handkerchief she held to her mouth was spotted with red.

The years went by, and she waited and did not die, and he still did not appear.

In her heart, she began to doubt. What if he really had died? For, if he were alive, would not he have come back to her by now?

She did not die, but neither did she live, except in the strictest and most technical sense. She watched her brother's children grow, and she lay in her bed and grew weaker and older, older and weaker, but she still did not die. She waited.

Sometimes they took her out into the garden, for the physicians said the fresh air and sunlight would do her good. She sat in a rattan chair amongst the early flowers, a quilt covering her legs, and, raising her face to the sun she thought, It is much too late now. If he were coming back, he would have done so by now. It is too late, and all my waiting has been in vain.

"Aunt Evie's crying again!" shrilled a high young voice, very close at hand.

"Adeline." An older voice, gently chiding. "Don't pester your auntie. Come on—let's get you cleaned up, and then have some cake, shall we?"

"Huzzay, cake!"

A swift patter of footsteps running through the grass. When she was certain of being alone, Evie opened her eyes again. The warmth of the sun was too bitter, too cruelly ironic. Perhaps they would forget about her, sitting in the kitchen, eating their cake and strawberries and drinking tea. Perhaps they would leave her out here forever.

Once she had waited, ever-hopeful, for her beloved to come home.

Now she simply waited to die.

H.M.S. *Prometheus* was rather an elderly frigate—she had served in the last war—but Captain Kermit Feldspar had a reputation for briskness and mathematical precision: he ran a taut ship, a ship in which royals could be set in under two minutes, a ship which could weigh anchor and put to sea with no more than a single order, and that spoken in conversational tones: none of that whistling and hooting and hallooing that went on in other, less disciplined ships (it might here be added that Captain Feldspar had unusually sensitive hearing, and that loud noises hurt his ears, which might explain his dear love of near-silent perfection). She might not be able to sail as close to the wind as some of your young, flash frigates; she might be something of a slug going large; but she was a trim and pretty sight riding at anchor in Umeboshi Bay, her brass gleaming bright, her yards as square and as black as art and the hand of man could make them.

The last of Captain Feldspar's dinner guests were going over the side now, being rowed back to their various destinations. The very last, Captain Acheron Zeal, paused and gripped his old friend's hand.

"I don't suppose I'll be able to return the favor?" he said.

Captain Feldspar shook his head. "I hope to set out before the evening gun. You know how it is: there's not a moment to lose—"

"—For wind and tide wait for no man," Captain Zeal finished, grinning. "Well, pleasant sailing to you, K."

"And to you." They shook hands. Captain Feldspar hesitated, then said, "Er... Listen, Ash. If I were to write to your sister..."

Acheron Zeal laughed out loud. "I wish you the very best of luck," he said. "Goodbye, now."

"Goodbye."

The marines stamped in unison and presented their arms, the bosun's pipe squealed, and Captain Zeal went over the side. "Give way," he said to his coxswain, and the men heaved on their oars and rowed him off to his own ship.

"Right," said Captain Feldspar, squinting up at the sky. "Looks like we may get a bit of a blow before nightfall," he said. "What do you think, Claude?"

His first lieutenant was a meager, weedy fellow whose hair was already beginning to thin on top, although he couldn't have been more than twenty-five. He followed his captain's example, narrowing his eyes at the western sky, where a band of gathering haze was barely visible.

"I think I'll feel more comfortable when we're putting in at Port Cullis, and we can get rid of our—ahem—our cargo. The men are already starting to talk." Claude kept his gaze fixed on the sky as he spoke.

Captain Feldspar raised his eyebrow. "I meant," he said, "what do you think about the possibility of inclement weather, Mr Ronson?"

"Oh." Lieutenant Claude Ronson cleared his throat. "Sorry, sir. Uh, yes, sir. Looks like it might, er, come on to blow...." He trailed off, acutely aware of his error. "I'll just go—see to the last of the provisions, shall I, sir?"

"Yes, Mr Ronson," said Captain Feldspar, "what an excellent idea."

"Aye-aye, sir." Claude touched his hat—and then fled.

It was almost nightfall before *Prometheus* set sail. The blue peter—a blue flag with a white rectangle in the center, signifying imminent departure—had been flying all afternoon, and now, emphasizing it with one final gun, Captain Feldspar gave the order to weigh anchor with quiet satisfaction. Those men desperate for one last pint of ale, one final romantic interlude, who crammed in all the pleasures they could stand up to the very last minute, were either aboard (looking greenish, crapulent, jaded, nauseous) or pelting toward the quay with frantic strength. They would find, to their infinite chagrin, that (just as the preachers always said) wine, women and song had been their undoing. They had, in fact, missed the boat.

Deep in the *Prometheus*'s hold, a man who could have told you everything you wanted to know (and much, much more) about the dangers of wine, women and song, raised his head off of his fettered hands. "Ah," said he, "so we're getting under weigh at last, are we? What a marvelous thing, to be sure." He leant back and sighed, getting as comfortable as his chains would allow. The air in his dim corner was dank and stuffy and reeked of the bilges—any candle you tried to light would burn blue for a moment, then suffocate for want of air—his fetters chafed him something awful, and it was as black in his little hole as the deepest pit of hell (as he had cause to know), but he was, for all that, cheerful. He would run his errand for Cousin Bayard, and then—why, then—

"You'll be your own man again, Flynn Freeborn," he said. "Aye, that you will!"

And, lulled by that charming thought, he was soon asleep.

He awoke with a start some time later—hours, days, or mere minutes, he could not have said; it was as dark as ever in his prison.

There was someone in there with him.

"Who—who's there?" he said.

"'Your own man'," said a voice. A familiar voice. A horribly, painfully, intimately familiar voice. Even that tone of mockery and disdain was one he'd heard a thousand times. His heartbeat quickened.

"Lu—Lucenza?" he said.

"Your own man," repeated the voice of Lucenza di Ladro. "Ha!"

"What're you doing here?" cried Flynn Freeborn, scrambling to his feet with a clash and a clatter of chains. "You're—you're—"

"Dead," she replied.

All this while there had been a sort of awful radiance growing around them, a pallid glow like that of luminous fungus—and when she spoke the word "Dead," with a horrible sound like a silent explosion, it blazed up, white and stark and terrible, and he could see.

"Oh, God!" he cried, recoiling.

Lucenza di Ladro had been, in her day, a beautiful woman.

She was beautiful no longer.

The long, sleek limbs were rotten and decayed, the once-smooth flesh hanging in rags and tatters, white bone showing through. The smooth face, whose lips he used to kiss, was a ruin, the skin bluish where it was not gone entirely, speckled with mold, eaten by fish. Her eyes were gone, but in the staring black hollows of her eye sockets, two lights glimmered, cold and malicious. And yet, most horrible of all, there was still, in this creature, this thing, this parody, a hint of the Lucenza that had been, a mockery of her once-vibrant life.

“Are you not happy to see me?” it said. “I have been wanting to see you, Flynn.”

“Get away from me!” he cried. “Leave me be! What have I ever done to you?”

“What have you done?” said the ghost. “What have you done?” Its voice spiralled up in operatic disbelief, just as Lucenza’s would have done. But if this hideous creature was Lucenza, he would eat his hat. With sauce. And maybe a nice side of greens, too. And a tot of grog. Aye, whiskey, wine or beer would be a grateful thing indeed, just at the moment—

“Look at you!” said Lucenza. “You are pathetic, Flynn! A shell of a man. You dream of freedom, but you are a slave, and you always have been. A slave to your weakness, your cowardice, your vice. Would a good man have left me to die, murmuring impotent excuses while he saved his own skin?” She waved one graveyard hand in his face, and the smell of corruption reached his nose. “Look at you!” she said again. “You are nothing! You don’t deserve to live.”

Flynn’s head came up at that. “Deserve?” he said. “Aye, perhaps it’s right you are, lass! Perhaps I’m not deserving of anything that’s ever come to me! But it’s alive I am, and alive I’ll stay, no thanks to you and your haunting and your guilting.” He crossed his arms and sat down on his bench, his jaw jutting stubbornly. “Now I’ll be thanking you to leave me be. Find some other poor fool to torment; I’ll not be taken in by you a second time.”

The ghost (if ghost it was) stared at him, frowning, biting at where its lower lip would have been, if lips it had retained. And then it smiled (a gruesome sight, rotting flesh gaping like shot-holed canvas, mandible showing through) and said, “Very well. I leave you for now.” She leant forward, thrusting her corrupted countenance right in Flynn’s face. “But wouldn’t you like to kiss me, Flynn?”

“Your soul to the devil!” Flynn roared, upstarting. “Get ye hence, demon!”

The spirit giggled. “Look to your own soul, Flynn Freeborn,” it said, and vanished.

Nighttime in Porta Bella, long ago. Before Baron von Death was anything more than an embittered schoolboy dreaming of world dominion and revenge, before the first airship soared through seas of sky and cloud, before the dragons descended from lofty Stratocumulopolis to mingle with the world again. After the straying Prince Remington had been returned safely home, new-wedded bride on his arm; but before cousin Bayard learnt of his own prodigal's return to his habitual waters, though reports of plundered treasure would reach him soon enough; at that time, Flynn Freeborn sat in his favorite tavern, getting loudly, exuberantly, gloriously drunk.

"A fine haul!" he roared, scattering gold coins from his fingers, just to watch them shine. "A fine haul!" The thieves, drunkards and whores who packed the Bad Halibut scrambled to catch a handful of the glittering rain, and Flynn laughed out loud. His new, lovely *Peregrine* had taken a treasure ship, so loaded with gold and silver its keel scraped the ocean-bottom; enough gold that every *Peregrine* in Porta Bella was a new-minted Croesus—though the morning would see them paupers again, no doubt. Paupers with incipient liver failure. That much gold can buy a lot of grog.

Young women (and some not so young, neither) surrounded him, giggling, simpering, rouged fingers reaching for his pockets. He slapped them away lightly. "None o' that, now, ladies, none o' that," he said, grinning. "There'll be plenty of time for that later, so there will. Now come here," hauling on the nearest one's blouse, "and give me a kiss—"

Then a new voice interrupted, "Away, harlot; I require a word with the Captain."

Crying protest, gabbling like a gaggle of geese, the women scattered. Flynn, disappointed, turned to face the newcomer. An unfamiliar face, though he'd have to say—eyeing her up and down—that he wouldn't mind making the acquaintance.

"Ahoy, there," he said, giving her his best roguish grin. She bared her teeth at him, and, taking it as an invitation, he circled his arm about her slender waist. "And what can I be doing for you, me beauty?"

She slapped him.

"Ow!" said Flynn, though he did not release her. Her eyes were dark black in her dusky face, and by no means were they the most interesting of her features. Scowling, she hit him again.

"Ow!" said Flynn, and this time he let her go.

"You are Flynn Freeborn?" said the dark beauty, shaking out her hand.

"Aye," said Flynn, rubbing his chin. "Ow. What'd you hit me for, then?"

"I am the Queen of Pirates," she announced. "No man touches me without my permission."

"And ... with your permission?" asked Flynn, with an acquisitive leer.

Her eyes flashed scorn under curving brows like lines of India ink. "Hmph," she said. "You're even more a fool than I thought. Perhaps this opportunity is no for you." And she turned to go, to force her way through the close-packed, drunken throng.

"Wait!" cried Flynn, starting up and holding out his hands—though he did not, this time, offer to touch her. "Opportunity, you say? And what sort of opportunity might you be referring to, then?"

For a year and more they sailed together, the *Peregrine* and Lucenza's *Stella Maris*, raiding, looting, pillaging, plundering. What grand times those had been! What a marvel it was, to be free and alive in those days, with no man to call master. Ah, and if the days had been grand, then the nights had been grander, once Lucenza actually gave her permission....

Oh, and if he could return to those times, what then? They were gilded in memory, sure, each moment blazing with sunlight and scented with the fresh tang of the sea—but look a little deeper, Flynn Freeborn, beneath the golden façade: what do you find? Joy and freedom? Or the stench of a blood-soaked deck, the groans of the wounded, the weeping of ravished women whose husbands, brothers, fathers you have killed? Squalid waterfront taverns, cheap whores, poverty and misery and pain, aye, and the blood on your hands that's soaked down to the bone. And how, then, will you ever wash them clean?

"Oh, my dear," said a voice at his side, "how did you ever come to this pass?"

Flynn's eyes flew open. "Mother?" he said.

There she sat, not as he had last seen her, hollow-eyed and weeping, her radiant hair shorn almost to the skull, as her new husband led her away—but as he liked to remember her, slim and smiling, her hair falling in rich coils all the way down her back. The same dim glow that had illuminated Lucenza outlined her as well. She lay one hand against his forehead, but he felt nothing, not even the lightest touch.

"We had such hopes of you, your father and I," said Vilmaris Peregrine, stroking his face with that intangible hand. "You would grow to be a good man, strong and brave, marry a good woman, carry on the legacy of our house. You could have been a force for good in the world, my son, but look at what you have become instead. Wasted, drunken, steeped in iniquity." She took her hand away, and though he had not felt its presence, its sudden lack he felt as keenly as a knife's blade. "You should be ashamed," she said.

Flynn struggled to sit up. "What could I have done?" he asked her—and had there been anyone to listen, he would have noted how the diction and accent of the indomitable pirate changed, becoming the tones of any well-bred young man. "How could I have helped? I was dead to you."

"Dead." Vilmaris laughed. "Your father was dead, Lysander. Your brother was dead. You were alive, and you did nothing."

"I should have died," Flynn said, looking down at his fettered hands. "When d'Urstwhil ran me off that cliff, I should have died."

"You should have," she agreed. He stared at her, aghast. "I would rather you had died," she said, "than know you lived on, and did nothing to help me."

"But—" he began.

"But," she cut him off, "you squandered your second chance. You wasted it. What could you have done, Lysander? You could have changed the very course of the world. But no. You chose the wide and easy path, and it has led to ruin—not just for you, but for everyone you should have loved, everyone you could have saved."

She got to her feet.

"Mother," said Flynn, standing also, holding out a hand to her. "Please—don't go—"

She turned on him a gaze of infinite disdain, of coldness to rival the eternal winter of the Pole of Wind. "I wish I had never borne you," she said, and disappeared.

He was twelve the year his father died. A hunting accident, they said. You know how Lord Errol had loved the chase. His horse had shied, and he had lost his seat and been trampled under the flailing hooves. A tragedy. A senseless, awful tragedy—and the widow with two young children to look after!

It was their nearest neighbor brought the news: August d'Urstwhil, a nobleman fallen on hard times, who sometimes hunted on Lord Peregrine's lands. He had seen the accident, he said, though from afar. He was sorry for their loss. Some men were bringing the body along. He would stay with her until they came.

Vilmaris did not believe him. Her husband was an expert horseman, had raised that horse from a foal. He would never have fallen. He knew these lands like the back of his hand. There must be some mistake.

But then they came, a grim entourage, bearing the body between them. Lord Errol's face was the face of a stranger, pale as wax.

"No!" Vilmaris shrieked, brushing off d'Urstwhil's hands, stumbling into the lane to fall on her knees beside her husband's corpse. She took his face between her hands and kissed those cold, dead lips, all the while weeping, weeping, and calling his name.

"Vilmaris." Strong hands caught her, lifting her up. She fought him, wailing and gnashing her teeth. "Vilmaris!" Cullen Rangle, who had married her husband's sister.

Her dead husband's.

"Easy, now, easy," he was saying, holding her wrists in a grip that was gentle but unbreakable. She lunged against that grip, weeping and pleading. "Lysander, run and fetch the doctor!" Lysander, twelve that year, bobbed his head and set off for the stables. He turned back once to look, saw his mother slump forward against Cullen's chest. Saw d'Urstwhil step forward, lift his mother up and carry her inside, as though she weighed nothing. There was a curious emptiness in his chest, as though all his innards had been scooped out. He dashed a hand across his eyes and ran.

Lord Errol was buried in the rain, his brothers, sisters, nieces, nephews, widow, sons all clad in mourning black, gathered around the grave while the chill rain pattered down. The priest spoke in brief (the rain was the nasty sort that finds every gap in your clothing, slinking like clammy fingers down the back of your neck, soaking you to the bone), then clapped his prayer book to and nodded to the sexton, who shuffled forward and began shoveling the damp, black earth over Lord Errol's coffin.

Vilmaris Peregrine, red-eyed but no longer weeping, shook off August d'Urstwhil's restraining hand (what a help he had been, friends and neighbors whispered, to the poor bereaved wife! Without his constant presence, it's sure she would have done herself an injury) and approached the grave. The rich, long hair that had been her glory was shorn to stubble; in her hand, a coil as thick as a ship's cable, heavy with rain. An outdated custom, you would have said, no longer practiced—except she had done it, and now she stepped forward and threw the rope of hair into the grave with the showering earth.

What was worse, Lysander could not have said: the black wound in the earth where his father's body lay, or the exposed curve of his mother's skull, naked and vulnerable now that her hair was gone. Neither was a thing easily to be borne. He stared unblinking at a point beyond the sexton's heaving left shoulder. He would not cry.

A small hand slipped into his. He turned and looked, biting back a cry of surprise.

"I'm sorry for your loss," said Evelyn Rangle, a soft and pretty girl his own age, daughter of Lysander's uncle Bartholomew. "Is there anything I can do?"

"I don't think so," said Lysander, looking back into the grave, almost full now. "But thank you."

Six months after that, Vilmaris Peregrine and August d'Urstwhil were married. (What a relief, said the local gossips, to have someone to help look after the boys!) Not long after that, Heathcliff Peregrine (never strong to begin with) died of a fever. Soon after that, Lysander Peregrine met with a fatal accident, tumbling off a cliff and into the sea.

In the due course of time, Vilmaris bore to her new lord a son. They named him Claudius.

Claudius d'Urstwhil grew up, married, and begat a daughter, whom he named Ellysandra.

Ellysandra d'Urstwhil allied herself with the man known as Baron von Death. Under his tutelage and direction, she murdered King Reginald Eustace I, thus setting in motion the wheels of a war that would plunge the entire world into darkness.

"A hunting accident," said Flynn softly. His face was wet; tears sparkled in the stubble on his cheeks. He scrubbed one manacled hand across his face, and his chains clattered like the bones of the dead. "The oldest trick in the book, so it is." He shook his head.

"Yes, the old burr-under-the-saddle gag," said August d'Urstwhil, appearing at his side. "A classic."

"Ah," said Flynn. "I was wondering when you'd come to take your turn."

If Flynn seemed inordinately sanguine about the constant presence of the ghosts of his past, well, it was only because he was, at this juncture, almost used to it. Since he had clawed his way, gasping, through the suffocating blackness and up once more into the world of men, they had been ever at his side. At first he had seen them only when he slept, and a liberal dose of grog was enough to keep them at bay—and keep at bay as well the memories, seen in hectic flashes like a twisted landscape lit only by blasts of lightning, of his time in the dark place—but there was a reason they called it that old demon rum, and at this point it would have taken an ocean of spirits to keep those other spirits away.

"I want to tell you something," said d'Urstwhil, settling himself on the bench next to Flynn. That same graveyard aura hung about him, the phosphorescence of rotting logs and the dank odor of the tomb, but he carried himself with a jovial benevolence that was, under the circumstances, rather off-putting. He slung an insubstantial arm around Flynn's shoulders, and Flynn cringed. "It's rather ironic, but I think, like me, you have a taste for ironies." He smiled, his eyes almost disappearing in the folds of his flabby face.

"Aye?" said Flynn, drawing indifference about him like armor—but what battered armor it was, rusted and full of holes! "Well, I'm a-waiting with baited breath, so I am."

D'Urstwhil's reptilian smile grew, if anything, broader, until the corners of his mouth threatened to meet at the back of his head. "I never had the chance to tell you how glad I was when you called me out. It played right into my hands—indeed, I couldn't have planned it better myself. How tragic! Poor Master Lysander, untimely deceased!" He clasped his pudgy hands to his breast. "Of course it would have been better, much better, if you had really died, but dead or not, you were out of my way, and that's what mattered."

"You'll be forgiving me, I'm sure, mate," said Flynn, raising one eyebrow, "but I'm not quite seeing the irony of it."

For a moment, just a moment, d'Urstwhil's aspect grew cold and grey: the face of a corpse, or the face of something that had never lived. "I'm getting to that," he said—and something flashed in his eyes, something chill and hopeless, a flare of hatred and despair, despair that feeds on hatred as a serpent eating its own tail, eternally damned to consume itself until all that remains is a cinder. And even the cinder still hates, and hating, despairs. Seeing that look, Flynn felt his own heart grow cold and small within him. Then resuming his former florid color (bleached out by the livid light surrounding him), d'Urstwhil said, "The irony, my dear impatient Lysander, is this: had you not challenged me, you would not have fallen off that cliff, would not have 'died,' would not have taken up a life of piracy and sin, would not, in short, have found yourself in your present unhappy circumstance. The irony, oh the sweet, delicious irony, is this—" Eyes slit in an awful smile, like a smug and bulbous toad, d'Urstwhil leant in close, putting his mouth next to Flynn's ear, and whispered:

"You are the instrument of your own downfall."

He rocked back and forth on the bench, tittering, pressing his fingertips together, as Flynn gaped.

"Think on that, dear son!" said d'Urstwhil, and vanished.

Flynn leapt to his feet. "Aye!" he cried. "And if you hadn't'a married my mother and murdered my father, that would have helped, you filthy bastard!" But his rage was the useless defiance of a young boy, and on the final syllable his voice cracked, and he clattered to his knees.

After a time, exhausted by his travails, he slept.

While Flynn is sleeping (poor fellow, he deserves it; as little rest as he's been getting it's no wonder he's seeing ghosts and hearing voices), let us creep from the darkness of the *Prometheus*'s hold (you have no doubt grown accustomed to the dank and bilgy smell, but I assure you, the air is much clearer up on deck) and walk about and stretch our legs. There is the quartermaster at the con, wearing a knit hat and a muffler, for the weather has grown unseasonably cool—though I trust you find the breeze refreshing? There is Captain Feldspar, wearing a griego, holding a cup of coffee in benumbed hands. See how the wind tears away the steam, carrying it off to leeward and shredding it over the glassy waves. In a moment he will order the topmasts struck down on deck, lest the ship's increasing roll send them right over the side. Unusual weather for this time of year; although the *Prometheus*'s route takes her up into the chill waters of the Bordeaux Sea, not too distant from the Pole of Wind, it is still springtime. There should not be the threat of snow on the wind.

Heading for'ard now; those seamen not occupied at some important task stamping their feet and blowing on their hands; one unfortunate at the head shivering with his trousers round his ankles ... but we need not go into detail, do we? Let the man have his privacy.

Turning to the southward, moving quickly now—the broad-winged albatross not half as swift as we—crossing miles of empty, slate-grey sea. Empty? No, not quite. Take note: a little ship, a polacca, far from its native waters, as close-hauled as it can be, beating up into the northerly wind. What business could such a vessel have so far from its home?

Well, it is no concern of ours—at least, not right now. South, ever southward we fly, leaving behind the forbidding sky, the greasy swell, the icy wind, reaching at last more congenial waters. Here sails another ship, one more closely related to our current purpose. You might take her for a ship of the line at first glance, built as she is along the same martial lines as a man-of-war, but no. Commerce, not combat, is her raison d'être; the *Pearl of Great Price* is her name. She, too, is bound for Camembert, loaded to the gunwales with merchandise from the Chai Empire. She also carries a passenger, into whose cabin we now will step, as silent as shadows, and observe her in her private moments when she thinks herself alone (for that is, after all, the writer's, and the reader's, prerogative, is it not?).

It was evening; the passengers had dined with the captain in the *Pearl*'s magnificent stateroom (Captain Doddard was not the owner of the ship, but a friend of the owner, one Norville Dunstan Ansley, who had sold all his earthly goods to purchase a single ship, the *Pearl*, which had grown into a vast trading concern, the N.D.A. Trading Company), those who desired remaining on deck to sip coffee or tea or something stronger and chat amiably with the officers and with each other, while the ship hove comfortably to, snug as an eider duck sleeping on a pond. Lethe Zeal, however, though an amiable young woman, felt no inclination for the company of others, and as soon as was reasonable and polite, she made her excuses and retired to her cabin.

There she sat, brushing out her long, golden hair, her arm moving up and down with the automatic regularity of a steam pump, her mind elsewhere. When she returned home, she would be married. To whom, she had no idea; the groom's identity was of little import. Any fellow would answer, she supposed. The thing was to be married at all. There were plenty of eligible young men (and some not so young) back home; no doubt her mother was already scheming and planning, arranging the perfect match.

The hairbrush caught on a tangle. With a grimace, Lethe set about working it free. She had no objection to the married state, as such, although she would have liked to choose her own mate. What young woman, though, is allowed such a liberty? She shook her head.

The knot came undone. She remembered, with a queer little thrill, the man who had danced with her at the envoy's ball, whose broad hands had guided her with such confidence, whose grey eyes had caught hers so boldly. What terrible things he had told her, but so matter-of-factly, he might have been commenting on the weather! She whispered along with her memory, "Oh, I'm a rogue and a sinner, and there is no virtue in my soul...." A flush rose to her cheeks, and the hand holding the hairbrush trembled.

She could never marry someone like that, not someone who boasted so openly of the horrible things he'd done! She pressed her hands to her face, hoping to cool the blood pulsing there. It didn't help. She kept remembering the look in his eyes, the desperate pleading as he pressed her hand with his. "Don't flee from me," he'd said.

But how could one do anything else? Should she acquiesce to the entreaty of his strong, sun-browned hands, the smiling eyes with the unspoken despair behind them? What though the thought of him sent the blood recklessly pounding through her veins, making her flushed and chilled by turns? Older, cooler, wiser heads than hers would chart her course; it were best to forget the handsome, smiling rogue, forget the lilting eloquence of his voice, forget the unfamiliar quickening of her heart.

What was his name? He'd told her, there at the end. Biting her lip, casting her eyes upward, she tried to recall. And then she smiled, lip still caught between her teeth. Just this once, she'd say it, just to try it, to taste the sound.

"Flynn," she said, and her heart raced.

"Awake at last, are we?" said a voice at his elbow. "Here I was afraid you'd gone and died, and we'd have to be tipping your festering corpus overboard. Ain't nothing like a corpus, there ain't, for bringing the bad luck."

Flynn's return to consciousness was slow, reluctant and confused. He forced open bleary eyes, unsure of what they'd see. His limbs felt heavy, waterlogged. He groaned.

"Aye!" said the voice. "I knew ye wasn't dead! Takes more than a bit o' damp to pull your card, aye, so it does!"

I know this, Flynn thought, befuddled. I remember this. "Where am I?" he asked.

A face, broad and beaming as the moon, swam into view, a face at once familiar and strange. Flynn knew it at once as the face of Cornelius Cid, the famous pirate, captain at this time of the *Wild Goose*, owner of the biggest, bushiest, grandest pair of mutton-chops in the whole Quadra Terrarum. But how did he know, when he'd never met the man, when he'd just now been pulled out of the sea, rescued from certain death? He shook his head, more turned about than ever.

A great black slit opened in the face, shaping words. "You're on me ship, you are," it said. "This ain't the best time of year for swimming, laddie, so it ain't, and this ain't the best ocean, neither." It roared laughter, and Flynn cringed and tried to cover his ears with his arms, the noise hurt him so. Then his fetters clanked, and he dropped his hands in confusion. He saw no chains.

"Ah, laddie," said Captain Cid, his rescuer from the deep, progenitor of his new life, "you can't see 'em, 'cause they ain't there, not yet. You'll forge 'em, sure enough, link by link and sin by sin, 'til they're long enough to circle the world and heavy enough to drag you straight down to the depths, but they ain't there yet. Just be patient." He chuckled.

Flynn struggled to sit up. This was wrong—this was not as he remembered. But—shaking his head, heavy with the water of his near-drowning—how could he remember it, if it hadn't happened yet?

His vision was clearing. There was Cid, stocky and stout, clean-shaven but for those ridiculous sideburns, one hand hooked through his suspenders, the other holding a pipe. A cloud of blue smoke drifted up from the bowl, but Flynn could smell nothing.

Cid turned to look at him, and Flynn's heart (which had been lying quiescent somewhere around the bottom of his rib cage) began to hammer against his breast, like a prisoner trying to get out. The eyes—his eyes were not Cid's eyes, those mild blue orbs: these were black, and cold, and desolate, an alien landscape under a dying sun, where nothing grows or lives or loves or hopes, and all that remains is a bleak, implacable hatred.

"And don't you wish," said Captain Cid, his old mentor, "don't you wish I'd left you to die? Aye, what a relief 'twould have been to you, I don't mistake, to drown an innocent babe, without all the filth and the grime a-weighin down your soul. Though perhaps, being lighter, you wouldna've drowned so quick!" At this he threw back his head and laughed out loud, a sound like hyenas baying. Then, putting down his pipe and unhooking his hand from his suspenders, he reached out towards Flynn.

"Cap'n," said Flynn Freeborn, "what are you doing?"

"What I should'ha done all those years ago," Cid replied, his broad hand covering Flynn's nose and mouth. "'Tis a pity, is it not, to be given a second chance to live, and to squander it on dissolution and villainy? Better, aye, better by far, to die here and now, innocent and unspoiled, than to go on to such an end as awaits the likes of you."

Flynn struggled, wrenching his head this way and that, but Cid's grip was strong, his cold eyes pitiless. But how can you know? Flynn wanted to ask, and would have asked, if he had the breath to say the words. If you kill me here, how can you know what I would have been?

There were stars bursting in his brain, blackness scrabbling at the edges of his vision. Cid pressed down with all his weight, his fingers squeezing the flesh of Flynn's face. His eyes were merciless, and so very dark.

Flynn woke with a gasp, jolting stark upright, one hand against his chest. The chains that bound him clanked and jangled.

"Bad dream?" said a voice beside him.

Flynn closed his eyes. "Oh, God," he breathed. "Please. No more. No more of this."

"What?" said that same voice—a woman's voice, rich and amused. "No more? That's not what you said earlier...."

He opened his eyes—then squeezed them tight shut. He didn't want to see another perversion of his memories. Not this memory. Let him keep something pure....

"Pure?" The woman laughed. "Pure filth, perhaps you're meaning? There's nothing good or clean or spotless in your life, Flynn Freeborn. Don't be fooling yourself." The hand lingered in his hair a moment, then traced a path down the side of his neck, along his shoulder, and down his chest. His bare chest.

Flynn yelped. Where the devil had his shirt gone off to? His eyes came open—and perforce looked into the eyes of the woman beside him.

"Do you remember me, then?" she asked. Catrionaugh Adaire, his captor, his lover, her red hair spilling across the bed cushions, the tangled sheets, her wicked eyes laughing at him.

"Leave me be!" Flynn cried, scooting as far away from her as he could. "Stop with you—putting your filth into their mouths, sullying them with your wickedness and lies! What do you want with me?"

"Oh, Flynn," Catrionaugh purred, running her hands along his chest (slim, strong, knowing, well-remembered hands), "why will you fight it?"

Fight he did, struggling to writhe out of her grip. "Why won't you leave me be?" he returned. "What do you gain from tormenting me?"

She ran her tongue across her lips and teeth—white teeth they were, and red, red lips. Her fingers curved into claws, and stabbed into his flesh, and the blood ran red from ten bright wounds. She dragged them down towards his belly, ten red slashes in his skin, and his spine curled with the agony of it.

"If you want it to stop," she said, leaning across him to whisper in his ear, "you know what to do. You have to end it."

"—End it," Bayard said, and turned to Flynn with an expectant look on his face.

"Uh—whuh?" said Flynn, blinking. The sudden change of scene, from a dim and alcoved bedroom to the great cabin of a ship of the line, disoriented him for a moment. Where was he now, and, more important, when was he? Was this the Bayard of sixty years past, young and dark-haired and vital, or the ancient Admiral of the present day, bent and stooped, his hair turned white where it remained at all? Even examining him keenly, Flynn could not decide. Perhaps it was both.

"End it, I say!" said Bayard, pacing near. "My God, cousin, how can you be so hard? If you could see her—!" His clenched fists shook with passion. Ah, thought Flynn, I do remember this. I know where I am now. "Every morning, every goddamned morning, she rises and says, 'Today's the day. Today he'll come back to me.' Every morning! But does he return? Of course he does not! He's too busy drinking and whoring and squandering his life!" He shot this last sally over his shoulder, like a stern-chaser's parting shot, and Flynn received it with stoical calm. It might hull him between wind and water, but he was not yet sunk, indeed he was not. Bayard turned back toward him, pleading. "It would break your heart to see her," he said.

Flynn clenched his jaw. "Then 'tis a good thing I haven't seen her," he said.

"Lysander—"

"Stop calling me that!" Flynn roared, surging to his feet, his fetters rattling. "I've told you before, but I'll not be telling you again! Lysander Peregrine is dead! He died on the cliffs that day, and all that remains is me, Flynn Freeborn, and I don't have the foggiest idea what you're talking about!" He ended, chest heaving, his nose mere breaths away from Bayard's, his chin jutting with rage.

Bayard's eyes were wide. "Have it your way, then. I'll trouble you no longer, *Captain Freeborn.*"

"Good," said Flynn.

"Now," said Bayard, "would you mind ... taking that axe away from my throat?"

"Oh." Flynn looked down at the boarding axe in his hand, its keen blade pressing the flesh of Bayard's neck, a thin line of red welling up along its edge. He tossed it away, and Bayard staggered backward, rubbing at the wound. "Sorry, cous."

"Yes, well," said Bayard. "On your head be it, Flynn Freeborn, if she dies."

Evelyn Rangle was Bayard's younger sister. She had not been a sickly child, and none could have predicted the illness that laid her low when she was still just a maid—nor could they have predicted the steely will behind her gentle exterior, which kept her alive when the best physicians in the country threw up their hands in defeat. When she was nine years old, she was engaged to be married to her cousin, Lysander Peregrine, who would be Lord Peregrine one day. Bartholomew Rangle had broached the subject to Lysander's father on a crisp day in late autumn, while the pack was snuffling about the hills in search of their fox, and at mention of the word 'marriage,' Lord Errol had almost fallen off his horse.

"Marriage?" he cried, while the horse danced beneath him. He was a large man, both tall and broad, and the horse that bore him proportionally large, bred to carry his weight without complaint (Errol—Lord Peregrine, that is—was an enthusiastic amateur horse-breeder), and it is surely fortunate that he did not give it a chance to plant its hooves in his anatomy that day. He retained his seat easily, however, stroking the beast's smooth neck, and turning to look at his brother-in-law with amazement. "Marriage?" he repeated. "It's a bit early to be thinking about that, don't you think?"

The pack's musical cry rose up in the distance, but Errol could not pursue a fox and negotiate the nuptials of his firstborn at the same time. The horse, impatient to rejoin the chase, didn't mind it, but then, the horse had a very poor grasp of marriage customs in Camembert during the reign of Queen Cynthia Leonara.

"Lysander's ten," said Bartholomew Rangle, grinning. "Evie's nine. They won't stay children for ever, you know."

"Is he ten already?" said Errol, mostly (it must be added) to himself. "How fast they grow! It seems just yesterday I held him in my arms, a purple, squalling, radish-headed infant."

"Will you at least consider it?" Bartholomew asked.

"It'll be years yet before he's ready to marry anyone," said Lord Errol (oh, truer words were never spoken, if only he had known it!), frowning.

"Well, you know what they say," said Bartholomew. "Gather ye rosebuds, and all that."

"Of course." But Errol still frowned. In the distance, a hound belled: the fox, the fox! This way, this way! And the rest of the pack took up the refrain. Errol's horse rolled its eye towards its master, as if to say, "The fox, you lackwit! Hurry, he's getting away! We must fly, fly, fly!" It snorted steam from its nostrils and stamped its hooves. Errol completely agreed. "Plenty of time to discuss these things later," he said. "Come on now!" Setting his heels to the horse's sides, he set off across the hills in pursuit of the pack.

Somehow, as a result of that inconclusive conversation, the matter had been decided. Evie and Lysander were to be wed when they were of an age; Evelyn being a romantic girl, much like her mother, she fell in love with the idea of being in love, and Lysander being, even then, a handsome lad, she was not at all reluctant to fall in love with him, too. They would be wed, and life would be lovely, lovely!

And then, of course, Lysander had disappeared.

She could have married anyone; even after her illness became too severe to hide any longer, she had several offers. She was a beautiful girl, and as her father, a sea captain, had not done too badly in the way of prizes, she had a beautiful dowry. Each would-be suitor, however, she refused, insisting that there was only one man she would ever marry, and she would wait patiently until he came home. Her family tried to impress upon her that Lysander Peregrine was dead, and that he would never come home; her brother, who knew they were incorrect on the former point, was in despair as to the latter. Whatever sort of man Lysander Peregrine might have grown up to be, Flynn Freeborn was stubborn, willful and intractable, and once he had set his mind to a course, there was no swaying him.

Thus the years passed, until came the day that Flynn Freeborn, adventure-loving pirate, intemperate lover of wine, women and song, unrepentant thief and killer, vanished from the very cabin of his own ship. Where did he go? Legends, rising up as swiftly as toadstools after rain, said that the soul of his dead lover, Lucenza di Ladro, had dragged him down to hell, vengeance for his ill treatment of her. Whatever had befallen him, it was true that no one ever saw him again.

Not, that is, until a certain young woman rescued him, quite by accident, from the cages of the Fisher of Souls, and Flynn Freeborn was cast once more upon an earthly shore.

Once more in Bayard's cabin, this time aboard the massive first-rate *Aubrey*, the lights of the city of Umeboshi glowing and wavering in the waters of the bay: "Tell me this favor of yours, cous, and have done," said Flynn.

Bayard—old now, weathered and worn by the years, an adventuring frigate captain no longer—smiled a withered, weary smile. "Go to my sister," he said. "Let her know you still live, beg her forgiveness for the wasted years. At any time you could have gone to her and made things right, but you were too damned selfish." Flynn was startled and appalled to see that the old Admiral was weeping. "Well," he said, "it's too late to make things right now, but by God, you will go to her now, and kneel at her feet, and confess to her the wrongs you've done! Perhaps I was foolish not to make you do it all those years ago, but I thought there was a spark of honor left in you. I thought I could blow that spark into a flame. What a fool I was."

"Cousin—" said Flynn, and there were tears on his own cheeks. "How can I? How can I face her? I—I'd be too ashamed."

"*Good!*" The old man's voice was fierce. "You should be ashamed, Lysander, of all you've done!"

"Aye." Flynn hung his head. His hair was filthy, lank, crawling over his shoulders like greasy snakes. The drowning of sorrows is not good, clean work. "Aye, and so I am."

"Then go to her, or by God I swear I'll see you hanged!"

"All right," said Flynn, his gaze fixed on his folded hands, and the clanking fetters that bound them, "I'll go to her." He glanced up. "I promise, cous."

The room had changed.

"Oh," drawled a voice from the shadows, "why wait? Kill him now! He'll never keep his promise!"

Bayard turned, a hideous smile stretching his face, holding out his arm to the figure stepping out from the darkness that pooled and puddled around them, sticky and viscous, like tar. She—and it was a female figure, though wasted and ravaged as by disease—stepped into the circle of his arm, snuggling against him, smiling out of a face like a skull.

The room swooped around him, and Flynn pressed his hands against his mouth, fearing he'd be sick. "Evie?" he said.

"Who else?" said Evelyn Rangle, breaking away from her brother's embrace. "I've been waiting for you, Flynn. Why won't you come to me?"

She was close, too close. He tried to scoot away from her, holding up his bound hands to ward her off. "No—no, leave me be!" he said. "I'll not go to you—your touch is death!"

Whirling in triumph, her long hair blowing about her like a funeral shroud, she turned to her brother. "You see!" she cried. "I knew he'd never come! He is a liar, a murderer, a sinner. He has murdered me by degrees these long, slow years, and now he will deal the death-blow! What were the words?" She leant in close to him, and the withered lips grew full and rosy, the sunken cheeks rounded and blooming—and Lethe Zeal stood before him, putting her face next to his, her lips so close he could have kissed them, if he'd wanted. But he was frozen, appalled.

"A rogue and a sinner, you called yourself," said Lethe, in icy-sweet tones, "with no virtue in your soul." Her blue eyes were veiled, accusatory. "You said you could see nothing beautiful but you'd want to corrupt it, and you'd sell out your own mother if the price were right. Isn't that what you said?"

"It's a fine memory you have, sure," Flynn stammered, trembling with fear and desire. He wanted, more than he'd ever wanted anything before, to bury his hands in the silken softness of her hair, to lose himself in the touch of her lips, the smooth perfection of her skin. But his hands did not so much as twitch; if he had touched her, he was deathly certain, that ripe skin would burst, revealing the rotted, maggoty horror beneath.

"Truer words!" cried Lethe Zeal. "Truer words were never spoken! You are a wicked man, a liar, so steeped in depravity there's no saving you! I would die before I touched you—and you should die before touching me."

He stared at her, shaking. Such words—such words should never come from such a lovely mouth. Such beautiful eyes should not flare with such malice and such hate.

Oh, God, he groaned to himself. It's true, it is. I've damned myself with my wicked ways, and I would have damned her, too.

"You're right," he said, bowing his head before her. "You're right, you are. I am a sinner, a weak-willed fool, a slave to my wrong-headed desires. What..." Raising his eyes to look at her. "What should I do?"

It was three weeks out of Umeboshi when the *Prometheus* sailed into a patch of dirty weather the likes of which her officers and men had never seen. Fell winds howled, and the air was filled with a blinding froth of ice and snow and freezing spray. Green and purple lightning split the sky, and sailors, ship and sea alike were shaken by the deep-voiced thunder's roar. Colored fires flickered along the tops of the masts, and the ocean heaved and bucked like a frantic horse. It was as though the world had gone mad.

For the first thirty-six hours, the officers and men had enough to do keeping the ship afloat, keeping her from foundering in the deep troughs of the grey-green waves. They had their hands full with not sinking, not drowning, not dying, and no extra energy for any other concerns. Captain Feldspar (wax in his ears and a cloth wound round his head, to save his sensitive ears) did not stir from the deck for a day and a half. At the beginning of the second day, however, when the captain was snatching a few winks of much-needed rest, several things happened at once.

The first was that the lookout, waterlogged and half-frozen, saw the icy fog part for just a moment, revealing the dark black bulk of an unfamiliar vessel, a polacca by its rig, struggling against the wind and water not a cable's length away.

The second came hard on the lookout's cry of "Ahoy, the deck! On deck there!" It was a scream.

A horrible, ear-piercing, wrenching, howling, ululating, gibbering, high-pitched scream of unspeakable agony, it ripped the air in two, louder than the constant thunder, shrill enough to shatter the stern windows and all the captain's wine glasses and his bottle of claret, sending the wine in a red gush across the deck, letting the wind and the blowing sleet come howling into the captain's cabin. Captain Feldspar gasped himself awake, clutching at his ears, as the scream went on and on.

“Mr Ronson!” he cried, stumbling out of his cot, blood trickling between his fingers. But his voice was a mere croak, after a day and a half of shouting orders over a howling gale, and he had not a prayer of being heard over that hideous wailing.

Still the scream went on.

Captain Feldspar stumbled across the pitching deck, slipping in spilt wine, treading on a huge chunk of broken glass. He reached the door of his cabin and flung it open. “Mr Ronson!” he shouted, into the teeth of the gale.

Lieutenant Ronson had been shoving his way aft, towards the great cabin, when the scream began. He was just in time to see his captain slump toward the deck, unconscious, blood streaming from his ears: red streams that the rain quickly washed away.

“Captain!” he cried—not that anyone could have heard it, over that monstrous screaming.

Then, mercifully, as though cut off with a knife, the screaming stopped. The relative silence that followed was a benediction.

The faces pressed in on every side, familiar faces, once-loved, now inimical and cold. Their voices crowded in his ears, harsh voices, cawing, laughing, taunting him. Was it not enough that they had tortured him day after day, that he was half-mad already, but now they must drive him over the precipice, as once August d’Urstwhil had driven a young boy whose only crime, then, had been a certain hasty rashness?

“End it!” said the voice of his mother. “End it!” urged Lucenza di Ladro. “End this torture—only you can stop it!” his father said. “There’s nothing here for you,” said Remy One-Eye. “One thrust of the knife,” cousin Bayard said, “and then it’s over.”

The ship was listing this way and that, the room reeling about him. The faces whirled together in his baffled vision, melting into one face, one white face that was not human and never had been, one red, laughing mouth, one pair of black eyes, hating, hating.

"Admit it," said this specter, "you've wasted your life. You'd be better off dead."

Words foamed out of his mouth—a scream—but Flynn no longer had the self-possession to know what he said, or if he spoke at all. "Leave me be!" he thought he cried, as the awful vision drew near, red mouth to devour him, white teeth to pierce his flesh, black eyes to sear his soul. He brought up his hands to ward it off, he raised his arms to cover his head, and the chains that hung from his wrists were flung up through the air, and came smashing down on his head, knocking him out cold.

"Well," said the apparition. "Bother!"

More voices, these quiet, human, soothing, their words soft and blurred, as though heard through a barrier of water. "Is this him?" someone said. "That's him," replied another. "That's the one I saw." Gentle hands lifted him up and bore him away, and he subsided into sweet oblivion.

At first there was only blackness, like a starless night at sea, and from the gentle rocking of the world about him, he knew he stood on the deck of a moving ship. There was no light at all, not even the hope of light; he could not see the planks beneath his feet, or his hand before his face. The ship's lanterns were unlit, and he sailed blind through a vast, implacable darkness. He felt, as he stood in that impenetrable night, a deep loneliness, and sorrow, and regret. He raised one hand to wipe away a tear, and flicked it off into the void.

The tear sailed through the air, flying farther than a single water-drop had any right to do, until at last it struck the ocean far ahead, and where it struck, a gleam of light bloomed into life, sweet balm to his aching eyes. As he watched, gripping the rail and leaning as far out as he could, the glimmer rose into the air, swaying with the motion of the ship.

"Why, bless my soul," he said to himself. "It wasn't my tear at all, but a star."

Such a lovely thing, the only light in the sky, in the world, gleaming silver and pure and true. The night had been silent, he realized, even the wind in the rigging and the water along the ship's side perfectly mute, but with the blossoming of the star's light there came a swell of distant music, and his ears yearned for that sound as much as his eyes longed for the light.

The star was growing larger and brighter—closer, he realized, swaying on the mysterious sea.

"Wrong again!" he said to himself. "No star at all, but a ship's lantern!"

By the light of that star, or that tear, or that lantern, he could see the other ship approaching: a beautiful, slim frigate, surging with infinite grace across the waves. He had never seen such a fine vessel, every line of her like a song.

Standing in the frigate's bows was a maiden, veiled in white, holding aloft the starry lantern that filled the sky with radiance. It was she who sang, a tune of such piercing sweetness he thought his heart would tear itself in two. Seeing him, she lifted her hand and gestured to him: Come to me.

Oh, yes, he thought, and began to climb up onto the ship's railing, to plunge into the sea and swim to her. Then the light of her lantern shone full on him, and he recoiled at what he saw.

Mud and slime covered him, head to foot, striped with blood and some other nameless feculence more horrible yet. He tried to wipe it away, but it clung to him like a disease. Weeping in bitter frustration, he scraped and scratched at his arms, trying to get them clean, but the harder he tried to scrape it away, the more there was to scrape. Shuddering, he scuttled backwards, out of the white circle of the lantern's light, back into the darkness. At least there, he couldn't see the filth that covered him.

"What are you doing?" called the maiden with the lantern.

"I'm hiding," said Flynn. "I don't want you to look at me."

"Silly," she said. "You have to come here."

"But," said Flynn, hiding in the shadows, "I'm filthy. How can I?"

"You'll have to swim," said the maiden. "The water will wash all that away." When he continued to hesitate, she said, "How will you come to me if you keep hiding there?"

"I don't want you to see me," said Flynn, abashed.

"I've already seen you," she pointed out. "It's much too late for that."

"Oh. Good point." He eased a foot into the circle of light, then hesitated. "And you won't laugh at me? You won't hate me?"

"My dear," she said, with infinite compassion in her voice, "how could I? Why should I? I have seen you at your very worst, and still I love you."

"All right, then," said Flynn. He hesitated a moment more, then took a running leap into the star's silver radiance, up onto the ship's railing, and then off, diving down, down, into the cleansing sea.

"Oh, God," groaned Captain Kermit Feldspar, opening his eyes, "what happened?"

All around him, the men of the *Prometheus* were waking up, like the courtiers in the fairy story who woke from their charmed sleep when the handsome prince kissed the enchanted princess. There was, however, no princess to be seen. There was no storm, either; the *Prometheus* sailed unimpeded across a smooth and sparkling sea, the evening sky deepening to indigo overhead.

"Sir!" said Lieutenant Ronson, raising his head off the deck. "Are you all right, sir?"

"Don't shout so, Claude," said Captain Feldspar, wincing. "I'm not deaf."

"Sorry, sir." Ronson dropped his voice to a whisper. "Are you all right, sir?"

"I'm not an idiot, either, that you need to repeat everything to me," said Captain Feldspar, climbing shakily to his feet. "Is everyone all right? What happened?"

"I'll find out, sir," said Lieutenant Ronson.

The man who had seen the polacca in the midst of the storm never had the opportunity to report it. At any event, there was no polacca to be seen now. It must have been an illusion, a trick of the chancy light.

No one aboard the *Prometheus* had been harmed, not even at the very height of the blow. Lieutenant Ronson had the ship scoured from stem to stern, and found not a single soul injured ... except one.

And you really couldn't call it "injured", per se.

Also, he was not actually a member of the crew.

The prisoner, Lieutenant Ronson found, the one entrusted to their care and keeping, was missing.

"Spirited away, by God!" Captain Feldspar breathed, on viewing the empty manacles—not broken or unlocked, simply empty, as though the prisoner, Houdini-like, had somehow slipped free. Other sign of him there was none. He had vanished without a trace.

"Oh, God!" said Lieutenant Ronson, his face turning white as whey. "What are we going to tell the Admiral?"

Another awakening, some miles distant, aboard the polacca previously mentioned. Flynn groaned and opened his eyes, immediately aware of several things. The first was that his chains were gone. The next was that he was covered with a blanket, lying on something soft and comfortable (he was not, however, as often happens in these circumstances, naked). And last he realized that, although he was not alone, wherever he was, the voices that had hounded him were gone.

"Take care," said someone at his side. "They may yet return."

Flynn opened his eyes. His vision swam for a moment, then cleared, revealing a man and a woman sitting beside his bed. The man was small and somehow delicate, despite his deep tan. The woman had black hair and black eyes; it was she who had spoken.

"Who are you?" asked Flynn. "And where am I this time?"

"This is my ship," said the man. "My name is Stavros Parhelion, and this is my wife, Phaedra."

"Stav—?" said Flynn, and shook his head. "I'll never be getting my mouth around that one, so I won't."

"You can call me Sundog," said Stavros Parhelion.

"Sundog, then," said Flynn, and they shook hands. (No more chains! Flynn's heart revelled in the freedom.) "And how did I come to find myself here?"

"We rescued you," Sundog replied. "From the hold of that Navy ship. We ... hope you don't mind..."

"Mind!" Flynn cried. "What a false, low, ungrateful discourteous wretch I would be, if I objected to your timely intervention! And how were you knowing I was needing rescue, then?"

"Phaedra." The little man put an arm around his wife's waist. (She was, Flynn observed, several inches taller than her husband.) "She saw it in a dream." He seemed inclined to elaborate, but Phaedra shook her rich, black curls at him, and her eyes sparked so dangerously that he broke off. Flynn, however, did not attend to this matrimonial dispute, but addressed himself to Mrs Sundog.

"Amazing!" he said. "Are you a wizard, then?"

"I have some skill," the woman replied, so forbiddingly that Flynn forbore to pursue that line of questioning.

"Well," he said, throwing off the bedclothes and swinging his legs over the side of the cot, "'tis grateful I am for my deliverance, indeed it is. Is there any way I can be repaying you?"

"Actually," said Sundog, fidgeting a little, "we had a hope that you could help us with something...."

"Name it," said Flynn, "and it's yours."

The married couple looked at each other, communicating with their eyes, as married couples will. Sundog appeared hesitant, Phaedra insistent—and in the end, as generally happens, the woman had her way.

"It would be a great favor," she said, "if you agreed to it. You will want to clean up, and refresh yourself, and then we will tell you all about it."

"Aye," said Flynn Freeborn. "An equitable arrangement."

Over dinner, lamb and vegetables cooked in the Fetan fashion, they told him what they intended, and why they needed him. Flynn shoved back his chair, scratched his head, tugged on his ear, drained his wine (a bold spicy red from Parmigiana), and contemplated. His hosts waited, Sundog becoming more and more Hangdog as the silence stretched on, and at last Flynn bounded to his feet.

"Aye!" he said, planting his fists on his hips. "Sounds grand, it does, sounds fine! I'll do it, I will!" And then he sank back down into his seat. "But I'll be needing to do a little something," he said, "before we begin."

"If it's in our power," said Sundog, "we'll help you."

Thus Stavros Parhelion's little ship, the *Leukothea* (mark II, since a certain captain of the Royal Navy had captured the first one), put in at Port Cullis in northern Camembert, and Flynn Freeborn set foot on his native soil for the first time in over fifty years.

"We will wait for you here," said Sundog.

"Give me a week," said Flynn, "and I'll return."

He hired a horse (trusting that riding a horse was like riding a bicycle in its unforgettableness) and set off along the road inland. When night fell, he took lodgings at a convenient inn, and the next morning, quite early, continued on his way.

She was sitting in the garden, watching the sun sink low behind the western hills and the ridge of trees beyond, when a tall silhouette interposed itself between her and the light. She squinted at it, wondering what it might be, and her heart, which had grown so flabby and dull, gave a great leap in her breast. She watched the man come striding up the hill, watched him approach the door of the house, and knock, and wait, and watched as he was admitted.

A little while later, a young woman came out: one of her brother's children, or perhaps a grandchild or even a great-grandchild by now. "Aunt Evie," said this young relative, "there's someone come to see you. Aunt Evie?" There was consternation in her face. Evie savored it.

"If it's another of those quack doctors," she said, "I won't see him. I'm tired. Tell him to go away."

"N-nooo," said her niece, or her great-niece. "It's not a doctor. I'll just ... send him out, shall I?" She patted Evie's shoulder and went away.

Evie waited.

She saw the man come out of the house, saw, through the gloaming and the brief gleams of fireflies, the niece or great-niece point him the way. He bowed, and the niece disappeared back inside.

Evie looked away as he began his approach; after so many years of waiting, she wanted to draw the moment out as long as she could. She heard leaves crunching under his feet, and once he gave a muffled curse as he tripped on a root or a branch. She sneaked a look at him anyway, and felt instant disappointment. It was a well-dressed young man—a young man, mind!—with a long pigtail swinging behind him, his gait the rolling walk of a sailor. She looked away again.

The young man knelt beside her chair.

"Hullo, Evie," he said, taking one of her hands.

She snatched it away. "I don't believe I know you, sir," she said. "What business do you have with me?"

There was disappointment in his face—a handsome young man, for all he was not the one she had wanted to see—but he did not, as she had hoped, get up and leave her be. "I've come to tell you a story, I have," he said, and in his voice she could hear the lilt and roll of the sea. "If you'll hear it, that is. 'Tis a long tale, so it is, and not a pretty one, I fear."

"Is it—" Her heart gave another fearful leap. "Is it about ... Lysander?" And held her breath as the young man hesitated.

"Aye," he said at last. "'Tis Lysander's story, so it is, and all the strange and terrible things that befell him. It's your forgiveness he's needing now, it is, if you've the mercy to give it."

Something about him—the timbre of his voice, or the shape of his face, or the color of his eyes, only dimly visible now in the blue shadows of deepening twilight—tugged at her memory, and she regarded him long and hard before reaching out and touching him with one frail, trembling hand.

"Lysander?" she breathed, still searching his face. "Can it be?"

"It can," he said, smiling gently. "It is."

"But ... how?"

He took her hand, pressing it with his own. "Will you hear this story, then? 'Tis a sorry tale, and long."

"Tell me," she said. "Tell me everything."

The sun sank in glory beneath the horizon, and one by one the solemn stars came out, and Lysander sat at her feet, telling of all the things he'd seen and done—things, dear readers, which you already know, or can mostly guess—and through this long confession he held her hand tight in his. The night grew cool and damp, and he took off his coat and tucked it around her shoulders, still talking, and she listened avidly to it all. The stars wheeled across the sky, and they watched them as he spoke. The moon rose, and bathed the still garden, the nodding heads of sleeping flowers, and the pair of them, in its argent radiance.

Sometimes he paused, and she would ask a question, and he would answer and move on.

It was grey dawn before his tale was done, a tale that wandered across almost seventy years, and all the lands of the Quadra Terrarum. The stars were fading when he released a last, long breath, almost a sigh, and then said,

"Tell me now, my Evie. You know what sort of man I am, and you know the things I've done. Can you find it in you to forgive me?"

His eyes were anxious, pleading, hopeful. With a weary sigh she reached out and caressed his hair. He closed his eyes.

"I am too old," she said, still stroking his hair, "to cling to bitterness any more. Once, a long time ago, I might have been angry, or hated you for what you've done." She paused, and felt him grow still beneath her fingertips.

"And now?" he said at last, when the silence had gone on too long.

She turned to look at him. "I have loved you too long to hate you now," she said. "Of course I forgive you."

The tension ran out of him all at once; he leant against the arm of her chair, eyes shut, and in the pre-dawn light she saw tears on his cheeks. "Ah," he said. "By heaven. How long I've needed to hear those words, and not known it."

"Lysander—" she said.

"Flynn." He sat up and looked at her. "'Tis Flynn now, so it is."

She touched his cheek. "It was Lysander I loved."

He smiled and took her hand. "Then I'll be Lysander to you," he said.

"And to yourself?" she asked.

She saw him consider it. At last he shook his head. "I've been Flynn a long, long time, so I have," he said. "Longer than I ever was Lysander. But who knows? Someday mayhap we'll see." He quirked an eyebrow at her. "And what was it, my

Evie, that you wanted to ask?"

"I thought..." She hesitated. Her hand was like a butterfly, cupped gently in his grip. "Am I dreaming?" she said at last. "Or dead? For the longest time I wanted to die, but I was afraid I'd never see you again. And now I am seeing you, and I thought, perhaps I have died, and that's why we're together."

He smiled—such a sad, knowing, tender smile it brought tears to her eyes. "Never think it," he said, and kissed her frail knuckles, one by one. "We're real enough now, so we are."

The sky's deep velvet black was fading to delicate blue, shot with ribbons of rose and palest gold. "Look," said Evie. "We've talked all night."

"So we have," he replied.

"Stay with me?" she asked him. "I'm a little afraid, now."

"No fear." He twined his hands with hers. "I'm here. I've come home. And I'll stay until—" His throat closed.

"Until I'm gone," she said. She looked not at him, but at the coming dawn, and she watched it with a fearless gaze.

"Aye," he said. "Until then."

"Good," she said.

They sat in the garden together, damp with the morning dew, hand-in-hand like children, and together they watched as the sun rose.

End of Book One.

Author's Note, and Thanks

The original edition of *The Voyage to Ruin* was released in 2007 as a bit of a lark. I had written a handful of fantastical pirate-themed stories during animation school to amuse myself, and when they were all put together they almost resembled a novel. In subsequent years I tried to make them slightly more resemble a novel (there is some connective material here that was not in that first edition), although there is still something episodic about the final result. Then a lot of life things happened, a lot of things changed, and I believed the airship pirates phase of my life was well behind me.

Yet the characters stayed with me, as an author's characters will do, and I still wondered from time to time, whatever happened to Flynn, and Drake, and poor Zeal, after all was said and done? The first step in finding out seemed to me to be releasing their first book, however messy, back into the world, all bright and shiny in a new edition.

There are things I would certainly do differently now, with twenty extra years under my belt, and I have done a slight whisk-through the text and cleaned it up here and there, but for the most part what my younger self wrote, I have let stand. It is my hope that in a sequel light may be shed on some of those decisions, and better decisions made.

Humble thanks to all the people who have supported me over the years, either explicitly supporting my artistic endeavors like my handful of loyal Patrons, or simply supporting me as a person, making sure I ate and got enough sleep and all of those necessary-to-life kinds of things. Love and thanks to my sword family, to my fellow artists, fellow mothers, most especially to my own mother who has graciously put up with me this whole time. And most deepest and explicit thanks to my husband, Scott Laurange, without whom none of this would be possible. *Forever and always, my dear.*

Find H.L. Trombley (who is really Kat Laurange) online at katlaurangeart.carrd.co, or on Patreon @katlaurangeart.

For more Voyage to Ruin things, visit VoyagetoRuin.carrd.co

Flynn, Drake and Zeal will return...

www.ingramcontent.com/pod-product-compliance
Lightning Source LLC
Chambersburg PA
CBHW020936310726
48980CB00007B/801/J

* 9 7 8 0 6 1 5 1 4 6 1 2 6 *